First published as a self-published Ebook in 2016

All characters in this publication - other than the obvious
historical characters - are fictitious and any resemblance to
real persons, living or dead, is purely coincidental.

ISBN: 978-0-9956499-0-3

Artwork

Carl Howe (thanks Carlos!)
http://moor-creative.co.uk/

Acknowledgments

Thank you to those people who have read and
commented on this work.

Geoff Kipling
Ruth Dutton
CW Perkins
C Pollock

Any errors – as a self-edited piece of work – are still my
own!

Dedication

To my boys – Ben & Jacob for being rays of light.
Mostly.

And to my Gran – always been there, always will
be.

Contents

PROLOGUE

Corsica, 1852

1. Awakenings

*

.

*

.Black

*

Eyes opened. Mirrors to the soul they were, which is why they were dead, showing nothing, certainly not life.

But open they did, of their own accord, no mechanics involved.

Well, not strictly true. He stood there because of the mechanics, because of the physic, because of his will to live and succeed. His desire to conquer.

That was why he was here, an untamed spirit that would not depart, because of a life unfulfilled.

His eyes opened of their own free will, his mind his own, controlling his body and driving the current to his desire.

His mind his own.

His eyes glowed like lanterns, his heart roared like bellows, haphazard sounds crackled and spat from his mouth.

Electrodes entered his shaved skull through neatly drilled holes. Closer inspection would reveal that the entire top of the skull had been removed at some point past, but then replaced by a gleaming brass tonsure. It made his head appear elongated and unnaturally domed. Beneath the metal bone, fine copper wires spread out from the electrodes like a spider's web, each entering a specific part of the brain, stimulating full mental capacity. The network created an electric field – a mild Faraday cage, shielding his mind from external influence and it powered his malice and hunger.

The drip of stinking water formed a puddle at his feet. The water came from the boiler on his back, and it hissed and wheezed as jets of steam punctured the air. The emaciated figure had neither muscle nor strength, yet weight meant nothing to him: an exoskeleton shouldered his burden. It clad his body, through which hundreds of cables penetrated into his withered limbs, allowing stimulation of former muscles. These were connected to the massive structure, and lo! he could move.

Every electrode was connected to a vacuum tube and each glowed orange to yellow to white, turning the figure into a human torch. The exceptions were the electrodes and valves attached to the brain. Valves here permanently glowed white, even the wires themselves flickered a fiery orange. Occasionally, the white light would become blinding, followed by a sharp crack, and noxious black fumes would pour from the ruptured glass. Further exoskeleton electrodes would glow orange as fully hydraulic pistons powered a second pair of arms that disconnected the broken item and replaced it with a fresh valve, which would again glow white.

Most notably, there were a small number that regularly cracked and oozed dark ink-like smoke, and these centred around areas of the brain that the accompanying scientist took for emotion – rage and hatred and desire.

He raged: his son was dead. He hated: his wife was a traitor. He desired: revenge.

He turned his body and moved across to the balcony window of the Bonifacio citadel. The ground shook beneath his weight and a crowd of pigeons fluttered away in alarm.

Below, in their thousands, soldiers stood in neat squares. Behind them gathered a disorderly hoard of wives and children. Barely a sound could be heard, merely an expectant hush.

"Mes ami. Mes enfants. Soldats."

The sound boomed, crackling and rattling at the faces below. They gaped in awe at the figure above them.

Not a man or woman doubted whom they saw.

"Soldiers," the automaton repeated in French. "You are here today at the dawn of a new era. The Royal Houses of Europe will soon be quaking at the thunder of our feet and the lightning of our war. No longer will we tolerate the rule of petty kings. No longer will royal bastardy decide our fate. Traitors of old will be brought to justice. Their families will watch that justice and their children will regard in inspired awe as the people of Europe rise up and reclaim what is rightfully theirs. What is rightfully ours. No more will a mere few dine on the fat of the land whilst the rest of us starve.

"You are a vast army of men. Twice before you failed me. You shall not fail again. You cannot fail again." He studied the army in front of him, and at a hidden signal, the ground shook. Men looked around, whilst others craned their necks to see over the person in front.

A line of a dozen figures, at least fifteen feet tall and eight feet wide, stomped out of the citadel gates to stand before the army of flesh and blood. They fumed black smoke and their very arms appeared to be wide-muzzled guns or great halberds. Men muttered at the sight and took a step back. All wore a look of fear because it was like nothing they had ever seen before, and to the minds of those simple folk, the concept itself seemed an impossibility. The automata before them appeared as Gods.

The figure in the tower raised its arms, causing gases to escape with a hiss. It was enough to catch the attention of the people below.

"There is soon to be a vast army of undefeatable warriors such as these. They will march with us. They will march *for* us. Their like has never before been seen, and they are irresistible. We will be a hurricane destroying the paltry forces set before us. We will reap vengeance on those that steal our food, take back the great houses built with our blood, and liberate the lands so woefully ruled by the fortunate few. This time you will succeed. WE will succeed, and Europe will once more be in my tender bosom.

"Soon we will march. We march for freedom, we march for liberty. We will march for VICTORY!"

In a single voice they shouted a feared phrase over and over again.

"Vive l'Empereur."

*

Mani Maurya stood within the crowds of peasantry watching, his aging, frail figure almost unique amongst the women and children. The hue of his brown skin appeared only subtly different to those of the sun-kissed Mediterranean folk. By comparison, his Hindi *dhoti kurta* garb shouted 'stranger' to all of those around him. When he had first arrived, people avoided him. He was too different.

Following several months of living on the island, his reputation for his skill with herbs had become such that the Europeans merely treated him with respectful wariness.

At the conclusion of the show – because it could be nothing more – he made his decision to leave as soon as safely possible. He needed to report back to London. Getting a message out had proven impossible, even using the most subtle of his machinations. Subtlety was, after all, a spy's greatest strength.

He knew that there must be others like him, but the organisation to which he belonged deemed it too dangerous to reveal other operators. Still, he believed he had spotted other spies, even if some of them belonged to nations other than Her Majesty's British Empire.

He waited several days. To all intents and purposes, he appeared as nothing more than a simple peasant who had a skill with healing herbs, another nameless face that had joined a secretive movement. No one could possibly anticipate that he happened to be something else entirely.

It occurred to him that those same herbs could kill, but it may not be possible to kill Napoleon again by something so mundane. That trick had already failed once, if that thing before him had truly had been the Tyrant.

No, the only way was to leave. Tricky, but not impossible. Boats were frequent, but those who left on them were not. A couple of people had managed to leave over the past few months, but they had not been especially clever, and they had been returned. One still hung in a medieval gibbet, now nothing more than tanned hide, black teeth and bleached bones.

Mani knew himself to be cleverer. Over the proceeding days, he watched and confirmed his knowledge of the habits of the men who so assiduously guarded the quays and wharfs. That mundanity always proved to be the weakness of any system. That same old dogged routine was Mani's best friend. Any Intelligence Officer of worth used this against itself. Man gets bored, man makes mistake. It should have been a mantra for every organisation in the world.

It was a simple plan, as they often had to be. He liked simple, and it always brought a smile to his face how the most complex plans so often went so wrong.

He smiled inwardly now. Wait until the dead of night. At two o'clock in the morning, the guard would change. They would desert their posts for a matter of minutes, and on the night where only a black moon shone, that precious time would allow him to steal a fishing boat and sail in to the sunset. Quite literally: he would sail west and south for a full day and night before heading south of east to Malta. The direction would confuse his trail, because no one would go west of Sardinia, a mere ten miles to the south, and then complete a journey of five hundred or more miles. Only a crazy person would do that! He grinned to himself. He grinned again. He realised that his smile was a bad habit for an Intelligence Officer, but it made him feel good, so he wore it often.

The night came, a chill wind blew from the north. It felt good.

The guards left their posts. Mani stole to the wharf. He undid the ropes and jumped in to the boat furthest from prying eyes. The current pulled him away from the wharf, and quite contentedly, he manned the tiller, not yet daring to raise a sail.

Dawn began as a vague light at his back, and as it did so, he raised his sails. Once that task had been completed, he studied the brightening sky back towards Corsica. He could make out the rise of its mass as utter blackness. He could see no signs of pursuit.

Yet doubt nagged at him.

He continued to watch for many minutes, and then, just as he turned around with a sigh of relief, fear struck him.

He whirled back round to study his rear.

There! A black sail, only visible due to the light of the morning, aimed straight at him. He considered the distance. Two miles perhaps?

He searched within himself. How could this be possible? His boat would still be invisible. He could only see the other craft because of her silhouetted against the pre-dawn.

He turned and tightened the sails, holding his course. To deviate was to lose speed.

A change in the light forced him to turn. Impossible! That word sprang in to his head. A *ship* loomed. Somehow, in the time it had taken him to tighten his sail, she had halved the gap.

Its prow pointed directly at him. It looked impossibly large.

He changed tack, aiming his boat straight into the wind. A larger boat would not be able to sail this course. If the enemy cut the corner, what would it matter?

He turned around once more. The ship more than loomed now, it seemed to cast its shadow over his craft. The pit in his stomach exploded with terror.

She did not slow. The wind did not seem to affect her speed.

Calmness descended on Mani. He watched in morbid fascination. The ship mesmerised him, all black and as huge as a medieval Spanish galleon. It scared him. Its presence was ominous. It petrified him.

The vessel approached and still did not reduce her rate. He heard the splintering as it struck. It seemed a distant sound.

The pain as the hull struck seemed irrelevant. He barely noticed the caress of the sea as it entered his mouth and lungs.

*

Mani awoke.

He recognised the figure stood before him. It – Napoleon – stood before him, impossibly large and – again – ominous.

He watched as it raised a hand, and could not force himself to move as long needles in the palm of its hand sparked blue electricity between them.

The hand descended and still Mani could not move. Pain registered, yet he did not scream.

The automaton forced needles through his skull, and then more pain. He could feel an interrogation, although he did not speak.

Blood started to run from his nose and eyes.

His mind started to fold in on itself. He could feel it happen. His bowels let go as his mind forgot. And finally, Mani's mind collapsed entirely. His body followed it. He slumped to the floor, dead.

It did not really matter.

Napoleon had all of the information he required.

CHAPTER 1 – HOPE FOR WILLIAM

"Heave y'lubbers, HEAVE!" screamed the bosun.

William Hope heaved and the bank of oars moved. Likewise, his counterparts on the opposite side heaved.

Less than a mile behind, the HMS Endeavour steadily gained on them, her motorised propeller easing the airship upwards towards the clouds and the pirate galley Bucentaur.

"Row, yer buggers," screeched the bosun with a crack of a whip sounding across the deck.

Becalmed, they had no choice. William continued to heave, sweat rolled across his body and his chest working frantically to take in precious oxygen. He may have been a slave, but Her Majesty's Airship Corps believed in shooting first and questioning survivors second, regardless of innocence. A smoking mansion below answered that question. Which is why he pulled and heaved and sweated.

"Fire!" yelled Duval, the Captain of the ship. The sound of a light artillery piece pierced the sky. The cannonball fell a hundred meters short. William could see a thin trail of smoke as it trailed off before plummeting to the ground below.

Soon after a flash appeared from Endeavour, followed by a resonating thump that rolled across the skies. It startled the enemy ship's Passenger pigeons, those augmented creatures that arose where biology met technology. They flocked into an indistinct cloud that shrouded the navy vessel.

A trail of smoke that seemed to have no perspective arced upwards, and it took William a moment to realise that a cannonball headed straight for him. He felt his bladder loosen.

The cannonball struck with a whistle that ascended to a shriek. It flashed murderously down the flank, destroying port-side oars like matchsticks. A lucky shot at that distance – but not for those oarsman on the opposite side to William. One was sliced in two by his oar from the force of the recoil. Two other men moaned in a state of pained semi-consciousness.

William continued to heave, the kites on the end of each oar inflating with air on each pull, the ingenious cams, springs and air relief valves allowing for easy return on release. Unfortunately, as nobody countered from the opposite side, the boat yawed rapidly to the right and the gap between the two boats closed swiftly.

It was an accidental but unexpected manoeuvre that brought the largest and furthest ranging cannons of the Bucentaur to bear.

Duval required no second invitation, and he hollered "Fire starboard cannons!"

An enormous crash resounded as the cannons hurled a deadly weight of lead towards HMA Endeavour. One ball hit and it tore through the rear section of the cabin, ruining Endeavours rudder.

The Bucentaur rose, spinning gently still, as the lighter-than-air gas propelled her upwards and in to the clouds. The Endeavour foundered, unable to steer. Replacement slaves climbed from the holds. Pirates manacled them to the empty seats still sticky with blood and oars were rapidly replaced. William breathed a sigh of relief.

"We might just bloody well make it," hissed the man chained beside him.

William found himself dragged back to the present.

"We're bloody lucky it's cloudy," he grumbled.

Under its cover, and with some clever navigation techniques (hard rowing on his behalf), they had lost the Endeavour. Admittedly, she had been rudderless, but all the same, no ship of the line relied solely on her rudder. Pressurised gases and relief ports enabled navigation, but without it, the fight was off against the likes of the Bucentaur. On the Endeavour, a whole swathe of emergency protocols would be required, necessitating lots of hustle and bustle, flicking of switches, moving of levers, orders written in triplicate, and all manner of naval bluster, etiquette and tradition. In a pirate tub like the Bucentaur, the sailors jumped-to immediately or suffered the cat' and any dysfunctional rudder only necessitated rowing to the helmsman's orders; and so she disappeared in to the clouds before the Endeavour could react.

"It's always cloudy this far north," his partner moaned. He was from Clerkenwell in London and had a thick Italian accent. "And cold. I thought we'd bought our ticket out of here, but the Froggie is good at this."

They had discussed a number of times about escape, but it seemed that the only time that a slave found freedom, it happened to be a short journey straight down. A short and unwilling journey.

"He is good. Very good. A bastard, yes, but a proper sailor. Still, another slip like that, and we might just be captured and freed."

"You're too optimistic, Hope. He'd rather die and take us all with him than surrender."

"I think Duval's rather pragmatic. He probably fancies that he could get the ship back if it was taken from him." The other man shrugged in evident disagreement.

Duval currently captained an airship that had been obsolete for over a hundred years. He had stolen it from an English maritime museum, if his wildly exaggerated tales of derring-do were to be believed. The pirates had escaped across the channel by conventional seafaring methods and then the Bucentaur had been refitted for modern naval flying warfare. Moments and gears did away with a large crew for rowing, and automation for cannons was positively brutal in effect. A modern ship of the line automated all of the loading, tamping, priming and only required a man with a linstock. A few prototypes had been tried with automated firing mechanisms, but so far it had been impossible to consistently ensure that the mixture of lighter-than-air gases and below-decks fire stayed appropriately far apart, something that sailors, a superstitious lot at the best of times, were very careful about. Some of the newspapers had reported most spectacular outcomes for experimentation on the matter, although London was now short of a few inventors.

The Bucentaur appeared small to William's eyes, but that hid the fact that it also made her light and manoeuvrable and so ideal for smash and grab air piracy. Duval used her for exactly this.

Mostly though, the Bucentaur was beautiful. Not just that, but a *thing of beauty*. She had history and all aboard could smell the grandeur of days gone by.

She had been Louis XVIIIs little play thing for cruising along the Seine on sunny days and, during the Terror, she'd been used as an escape vessel for the King of France. England had harboured him, and he had donated the vessel to the maritime museum. All gold in colour, exquisite carvings, opulence, splendour and wealth personified. Exactly the reason that the Terror had taken place and Citizens had come to rule.

*

William was marched, manacled and chained, down to the slave hold, where dinner was served. A delicious steak served blue, rosemary and garlic roasted potatoes, Chantenay carrots with a honey and mustard glaze, and a rich ruby port. It smelled delectable, and the bouquet of the port intoxicating. All followed by a decanter of brandy whilst they talked over piquet and cigars.

Or not.

Grey gruel, with white globules of some nameless fat, served with brown, brackish water. The smell was death and ash. Retching and dry heaving, William downed the lot. His stomach continued to growl and grumble.

William and his fellows were then ordered to their hammocks, where he carefully unfolded the copy of The Times that had been in his pocket when he'd been snatched. As well as his only reading material, it also supplemented his blanket. Nights were cold at altitude.

"Anything in the news today, William?" a fellow slave quipped.

Hope smiled at the tired joke. "Always doom and gloom. It was the same yesterday, and will probably be the same tomorrow."

He re-read the front page, a page that was becoming increasingly tattered and worn. He had to squint to read the small print, partly because of the light, but mostly because of its creased condition and the damp that caused the ink to spread. He sighed audibly: it *was* always bad news, whether he re-read this same article every day for a hundred days or whether it had been hot off the press. Cholera had struck the East End again, although it seemed that the severity of the outbreaks was reducing over time. There were riots in the East End. The East End was on fire. A brutal murderer was on the loose.

It always centred on the East End, and William could not understand why the events that occurred in other working class towns were totally ignored. Workers in those mills in Hyde, Marple and Macclesfield, where he himself had investments, regularly gave way to unrest, whilst the poorest areas of Manchester were often ablaze or infected with some form of horrendous disease. The poor were getting poorer all over the country, not helped by the large numbers of maimed soldiers from the Rambling War who were unable to find work. Food was scarce and the populations who made up the poor were growing rapidly.

"Lights out," came the faceless cry.

William struggled into his hammock, leg and arm muscles shrieking in agony, wrists and ankles raw and bleeding from chafing against the heavy ironwork. He covered himself with an old piece of sail-cloth and day-dreamed of his four poster with its silken sheets, a nameless but beautiful concubine and bucket of celebratory champagne. He closed his eyes and immediately went to sleep.

Bang!

William fell out of his hammock in shock.

"What the..."

Bang! Bang! Bang!

It could only be a full broadside.

The fall saved William's life as cannonballs tore through the slave hold at hammock height. Splinters of hull, some the length of a man's arm, eviscerated fellow slaves in the hammocks either side of William. Blood rained gently on his prostrate form. Moonlight pricked through holes in the hull and screams filled the place. Heavier gore splattered William, a wet slap hit the floor, and there were more screams.

The large hydrogen balloon of the attacking dirigible blocked the faint moonlight. Bright flashes from its gun ports momentarily blinded William. The sound came a moment afterwards.

Bang! Bang! Bang!

The shock of impact shook the Bucentaur. Moonlight returned as the enemy airship fell away, dropping below the line of vision.

whooOMPH!

William's stomach plummeted as the prow of the Bucentaur fell forward and heat tore through the slave hold. William leapt head first out of a hole produced by cannonball, immediately followed by a mass of flame that quickly dissipated at his tail. He was still holding the sail cloth, and this filled with air above him. It erupted in flames. He gasped and let go and he felt his hair set on fire. His clothes smouldered, the stench of burning pork filled his nostrils and his manacles dragged him down at a breakneck speed.

William plummeted for an age that lasted seconds;

His breath was knocked out of him as he landed on top of the dirigible below and he slid down its inflatable, pain wracking his head, disorientated beyond reckoning, struggling to draw breath through scorched lungs.

Over the side of the great hydrogen balloon he slid jangling and teetering, and finally gravity pulled him down... approximately ten feet to a catch net below. Bouncing gently, he slipped into unconsciousness.

*

"aaaaaaarrrggGGHHHH!".

"He's awake, sir," said a young voice.

"So I gather," said a much older gruffer voice. Amused.

There was a pinprick in his arm and the pain subsided immediately, ravaging agony reduced to severe discomfort. Footsteps clicked across to the bed.

"Pirate. Look at me."

William looked, peeling his eyes open, grimacing at the distress of so small an action. He squinted myopically at the brightness that blinded him.

"I have saved your life so that I can see you hang." The speaker was a ship's Captain, if the epaulettes were anything to go by. Shiny, big, gold. Officious.

William tried to speak, but no sound came out other than a rattle of air through his scorched lungs.

"Water, please, Brown."

The young voiced man brought a glass of water and tenderly tipped the glass to William's lips and he drank gently, barely able to move for the torment racking his body.

"Thank you," croaked William, the words acute pin-pricks of distress.

"Name," barked the Captain.

"Sir William Hope. And I'm not a pirate, I am a Gentleman and a naturalist." He spoke very slowly, and at the end of the sentence closed his eyes, breathing raggedly. He slowly raised his arms and gently jangled his manacles.

"A knight of the realm AND a pirate, eh?" The Captain smirked at William, not believing a word of it.

"I was press ganged in Paris," William rasped. "The bastards hit me with a cosh and then stole all of my belongings. Manacled me to that bloody ship."

"Paris, eh? Bit dangerous for an English gent, I would have thought." The Captain still wore a sardonic smile to his face. "What business did you have in France?"

"None of yours," William said tartly, even though it hurt him to speak in such a tone. He relented slightly on seeing the face of the Captain. "I'm a bloody member of the Royal Society and we do not tend to adhere to such petty things as national rivalries and histrionics."

"But Sir," Brown's young voice, barely broken, sounded, "the French hate us. Isn't that rather dangerous?"

He was right. The French did hate the British – and the rest of Europe, truth be told. Harbouring renegade royals was the official reason for certain Anglo-French tensions. But there had also been the war across Europe, the rape and pillage of France's wealth, the installation of a French puppet government (read Anglo-Prussian) and the imprisonment and death on St Helena of Bonaparte. Arsenic in the wallpaper apparently, although licking wallpaper didn't exactly seem normal in a person, even Bonaparte. Arsenic in his tea – William could see that.

The French people, a lot of whom still adored Napoleon, simply believed that he'd been slowly murdered by his British gaolers. And they were probably right. They were also a bit testy about the burial at sea, and the flat refusal to release the body for a state funeral. Oh well.

The boy reddened as his Captain glared at him. He stammered a bit more and then fell silent, eyes downcast.

"Quite right, but moving in my circles is a bit different to most others, lad," Hope said.

The Captain stared unremittingly at William. He sighed and told the story of his capture.

*

William walked through the streets of Paris. He could feel the tension, from the hooded looks on the womenfolk, to the naked aggression of the men. More than once during his short journey he'd had the need to swat away a grubby urchin's attempt at picking his pocket. Neither had been higher than his waist.

The ordure of the city pervaded. He silently thanked a nameless god that the narrower street he needed to take appeared to be free of people.

The city had gone steadily downhill since the end of the war. The rate of that decay had accelerated over the past year or so. Ramshackle houses reached for the sky, hovels stacked one on another. This once splendid region of the Sorbonne, as well as many other well-to-do areas of Paris, had rapidly been encroached upon by slums expanding their kraken-like tentacles.

William walked down the street. A sound came from just behind him, but before he had time to look around, a figure stepped out from his front. His barrel chest and cudgel were the only marks of note.

A hand clamped on William's shoulder. He jumped, because he had not heard another sound from behind.

"Mr Hope, you are to come with us."

A torrential rain started. Ridiculously, he suddenly regretted forgetting his umbrella.

The pressure on his shoulder increased and began to turn him. The brute in front approached. Fear started to freeze William into rigidity as the tug on his shoulder became insistent.

His instincts came through, those instincts honed over many months in the boxing ring and dojo.

He used the grip of the man behind to accelerate himself round, forcing the thug off balance, and that leverage gave him a momentum that turned his fist into an anvil. It thudded into the juncture of jaw and ear of the man who had gripped his shoulder. The joint splintered audibly and William felt pain as a shard of bone speared his knuckle.

A noise behind.

Damn!

He felt the cudgel strike home. Blackness enveloped his vision.

Hold on! They know my name!

Consciousness waned and waxed. The rain buffeted his body. Hands rifled his pockets. He dimly heard the click of his briefcase being opened.

Light entered his eyes. He saw a purple photograph wash past in a rivulet of water.

He heard a groan stifle to a throaty whine.

The big man hauled William to his feet. He could make out eyes peering out at him from behind twitching curtains across the street. A bag went over his head.

"Don't damage him too bad," a coarse voice pleaded.

A blow landed in William's midriff and all air whooshed out. He doubled over, choking for breath, before a thud landed on his head, and this time the blackness only waxed.

*

What William hadn't revealed was that he had been in the Catacombs in Paris with his photographic equipment gathering evidence in support of his paper for the Royal Society.

The results had been fascinating. Remarkable even. Most modern photography relied on silver nitrate, but William had discovered a small alteration – not using silver nitrate – gave interesting results. Astonishing, he supposed, if the daguerreotypes were anything to go by.

William had found that soaking paper in a solution of carbon black, potassium permanganate and horse-glue, dried with a finish of gelatine, produced photographs perfect for the modern printing press. However, the addition of hydrogen peroxide, and then setting off a phosphorous flash (in the presence of the dead, naturally), burned an image of such sharpness and clarity, magenta on black, that William had at first wept.

Unfortunately, the photographs were now in a gutter somewhere in a back street of Paris.

What they would have shown – if not for the rain and the filth and the piss – was that the catacombs were infested with the spirits of the dead. They didn't appear malicious, just lost. They were somewhere they should not be without an idea of how to escape. In fact, they didn't even know that they could escape. They were futile. His futiles. *Les Futiles.*

*

William looked up at the people in the room. Brown looked amazed, the Captain seemed marginally less smug and the Doctor, still holding the syringe, considered William with a certain respect.

The boy showed bravery – or youthful foolishness – because he looked directly at William, even though his Captain's eyes still burned into him and made a further comment.

"I still don't understand how you even consider travelling alone, Sir."

"Scientists and explorers tend to be accepted, immune to politics. Which is why movement across borders is generally easy. A good reputation in the correct fraternity gives rise to invites to seminars and presentations of scientific breakthroughs across Europe." Nowadays, this was William's world. He'd had enough of foolhardy adventure. He was in his thirties and it was time to settle down.

"Admittedly, there are a number of underhand rivals because some scientists are extremely precious, but I've never heard of anyone stooping to such levels as press-ganging." No – that was just paranoia.

He looked at the Captain.

"Not a pirate," he croaked, his voice giving way once again.

The Captain paused. Even through the pain and damage, William spoke in the clipped tones of an educated man; more even, possibly a noble.

A shake of the head.

"Pirate, until I learn otherwise, you are to be hanged. Doctor, mend him so I can watch him swing." And with that, he stalked out of the room.

The Doctor came in to view, shaking his head ruefully.

"I have injected you with an opiate to manage the pain," the Doctor said gently. "I hope the Captain hasn't unsettled you too much."

"What happened?" whispered William.

"In short, we blew up your ship. Heated grapeshot into the balloon, it's a new tactic apparently, although I can't say I like the idea of a furnace heating up lots of little metal balls on a dirigible."

The doctor started rubbing a salve of marigold on to William's skin: hands, arms, face, chest and scalp. The effect, very temporarily, was wonderful. Until the Doctor and the boy turned him. In fairness, they were remarkably gentle, but even so, William screamed as the pain wracked his body. The Doctor applied more salve to his back, shoulders, and the back of his head. There was no hair left.

The doctor and the boy turned him again, and this time he stifled the scream to a low, agonised groan.

*

The morphine dragged William's consciousness under and over the proceeding days, he found himself in a maelstrom of waking hallucinations and painful dreams.

Mostly, painful dreams. His mother, his father, his brothers and his sisters.

*

Oh! The Pirate Queen, how William had yearned for her... lusted for her....loved her.

And she'd led him a merry dance, quivering at his touch, begging him to help her, looking at him with those eyes, eyes dark and soulful, an abyss of emotion. She'd given herself to him, whispered how she loved him, yearned to be with him forever, she'd paraded him around like a prized trophy, head held high with pride.

And then, when the Pirate Captain hung from a gibbet, the Pirate Queen took his seas and cast William overboard into the shark-infested waters, and as he bobbed there helplessly, she laughed and cackled and shrieked as she tormented him, about how she could never love a white man, that his pleasurings were tedious and clumsy, belittling the size of his manhood, the stiffness of his upper lip, and whilst choking on sea water, he burned with shame.

And then she had taken a kind of mercy for him, she threw down a ramshackle raft, pointed in the direction of the setting sun and told him to paddle if he would save his worthless skin.

He had lain there watching the pirate ship sail towards the eastern horizon, he had lain there watching the dark space where she no longer was, until the sun rose and burned. And then he'd paddled ineffectively for hours before being rescued by a Royal Navy ship. A ship that followed the faded wake of the pirate barky, which caught up with her and hung her from the main beam.

And William had cried with misery and cursed with hatred as she cast never a look in his direction, not a plea of mercy; and he cried as she was hung, so full of grievous pride, hung without uttering a sound; and he cried as she swayed gently in the breeze, no longer capable of sound; he cried until he was utterly dry of tears and he became filled with hatred when they displayed her mouldering corpse throughout the port town and felt nothing, bar hatred, as they nailed her up next to the Pirate Captain as a warning to any who should dare to trouble the seven seas again.

*

William woke one evening, his mind hazy and with an ache of pain swimming around somewhere in the background. A tall, strong fellow wearing a marine uniform sat by his bedside. He had sandy hair and a chiselled jawline as if imitating a pin-up poster of a soldier with a glint of heroism in his blue eyes.

"Good evening Sir William, good to see you awake and looking much better." He spoke in a deep voice, re-assuring but measured.

William croaked, his mouth parched. The marine passed him water.

William drank, and managed to get some words out. "Evening? What day? Who are you?"

"In that order? Yes, evening, it's a Friday, but to be more exact it's Friday the fourth of March, eighteen hundred and fifty-three. My name is James Smith.

I'm what would once have been called an Exploring Officer, although it is much more covert nowadays. I'm on Lord William Melville's staff."

"Melville's staff? Here?"

"Yes. Revolution has struck. Italy is in flames. There appears to be no reason for it, it almost happened overnight." He paused to study William. "And there's a trail that leads here, even though it is fairly tenuous."

"Revolution? Italy has only just been unified. The subsidies make it the least poor country in Western Europe. And how on earth does a backwater of the Empire like this place come to be implicated?"

"We don't know yet, but Brocklehurst isn't the most stable man. Nor the most trustworthy. Outwardly I may be a marine, but I have additional duties."

Hope was fully awake now, although he could feel the morphine lethargy in his limbs. "You're being rather frank, almost to the point of rudeness about a peer of the realm. I've yet to meet the man."

"Lord Melville has fully appraised me of your relationship. I judge that in the current circumstances, frankness is required."

"I don't understand."

"You couldn't. Tell me your story. If I deem you suitable, I will tell you more. I don't need the death of an amateur on my conscience."

"Now hang on one minute! You can't come in here demanding that of me. You're a complete stranger!"

"I know, but I need assistance, and nobody else can get in here. I've tried and recently Brocklehurst has resisted anyone he hasn't specifically requested himself. It's now a matter of national importance. No, strike that – international importance."

William studied the man before him. He didn't have the look of melodrama, in fact he was serious and composed.

"Why not speak to Melville directly?"

"I have, but his hands are tied. Politics." He spat the last word.

"I don't understand. I'm in the middle of sheep farming territory. What on earth is happening here?"

"Ahh, Sir William, that's the crux of it. This facility is a secret weapon. We're manufacturing what may be the most versatile and deadly armed force that the world has ever seen. Maybe will ever see."

"Here, in Cheshire? You'll have to tell me more."

Smith lowered his voice to a conspiratorial whisper. "Well, Brocklehurst is some kind of genius, which is the reason that he has been employed, only he's possibly quite unstable. He's definitely unreliable, to the point of being willing to work for the highest bidder."

"How do you know I'm capable of helping you out?"

"Melville. He tells me that you're capital fellow. He's let me know some of your history." There was a pause. "Do *you* think that you're capable?"

It was a shrewd question and was matched by a shrewd look on Smith's face.

"What is the help you need, and what exactly has he told you?" There was an edge to William. They were discussing his personal life, personal not just to him, but also his family.

"Fear not Sir William! He only told me what I needed to know."

It occurred to William that this would be an excellent way of gauging the man. Bill Melville had been a friend of his father, and the acquaintance had been maintained. If he really was an agent of Melville's, then the extent of his knowledge would indicate that.

"Elucidate. Humour me."

"The day your father died, you were taken by pirates. Once home and a number of months had passed, you had overcome the shock and actually started to apply yourself. You became the head of the family, not just by right to the titles, but by stubbornly asserting your strength of will and your insistence of governing the family estates in a manner that you saw fit and against which none could gainsay. In short, you became a man. You were still young, very young, for such responsibility and you often went astray. You found drink and often found yourself in brawls, usually on the receiving end of a beating."

Smith delivered this as if he was reading a formal report, but now he paused and looked at William.

"Lord Melville claims that there was a hollowness in the core of your soul. You were an orphan, and it burned you up. Your sister Mary was rarely seen in public and barely more frequently seen around the home.

"You were an orphan with no support, no way of explaining the loss, no way of expressing the sorrow. You had lived with that sorrow for months during your captivity, but that time was no catharsis, it only made you more fearful of what might become. There had been an even more terrible spectre of hope, that you may eventually be freed. That sort of baseless optimism can do things to a man.

"Mary still endlessly re-lived her ordeal, you could hear her screams at night. Your younger sisters were slaves somewhere, and you tormented yourself about them. Who knew where they were? What sort of world did they live in? How terribly harmed were they?

"There was more. You had lived completely in a world that did not contain this sort of thing. How had life up to that point not included some sort of education of these things? How could you have been so blissfully ignorant?"

William picked up his own story. It was easier to tell it than listen. It was his story, after all.

"So I had to understand. I chose to study people. The literature was pitiful, from Greek homoeroticism to Elizabethan high-born denial. Which made me study mankind. Not from books, but by studying the people themselves. I travelled far and wide, normally alone. I preferred my own company and I still do to this day. During good times I would attend balls and lectures, talking and watching, and during those darker days, and there were many, I would find himself in slums and back street public houses, whatever continent I was on.

"People confused me at first, it didn't make any sense, you see. At both ends of the spectrum they talked lots and said extraordinarily little, all of them too afraid to appear weak or foolish. They were, almost to a man or woman, braggartly and scornful of others. The dominant males and females throughout were the same – ruling by fear and intimidation, whether a beggar or a prince. It took me some time to realise that the sole distinction was upbringing, and in poverty desperation, in wealth, desperation – either desperation to live or desperation to retain wealth, even not to reveal poverty.

"I studied the middling classes a few times, but they were simple creatures and to be fair, I dismissed them as an irrelevancy fairly rapidly. They're too afraid of both the lower and upper classes, not wild enough, not powerful enough. Whilst they make up the majority of society, they are the most mundane, too busy earning a crust to challenge the upper classes, too civil to fight the lower.

William's tale flowed as if a dam had burst, and his words tumbled out faster and faster. Smith listened fascinated.

"I would vanish for weeks at a time, sometimes months depending on my state of mind, without word, often reappearing dressed in rags, dishevelled and stinking. I could sleep for days afterwards before returning to my rightful duties as the family head, a brother and an employer." William smiled at the memories. "I'm afraid I wasn't really very good as a brother."

"I always managed to do just enough in the family business to keep it running and I spent so much time training, it was endless. There was armed and unarmed combat. I hired the best karate sensei I could find, I learned wrestling, boxing, bushido, fencing and then there would be grass before breakfast, gutter fights and gouging. I was becoming a spring-heeled Jack figure in the slums, and an infamous duellist in the upper classes. I became obsessed to the point that I was actually turning in to the type of bully that I most loathed. The type of bully who would use those weaker than himself and then take pleasure in it. It had to stop."

William broke off and took a drink. He was parched, but it was also a way to hide the raw emotion that thickened his throat and clenched his stomach.

"And I couldn't get my Elisabeth and Victoria, my little sisters, out of my mind. *They could still be out there* was my prevailing thought. So, I set my affairs in order, hired a trustworthy, competent estate manager, wrote a farewell letter to Mary and simply disappeared. I didn't really expect to return. I was nineteen, and thought myself fully a man. My will was to be executed when I reached the age of twenty five. I returned aged twenty-three. I was a different person, both physically and psychologically. I arrived like a stranger, nut—brown, physically scarred and mentally at peace. Eventually, only this showed, though." He pointed self-deprecatingly at his nose, which was misshapen.

"Most importantly, I returned aged twenty-three with two sisters in tow, scared, frightened young things, both grim and stubborn, wild hellcats who listened to no-one, stole and lied. They were the ringleaders of the two dozen other children that came back with me. They caused pandemonium." He smiled at the memory. It was a decade past.

Smith continued the story, partly to allow him a break, partly to complete his demonstration of knowledge – and trust. He hoped so, at any rate.

"You loved them endlessly, William. And thankfully, due to the resilience of their youth, and the love of their family – especially your own love, for Mary was shocked to almost muteness at their return – they became almost normal. You taught them, pampered them and scolded them. They may never become ladies in high society, but they are human, and they have a life that is less scared and far longer than it could have been.

"But William, you still harbour a hatred of those things that stole your sister's innocence. Passionately. Even those – especially those – that are dead. It still shows, even today."

He didn't know why, but William felt better for the telling. For the sharing. It had been a long time, but he still woke from nightmares on occasion, especially about that place that he'd had to rescue his sisters from. And he still missed *her*. His Pirate Queen. He shouldn't, but his bitterness had mellowed, and he remembered her more fondly. He remembered her physical form, and it made him become hard at the memory, even now. He believed less, as the years passed, that she had truly meant her parting diatribe, that abuse, that bile. There would never be anyone like her, certainly not in the society that he was now a part of.

William felt drained and on seeing his condition, a nurse ordered Smith out of his room.

"We will speak more tomorrow, Sir William."

He moved his mouth closer to William's ear and hissed a whisper that the nurse could not hear. "We *must* speak again. Trust nobody."

William could only nod.

The nurse took over.

"You need to rest. This will help you sleep." She tipped his head forward and he drank his dose of morphine. He sank into dreams, dreams that remembered painful memories...

*

The ship sank slowly, holed repeatedly by Caribbean pirates. A few people panicked and leapt overboard to clear themselves from the peril. These were the lucky ones – the sharks were hungry and the turquoise sea soon frothed pink. For them, death came quickly.

The senior Lord Hope, William's father, as the primary guest on board the once-gorgeous cutter, had been chaperoned to the most seaworthy lifeboat on board, along with his family. A host of small, frightened children, huddled around their mothers, remained on the sinking ship. Lord William had taken charge and physically removed some of the menfolk already seated in the lifeboats. Only women and children and a small handful of sailors were allowed. It emptied the cutter of those who could not defend themselves. The captain protested at the usurpation of his command, but the force and power of Lord William had soon silenced him. Normally gentle and mild, he could be moved to implacable when driven by his emotions. Never had William seen his father driven to such passions.

Two of his brothers remained with their father, and he gave William command of his mother and four sisters. A dozen other truncated families huddled in the lifeboat, mostly young children and swooning mothers with panic written over many faces. William tried to appear brave, but inside his stomach churned and his heart beat more rapidly than he thought possible.

Even the sailors looked nervous, but then it was their job to extricate the boat from the pirates, and enough tales were whispered about what happened to people caught in these waters. They didn't hold out much hope of survival, but their deaths would be mercifully quick. One of the older sailors glanced around the boat at the women and children and grimaced. *Their* fates would be much more painful.

Eventually, a group of sailors dropped the boat heavily into the sea on the blind side of the pirate ship, which was currently manoeuvring in fitful winds to board the cutter. Desultory canon fire continued but both ships understood the steps of this particular dance. Sailors, armed with cutlasses and ancient flintlocks, were massing on the starboard side, ready to try and repel the boarders, whilst the emaciated men of the pirate ship massed on their larboard. They outnumbered the sailors by more than double and William could see the grim atmosphere amongst the sailors on the injured cutter.

A sailor on the lifeboat manned the tiller, whilst another half dozen raised the sheeting. Yet another half dozen rudely shifted people off benches and started rowing. They achieved little, but they understood that just a little could mean the difference between life and death.

The wind slapped in the sails before finally catching; their only hope was that they would get a head start whilst the pirates pillaged, bloodied and burned, and then for night to fall rapidly, a dark, dark night full of cloud. The turquoise sea, twinkling whitecaps and pale blue sky belied the hope, but it was all they had.

Whilst the pirate ship was coming round, it too was dropping off a lifeboat, a maggoty, worm-ridden, stinking affair that barely floated and carried fewer than thirty wild-eyed brigands, their weapons notched and blunt.

Four other boats had been put to sea by the cutter, elderly men and low born women sitting petrified on their benches, water lapping gently around ankles as a few sailors spared to the task bailed and sailed.

These boats were utterly ignored, and, if you would like a happy ending, one of these made it to land without capsizing, sinking or being captured, they made it without male children murdered, older women raped and then murdered, younger girls raped before being sold in to slavery, younger mothers being turned into whores and passed around the pirate ship, until they too died of the bodily grievances inflicted. One boat made it, marooned for months, before being rescued by the Royal Navy, starving and feral.

William's boat, however, was the first to be taken, wily pirates taking the most prized possession first. None on the boat were harmed – initially. All of these folk could potentially be worth a great deal of money in one form or another – the boys could be ransomed unless particularly pretty, in which case their end would be a fate worse than death. Ladies and rich wives, likewise, could be ransomed whilst the younger girls could be turned into money in any number of ways.

One exception: the sailors in charge of the lifeboat had put up a brave fight, killing a few of the pirates, but the pirates swiftly overcame them, killing them to a man.

Dimly, through the tears of pain and anguish, William could see the cutter, flames leaping from her decks, screams echoing across the water, the pirate ship sailing free from the vessel. He never saw his father or older brothers again.

William hugged his sisters, even Mary, the eldest sister, and gratefully felt the arms of his mother enfolding them all. His youngest sister, only two, screamed inconsolably, only aware that bad things were happening. The older two sisters were petrified beyond this. Aged eight and nine they knew their peril without any real concept of the hell that potentially lay ahead. Mary was almost in a dead faint as William winced at the tightness with which he was being hugged – bruised ribs, chest slashed and a broken nose. He had tried to help the sailors prevent the boarding and thankfully he was no longer a pretty boy.

Placed in a pen with a number of other captives, their bodies had been squeezed painfully together, barely room to breathe, never mind urinate or empty their bowels... which unfortunately had to happen for a number of days without remorse.

Only minute quantities of water had been given in order to keep them alive. Port had been close enough not to require food, a large town being their destination, the Captain brazen and bold with his catch, fearless of the Spanish and Dutch naval vessels in port. They studiously ignored the plaintive cries from the pirate ship, even though some of those cries were in their native language.

The Pirate Captain had a town house, where he and some of his trusted crewmen berthed. The rest had been given gold which they rapidly drank away until they could no longer stand and they slept where they vomited.

The Pirate Captain towered above everyone, a veritable giant of a man with his huge barrel chest, ebony-black skin and a shining bald pate. His had a pugnacious face and vastly ugly, with many scars and hostile eyes. He interviewed them all in turn. He hadn't been gentle and a young William had had the truth beaten out of him. More ribs had been broken and teeth smashed; rapidly, in truth, did he concede.

He had been sold for ransom, back to his family and a year after being captured he arrived home again, quiet and withdrawn. Guilty.

His mother had not been so lucky; the senior Lord Hope had married for love, not wealth or connections, and so it transpired that she was worthless as a ransom. She had no heir to a family title, merely a dowager at the age of thirty five.

Her screams echoed around William's morphine-addled mind, much as it had when he'd been returned home by the Royal Navy.

His elder sister had also been returned, the benefit narrowly offsetting the trouble of finding the right buyer. At fifteen, she had been too old to be overly valuable.

His three younger sisters were the least lucky. The youngest was too young and too much trouble to nursemaid and so she was murdered out of hand. The Captain had laughed uproariously when he repeatedly told William of her fate during his long months of captivity.

His two sisters were sold to a very rich black paedophile.

And so William had begun a hatred of Negroes and pirates. He had always been sickened by paedophiles – all sane people were.

*

William limped around the grounds of Birtles Hall. He stumbled and was surprised to find himself caught by the elbow, a strong, firm hand pulling him upright.

"You're up, Sir," said the voice of Smith.

"Ah, Smith, yes. And thank you for the assistance. I don't know that I've ever felt so weak."

"Enslavement, fire, shock and morphine can do that to a man."

"And you would know?"

"Not personally, but I have seen similar effects in others. Have you ever been to Limehouse?"

"Chinatown, yes. I understand your meaning, although from experience, the notoriety of the opium dens are greatly exaggerated." William smiled up at Smith. "From my own humble experience, at any rate."

Smith spluttered with indignation and then burst in to laughter. "My, my, you really are a dark horse, my Lord."

"My tale was not exactly fabricated, you know. Now, what story will you fabricate today. I've spoken to Brocklehurst, and he seems quite well reasoned. A touch of that eccentricity that can touch those with genius, but certainly not unstable."

"I did not claim that he was approaching insanity, Sir William," Smith said sternly. "I said he could not be trusted and I need someone who could not possibly be suspected of being a spy to be exactly that. I need information that I'm entirely unable to get."

"What information, and why can't you get it?"

"As I said, I'm merely a guard. I've no right to be asking questions, and I don't think Brocklehurst trusts me. I need to know where certain packets of sensitive information are being sent. Not lots of information, but a bit here, a bit there and some of it has been rather embarrassing. What I really need is some proof, definite proof, that there is a link between the Italian uprising and this place."

"What information could there be that would matter to such a conflagration?"

"Little things. Disposition of forces, weak diplomats, that sort of thing. We even suspect that blueprints of weapons have been leaked. It's not the only place such information could have come from, and I'm not the only Exploring Officer performing this kind of reconnaissance, but the other potential sources are pretty well spoken for."

"Whispers in dark corners – it's nothing more than that?"

"Not really, no. But a more respected man than myself may be able to get through him. Technical talk, give his ego a massage." Smith looked exasperated. "Please, Sir William, you must try, before it is too late."

"Too late? Too late for what exactly," William asked sharply.

"I'm not sure exactly, but I can smell it, it's why I'm good at my job. There's an odour of finality."

"Bloody, bloody, hell. Can a man not even convalesce in peace?"

Smith smiled at William. "No, my Lord. No, you cannot."

CHAPTER 2 – RAPE

A young lady sits in the dark. Alone. Weeping.

She is bleeding lightly, a dark trickle between her legs. Yet, there is no physical pain. She is numb, physically and mentally, the tears a subconscious reaction, as if she almost should be crying, rather than actually wanting to, *needing* to.

Her skin is dark as night. Long slender arms tremble, goose bumps impossibly large. Short cropped curly hair crowns a near-gaunt face the shape of a teardrop, a face that boasts puffy almond eyes that are the colour of an indigo twilight overshadowing high prominent cheekbones. From her neck to her thighs a long sleeping shirt covers her slender figure to near shapelessness; only small, erect papilla jutting forth from small breasts crease the garment. The hem is stained in wet blood; and from below the hem stretch long, ever so long, smooth luxuriant legs.

She is remarkably beautiful.

This is why she has just been raped.

*

Amara had been walking alongside the River Abys before it had happened, the wide water's slow, meandering journey broken only by large rocks and boulders that occasionally came crashing down from the rock face on the opposite side. Over the years, the passage of the water had scooped out the lowest parts of the rock face leaving yawning overhangs and shadows where fish shaded themselves from the heat of the midday sun. On the side of the water that Amara walked along, some twenty metres from the rock face, it was as flat as the other side was sheer. Tall stark trees lined fields, mostly devoid of leaves, except for the occasional russet survivor. Crops grew here during the summer, but in the twilight of autumn, the soils had been freshly turned in readiness for the spring. And across from the fields and rocky outcrops, far below as the fields ended and the hillsides sloped downwards into brown savannah, the sun had been setting. It had moved visibly as the last few inches travelled to the horizon and beyond, ochres, purples, reds and oranges intermingling, unravelling, fusing and melting, shouting out to all who could see that this was the days end.

Amara had watched the sun set until the only clue that the sun had ever been was the blue gradient from the horizon to the rock face, a warm pallid blue to deep cobalt, where stars began to show.

As the blue deepened on the horizon, she had turned for home, for without the sun the air had been chill.

Arriving at her small home, she had intuitively known that something was wrong – a sensation of foreboding, an indefinable feeling that something was out of place. Opening the door, almost cautiously, the first thing she had noticed was blood: copper tang and crimson hue. The small kitchen into which she entered had been almost repainted in sticky redness. Rough hands had grabbed her and she had cried out, not at the rough hands, but at her husband's corpse, carelessly tossed into a corner. His eyes stared sightlessly across the room, a blades deep, jagged rent across the smooth black skin of his throat.

Then she had been punished, although she had felt nothing, had seen nothing; nothing but the face of her dead husband who watched her shame through those glassy eyes.

Dimly, at the end of her ordeal, she had heard one of the white men say, "Shall we kill her?" In the subconscious periphery of her vision, he had been holding a wicked serrated hunting blade. "No," replied another, the first to rape her. "Let her live." His face had creased as if he found the idea humorous. They had left with a full moon lighting their way.

Her fear left her.

*

Now, slumped on her bed, dawn light blinding her unseeing eyes, Amara rose. Her guilt was immense, not at the rape, but that she had survived whilst her husband had perished. All her fault. Her escape attempt had been futile.

Like an old lady she shuffled across the room, through the copper and crimson kitchen and out of the house. Her body was an agony of aches and bruises. Especially *down there*. She hobbled to the river, down the shallow bank into the water. She continued walking until the water was at chest height, and then cast herself in, coming to rest face down in the water.

Only a short time passed before, spluttering, she threw her head back and attempted to stand. She flailed wildly for a few moments, panic briefly setting on her face, before her feet found purchase. She had never been strong enough. She had never loved her husband as he ought to have been loved.

Almost vacantly, she waded back to the bank, tears streaming from her unseeing eyes. Stumbling up the bank, she returned to the house. On walking into the kitchen, she glanced at her husband. He had been a good, honest man and deserved a better end than this. He religiously tended to their fields and cattle, always putting food on the table; and he loved his wife with a fervour. They had been trying to start a family, but their beautiful marriage would now end barren.

Dimly, she wandered through the house with a bag in her hand collecting various miscellany, money, clothes and any item that her misted mind deemed to be of use. There was not much in that bag. She barely registered the state of her normally pristine house, the wardrobe overturned, drawers emptied, wall panels hanging loose and the hearth physically upended. She changed her clothes, donning a long cotton smock the colour of mint, hemp moccasins a thin cloak that she wrapped around her shoulders. Finally, she returned to the kitchen, taking several knives. She put all in her bag, barring one, her husband's hunting knife, which she put under the belt of her smock.

Without a backward glance, Amara left her home and never saw it again.

*

She walked westwards, tracking the banks of the River Abys. A mountain peak ranged high above, and the steppe upon which she walked ranged to the west, descending slowly. As the land dropped away, the river became narrow and deep, moving with a far greater speed, its noise almost deafening her.

Late flowers were still in bloom, clinging to the weakened warmth from the sun and wild Ackee trees still bore over-ripe fruit, tasty and lethal. She sometimes used the seeds to poison packs of wild dogs, and more than once on her journey to the plains below she became absently tempted to do the same, to put herself down like those self-same wild dogs. She never felt sufficiently motivated to perform the task.

At this altitude, the snows would arrive in a matter of weeks, the weather changing rapidly, and all would be a blanket of white. It would still appear green and verdant in the lowlands, where instead of snow, the rains would fall for many weeks, with the Abys bursting its banks to sluice the land with its orange mud until the rains subsided, signalling the start of spring. The savannah would then erupt in a riot of colour, starting with a creeping green carpet of wild grass, which would then be interrupted after only a few days by yellows, reds and blues of savannah flowers.

Amara's moved stiffly, like an automaton, with no arm movement or rocking of the head. She stumbled frequently on the rough track, and saw nothing, not the late flowers, distant savannah or blue horizon. Occasionally she would sit and rest, eating and drinking a little, the actions entirely independent of conscious thought. She carelessly ate the Ackee fruit, somehow managing to eat only the edible parts, inattentively stuffing the remains in to pockets or her bag. Always her path lay downwards, descending on a winding trail towards the plains below. Sometimes the going was steep and treacherous, and other times gentle, at which times the river would slow and widen.

Amara journeyed down the mountain for two full days and nights. During the nights she lay down in a parody of sleep, eyes closed, body still, but without the deep dreamlessness that was required for her body and mind to heal. Both were bruised and broken, oozing pus and beginning to stink as a rot set in. Any sleep she did get was light and interrupted by terrible dreams. In one dream she was being hauled up a tree by a leopard, teeth gripping her broken neck. Amara still lived in this dream, and the pain was horrific as her head lolled unnaturally. In another dream, she had her husband's knife, and this she plunged repeatedly into her own stomach, pulling out a still born child with her vital organs. Following every dream she awoke with tears streaming down her face.

She saw no one as she dropped down towards the plains. Few people had reason to come into the mountains at this time of year. As the mountains ended, the land rapidly flattened into rolling countryside. A village existed on the banks of a lake formed by the river.

Amara walked into the village, and all who saw her stared, although none seemed to recognise her. Her face displayed a cacophony of colour, bruises pale yellow and livid purple. Her eyes were shot red, and her hair unkempt and unwashed. Pus had encrusted her shirt to her back, the legacy of being lashed for failing to make a sound or utter a whimper whilst being raped. She had not uttered a sound under that lash either. An old, bent lady attempted to stop her as she passed by, and as Amara walked past the lady without a glance, the lady gasped in shocked recognition.

Amara walked on for several paces more before collapsing in the street.

*

Amara came too in a warm, close room. The smell of wax candles pervaded. A young white man sat on a chair by her cot. She had rarely seen a white man before being raped by one, although this one perhaps appeared tantalisingly familiar. Maybe they all looked the same. She simply could not find a way to react in anyway. A man – a white man – sat in her bedroom.

"Mademoiselle" he exclaimed, on seeing her, "ça va?"

Amara looked at him further, understanding him perfectly, but comprehending not at all.

"Mademoiselle?"

Amara continued to stare incomprehensibly, unmoving, not even blinking.

"Do you remember me? I'm an explorer. You're exactly what I'm looking for. Or rather *who*."

Amara gazed into his deep blue eyes, gazing without any focus.

"My darling, let me explain. You are lost, I can find you. Now, don't misunderstand me, you aren't lost. You're *lost*. I can see it in your eyes, those beautiful violet eyes".

Amara's gaze remained unchanged, but the temperature fell with apprehension and fear. Her body remained bruised, abused, and her person was in shock, physically and in her psyche. She had been raped.

The white man smiled gently. "Worry not, mademoiselle, I say again, I can find you. I do not mean that in any way untoward. I only want to help".

Amara continued to gaze, the chill continued. She no longer wanted to be in the room with the man, but she had no way to remove herself in her current state. Physically abused and exhausted, husband murdered, she had nothing to live for.

She blinked and turned over, eyes still gazing.

Seeing the white man, she considered herself. She did have one thing to live for.

That thing was revenge.

*

Amara awoke. A decent sleep this time, and she felt almost fresh. She had eaten, drank, slept and woken a number of times; sometimes the young white man was there, sometimes the chair was empty. Sometimes, an old black crone sat in the room, skin like leather, but if she noticed that Amara watched her, she gave no sign.

One morning Amara's eyes opened to see the young man watching her intently. She swung her legs from the bed and rose. She undressed completely, her body almost completely healed and it was lithe and beautiful, luxurious even. The young man's eyes widened, his face reddened, and he spluttered incoherently as he ran from the room. At the end of the bed were her own clothes, folded neatly, which she donned. The old lady came in to the room and seemed ready to protest that the girl shouldn't move, but she took one look at Amara's face and held her tongue.

No emotions played on her face, no emotions were present in her head, only the tight control of a task to be performed. The fear had drained and returned, and had to be conquered. That fear that had led to her taking her man before loving him. She felt her talent ticking at the back of her mind. She pushed it away, trying to squash the fear that came with it.

Fully dressed, Amara gathered her belongings and walked from the room, brushing aside the old crone who this time did try to stop her. The man stood on the porch of the building, and he hurried to catch up with Amara who walked in the opposite direction purposefully to avoid him.

"Mademoiselle."

He bustled behind her as she showed no sense of having heard him. "S'il vous plait!"

Amara lengthened her stride.

"Amara."

Her stride faltered for a brief instant as bewilderment registered on her brow. And then she walked even more quickly, head held militarily high, still ignoring the white man.

"I know who did this," gasped the man.

Amara stopped, and the man walked straight into her.

She flinched at the contact and twisted sideways, hand holding the hilt of her husband's hunting knife.

"Je m'apelle Jean Nicolas Arthur Rimbaud, that is, my name is Arthur Rimbaud." He pronounced Arthur 'Artur' which struck a pleasant chord with Amara, the first pleasant thing she'd felt in an eternity.

He proffered a hand which she ignored.

"The men who did this...I am ashamed to say they were my countrymen and I travelled with them."

As fast as a striking snake, Amara had the hunting knife at Arthur's throat, a tiny nick leaking a small stream of blood down to his chest. People stopped in the street to watch.

"Please, I have vowed to kill them, or be killed in the process. I have waited for you because in your place I would want the chance of revenge."

Amara withdrew the knife and smiled. Not a pleasant smile to light up her beautiful face, but a horrific manifestation that contorted her features into a nightmare that made Arthur flinch.

"We go now," she said.

He could only nod.

*

Rimbaud insisted on getting provisions for the journey before setting off. She could see the logic, and so allowed the small Frenchman this concession. Once the logistics were organised, Amara walked side by side with Arthur as they left the village, looking neither left nor right. She did not see the path ahead, she merely walked.

Arthur could not help but to continuously side-glance, watching her out of the corner of his right eye. He was nervous – very nervous. But he needed her badly; his work could not suffer, and he must do what he had to do. So he steeled himself to the inevitable conclusion. He gazed further down the track heading northwards. It would not be long now.

It was incredibly hot and humid. Trees and Jurassic vegetation surrounded them, making Rimbaud feel claustrophobic, air unbreathable, the world closing in. After about an hour of walking in silence – excepting the screeches of tropical birds in the trees, the buzz of insects that attacked Rimbaud with a frenzy, and the screech of the Colobus monkey high-up in the trees – a single alien sound was heard. Arthur was startled, even though he knew what was coming. Amara's hand went to her knife.

The sound was that of a gun being cocked.

On the path ahead, a bearded white man stepped out, a wicked grin on his face. Another man, much younger, joined him. Amara screamed, a high pitched ululating scream and without thought, sprang towards them. Arthur, shocked beyond belief at her action, did not move.

Amara's fear ceased to exist.

Knife in hand, she covered the distance in a ludicrously short time, that very time compressing into a tiny bubble as she leaped high in to the air. The younger man reacted and stepped towards her, raising his gun. He was too slow, much too slow. Amara landed on his chest, knees first, knocking him to the ground. A pain lanced into his neck, and he had a few seconds to watch Amara withdraw her husband's hunting knife and plunge it again in to his throat, a fountain of blood rising, before the light dimmed to monochrome except for a scarlet flood, and then he was no more.

Amara plunged the knife in to the dead man again before a small torch shone at the back of her mind. Just as she again withdrew the knife, and turned to face in the direction of the bearded man, a shadow passed the sun and a crack struck her hard on the side of the head, knocking her unconscious. The man booted her form in the side and would have repeated the kick until she was no more, had Arthur not prevented him.

The dead man was, after all, the bearded man's son.

CHAPTER 3 – GEORGE AND THE DRAGON

George Chapman sat in a comfortable library in a rather fashionable suburb of Paris. He wore a midnight blue suit with a scarlet waistcoat and blazing yellow cravat. Rain spattered the windows, the light a dull autumnal grey. He had leafed through a number of tomes, those that had caught his eye, and he longed for a relaxed period to be able to revisit the shelves. But then, he was anything but relaxed as he frequently rose to pace the room, an anxious crease wrinkling his non-descript features.

He had also been there long enough to allow his mind time to wander.

He mused on his most favourite pastime. Currently, this was murder.

As a student of learning, he was desperate to again become a fellow in the Royal Society and he fumed that he hadn't yet been invited, even though he had been quite brilliant during presentations of his research before the misunderstanding that led to his being black-balled.

Nominally, he studied society and how the wonders of modern science could integrate with the neediest in society, and indeed, across the known world. He'd even provided assistance with steering scientific research to concentrate on certain facets of development.

As a younger man, this study of society had shown him the darker sides of humanity, and, whilst on a research trip through Africa, he had partaken in a Vodun ritual. He had been impressed with the religion from the beginning, recognising its sympathetic nature and its innate goodness as a tool for community and togetherness.

But the ritual had a darker side, probably not even recognised by the locals, or just so *normal* as to be ignored. Maybe it was his superior white intellect, his more evolved mind that recognised the darkness.

He'd then attended more rituals, focussing on the language and ascertaining the key triggers to show the darkness. Swimming in the background, in a fume of its own oily smog, stalked a dragon.

This was especially obvious to him during animal sacrifices performed by the African Negroes for celebration feasts to a particular deity or spirit. And the more complex the organism that was sacrificed, the darker and more real the dragon. He became hooked in an instant. The dragon signified death and he had to conquer it. He'd not only *own* the Royal Society, he would almost be immortal.

As a man of science, it was therefore necessary to experiment, and on the most evolved species of them all: humans. A few victims from Whitechapel shouldn't have been missed. He had used his imagination somewhat, though. Rather than just sacrifice them, he may have gone slightly over the top.

But how very wrong he had been. His antics were all over the sensationalist press as a result. He had had to slit their throats of course, but some other facets of the sacrifice meant that he'd had to disguise his ministrations. He'd been excited and aroused. Maybe he had gone too far. It was done with for now. He had learned little of worth from them. He considered a trip to Africa. Maybe he would have better results with believers, but the idea sounded specious, and he viewed a trip with scepticism.

The murders were untraceable, but a certain nervousness raised his pulse somewhat. A cryptic, but very pointed telegram had forced this urgent journey, dragging him here to Paris. The telegram was from one Wilhelm Stieber, a name to strike fear in to any person who knew it, or had heard rumour of his dealings. A Prussian Spymaster General stationed in Paris, aware of everything important and a lot that seemingly was not. He was responsible for the removal of French antagonists angry over the farce of the French Government, the interrogation of foreign spies; he moulded and shaped the very future of Europe. He was the advantage that Prussia had over the British in shared France.

A newspaper headline caught his eye, and he read the article, one eyebrow raised.

"My god, where do these reporters dig up this rubbish" he muttered to himself. "In fact, where do they dig up these bloody rubbish reporters?"

Spies!

The Russians attack Paris!

A Russian spy has allegedly been captured in the governing halls of Paris. Armed with incendiary devices, he has been positively identified as Pyotr Rachkovsky, a member of the Russian secret service. Prussia and Great Britain have expressed outrage at this attempted terrorism and demanded an unconditional apology from the Kremlin. They have also insisted –

most brusquely – that they immediately withdraw the forces that threaten the Pomeranian borders.

"Tsk!" muttered Chapman to himself. "The bloody Russians wouldn't apologise for fear of denting their pride, never mind that they risk millions more of their own people. And who gives a damn about Pomerania. They're just a bunch of turnip eating pygmies!"

Chapman was eventually ushered into a beautiful office. It contained the finest mahogany furniture, beautifully upholstered in leather. Crystal glasses of breath-taking clarity adorned a small bar to one side, beside which were a range of the finest brandies and wines that any connoisseur could name. Gold framed art lined the walls, and everything spoke of breeding and wealth.

Almost, that is, Chapman mused. There was a technical drawing of one of those motorised bicycles that had so become the trend with the rich, terrorising country roads and killing themselves in equally abominable numbers. The diagram was placed onto a large drawing board to one side of the room with a number of annotations made in expensive red ink.

With some surprise, Chapman noted no evidence of the more kingly sports, such as hunting or coursing. He had imagined that the office of a bloody – quite literally bloody – tyrant such as this would have been bathed in trophies and weapons. But no, there were none. In fact, a book of romantic poetry sat on the edge of his desk, obviously well read.

The figure in the chair did not fit in with the surroundings. Ignoring his presence entirely, sat a short, bespectacled man, with an unkempt, bushy moustache and a balding pate, his bowtie lay at an uncouth angle, and food stained a rather old and threadbare black coat. He was clearly disorganised, a mass of papers strewn across his desk in various untidy piles. Chapman relaxed a little and began to consider that the reputation of this individual may be somewhat overblown.

"Mister Chapman, please take a seat," said Wilhelm Stieber in an almost flawless English accent. He had not so much as looked up from his writing.

"I hope the wait was not too inconvenient."

A total of four hours had passed in the waiting room, and whilst he had been fairly pampered, it had been a deliberate ploy to exhibit where the power rested. In fairness, the telegram demonstrated that with cryptic clarity.

Stieber put his notes to one side and looked at George for the first time. There was a smile and this made the domination of the man clearer still. He had the look of a cat licking its lips in anticipation. His eyes gleamed.

At that look, Chapman paled and although he didn't show it, he suddenly needed to urinate.

"Thank you Monsieur, sorry, Herr Stieber. There was no inconvenience," he stammered.

"To business then, I can't abide banal meaningless pleasantries."

He shuffled some paper and glanced down at them. He smiled again.

"It has come to my attention that you are somewhat of a formidable and resourceful scientist, intent on becoming a member of the Royal Society, ah, again," he stated as fact, but looked enquiringly at Chapman, who nodded jerkily.

"And that you have made an intensive study of Vodun?"

Again, Chapman nodded mutely. Inwardly, his mind was whirring madly from one side to another, up and down and then round again. *What in heavens name could this possibly be about?* was the only properly lucid thought in his head.

"A colleague of mine has also been studying, quite closely, some of those same rituals. I believe he was inspired by the conclusions of your report. Even more so by your notes that were omitted from that report. You see, as a former colleague of yours, he was surprised that these were not brought to his attention at the time."

"I'm sure I don't understand, Herr Stieber. What unpublished notes?" George squeaked as he spoke, and sweat dripped down his back. He realised that this was a futile attempt at deceit.

"George – may I call you George?" Without waiting for a reply he continued. "I have read your report, your unofficial notes and I am fully appraised of the missing persons mystery in your London. Please do not try my patience with ridiculous denials. I wish to help with your research and I believe I have some useful research notes from a colleague who has also studied in West Africa. Along with the whereabouts of a particularly useful gift."

George's mouth opened and closed again. And then opened again. "I don't understand."

"Of course you don't. Let me simplify our arrangement significantly. I direct your research. You essentially do as I say. If I believe you are disobeying me in any way, I will hand you over to the authorities in London with irrefutable evidence of you being the London murderer, Jack the Ripper. In return, I will see all of your research, and will make sure you become a member of the Royal Society. Is that understood and acceptable, Herr Chapman?" Stieber's eyes glittered and the lack of fear-inducing smile was somehow worse.

George could only gaze at Stieber slack-jawed.

"As you have no alternative, I'll take your silence as an affirmative."

Chapman gulped and nodded.

"How could you possibly know?"

"As you can see, information is power and so I have agents everywhere. You were rather zealous in your slaughter."

"Well, yes, I may have become a touch carried away."

Stieber continued. "Pray, tell me, what was the reason you were removed from the Royal Society?" He glanced down at a sheet of paper laid out in small German script, numerous annotations once again in red ink.

Evidently Stieber already knew the reason, but he seemed to be enjoying himself and Chapman, shocked by the bland statement regarding the killings in the East End, his heart beating at the revelation, and even more so at the promise of re-admission to the Society, was agog with attention.

"Well," he stuttered. "It was all a most unpleasant misunderstanding, to the best of my knowledge."

He blushed as he remembered standing before Sir William Sabile like a naughty school child, the man's Dublin accent raised to its finest martial pitch as befitted a former artilleryman.

"How bloody well dare you bring my Society in to such disregard. My arse has barely warmed this seat and you shame me man, shame me! You shame us all."

"Now get out and never darken these doors again." This was Sabile's sad lament on the matter. Chapman had left at this, angry at the short-sightedness of the horrible little military man.

"Come William," said Stieber, shaking Chapman out of his recollections. "It was a little more than a misunderstanding, surely?" Stieber was taunting the man in front of him, laughing inwardly at the slumped shoulders and the reddened cheeks presented before him.

Chapman found some pride and straightened in his chair, a momentary show of courage on his features.

"I was accused of plagiarism and my research ethics were questioned. Most unfairly." A stubborn jaw jutted forth.

"Quite," said the Prussian with an arched eyebrow. "Still, to relevant business. Your former colleague who was veritably flabbergasted at the, ah, *unabridged* report is a certain Arthur Rimbaud. Do you remember the name?"

Chapman did. That weak little man had been the expedition leader. He couldn't stand that pious Frog. Far too intelligent for his own good, and with none of the force of will that characterised an Englishman.

"I recall him." It was a grudging accession.

"He recalls you also." A smile twitched one corner of Stieber's mouth. "Perhaps I overstate his surprise."

There was a long pause as Stieber fished around in one of the drawers of his desk containing more paperwork, also seemingly disorganised.

"My aim is to speak to these people." He dug in the middle of one of the piles of papers, immediately finding what he required, and pushed across several photographs, all slightly disturbing in their vivid purple colouration. They were in poor condition, obviously having been wet at some point. Chapman couldn't even tell what they were meant to be. Until, with a gasp, he caught the image on one daguerreotype, and then all of them fell in to place.

"What on *earth* is that?"

"They appear to be spirits. They surprised even me."

"Where did you get them? Where were they taken? They're astounding!" Chapman's eyes gleamed greedily and he leaned eagerly over the desk.

"THAT is none of your business," snapped Stieber, suddenly fierce with unexpected anger, and he gathered up the photographs

George's mind whirled, but Stieber's glare forced his greed into submission, bringing him sharply back to the present. It reminded him of the look on Sabile's face as he was frog marched from Royal Society premises whilst being barracked remorselessly.

"Depraved behaviour, unheard of in the annals of our proud history, damn you, damn you to hell. Plagiarism, well, I find it bad enough, enough to tarnish a reputation, but the repugnancy…"

There was a long pause.

"…I don't care about the results, the methodology must be untouchable, the hypothesis justifiable. Zealotry is unforgivable and groping aimlessly for results is diabolical. And the tactics used! How dare you drag our great Society into such sordid drudgery, little better than…"

Another long pause.

"…you, Sir, are a cad and a bounder, a villain of the highest order. The records will show this. You will never be re-admitted to this great Society again…"

Chapman had felt like a new recruit on the end of a tongue lashing by a particularly irate sergeant. He felt like that now.

The temperature in the room had suddenly plummeted, and as the German's temper had risen, his accent had become more pronounced. Chapman became petrified. Maybe it was the added memory of old Sabile that made him tremble.

"I need to communicate with them. To that end, you will go to Cheshire in England, kidnap the Negro housemaid at Birtles Hall and perform your ritual on her. I believe she is a Vodun adept and a virgin, both of which I believe may aid your research. Her presence will not be unduly missed. You then need to come back and report. Depending on your conduct and your results, my colleague may have another subject for more extensive study." Stieber gathered up his notes, entirely ignoring his guest, who did not dare move.

After a few seconds he looked up. "I believe you have a task to perform?"

George nodded, rose and turned to the door.

"Do not fail me, George, for you will fail yourself."

Chapman looked over his shoulder and nodded spasmodically. And then he fled.

*

The man, a most unremarkable looking man, awoke in a dream. His clean shaven features were non-descript, his eyes brown, his build neither slight nor large. He was neither tall nor short, fat nor thin and his hair was a most unremarkable blonde-brown, as were his thin eyebrows. The dream was one he had desired above all else, but at that moment it was the last place he desired to be. A dragon was his guest; or rather, he was the guest of the dragon. The dragon was the colour and texture of deeply tanned leather, wings furled upon its back. It lay on its soft underbelly, countered by the armoured scales upon its back and sides. Like a cat, its legs were positioned to seemingly allow it to pounce. A barbed tail lay coiled motionlessly on the floor. Black smoke oozed fluidly from pointed nose, fanged maw and the corners of its eyes. Its eyes were open, and they regarded the unremarkable man. Mesmerized, the man gazed helplessly into the black, swirling, oily surfaces that were the dragon's eyes. The man did not notice the dragon's sudden activity, the swish of the barbed tail, nor the foreleg of the dragon, which reached out, its taloned claw enclosing around him. Nor did he notice when he was effortlessly picked up and transported to the unnoticed widening of its mouth. The man only noticed that all of this had happened when he was entering the mouth of the dragon and contact with its eyes was broken. By then it was far too late.

In his head he heard a fathomless laugh, a noise from the bowels of the universe that contained no mirth, only pain and suffering.

The man screamed.

And screamed.

And screamed for a long, long time, until he awoke.

*

The unremarkable-looking man, who just happened to be George Chapman, no longer looked quite so unremarkable.

Agreed, he still owned non-descript features if one but had the temerity to look for such a thing. However, he now towered to a height of nearly eight feet tall. His limbs seemed to have been stretched and as a result had become skeletally thin with sinuous muscles ripping through a skin dyed to ebony. His hair had grown and descended in perfect straightness to the base of his spine. It too had become as black as jet in colour. His eyes had no whites, nor could any pupils be distinguished. They had become a soulless, dull black. Those eyes could quite easily have belonged to a corpse. A long black beard hung from his face, hiding thin, pinched lips as pale as ivory. His skin was nearly transparent through the ebony, small blood vessels evident below the surface. Long bony hands and fingers protruded from the black shirt he wore. The transparency of flesh, the elongated gauntness and the bleakness of expression, all insinuated at that of a mythical Nosferatu, desolate and terrible.

He no longer recognised the name George Chapman. His name was Rune.

Most remarkable of all the changes in the man was his age; it appeared as if he had aged a millennia. Indeed, in his own mind – if his own it was – he had screamed for all of those years whilst he had been broken and re-shaped into this parody of humanity.

He stepped through the cave that had been his home during the dream-nightmare. The darkest mid-winter had waxed to sharpest spring; no trees yet bore leaves, but early snowdrops and the beginnings of a certain lush verdancy combined at the edges of his cave. It was morning, an achingly beautiful morning with the hint of a light frost lacing the rolling hills. Chapman would have revelled in the moment, if he'd ever have been up this early. Rune saw none of it.

The vestiges of his fire had been scattered by the winds these long days past and the remains of his food had rotted, even the cured meats past redemption. Strangely, nothing seemed to have tried to disturb his dream-nightmare, no wolf, fox nor carrion bird appeared to have visited. Indeed, there appeared to be no animals at all in his vicinity. The bones of the dead Negro woman had been bleached white.

Looking around himself, he studied his surroundings further, and calculated that it must have been many, many weeks since he began his fugue. The rite had been his last external memory, the screams of the woman echoed still.

Evidently, or so the small sliver that could was the real George Chapman told him, he had made further errors and things had gone drastically wrong, although he couldn't remember feeling this right, this *knowing*.

His time within the ritual was full of vast, all-encompassing pain, certainly not a pleasant recollection. But, to a zealous scholar, the weeks inside the burning, acrid dragon had been achingly informative, and he now knew about things he had never known even existed before, and in this knowing, he now desired more knowledge – and he desired…other things.

He had visited the past, studying for long years lore unheard of in this present age, a lore defeated eons ago by a lore also lost. He had visited the future and seen the possibilities in front of him, enabling him to shape the present to his own ends, to the dragon's end.

The dragon. What exactly was it? A real dragon? He did not know for sure. What he did know was that it was strong and deeply learned; as a scholar, he had nothing but respect for that, and as a zealous scholar, he had nothing but ardent desire to know more.

For now though, he was hungry, and the knowledge would have to wait. Walking to the mouth of the cave and beyond, he planted bare feet onto green earth. His feet stretched and twisted, bone warped and sinew writhed beneath transparent flesh. Tendrils grew from fine hairs, slowly at first and then more quickly. Like autonomous snakes, they shivered and shook in the morning breeze, and then as one descended, burrowing violently into the earth below. His skin deepened in colour, losing some of its transparency and his eyes gained a dancing gleam of eerily reflected light. All around him had become desolation. Branches lay bare, bark twisting and crumbling, the grass just no longer existed. Even the soil was grey and powdered and barren.

He was hungry no more.

CHAPTER 4 – UTOPIA

Lucas was cold, hungry and lost.

He was cold because he stood on a pebble beach by a huge lake, surrounded by snowy mountains. The air felt thin and he wore nothing but a white and badly worn wool shirt, stained white trousers and a pair of holey old boots.

He was hungry because….well, just because he was. Not the ravenous, emaciated hungry of a starving man, just the hunger of someone who hasn't eaten in hours. Hungry.

And he was lost because he didn't know where he was. He *really* didn't know where he was. Or how he'd come to be here. It was no place he recognised. Looking about in a circle, the sun glinting off icy peaks, the cloudless light blue sky, the eerily still, dark blue lake sparkling with the sun's rays, he realised this place could possibly be utopia.

He barked out loud with laughter, the harsh sound cutting through the silence.

Utopia. No place.

Or rather, no place he knew. So what to do?

"Walk somewhere, find someone" he muttered to himself. "But where?"

Straight on. Not an option, unless he'd suddenly developed the ability to walk on water.

Left and right, alongside the waters' edge, his eyes scanned for signs of life, but he could find none and the absolute quietude began to unnerve Lucas. No paths could be seen, no signs of human life – cognisant life – were evident, not even a bird in the sky. The only visible signs of *any* life were plants and grasses on the sheltered sides of larger rocks, flora that was made short and stunted by the cold and wind.

He moved to the water and peered at his own reflection. Luxurious white-blonde hair cascaded down to his shoulders and piercing blue eyes full of humour and warmth twinkled in the light. High cheekbones and fresh, tanned skin framed the eyes, with full lips. He barely recognised himself. If anything, the only defect in his countenance was a small, sharp nose. Everything else was flawless

Turning round to face the mountains, he scanned for a path, but after several minutes looking could find none. All he could see were pebbles and rocks of the darkest grey, vague stunted greenery and then the snow that contrasted harshly with the stone. Those mountains climbed massively before him, the white peaks sharp and foreboding. He could have been standing in the gaping maw of a biblical behemoth looking up at its vast teeth. There could be no way over those peaks.

Then, a quiet noise behind him, water gently slapping an object, and a creaking sound. Lucas span round, his heart rising into his mouth. The prow of a wooden skiff was just visible, approaching through the mists on the lake.

Shapes danced in the mists at the corners of his vision and the water seemed to broil unnaturally, although it appeared calm when he turned to look directly.

Lucas suddenly realised the enormity of his situation. A moment ago it had been bright and clear. *Utopian.* Now the lake was shrouded in rolling white mist, the mountains ahead invisible. He turned, and the mountains behind were still clear, sun glinting off the snow and ice, but the clarity seemed strangely dim and the brightness oddly gloomy, like viewing something through a smoky glass window. Apart from the fact that no glass existed, and the sun glinted clearly on the peaks. Only darkly.

In that moment he almost soiled himself with realisation, his lower stomach and bowels growing weak, blood flowing away from his face and dark spots swimming nauseatingly in front of his eyes.

"Mother Shipton", he swore softly, as the moment passed.

Lucas returned his attention to the wooden boat. As it appeared through the gloom, he was unsurprised to see that it appeared empty, except for a grubby tarpaulin heaped in the stern.

He had a feeling that not a lot else could surprise him today.

Closer it came, and then slew up onto the pebbles, utterly shattering the quiet and solitude, stopping a matter of inches from his feet.

As it did so a loud bark issued from the boat.

For the second time that day, Lucas nearly soiled himself, and he stumbled several surprised steps backwards.

The tarpaulin in the back of the boat appeared to come to life, almost laughably like a small (*large!*) child draped in a blanket, until a brown canine head poked its head out, tongue lolling. For a moment it regarded a trepid Lucas with brown, intelligent eyes, and then turned around and started snuffling around underneath the tarpaulin, a long tail, wagging pendulously, escaping from the place where its head had been.

It – she – bounded out of the boat at Lucas, who took another small, slightly horrified, step back. The dog skidded to a halt in front of him, and sat obediently, neck drooped downwards almost to her knees (*and what a long neck!*) and wounded puppy-dog eyes looking up from her face.

This wasn't just a normal sized dog, no Labrador or Alsatian. For starters, she probably weighed more than Lucas. Her shoulders were at the same height as Lucas' sternum, and she appeared to be almost as wide as the man that studied her. Long mahogany hair was interspersed with short mahogany hair along her flanks, as if she was moulting. The dog's four paws were huge, comically so (*you could use them for snow-walking*) and her head was the size of a football, with a long snout protruding (*best not get too close*). The longest neck Lucas had ever seen on a dog connected her head to her body, giving a ridiculously disconnected feel between head and body. Given the whole, it looked like someone had taken various parts of various animals to create a hybrid. Except she definitely looked all dog.

Lucas stood there, motionless, frozen, looking at her.

"More like a horse" he confirmed ever so quietly to himself, almost as if by thinking loudly the dog may be able to hear him.

The dog sat motionless (except for its ever-pendulous tail skimming across the pebbles) studying Lucas. Expectantly.

Lucas realised he'd stopped breathing, and exhaled slowly...which kind of made him act, as if the very action of breathing made him realise he should do something. So Lucas squatted down to eye level with the dog and proffered a hand. He hoped that the dog wouldn't take too much of a fancy to it.

Thankfully (and slightly perturbingly at first) she gruffed at the hand, and then she barked properly, a deep rolling "ruff", and nuzzled Lucas' chest. Which, given the size of the dog, hit him more like a head butt.

And with surprise etched over his face, Lucas fell backwards onto the pebbles.

After picking himself up, dusting himself down and allowing his heart rate to reach something approaching normality, Lucas' attention turned to the skiff. He moved over to the boat, wetting his feet in the process (*damn cold*). The water seemed to rise to greet him, seeping up and through the gaps in between the pebbles.

If the water seemed sentient, then the wood of the boat had a pulse and spoke to him in the voice of his Grandfather, a deep, wise and mellow tone.

The skiff didn't actually speak. Obviously, it didn't. It couldn't.

But the skiff did seem to make his head thrum gently, massaged his scalp, caressed his sinuses and warmed his brain. All at the same time. Yet there was more; the hairs on his body – all of them, it felt like – stood to attention, as did his penis, his cheeks flushed, his muscles flexed, his finger and toe nails pulsated, whilst the fingers and toes arched in a luxurious stretch-flex.

Lucas began to feel his consciousness slipping (or it might have been a loss of control over his consciousness), fingertips massaging his brain, his mind, probing his emotions, penetrating his whiteness and his blackness. And the greyness. That portion of his mind, both the strongest and the weakest, the part – the largest part – of his emotion that eyed the world without colour, that segment that in most people is smaller, less repressed, more expressed. It was the grey of his mind that refused to accept friendship easily, a blandness that could easily be mistaken for charm and dryness – or apathy. A part of his mind that absorbed boredness and excitement in equal measure, disallowing extreme highs and lows. A greyness, partly of pride and stubbornness that he'd moulded it into, allowing only a rare show of emotion, and that had turned into a habit. All told, a gift and a curse in equal measure.

This wasn't to say that Lucas was an unfeeling shell. He wasn't. Lucas was capable of the darkest of moods and also the most impulsive overblown gestures of kindness and love. It was just that all too often Lucas didn't really care, was immune to many of the tears and laughter that came so easily to some, the penetrating facility to understand the crux of humour or sadness or excitement. He could see death and then shrug his shoulders and move on. He was able to walk away from a *belle* into which he had invested much time and effort (and yes, he certainly *did* try) without shedding a tear. In some ways, he knew, this could be good. The ability to just pick up the pieces immediately and just get on with life. At other times felt as if he missed out on the larger picture, or worse – he just missed out.

All of these thoughts, these feelings and memories, coursed through Lucas in the twinkling of an eye and Lucas felt compelled to climb into the boat.

In an attempt to access the highs that other people seemed to have, Lucas had frequently taken opiates in the seedier parts of town. They were good, making you feel like you were on top of the world, but (*coup de foudre*), whatever this wood held, it worked better than any drug. Much better.

Or much worse.

The skiff had moved on from the opiate-like high, and had agitated his senses, as well as his physical being. This agitation of the mind had brought down sharp barriers. Lucas' greyness, if the truth be told, and being *compelled*, as if by an unseen hand in the middle of his back, provoked Lucas' greyness. The stubborn part of it.

So he didn't climb into the boat.

He simply removed his hand from the wood. And my, hadn't the water risen around Lucas, making a miniature mountain of water up to his knees.

The water now withdrew – mostly – when he removed his hand, now being a mere hillock over his boots.

Lucas stepped out of the water, boots soaking wet with puddles inside. These he removed, and emptied before putting them back on again.

The boat waited, the dog watched.

Lucas decided to walk around the lake into the mist, keeping close to the shore. The dog followed him, as did the seemingly sentient skiff. The mist seemed to be just over the lake, because the longer he walked the more he could see of the gleaming white mountains which had been towards the opposite side from when he first arrived. Away from the lake, there appeared to be little change; there were certainly no paths visible, and no animals or birds were apparent, which was odd, in his opinion.

Lucas' feet were beginning to hurt after a few hours of walking, the wet boots giving rise to blisters. The sun didn't seem to have waxed or waned, the dog still followed him, and the skiff still tracked him. Creatures still broiled in his periphery.

It also appeared that the mountains were a painting – they didn't seem to change, instead mirroring each other in height and shape. This truly was utopia, because no place on earth could be like this.

He stopped and sat down. The dog did the same. The skiff halted.

Lucas put his head in his hands, shaking it gently in denial.

"I'm going to get in the boat," he said impetuously to the dog. "But if it tries *that* again, I'll burn it, OK?"

"Woof!" said the dog.

He climbed in and the boat turned itself around. It sailed in to the mist and Lucas knew fear, because the creatures from his periphery existed.

CHAPTER 5 – EXPLODING UMBRELLAS

"Well, the scarring shouldn't be too bad."

"Thank you, Doctor," William replied.

Skin taut and the flesh of his head glowing, William rose from the cracked leather seat, wincing as his lower back parted from the flesh of the chair.

"Here, take this."

William took the offered pot of green-yellow unguent of gold-bloom & Zanzibar aloes rendered in to some nameless grease. He'd been using it for weeks, and the smell of rancid fat still made him retch. It did, however, seem to work, as the skin of his scalp and shoulders no longer oozed a bleak yellow pus. Hair had even starting to show on some areas of his skull.

The doctor put away his examination spectacles, a marvel of optical design, with slots for various strength lenses, and a small winding mechanism to enable ultra-sharp focussing.

"Can I borrow your spectacles, please doctor," he asked.

"Hmmm, I have an older spare pair, if you'd like. I'm loathe to part with these; they're unique you know, my very own design, machined by some of the marvellous micro-engineers we have here. My spares are the prototype and need some extra twiddling to get the sight crystal clear. Here they are."

"Thank you, doctor."

"You may keep them if you like."

"Ahhh, the news, I can read properly again without squinting."

With a smile, the doctor turned away, and William left the room, returning to his quarters, paper in hand. He lay back and read the headlines on the front page.

Нарушитель!

```
(Intruder, in Russian)
```

```
Russian    newspapers    report    that    a
British    mercenary    has    been    summarily
executed    by    the    Russian    Military    for
stealing    military    secrets.    The    Russian
government    has    angrily    accused    the
British    authorities    of    being    behind
the    failed    attempt.

Britain    has    denied    all    involvement,
stating    that    he    had    been    hired    by    the
Russian    military    to    advise    on    tactics,
and    that    if    they    couldn't    control
their    own    employees    "then    tough
titties!"
```

"Bloody politicians," snorted William disdainfully. "They should get a proper bloody job. Tosher would be about right."

His new quarters were a big improvement on his original quarters. Those had consisted of a small cot with a metal pot in the corner. And a locked door.

Now, however, he had something that could realistically be called quarters. Running water to a sink, a metal tub plumbed in to hot water and cold, even a sanitary design toilet with a u-bend to prevent foul smelling odours. Extremely rare, as was the concept of the 'flush' toilet.

William peered in to the mirror above the sink. He looked awful. Mere stubble existed where his luxurious moustaches had once been, and it looked odd to have a top lip. He sighed; it would be at least a year before he would look proper again. Small areas of salt and pepper stubble showed through on his scalp. At least his eyes were the right colour – hazel – and the whites were once more mostly white. They'd regained most of their merry, mischievous look. His face still showed signs of puffiness, but most of the swelling had gone down so that his face was once again almost muscular, a slender nose and narrow jaw, high strong cheekbones and broad lips.

He removed his gown to see a body that had wasted somewhat during his recuperation. Goose bumps raised on his flesh as it tasted the fresh air of Birtles Hall.

He dressed and walked in to the grounds which contained a number of exotic shrubs and trees. Of particular interest was *Eucryphia nymanensis*, an incredibly rare exhibit only just introduced from the South Seas. Unfortunately the leaf buds were only just starting to thicken, with a large area around its base still protected by straw in an attempt to keep the frost away from its roots, which could still be seen on some of the higher peaks. He made a mental note to visit again in late summer to see it in bloom. One or two early rhododendrons were blooming, leftovers from Lord Hibbert's Hare Hill retreat a mile or two away.

William mused on the popular news from that time. Hibbert, now deceased, had transferred ownership to Lord Brocklehurst on his deathbed, an unusual twist from the original will of Hibbert. Brocklehurst, much to his families chagrin, had donated a large estate of his own to Hibbert's heirs somewhere down in Somerset.

It was a bit clearer now (there had been a big scandal at the time) – Brocklehurst had wanted the estate to have expertise at hand and, being a Royal Society colleague of Hibbert, had arranged this swap.

Looking around him, William would never have guessed the degree to which the estates extended underground, and how the surrounding woodland was a powerful part of Brocklehurst's master plan in the battle for Britannic supremacy over Europe. The Prussians, nominally allies, were twitchy over France. The Austrians, Hungarians and Spanish were twitchy over France and the Anglo-Prussian alliance – and the power of their armies. The Dutch...well... just twitchy. Part of their national make-up. And the Russians were flexing their muscles. War seemed imminent somewhere in Europe. And quite soon.

He sighed in admiration. The clever thing about Brocklehurst's plan was that whilst the immediate area was famous for its mysticism, druidry and witchcraft, just a few miles down the road lay the conurbation of Manchester, a vast cottonopolis famous for its engineering, gadgetry and inventiveness.

From Ancoats there had been the steambulator, a beautifully engineered, minute, steam engine fixed on to a large sofa chair. It even included an umbrella holder for those inevitable Manchester drizzles.

Rochdale had produced a number of pointless automatons, small foot high water-powered figures that could walk in a straight line, or possibly fall over on cobblestones.

Stockport had invented a range of hats, from self-defence trilbies that exploded when thrown, to automated sou'westers that unfolded in to a waterproof over-coat when rain fell. And this by the power of the sun! Incredible!

In fairness, most of these Mancunian inventions had been ridiculed, but Brocklehurst had seen through the gadgetry and had concentrated on the beauty of the detail – a steam engine the size of a child's fist; using motion to almost perpetualise the re-circulation of water; harnessing the power of the sun! This was genius at work. And to top it all, Brocklehurst had the intellect to bring all of it together. Imbued with the power of nature, in the form of powerful mysticism gifted by the local crackpots (crackpots! Ho! Genius!), Brocklehurst had redefined science, although this was still top secret.

As were the automation experiments in all the other power houses of Europe, those very developments and technologies that every government knew each other worried away at in secret. The Russians had the *Vezdekhod*, an armoured vehicle that was apparently causing problems – the armour did not prevent occupants being killed when explosions occurred inside the machine. It was mostly developed, however and a few tweaks to the engine would have it up and running. If they combined forces with the Prussians, a most formidable weapon could be born, as an American, Hotchkiss, had reputedly developed a motorised rifle for them that could propel ten bullets every second over a distance of five hundred yards. Whilst the gun worked, unfortunately ammunition production was not yet sufficiently automated. That concern had almost been solved, but the actual production of the number of shells necessary to provide a reasonable stock would take some time – ten guns firing for ten minutes would require sixty thousand shells, therefore to provide for a full army would require a cache of millions. There were some minor design issues also. Occasionally the gun itself would get so hot that the whole thing would explode as it overheated the ammunition. There were rumours that somewhere in the British design houses a water cooled version had been built to combat the problem.

Even the Dutch had been at this innovation malarkey, building some fantastic dams - they didn't even need to paddle anymore.

Spy networks everywhere had stolen designs for these inventions, and, thankfully, the initial blueprints to the British automaton inventions had also been stolen. The European powers could design similar contraptions to their hearts content – because the one part that hadn't been written down – anywhere – was the requirement for nature to lend a hand. Brocklehurst had even gone to great lengths to ensure that his blueprints *were* stolen. They included faulty steam engine design and materials that could not possibly soak up the sun's rays and then convert it to power. The quasi-perpetual motion design was Brocklehurst's favourite, because it amounted to little more than a bucket with a hole in it. That you had to refill manually.

*

"Ah, Sir William! How are you today?"

Shaken out of his reverie, William looked around. "Lord Brocklehurst. Weak as a lamb, I'm afraid, although I am getting stronger daily. Your physician is a tyrant, it took all of my powers of persuasion to let me out in to the grounds."

"Yes, he is rather obstinate, but then he is rather brilliant in his field. He's a bit wasted here, to be fair, there are very few injuries other than the odd burn from the steam engineers."

"I mean for him to officially let me walk in the hills somewhat over the next few days. Would you care to join me?"

"I'd be delighted, although it will have to be in three or four days, as I have to go and visit old Purse Strings."

"The Prime Minister? You do socialise in rarefied circles, Lord Brocklehurst."

"Socialise – ha! Gordon wants my guts for garters. I'm over budget and beyond the deadlines he set, no matter how I argued that deadlines couldn't be set for this project. The man's an imbecile; absolutely no learning. He went to Cambridge of all places. Bloody commoner!"

"Things go badly, then?"

"My God, no!" exclaimed Brocklehurst. "It's miraculous what we've managed to achieve. We've managed to perform a fair number of imbuings, and now we're improving their conditioning."

"Conditioning?"

"Yes, conditioning." Brocklehurst looked a tad impatient at having to explain such a simple notion.

"We have to be able to give them orders; they're automatons, in the broadest sense, but in order for them to operate in anything other than straight lines, they need to be able to communicate and obey. Conditioning."

"My goodness, I didn't realise things were so advanced!" exclaimed William. "How is it carried out?"

"How we perform the conditioning is top secret although I may let you in on the matter in the near future, depending on how things further progress. It's based on the practice of Vodun, however. I first witnessed various phenomena whilst I travelled in Africa, but I didn't really take much notice. Inventing isn't my thing, you see. Innovation is where my talents lie. Anyway, another Royal Society colleague mentioned something similar whilst he trailed around after some Froggie scoundrel, and with a bit of this and that, we've managed to hit on a way of doing things around here. Only we use good old British ways, not of those foreign superstitious things."

A thought occurred to William. "So we're here near Alderley Edge for the druids?"

"Yes, pretty much."

"White superstitions over the black ones *must* be far superior then."

There was a twang to his voice that made Brocklehurst glance sharply at him. He went on regardless.

"Our first test subjects were a little trying; it seems to depend on the captured spirit. Some were evidently sailors and only understood starboard and larboard, for example, whilst one couldn't initially manage any form of direction."

"Probably a female then?"

"Yes, my thoughts exactly."

*

They met up following Brocklehurst's trip to London. There had been raised voices on his return, and two days of clandestine meetings with various engineers and scientist following that arrival. Now he was free for that walk with William, and he looked mighty pleased with himself.

"So, how are the conditionings going, Lord Brocklehurst?" William enquired.

"Please, call me Francis," said Brocklehurst. "They're marvellous. We believe we may be able to mass-automate with some fairly simple jiggery-pokery."

"Mass automate? You mean giving them mass orders, like a hive mind?"

Brocklehurst nodded. "Yes, but there do seem to be some shortcomings with the druidic way. We may have to resort back to some Vodun principles. There's been some correspondence, and we should have results very soon."

"Extraordinary. Who's the correspondent?"

"Top secret, my man. Top secret!" He gave Hope a conspiratorial wink. "Still, it should all be very obvious within a not inconsiderable amount of time. We'll almost have a new model army."

"But they're only being imbued singly. Surely to obtain a larger force, that will be a major constraint?"

"Not at all, I believe we should be able to do create the blighters *en masse* once we have the Vodun hypothesis confirmed. The government should be more grateful for my efforts. Without me there would be nothing, and London would stay bottom of the dung-heap. Maybe it should, that would teach them a lesson"

He went off on a rant. "By God, don't they know that what they have here is the keys to Europe. There could be peace, and the bloody commoners would be so petrified that they wouldn't dare to even consider an uprising."

"It sounds very peaceful."

Brocklehurst bestowed William his oft-practiced glower.

"It would mean Britannic dominion, Sir William. No more pandering to the Prussians. Why the hell the politicos cannot see that is beyond me. The guff they spouted over the past couple of days was appalling. Still, I'm sure that they'll sit up and take notice soon." He offered William an enigmatic smile. Before Brocklehurst could be questioned more closely, he carried on."

"Now see, before we set out, here's one that I'm using as my personal valet."

A thundering stomping metal robot of brass and some type of burnished metal approached bearing a walking coat for Brocklehurst.

"Bloody marvellous invention, never needs to sleep, never ties a knot too tight or too slack, makes the perfect cup of tea."

"What's his name?"

"Her. I call her Bob, a good working class name, as I couldn't get over the fact she would – as a woman – would see me anything other than turned out. She's a complete pacifist though, useless as a weapon, which is why she's my slave."

"Slave?"

"Well, more of a valet, really. Splitting hairs a bit though, don't you think."

After helping him to don his coat, Bob stomped off, the floor resounding with each footstep.

"You've actually tried arming them, then?" enquired William.

"Of course. They'll be an absolutely unstoppable army, and no-one gets hurt."

"No-one on our side."

"Quite."

"And Bob wouldn't fire a gun?"

"No, regardless of even more advanced techniques for, ahhhh, re-calibration. Brainwashing, I suppose you could almost call it, although that sounds rather blackguardly, not a term I really like to use, as of course there's no brain. No person."

"Has she a conscience then? A personality, even?"

"I've no idea, nor do I care as long as she behaves. Frankly, I can't say I give a damn."

William's mind brought back his conversations with Smith. He was certainly lacking consistency in his moral fibre.

"Lord Brocklehurst, to my humanity, that sounds excessively cruel; barbaric more or less. How can you press on with this without understanding the subjects? On an entirely different note, from a control point of view, it seems fatally flawed, the whole project."

"Damn it man, damn your impertinence. It's a freak of nature, nothing more than a damn good slave."

"But what about the rest of them?" pressed William. "How can you assure their unswerving obedience?"

"The scientists and engineers have managed to come up with a system, a rooting placed into the base carbon of the control mechanism. They have a term for it, ahhh, programming, I think. It's better than ninety-nine percent successful. Unfortunately, there doesn't seem to be a retrospective method for the likes of Bob."

"And the remaining one percent enter servitude, I take it," William snapped somewhat waspishly.

"Oh no," smarmed Brocklehurst quietly. "Most of the rejects are used to demonstrate the success of the ninety-nine percent."

William gaped at Brocklehurst as realisation dawned on him.

"You don't mean….no, surely, it's too cruel…"

"War is cruel," Brocklehurst snapped sharply. "And it demonstrates that unswerving obedience you seem to feel strongly about."

"But surely the druids are dead against such practise? Even if they are already dead, killing a spirit again..." William did not know how to complete such a sentence. It amazed him that he could even discuss this in a supposedly rationale fashion.

He gave William a sly smile. "The head druid, Allan, is rather compliant in the matter. He has little choice. Come, let us be off."

Walking at a moderate pace for William's sake, they passed around ploughed fields, more mud at this time of year. Hawthorn and blackthorn hedgerows were bare, barring naked spines and thickening buds, whilst snowdrops littered the bleak rolling landscape within the naked woodlands.

William was deep in thought for many minutes, a growing dread and suspicion dawning further the more he considered the conversation.

"Are we headed anywhere in particular?" asked William.

"I thought we'd do a short walk to the Edge, Sir William. Nothing too strenuous, just something to loosen those hams."

"Is there really anything in those old stories? I've seen things in the Catacombs of Paris that would be the stuff of most peculiar nightmares."

"Oh yes, there's certainly an aura around the place. It's very subtle though, I wouldn't like to over egg the place if you are after cheap thrills. The local druids though…"

"I'm not sure I understand."

"Apparently, there are denizens that wander in from afar, and the druids around here are supposed to ease them on their way to a more restful place."

"Really? I must have access to your laboratory, chemicals and a camera, if at all possible. If it's what I think it is, I can show them to you."

"Certainly," said Lord Brocklehurst with a wry smile.

CHAPTER 6 – ROMANTIC ROME

Amara woke in a shroud of pain, jostled and bounced in the back of a cart. Sunlight speared through a migraine, and every jostle wracked her ribs. A low groan escaped her lips.

"Ahhh, my darling, I'm sorry about this, but you really are the one. My man here mistook you and your husband for common people. Still, we couldn't have the old boy hanging around, I'm sure he'd have been most displeased at us carting you off, so to speak," Arthur tittered wildly. "It's as well we don't need you to be a virgin, or that would have been awkward. You're very important to my experiments."

A frown swept across his face and he started to gabble.

"I'm sorry, dear heart, but you will eventually be free to go...once my master says it's ok. I made him promise that no-one important would come to any harm."

Amara squirmed in her undergarments and realised that her undergarments weren't quite right. They had been removed and replaced most inexpertly.

A tear of ubiquitous despair ran down her cheek, and a vast chasm of darkness opened up in her world. Husband murdered, home looted, raped, and now captive to a madman, a subject to be locked in a cage and experimented on. Needles stuck in her, limbs removed and reattached, eyes blinded, her...womanhood defiled. A well of despair started to drag her away, but as a proud woman, she swallowed with difficulty, refusing to let him see her discomfort.

"Water," she rasped harshly.

"Oh, my sweet, of course," gushed Arthur, "how silly of me not to offer."

Gently, he dribbled water on to her dry lips, and looked fondly in to her eyes.

"It's nothing personal you know, you're just so special."

A stony gaze was his only reply.

"Look, my master is a very fierce man, and I'm very passionate about my work, as well he knows," he babbled. "And I simply must have only the best subjects to work with, which is why I was sent here, and to you."

Amara gazed on, unblinking. A sweat appeared on Arthur's brow and his prattling for forgiveness and understanding in his test subject continued.

"My work, it's revolutionary, ground breaking. It will end all wars!"

She stared on.

"One life! That's all! It will save the lives of millions! I'll be a hero. So will you!"

A snort from the front of the cart brought a red flush to Arthur.

"Just bloody drive, and shut up," he snapped without turning.

"Careful, little man," the deep tones of a rapist sounded.

A look of fear crossed his face, and then he flushed, this time with anger. The woman in front of him smiled a pitying smile, and in flames of agony turned her back on him.

"There is one thing you need to know," said Arthur. "You're pregnant."

CHAPTER 7 – OVER THE EDGE

A couple of days later, William and Brocklehurst retraced their steps back to the Edge, this time accompanied by a rather strange individual who Brocklehurst introduced as Allan, a fellow member of the Royal Society, a naturalist and a druid. He rarely left Cheshire – and his flock – for London, which is why William had never met him. His eyes were those of a shrew, and he had lips so narrow as to be barely visible, giving him a permanently sour look. He was barely five feet tall and had a scrawny neck like that of a turkey. He did not look pleasant to William's eye.

"Are you able to see the spirits?" William asked of Allan.

"No, but I can feel them. They are as human as you and I; barring the fact they have no body. Nor a purpose."

"So you've seen fit to partake in Lord Brocklehurst's experiments? I would have thought the spirit sacrosanct?" He could feel Brocklehurst staring daggers, which he ignored.

"It is, but this is temporary, nothing more than gazing at possibilities before we wend them on their way."

"We?"

"Yes, there are still a few of us who hold by the old ways."

"And the second deaths procured on those automatons? Those who didn't comply with the conditioning. How can you justify that Allan? It feels to me…murderish." William was being purposefully inflammatory, his natural sense of justice simmering below a transparent surface.

Allan paled but remained silent. He was naturally self-controlled, it seemed. Brocklehurst's temper, however, got the better of him. "That's enough!" he snapped at William.

They walked further, William's brow furrowed in deep thought.

"So exactly how are they integrated in to the machines?"

It was Brocklehurst who replied. "The energy of the sun. That ridiculous device made by that fool of a hat maker from Stockport concealed an incredible invention that has the ability to transform light from the sun into electricity. In conjunction with this energy, there is some kind of druidic communion that transfers the spirit to a cell of carbon stored within the automaton."

"Carbon? In what form? Diamond? Some form of resonance?"

"Oh no, don't be ridiculous, it must be able to conduct electricity. Our engineers here have been able to refine natural coal into graphite far purer than on any scale previously seen. It really is marvellous watching these groups of specialists work together. Druid, scientist and engineer. It ought to be chalk and cheese, but it actually seems to be more scone, jam and cream. Once they get started, their discussions are unfathomable. We believe the Vodun method may be an efficiency improvement on that."

William's mind whirled as they walked. It was difficult to comprehend exactly how all of this had started. This was *farming country*!

A mile or so of relative silence passed as the hills became steeper, first up and then a scramble down to a railway line that disappeared into a hillside. Situated in a small hollow there was a stone table and a number of wooden stumps arranged in the outside clearing.

"It's odd, the very place where spirits flow at the zenith around this place is exactly where the miners made their first hole," spoke the druid conversationally.

"Are they here now," asked William.

"Always."

William set up his photography equipment and looked about himself, gauging the light conditions for the required exposure and flash. He hummed tunelessly to himself, perfectly unconscious of Brocklehurst and Allan. These two smiled gently at each other in mild humour.

Some forty five minutes later, William had used his supply of photographic media.

*

"Lord Brocklehurst, I must return to that grotto!" William exclaimed, some days later.

"Certainly – tomorrow morning I'm free and I need the exercise." Brocklehurst paused. "May I see the results?"

William passed Brocklehurst a handful of daguerreotypes. He browsed through them, eyebrows raising impossibly higher with each image.

"They're marvellous, Sir William, it's just a shame they're not a little clearer."

"Now that I have a few background snaps, I believe I can marginally alter the chemical formulae for the film coating, and as I know exactly where to pinpoint our friends, I believe I can significantly improve the images you see."

"Nine a-m?"

"Perfect, I will make use of your laboratory immediately."

*

Next morning, William left the breakfast table at Birtles Hall, and started the trek back to his room to change in to his walking gear. He had a lot to think about. He was being used by Brocklehurst, and the wretched man knew far more than he divulged. This, combined with Smith's reports about keeping an eye on the man, made William pensive, especially as he had found nothing untoward, barring Brocklehurst's morality – or lack, thereof. It niggled William to the point of irritation.

Rounding a corner, he walked straight in to Bob. He grunted painfully. She was hard.

"I'm sorry Bob, my mind was entirely abroad."

Bob tilted slightly at the waist, a bow of some sort that William couldn't entirely interpret, but which he took as part apology, part acknowledgment of Hope's apology.

"I say Bob," William exclaimed in a flash of revelation. "Can you communicate?"

Rather dextrously, her fingers and hands twirled. The hands were a marvel of engineering science. Taut springs, some only a few millimetres long, connected the joints of the fingers and the intricate connections within the hand. Antagonistic pistons acted as muscled. The technical parts were all brass – easy to work at such small sizes. Covering the mechanisms on the back of the hand was some unknown type of burnished metal, no doubt there to protect the mechanisms and probably act a significant weapon, if her bulk was anything to go by. Fully seven feet tall, she was almost as wide as she was tall. Eyes glowed a deep sea green, around which was a heavy brass and burnished steel skull. There was no mouth or nose. The same alloys protected her torso, completely hiding the secrets of automated life inside, although a warmth emanated from the metalwork. Arms and legs showed similar mechanisms to the hands, only these were necessarily bigger and stronger versions.

William looked back to the hands, and his eyes widened as he recognised what she was doing. Sign language. Whilst this had been almost entirely removed from the education of the deaf as it was no longer fashionable, it hadn't yet been removed from use by the deaf themselves. It appeared that their preferences still prevailed over the preferences of the experts who themselves weren't afflicted by deafness or muteness.

William himself knew sign language due to the volunteering work he'd carried out at the veteran's hospital at Dunham Massey, where sign language was a popular method of communication for those such afflicted. Indeed, the methods of communication in these places were a bastardisation of the spoken word, sign language and the use of interpreters where communication between some individuals was not possible.

"Yes, although I get little need," signed Bob.

"My Good God," whispered William. "How do you cope with all of this? If it's not too personal a question – are you all there?"

"Yes, my cognisance is normal. And I have no choice but to cope."

"How do you manage with working for that bore, though? Why don't you just leave? His cruelty to you – and the others – is astounding."

"Where would I go, Sir William?" Bob signed. Her signing was a mixture of spelling out using the alphabet, and using common gestures for certain words.

"True, true," mused Hope. Indeed, where would she go? She'd instil nothing but terror in any populace in Britain. Well, except the Celtic Northmen, they'd probably deify her. He smiled at his own quip.

"Do you have a full memory of the past?"

"I have little memory, merely fleeting images. A small child, a sad man, a beautiful woman. I don't recall my name."

Somehow William didn't believe the last part. Her eyes momentarily changed colour and he suspected that these could indeed be used to gauge her mood.

"How do you hear?"

I can feel the vibrations when you talk, and when I can see you talk, it helps a lot.

"Does Brocklehurst know?"

"No! He knows I can understand rudiments and simple commands, that's why I wasn't murdered along with the others who refused the programming. I became useful."

"You could come with me," ventured William. "I would not see you continue this level of servitude to that man."

"And what would I do for you? How would things be different for me?"

"Well, you'd be free. Not a slave," he stammered.

"But the outcome would be the same," signed Bob.

"I'm afraid there's nothing I can do about that. I can only offer you kindness and respect."

"All I really want is to die again. To move on."

The lights in her eyes dimmed slightly and changed to a turquoise hue. Her shoulders seemed to droop in sadness.

William felt a tear running down a cheek. Roughly he cuffed it away. "Well, you know where I am if you want something different."

There was a pause as they both appeared to be about to move in their separate directions. And then she signed again.

"He knows, you know, about your photography. Something's going on. I don't know what, but you being brought to Alderley Edge is not entirely an accident, even if the way you arrived was."

"What?" William was astounded. How could anybody possibly know about his work?

"It's true," she signed.

"But how. Almost no one knows, excepting a very few trusted colleagues at the Royal Society. Their discretion is absolute."

There was movement behind Bob rendering further discussion impossible, an engineer walking their way dressed in greasy overalls. William gave a curt nod to Bob and continued along his path.

*

At nine 'o' clock sharp, William and Brocklehurst strode purposefully through the spring woodland; beech leaves were ripening, leaves in Elder green were starting to show and a pale blue sky shone to near insignificance against a fresh, vivid sun. Morning dew glistened on the grass, a myriad of miniature rainbows refracting from the cold sun.

"Bloody glorious, what?" exclaimed Brocklehurst.

He was in a rare good mood, a beaming grin fixed across his face.

"It always fascinates me that *Aesculus hippocastanum* has evolved to form a sticky leaf covering, dear William. I wonder what our friend Mr Darwin would make of that. What evolutionary challenge triggered that, precisely? The man is an idiot, and I pray daily that the damned Catholics find him and burn him with his ridiculous notions."

"Maybe it was a straight mutation, Lord Brocklehurst, and from there it had such a survival advantage over other individuals of the same species that it became the norm," William said, somewhat waspishly.

"That barely supports his concept of evolution though, dear boy. These specialisms are supposed to develop over thousands of years, tens of thousands - hundreds of thousands, even - of generations."

"True, but evolution doesn't rule out genetic aberrations that lead to an individual becoming far more successful than its peers."

"I suppose not," gruffed Brocklehurst. "My lord! There's a sight to behold. The nuthatch, *Sitta europaea*, I simply adore watching those little mites. Have you observed them in autumn? They collect winter supplies, and I remember sitting watching one once, repeatedly hammering home hazelnuts into a hole. Waiting on an adjacent branch was a simple *Passer domesticus*, and it kept stealing the nut, only for the stupid bird to repeatedly return with another nut. A simple sparrow wiping its eye! I laughed so much, I nearly cried."

William frowned at Brocklehurst's odd behaviour. He wasn't exactly famed for his idle chitter-chatter, and his mind creased further at this continued demonstration of a darker aspect to Brocklehurst's psyche.

"I say Lord Brocklehurst; I noticed that the union flag hasn't been raised this morning. I mentioned it to one of the man-servants and he said it was at your orders."

"MY orders? Ridiculous! I'll have the lying toe-rag beaten and tossed out of my service. Which wretch was it? Smith? He's always looking at me sideways."

"I don't remember, I'm sure, but it wasn't Smith," lied William.

A frown remained on Brocklehurst's face and they continued in silence. It was a relief for William not to have the challenge of such a direct conversation so early in the day.

They arrived at the pit and entered. This time the photography took much longer. At about midday, some two hours later, they left the cold, damp caves and started their return trek to Birtles Hall. When they were a quarter of a mile away, a journey made in absolute silence, William noticed an increasing eager giddiness playing across his companion's entire body. He walked jauntily, a gay look playing across his features and his eyes were fixed, glittering malevolently, at their destination. William looked ahead more closely. He couldn't see a soul moving, the gates of the normally secure grounds appeared to be open and askew and an unusual spire of smoke twisted lazily upwards. As they got closer, William thought he could see prone figures on the pristine grass.

And then it caught his eye: At roughly nine o'clock from their own path lay a blackened swathe that stretched from the rising hills further away, right to the gates and then further in to the grounds. And within the grounds he could see twisted, blackened shrubs and trees either side of the swathe.

With a rising dread, William dropped all of his equipment and started to run towards the grounds.

It turned in to a sprint when, from behind, he heard an insane cackle emanate from Brocklehurst.

*

William's sprint slowed as he reached the gates. The wrought iron portals, normally burnished to a gleaming shine, were rusted beyond belief, pitted and flaking, the hinges rotten to failures of red, orange, and ochre. The long, broad driveway was bordered by blackened, brittle grass. The streak cut a straight line across a bend in the track and William barely noticed the seemingly cremated remains of the *Eucryphia nymanensis*.

A figure stood under the portico at the entrance of Birtles Hall. To William's eyes, it was humanoid at best, but he barely noticed it. The entranceway, normally alive with the movement of scientists, engineers, druids and menial staff was still and lifeless. Bodies littered the area where vehicles normally parked and rusting hulks occupied places where steam cars normally chugged and puffed plumes of water vapour. Some of the prone figures looked like they'd been attempting to flee, others attempting to engage the motionless figure. Smith's body lay face down, his face turned to one side blackened and charred, his mouth a silent scream that was starting to flake in the light breeze that spread across the courtyard. Only half a head of that distinctive sandy hair remained, the rest made up of burned skull. His body was one that had run towards the figure blocking the entrance to the hall. His pistol lay a few feet away.

A high pitched cackling laugh sounded from behind William, and he realised that the inhuman noise was from Brocklehurst. He turned fluidly and ran directly at Brocklehurst, whose high lilting laugh stretched over a distance of fifty yards. Before he had covered ten yards, William found himself lifted bodily, legs still pumping furiously. Higher he went until he was thrown violently back to the floor, where he lay badly winded.

Regardless, he attempted to rise again, choking and gasping, staggering towards Brocklehurst who was now screaming with hysterical laughter.

Entirely insane Hope thought as he scrambled and staggered in Brocklehurst's direction.

And then a great weight was upon William's back, and he could no more move than he could breath.

"My dear William! I see you have met my friend," tittered a gasping, breathless Brocklehurst, eyes streaming. "Actually, I believe you already know him, or should I say *knew* him."

The weight of what felt like a small elephant was removed from his back and a tentacle wrapped around his ankle, lifting him upside down along the whole length of the figure.

The figure was ridiculously tall, a rising journey that took William an age to pass from foot, to knee, to groin, navel, chest, neck and finally head, face to face with an alien, or rather a freak, because the face was humanoid.

And as he looked, he saw and it took several seconds for him to realise that he *did* know the face, it made his mind reel in that flash of inspiration.

"Chapman…."

If it wasn't for the blood flowing to his head, William would have paled to the point of virtual transparency. What had happened to the man?

The face before him was ebony instead of white, but not a natural black skin because none could be this black. It was black to the point of drawing light in to it. Black eyes pierced William and he found himself sinking in to an abyss that spoke of no soul, only pain and cruelty. Uncontrollably, he pissed himself in fear; nay, utter terror.

A portion of a tentacle broke free and roamed over his face, prodding painfully with its barbed point.

Laughing asthmatically, Brocklehurst spoke from behind William. "I think it's time for you to die, Mr Hope."

The independent shard of tentacle began to turn painfully in the centre of his forehead, speeding up as it started to burrow into the flesh. William screamed in pain and terror as the shard struck skull, and he began to thrash uncontrollably as blood ran into his hair. The tentacles gripping his legs held firm.

A crunch on the pathway behind Brocklehurst sounded, a resounding thud resonating through the ground. Brocklehurst turned his head to see Bob approaching, and as she drew close, her arm retracted and swung through a half circle to hit him sideways, sending him sprawling several feet away. Unconscious.

Bob advanced further to a living creature who could not sense the metalwork approaching from his blindside. A towering fist thundered into Runes ribs, a thousand screams sounding from a multitude of appendages that promptly spasmed in self-defence, dropping an agonised Hope. A tentacle shot out and grasped a metal arm which yanked powerfully, pulling Rune closer before the tentacle hurriedly let go.

Too late: a second fist smashed Rune full in the chest, a crunch of mangled ribs accompanied by a brain-piercing shriek that caused William to pass out. Rune flew a dozen feet though the air, crashing heavily to the floor.

Tenderly, Bob picked William up in her arms and began to run, slowly at first, but faster and faster as her mechanical legs started to pump powerfully. It was a jarring, crunching run that caused William to stir through his rather pained consciousness, his bones flailing in secondary agony.

Rune flicked his arms, and ten fingers flew through the air in the direction of the fleeing robot. Hitting the ground, they began to scamper in Bob's direction, who's pace continued to increase, as did Hope's pain. The fingers scurried at a pace of a fleeing fox, but Bob's pace was that of the fleeting deer, and Rune's control, immature as it was, only lasted for a few hundred yards before the fingers started to erratically founder, twitching and circling uncontrollably, until he approached, an oily smear gleaming in his eyes. He redrew the appendages back into his whole, watching as the couple fled in to the Cheshire plains.

CHAPTER 8 – THE ART OF TREPANNING

Amara felt the ship grind gently against the wharf. She hadn't seen light for many days. Her head ached and she suspected that her skull had been cracked or dented. She could only breathe properly through her mouth because of her still-swollen nose. Given the heat of the hold, it half surprised her that she hadn't died of dehydration or even choked on her own tongue, which was dry and engorged, although being alive may not entirely be a blessing, depending on what the future held.

She worried at her pregnancy: she could feel nothing growing inside her, almost as if nothing were there. Did Rimbaud speak the truth? Or had her treatment led to a still-birth.

Mostly she worried about one thing: If a baby did grow, who was the father? Why would she raise a rapists get?

The makeshift door opened to her makeshift cell and the white rapist appeared with a sack cloth.

"Put this on yer barnet," he snarled.

Amara looked confused.

He flung it at her and spoke loudly and slowly, as if to some dumb foreigner "Put-the-bag-on-your-head…savvy?"

Amara wasn't scared of the man. He had taken everything away from her, all she had was her life, which, she quite objectively considered, seemed more or less worthless. So she gazed at him not moving a muscle.

The backhand came across so fast that she barely had time to register it – indeed, he'd moved several feet forward and hit her very hard, very quickly. She reeled backwards banging her head against a wooden bulkhead. Her ears rang and black spots swam in front of her eyes.

"Stop that this instant," squeaked a little voice from the door.

The rapist turned, raised an eyebrow and smiled at Rimbaud as if he was about to devour the man. Stooping he picked up the sackcloth and flung it at Amara.

"Put it on, bitch." No emotion showed on his face this time, and she felt her bladder turn to liquid, and only stopped herself urinating by the finest of margins. He stalked out, shouldering Rimbaud out of the way.

"Where are we, murderer," asked Amara in a matter-of-fact way.

Rimbaud stammered for several moments and then steeled himself, glaring at her.

"Rome, the most romantic city in the world," he snapped.

She put on the sackcloth over her head. She felt the coarse hands of the white rapist tightening the strap around her neck. For a moment she panicked because it was too tight and she could barely breathe. But once the hands were removed, breathe she could, so she shouldered the burden, a small burden among the many, and did not complain or behave awkwardly as she was led out on to the quay.

The deep rush of the widest of rivers sounded below her feet as she stepped along the gang plank, the flow of the waters forming a pleasantly cool breeze that caressed her ankles.

A horse whinnied on the cobblestones from close quarters and she shied away at the sound. Fresh manure assailed her senses, but it only dulled the pervading stench of death and decay that palled the city. Bells rang in the distance and a high pitched scream could be heard from afar. Amara drew into herself; after a lifetime in the open, the smell of the land her only company, she became scared. The more she became of aware of her surroundings, the more she smelled and heard. Almost all of it was alien. A distant clamour of people, breaking glass, fish guts decaying on the wharf, the stomp of booted feet. Only partially aware, she was manhandled – none too gently, nor gentlemanly – into an awaiting carriage.

Here, the senses were assailed differently. No longer was there the tumult of the city and a million disgusting odours: there was quiet and cigar smoke and fine leather.

Following an interminable stay at sea, this was more of a shock than the stench and alien sounds of Rome.

"I think we can, ahh, dispense with the hood gentleman."

The buckle around her neck was loosened, and Amara beheld a well-lit carriage. On a seat on the opposite side was a small, scruffy man with glasses and a large moustache, which surprised Amara as the voice had been deep and rich and obviously in charge.

"My word, your beauty is remarkable, even forgiving your condition. I think a hot bath and a good meal might sort things out – you look like bone and skin, and, if you pardon my, ahhh, rudeness, you smell rather bad. Oh, you do speak English, I take it? Nobody seems to speak German anymore. Bloody New Worlders."

He man careened off into very poorly sung opera, singing it twice, once in German and once in English. Both versions were truly awful.

Hieher, Verlor'ne!

Laß' dich nicht seh'n,

schmiege dich an uns,

und schweige dem Ruf!

Hieher zu uns!

Be thou not seen,

hide thee in our midst,

and heed not his call!

Be hid by us!

Then hide, thou lost one!

"Ah, Wagner, how I love the man! You find me in rare good spirits, girl! Name your heart's desire and it will be granted."

"Home. Husband," was all she managed before she collapsed into floods of tears, uncontrollable hysteria, a wreckage beyond the minutest comprehension of the men present, all due to a small act of thoughtfulness, the first visited upon her in a recent memory.

*

At the sight of the sobbing girl, the rapist raised his hand to strike, but Rimbaud caught hold of his arm, an automatic reaction with no thought involved.

"Little man, let go," he growled.

"Leave the girl be, you beast," squeaked Rimbaud, his eyes wide with terror. "You have done enough rape, murder and beatings."

A fist struck Rimbaud full in the face and he momentarily blacked out. His subconscious heard the sound of sliding metal and he regained his vision just in time to see a sword point exiting the rapist's ear. The sword stuck fast into the fine leather upholstery by Arthur's head.

He stared wide eyed as the body of the rapist twitched in its death throes. Even Amara only whimpered, also transfixed at the macabre scene.

"I gave strictest instructions to you both zat zis specimen vas to be entirely unharmed." Fire blossomed in the man's eyes and the Prussian accent became thick and fierce.

"My Lord Stieber," cried Rimbaud. "I have tried to protect the lady from that animal. First he walked off into the hills on a wild goose chase, murdering her husband and causing the most grievous form of harm upon the girl. The buffoon didn't even realise who she was."

Rimbaud's incoherently fast babble continued as Stieber's fires had not yet died down.

"And then he hit her and threatened me, and no matter how I entreated him to better behaviour and less violence in the name of our Lord, he would not listen. You saw what he was like, even the threat of your good name never did any good."

Stieber remained mute, but thrust the sword more deeply, twisting the blade as he did so. Blood and white matter flowed down its central groove as Rimbaud watched the cerebral matter in fascination, before vomiting violently in to the rapists lap.

An undulating, uncontrollable laugh sounded from beside Stieber, wild feral eyes gleaming whilst tears rolled down her face, and her body shook uncontrollably.. Ivory white teeth shone against her black skin, teeth bared like a feral animal.

Stieber rolled down the window and ordered the driver to "make haste, make the greatest haste". His eyes still gleamed dangerously, but a green tinge had coloured his gills.

"I hate vomit," he muttered.

*

The carriage clattered noisily through the streets of Rome and finally stopped at a large townhouse that had stabling attached behind large gates.

Stieber leapt lightly down, lithe for a man of his stature and bearing. Between himself and Rimbaud, they managed to extricate Amara from the coach; she could not take her eyes from the rapist. When eye contact was broken, she snapped. Rounding on Stieber she punched him with all of her might square in the face, shattering the glass in his glasses, snapping the frame and breaking his nose. She kicked him hard between his legs, and as he groaned at that particular agony, her knee connected with his forehead. He went out like a light, blood leaking from any number of glass cuts.

A number of stable hands raced out and restrained her physically before she could mete out more punishment, the strong muscled arms of a blacksmith pinning her arms to her sides.

She spat on Stieber. "That bastard was mine to murder."

She spat again, and then again at Rimbaud, who flinched away in terror at her wroth.

She continued to struggle and the blacksmith tried to calm her down in gentle Italian. A maid came to his rescue, taking one look at the black girl and cradling her head whilst stroking her unkempt mane of hair. She barked orders at some of the boys lollygagging at the scene, and they set to do whatever it was she had ordered as if the Valkyries themselves were on their heels.

Thirty minutes later, Amara was in a room near the top of the house behind a screen. On the other side was the blacksmith who refused to leave the small army of women tending to her. Amara guessed it was more for their safety than her own secure keeping, although the presence of a man so close to her nakedness made her shiver slightly.

She rose out of her reverie.

In the last ten minutes, Amara had been undressed and coaxed in to the steaming hot water of metal tub. She had never seen a bath of hot water before, and passed her hand suspiciously through the steam a number of times. She had rapidly dropped from her state of hysteria and fire, the tunnel vision of her feral self returning to something approaching normal. Her tempers had always been like this, so different from her husband who had been patience personified. A gentle man for a gentle, simple life. All gone.

She felt comfortable around the women because they were obviously simple peasant girls, much like herself... although the one whom had rescued her was as sharp as a pin.

She felt cold, emotionally drained, exhausted. So she let herself be scrubbed, her hair cleaned, unguent oils spread over her luxurious skin, all amidst the 'ooh's and aah's' of the ladies who attended her as they found yet another bruise or scrape. She caught the knowing glances at the disrepair to her womanhood, not yet fully healed although a month had passed since the brutal rape. The ladies tended her nails, combed her hair and then towelled her dry. They brought out beautifully soft clothing that hung with a lingering odour of softness.

Amara felt better physically than she had in a long time now, the bath, pampering and clean clothing reviving her, and it was a temporary balm to her spirit.

*

At the allotted time, a girl took her down to a large ornate dining room. Servants lined one wall and the smell from the kitchen was divine, although she hadn't a clue what could be cooking to produce such a smell.

A large table dominated the space with ancient candelabra equally spaced down its length producing a subdued, warm glow. There were twenty chairs down each side, with more ornate (*thrones*, thought Amara) versions at the heads of the table. On one sat William Stieber, almost in shadow at the far end of the room. Sat on his right was Rimbaud, and on his left a willowy, pasty blonde lady. She was almost as beautiful as Amara.

But not quite, and from the extended pout, she knew it and hated her for it.

"Amara, you look ravishing darling, so much more civilised," gushed Stieber nasally as he snuffled through his broken nose. His entire face seemed to be blackening. The compliment earned him a look of pure disdain from the woman next to him. He ignored it, as both himself and Rimbaud rose to their feet.

"Amara…you're positively radiant," blushed Rimbaud, quite obviously moonstruck at seeing her for the first time without dishevelment (although, he noted, not without bruises).

Amara gave a sweeping, haughty look around the room and seated herself with a discordant scrape of chairs on marble, at the other head of the table, as far from the others as possible. She was rather shaky from prolonged abuse and hunger, but stubbornly refused to show any weakness. Instead, she glared haughtily down the table.

The two men sat down, and as all three studied her, she felt like the main attraction at a travelling menagerie.

"So why am I here? And why have you murdered my husband?" she crashed out, as discordant as the chair legs on marble.

A satisfying silence stunned the room, even the servants stiffened, and Rimbaud physically squirmed in his seat.

"That was a most unfortunate accident," said Stieber placatingly, offering open arms as if to bring Amara in to their fold.

"Yet murder him you did." Her face was devoid of all emotion. "And you will pay with your life."

Stieber smiled broadly, "Fraulein, we can do things the easy way or the hard way. The easy way will be better for us all. The hard way will mostly only be hard for you."

What he didn't understand of her, and her way of life, was that it was hard anyway. Living in a small village in Africa was difficult, living alone more so. The weather was capricious and living in solitude left you prey to bandits and thieves, never mind packs of wild animals. Working the earth was tough, growing and storing food was tough, keeping livestock safe and fed was tough. Ergo, Amara was tough.

Not only that, she was intelligent, very intelligent, although she had no formal schooling. Her mother had been the local Vodunsi, the most learned in the village, a Vodun adept. She had no idea who her father had been, and talk of him had been forbidden. Indeed, the very reason she had left to live in the mountains was that she saw more in the flames than her mother could conceive, and so when she had fallen in love with her beloved, they had eloped and built their life afresh – tough work, but all theirs, every stone of their home laid down with love and tenderness.

People such as these seated before her could never understand the tenacity and strength of character that it took to build such a life – and for ones happiness to be enriched because of it. Stieber, whose life was pampered from dusk until dawn, who had people at his every beck and call, a man who only ever destroyed and criticised, who had never built anything of value, well, a person such as that could in no way comprehend this.

Amara laughed out loud at Stieber and he flushed in anger at her standing up to his authority.

"We do not need your cooperation, Fraulein. We can just take what we want."

He snapped his fingers and the servants immediately began serving starters and refreshing beverages. An hour passed over the meal, and not a single word passed between them.

Suddenly Stieber clapped his hands and servants moved everything from the room. Everything. Table, chairs, rugs, even themselves. The fire roared in the magnificent hearth. Stieber moved over to the fireplace and gently pushed the navel stud of a noble Indian statuette.

There was a spit, a hiss, steam started to rise from a grate in the floor, somewhere below pistons rose and fell, a camshaft rotated, and a resounding crack resonated through the room. The floor started to fall away in the centre of the room, not a random catastrophic failure, but in a carefully controlled sequence of coordinated events. Heavy oak beams clicked in to place to form an elegant stairway heading widdershins into a well-lit chamber.

They descended, Amara being motioned down first. At the bottom, was a vast cavern of roughly hewn rock, but warm and well tended. A sharp light came from electric lighting, softened by the diffuse, warm glow of burning brands. Lining one wall was a row of people, all women. Vacancy and emptiness filled their eyes and Amara gazed on unblinking. A series of copper wires encased their scalps, great holes trepanned through each skull. The wires glowed red and dimmed in a seemingly random fashion.

"These are some of my slaves Amara. You can become one of them or be a part of my masters greatest revenge."

"Your master?"

"Yes, my master. I'm an excellent slave myself, dearest; I don't have the cognitive capacity to lead or have such brilliant designs, nay, visions. I merely make things happen."

"Who is he?" asked Amara, slightly awestruck by a being with more power than Stieber, who had entirely ripped her life apart.

"All in good time, beautiful darling."

"What do you want?"

"I want your talent. These ladies here were unable to help. You, we believe, are the answer."

"Me?"

"Yes, you. You are Vodun, like your mother before you. You know and understand the living and the dead, life and death."

Amara laughed. "Surely you need a virgin. You failed. Your man saw to that. You remember – that rapist you murdered today"

Rimbaud gasped, a hand covered his mouth.

Stieber only chuckled. "Amara, my love, sex and sexuality mean nothing; only your sex can help. We believe that the influences that drive your monthly cycle are important, and being Vodun is critical. Whether you are intact or not is unimportant."

"I was Vodun, but I have rejected it, it is nothing to me."

"Ahh, but has it rejected you? I think not. In fact, it is irrelevant. You have the knowledge, the truest insight in to the dead and the living through your upbringing. Vodun be damned, it's an education thing, nothing more, nothing less."

"Where are the men?"

There are none, my dear. They just die. We have tried, believe me."

She looked around helplessly, no argument could brook this ridiculousness. "What are they?"

"They are your predecessors. Technically, I think they're probably dead, my dear."

"Dead? How? What have you done to them?" Again she stared unblinking, afraid to even hear his reply, expression aghast.

"Well, certain areas of their brains are alive, hence the wires; it's basically some form of electricity bouncing around their heads. I don't understand the science, but I've got a man who does and he hypothesises that the parts of their brain that are alive are basically stimulating those parts of their minds that are technically dead with their own intrinsic electricity. Take away the pretty wires and they're corpses."

"And I'm different how, exactly?" asked Amara somewhat tartly, as she realised she was nothing more than another guinea pig.

"You won't be murdered by the dead."

"The dead…?" Amara continued to gaze at the so-called corpses. At a nod from Stieber, one of them moved and took Amara's hand and led her deeper underground. She went without resistance.

*

She didn't really care, she was almost giddy with not caring to the extent that she thought death may be the best way out. Dealing with that beast – not that she strictly dealt with him, but seeing him shook her badly enough – and she had suspicions of what he was – was terrible. Furthermore, she really felt like she knew him, both the physical being and the thing that it was. Both of them, for they were surely different.

He rarely seemed to eat or drink, but occasionally, very occasionally, he would drink water down in the bowels of this townhouse whilst he watched Rimbaud perform his preparatory experiments.

The previous night, whilst the house was asleep, even the guard at her door from the sounds of the snores, she rooted around in her bag. In the bottom were a number of dry Ackee seeds. Her bag had been searched when she'd been captured, but nobody had an idea of what the seeds were, so they'd lain there. Her knife was gone, of course, and anything valuable was now probably heavy in someone else's pockets. But the seeds were still there, so mundane as to be entirely overlooked.

She crushed them as finely as she could and wrapped the grains in a handkerchief, secreting it about her person. She had no doubt that she would be back underground that morning, and the small barrel of water in an alcove would be an ideal place for her to scupper this wrong-doing. She could kill Rimbaud, Rune and Stieber if she was lucky, although she suspected that Stieber wouldn't be downstairs, he'd be too busy making preparations some journey he continually referred to, all of the time willing her to ask "where?", and all of the time her not satisfying his desire for control.

She lay back down in her bed again. It was too soft and she was too warm under the covers, so she threw them back to allow the faint breeze to cool her skin. She still couldn't sleep, though, a surge of excitement flowing through her. She could end this nightmare!

Eventually, well after midnight, she must have fallen asleep, because all too soon she was awakened by a jangle of keys in the lock to her door and then the bolt was sliding back.

Rune entered. A most unusual occurrence. She suddenly remembered her plotting of the previous night, and she flushed at the thought, which was immediately proceeded by the thought *He knows*.

He didn't. He just stood to one side whilst one of the maid servants entered the room with a bowl of steaming water for her morning wash. It was very early, the sun still below the horizon and she felt muzzy-headed with a lack of sleep. She indicated that first she needed to perform her morning ablutions, so she was taken down a long corridor to a corner room that was only used by the great and good of the house. As she approached, Stieber's woman left. She smiled quite foully at Amara, a smile that said *You're nothing, just a slave. You're below my every consideration.* Which Amara clearly wasn't, the very smile a contradiction of itself..

In a clear voice, accented with a lilt of French, the black woman said "Don't forget your make-up."

The smile turned in to a scowl and she spat at Amara's feet, but she kept her council. Amara laughed, a beautiful fluting laugh. She fully expected today to be the last day of her life and she was determined to enjoy it. Her sleepiness had vanished, a surge of electricity coursing through her veins. She blew the woman a kiss, and continued her way in to the smallest room.

Before Stieber's woman could leave earshot, Amara said in a loud voice "It *really* smells bad in here!"

There was a slam of a door.

*

Amara, once those morning routines had been completed, was taken down to breakfast. She was sat alone with Arthur Rimbaud, Rune and Wilhem Stieber. Grapefruit was served with a sugar topping that crunched pleasantly as she ate.

She became aware of a fluffiness in her mind as she ate. It was almost a tickle, a feeling almost like that of being caressed. It felt familiar to her, like her husband was stroking her skin. The sensation was pleasant and she started to look at it, looking almost inwards at her very own mind, that throbbing pulsating grey matter so infused with blood. She felt herself sinking as she chewed her grapefruit, but then something about the mastication, possibly a sudden gush of bitterness over her tongue as the sugar dissipated, brought her to the fore. She looked alarmed, eyes wide. She could see the look on her own face, as if she was dissociated from her very own body, a look like a gazelle faced by a hunter, eyelids drawn back into her skull, the pupils small pinpricks and shock written all over her face.

Amara returned to her body with a snap.

Her beautiful black faced looked around the table. Rimbaud was oblivious to the apparent goings on, whilst Stieber was at the far end watching intently. Rune was in the middle, side on to her and Stieber. He – it – was not looking at anything, he barely seemed aware of his surroundings, barely seemed to be even alive.

Amara could feel the caress returning again, a subtle touch, more subtle than last time, and closing her eyes, she dropped herself into a kind of trance, immediately going under. This was not normal. It usually took several minutes, sometimes longer depending on the prevailing emotion, but this time it was instant. There was a path of shadow in the grey. It wasn't a real grey, any more than it was a real shadow, but it was an imagined manifestation of this mockery of a ritual. She followed the dark streak and somehow she could feel herself tiptoeing gently down the table so as not to alert the black vein, right down its centre before veering off to the left about half way down.

Still possessed of her manic fatalism she did not think. Her war cry *Ai, ai* came out in a mental blast and she hurled herself at the creature that was Rune. She was met by a solid wall. No – not solid. Almost solid. She could feel it sag imperceptibly, if such a corporeal description could adequately define the feeling.

It was like the molecules of the shadow seemed to bend inwards and part. Some winked out of existence as her own grey was almost enveloped by Rune's blackness.

For a moment she panicked, her strand of colour almost entirely enclosed by Rune's blackness as she pushed too far, she could feel her breath constrict in her body and then she was pushed, hard, back to that living shell. She re-entered herself and could feel the blood coursing through her veins, a ragged breath shuddering through her body and a pulsating awareness of what exactly this beast may be. She felt fear, exhilarating and constricting her simultaneously.

She vomited, her grapefruit unfinished.

No words were spoken. She was led downstairs.

*

Amara sat in a sterile white room in which was a silver-steel chair. Both the room and the chair were immaculately clean, as was the surgical table to one side. She was alone with Rimbaud. She could feel blood drying on her skull, minute scabs forming on a head that was now bald.

"Why do you do this? You're not like him."

"I have no choice. It started with the science of it all. It's like a drug, peering in to a world the like of which has never been truly seen. And I was hooked; I'm still hooked. I'm convinced it's for the greater good in the long run, mankind can only benefit."

"I believe you're basically a good man, Rimbaud, if a little misguided. Perhaps a little insane." She spoke mildly, as if commenting on the weather. Not that she could see the outdoors, and hadn't in a while. She missed the wind in the trees, the sun on her face. "No matter what you've done...you're not an evil person, like him."

Rimbaud's face dropped in to one of utter, utter despair. "It's too late for me. All of those women I've murdered, and maybe you next. I murdered them all."

"Redeem yourself."

"No. I can't."

They stared at each other, one coldly, the other helpless.

"Please, this way." Rimbaud touched her arm and she flinched.

"I can manage."

She levered herself up, her head aching terribly from the chloroform that had been used to render her unconscious before the operation was performed. She suspected her head would have ached anyway, even though she'd been told there would be no pain from the operation itself. It felt queer, a tugging sensation on her scalp whenever she frowned. She hadn't yet had cause to smile. Her head was cold, also. She had no hair remaining.

With revulsion, she again noticed the table beside her, upon which rested a revolving device that held a hollowed and sharpened tube. This had been used to burrow into her cranium removing corks of bone to expose her brain beneath. Those corks were in a brass bowl, also on the table, blood sticky upon them. She had been washed whilst she'd slept and freshly dressed by one of the disquieting corpses that tended her without emotion of any sort. Amara could feel emotion and this corpse had none. The woman would have been pretty. Was she someone's wife or sweetheart? Did she have a gaggle of small children mourning her disappearance? Did anyone here care?

"Who are they, Arthur?" she asked quietly.

"I don't know," he replied, equally quietly, almost mournfully.

"Have they husbands, lovers, children?"

"No-one knows. I suspect they were vagrants brought in by Stieber or Rune." He shuddered.

"This way, please," he invited her politely.

"Where are we going now?"

"We must insert the wires, the Faraday cage. Unfortunately, we need to be able to see any reaction that you have, so there may be some mild discomfort."

She'd seen the women. She stopped dead.

"Explain."

"The copper wires need inserting into various parts of your brain. We've managed to hone our skills so that there is virtually no incorrect placement, which can lead to, ah, difficulties arising."

"Difficulties?" spat Amara, disgust evident on her face.

"Death," he said putting on a braver face than he felt. "But it could not possibly happen now."

He moved to touch her again in what she took was meant to be a reassuring manner, but she stepped away from him again.

"Keep your hands off me, pervert."

"Amara, this small sacrifice could save millions of lives, it could stop all wars forever. With the aid of these spirits, there never needs to be the threat of another bloody tyrant like Napoleon."

He grabbed hold of her now, not ungently, but firmly all the same.

He took her in to a small room that led from the (*hospital ward* Amara thought) room that she was in now. In it there was a cold white chair and a large wooden table. The chairs had manacles attached, to which her eyes were drawn and Rimbaud noticed immediately.

"They're for your own safety. It apparently feels somewhat strange. Or so I'm led to believe."

"Really?" said Amara sardonically.

"The thing is, is that it's a delicate operation, so that if you try to interfere there's always the possibility of the most terrible of consequences."

Her eyes were drawn upwards to the pole bolted to the back of the chair. Attached to it was another restraint.

"For the same purposes?" she asked.

"Yes, my dear."

The table contained a large variety of items. Spools of copper wire were arranged neatly in size order, some almost as fine as the hairs that used to exist on her head. Some were far thicker. A large wooden device sat in the centre of the table, a thick spiralled wire connecting to an even larger metal-cased device that sat on the floor. It seemed to emanate slightly. Emanate what exactly, Amara could not be sure. Leading from the other side of the metal casing was a thick sheath of wiring that plunged through the floor of the room.

From the large wooden box on the table, a pair of wires extended to the other side of the room and a large glass dome the size of a man. Ridiculously, in the centre, was clamped a black rectangle the size of an envelope. A final pair of wires left the wooden box to be clipped gently to a crown that sat reverently on a small plinth behind the chair.

She sat herself down without being told and Rimbaud set himself to the task of securing, all the murmuring to her that it would all be well, no harm would come of the procedure. It sounded to her ears as if they were in the confessional, that she was the priest expected to give absolution for his sins. She kept her mouth closed, offering no such gift to the Frenchman, but her eyes followed him about his business, and he could not meet her gaze.

Lastly, he tightened the metal band around her forehead, and then the chair was reclined slightly.

She could not see him, but she could hear activity on the metal table. And then she felt a sensation. It wasn't pain, nor was it especially unpleasant. It was merely queer.

And then another stab of queerness, only this time the sight in her left went blurry for a moment before steadying itself.

And then there was the smell of almonds.

There was a blur in her right eye.

The pleasant smell of vanilla.

A twitch in her right leg.

Salivation.

The world in black and white.

The pungent smell of cigarettes.

A tingling sensation in her face.

A spike of agonising pain through her teeth.

And then it was over. The firtling ceased. There was a moments respite where Rimbaud could be heard shuffling items around, then …

… all of those sensations seemed to fire off at random times rapidly and after a minute or more of such disorientation she felt all of them at once. She wanted to scream, she felt her mind slipping into insanity. There was a hum, clicks of electricity...

...and then it all went away. There was the smell of molten metal, and she gasped as a tiny fragment twitched on to her skull.

She gasped, all normal sensation returning. Her body was covered in sweat, she could feel rivulets running between her breasts, down her back and pooling at her behind.

There was a snap, and her hands were suddenly free, followed by her ankles.

"Oh praise be!" Rimbaud's enthusiasm was audible from behind her. "Oh, praise be!"

Amara remained silent, concentrating on her own breathing. More, she tried to concentrate

"You should regain your breath before I release your head, Amara. We need to make sure that the metalwork has cooled, and you need to understand that the wires must never be disconnected. The crown is fragile. You must be careful never to damage it. Doing so may hurt you." He was earnest in his words, really meaning everything he said.

"What happens if I just take them out?"

"You won't be able to, you'll be physically incapable of withdrawing more than one, and then only probably partially."

"And what had happened to the others after your defilement?"

Arthur walked around to look in to Amara's face. He looked wounded. He seemed to be unable to comprehend the hurt that he had done to her.

"Defilement? Amara, I do what I must do. Once this is over, you will be free to go. The abilities that you may gain because of this are undiscovered, think of the potential, the opportunity!"

"You do not understand, *cochon*."

Rimbaud flinched at her use of French. "I am not a pig. This is science in action."

"You dissemble. What happened to the other women at this point of your *defilement*?"

"They became as you see them, They are merely shells, although one or two are still open to suggestion."

"You sicken me, Arthur. Where is your humanity? Look! What do you see before you?" He gazed at her, and he looked about to speak, but she forestalled him. "I believe that you see an experiment. I believe you see some kind of phenomena, a hypothesis to be proven. I am not. I am a woman, a human being. Do you know what I see?"

Rimbaud shook his head, tears in his eyes.

"I see someone who has no humanity. I see a defiler." There were tears streaming down her face now, and they matched the rivers that flowed down Arthur Rimbaud's cheeks.

"I am…"

The door to the room opened and Stieber entered the room halting any further conversation. She couldn't see him, but she could tell it was Stieber by the footsteps.

"Is it done, Rimbaud?"

"Yes, Herr Stieber. It is done. She still seems to be normal, although we may have to wait a short while to see is her body rejects the machinery."

"I want an attempt now."

"Now? But she's only just been processed."

"Now, Monsieur. Now. I would like to watch, so continue."

"Y-yes, Herr Stieber, although I do require quiet. Perhaps if you could take a seat over there?" He gestured to one of the chairs that sat beneath a high window.

"Of course. I would hate to break your concentration."

Arthur busied himself behind Amara. There was the creak of metal hinges, the crackle of naked electricity and a fume of burning assailed her senses. She felt the crown on her head being manipulated in some way, and then an insistent tug as if something were pulling on her scalp.

The hum that had been in the background rose in pitch and volume, it came to the fore, and suddenly Amara's mind was whipped in to a space. It was like a Vodun ritual, only here there was darkness.

No, there wasn't darkness, it was a tunnel, and it was grey, only a very dark grey. It felt diabolical, as if there was no hope left in the universe. Suddenly she was in a green verdancy that clarified itself into a woodland, lush and invigorating as if spring had just come, and had just been washed in a cleansing rain and dried by a hospitable sun. It was beautiful.

She felt and heard an approach. She turned to see a young man in a bedraggled uniform approach. She lifted her hand to wave, but he looked straight through her and didn't seem to be able to see her at all.

"Run boy, run," she called to him. He stopped, appearing to search for her, but then continued on his path.

"Run as far and as fast as your legs can carry you!" she shouted more loudly.

She suddenly remembered what she was, where she was. She watched the young man approach, an enormous dog at his side. It gambolled like a new-born lamb through a field of yellow rape, which she ought to be able to smell, but couldn't.

And then the world went black for a moment, before she found herself in a bower.

*

Lucas walked along a rocky shore. The boat had brought him here, the dog leaping around like an over-excited pup. He'd called the dog Mudasir. Ironic, considering he *wasn't* a handsome dog. But he was sure he had known someone of that name – fought besides them, even – and that they had been good friends. More, he was sure that his friend would have appreciated the joke.

Past tense. Perhaps he lay dead now. Lucas could not be sure.

Nothing of importance yet appeared in Utopia, and strangely he did not feel any hunger or thirst; yet the boat ride had lasted an age, a freezing journey of strange apparitions that flew straight through him, but caused no damage. There had been other things too, fleeting and incoherent, and they had made his eyes water to try and focus on them. He did not fear the beings in the mist, though. That made him afraid in itself. He felt altogether too phlegmatic, and it was only this that made him uneasy.

Still, at least it was warm now. From his vantage point, the land sloped gently downwards, fresh spring green below rich azure skies, and across yellow fields swaying with tall rape, the scent filling the air. It reminded Lucas of Belgium: fields of rape in the spring, wheat in the autumn, blood ubiquitous.

It *was* strange though, he considered, for he understood none of it.

A path beckoned through the field, and clicking for the dog to follow, he strolled down the path, hands brushing the yellow flowers. He descended gently along the lushly grassed path with no thoughts and no worries, only smiling at the dog who still ran like a pup through the flowers. He removed his jacket as the sun rose higher and the path stretched as far as he could see through the undulating fields, the endless fields. An awful lot of steam engines need lubricating, thought Lucas.

The air in front of him shimmered gently. He stopped suddenly. The dog sniffed cautiously.

There wasn't much to see, a blur like a heat haze, blocking his path.

RUN BOY, RUN it spoke to him.

RUN AS FAR AND AS FAST AS YOUR LEGS CAN CARRY YOU

The haze disappeared as suddenly as it had arrived. Panicked beyond, Lucas ran and ran and ran. The fields continued, the path unerringly straight, until suddenly he was in a clearing of large oak trees, trees that surely hadn't been there a moment ago, with a grove in its centre. Abruptly tired, he lay down at its centre and before his eyes were properly closed, he was asleep.

Lucas awoke in the clearing, a searing pain stabbing his skull repeatedly, like a large blunt needle being inserted, removed and then reinserted into his brain. Then another needle, and another and another and another.

The pain was so great he was unable to scream.

And then the pain left him; not entirely; a balm was poured on to his imaginary wounds.

Panic

He felt it, she felt it. Sentience.

Panic

Quick, look around, like a doe in the forest

Breathe

Calmer

A voice resounded around his head, although there were no words. She knew him. Could feel his mind, could read his every thought.

Shhhhh....Lucas....Shhhh

Panic decreasing

In both places

There was communication, that of a God appearing before a Believer. No words were necessary and understanding was perfect, no nuance, hint or subtlety. Lucas knew. She knew.

And finally.

Run, Lucas, run, never come to this place again

Lie down, rest, accept

And then she was gone.

The pain went. Suddenly, not gradually. It was there, it was gone.

Run? Accept?

Really?

Lucas was dead. He should have known it, he realised on introspection. A fleeting memory of smoke and rotten eggs flashed through his mind, there his memory ended.

*

There was a crack and then the splintering glass disintegrated, filling the chamber with a fine powder, like sand in a desert storm. There was a flash as the small black object combusted of its own accord.

A shockwave followed the fire, not physical like compression after an explosion, but mental.

It rendered both Amara and Rimbaud unconscious.

CHAPTER 9 – THE RAMBLING WAR

"Napoleon has humbugged me!"

Sir Arthur Wellesley surveyed the terrain of a rather obscure part of Belgium. His ragtag army was tired and dispirited. It reeked of defeated and it looked in no mood for a proper fight. Admittedly, they would prefer to fight and get it over with rather than carry on fleeing with their tails between their legs. But the reek was most definitely of failure.

Unfortunately for them, it was Sir Arthur's job to win. His nose twitched and he sneezed violently. If he didn't give Boney a damn good hiding soon, then England would soon be speaking French.

Marshal Ney had done a damn good job though, harrying his advanced positions and eventually taking the Quatre Bras crossroads in a battle of such depravity that Wellesley had questioned the written reports he had received. The Duke of Orange had died in that place and Ney had won through for the French and then harried Wellesley's force all the way to the ridge before Mont St Jean. The wet ground had prevented the French Cavalry progressing, but it had meant the destruction of a significant portion of the Allied artillery, which should even now be crowding the ridge where cold and damp soldiers were now huddled. Instead, they had been destroyed by Wellesley's own troops to prevent their use by the French.

A low mist still clung to the low ground below and la Haye Sainte was almost invisible just below. It was the most southerly place that Allied troops still held, and only then because night had fallen on desperate, vicious fighting, and the rest of the French advance had had to stop.

He could see the French massing on la Belle Alliance. The ridge bristled with artillery, and at the foot of the rise, the French infantry were rousing, the smog of damp camp fires mingling with the morning mist. It was so sodden down in the low ground that Sir Arthur expected any attack to be delayed by some hours. It just wasn't practical, the cavalry couldn't mass on the flanks and the artillery couldn't be brought up in support.

But still he did not like it. His proboscis detected that distinct smell of defeat in this particular setting; alas, it couldn't smell Blücher and the Prussians and that was bad. Communications had gone awry, they could be anywhere. They should be *en route* to join up this day, but because the weather had been so dreadful, they were probably bogged down somewhere fighting the Crapaud brigade commanded by Grouchy. Surveying his own army's escape route to the north, should he stay and fight and the worst occur, Wellesley did not much like the idea of marching routed men over what were effectively Irish bogs, akin to those of his own upbringing in Dublin.

"Damn the Prussians," cursed Nosey under his breath.

It was a difficult choice to make, one that would have lasting repercussions. To retreat further north in search of terrain better suited to his tactics and men would mean splitting the army because there wasn't the slightest hope of avoiding some form of disaster if they stayed together. But then disaster would occur if half of his army met all of Napoleon's might. Whatever happened, Brussels would fall. It just wasn't defensible.

"Damn the Prussians!" he cursed more loudly.

"Sir?" enquired an aide.

"Nothing, nothing," said Sir Arthur. His hawk-like eyes studied the aide.

"We must retreat further north." He spoke softly, but torment showed on his face. "We need to split our forces; one will divert east to meet up with Blücher whilst the other half will try and split Boney's forces and take them to the west. Maybe we can manoeuvre him within the month back to somewhere I like, and with the damned Prussians in tow."

He paused somewhat melodramatically. "Waterloo. How could I ever refuse?"

*

In the event it took a bit longer than a month to rejoin a decisive battle. On the 17th June 1815, Wellesley was forty six years old. He was sixty and still in charge of the British armies, as well as being Commander-in-Chief of the allied forces against France and her allies when the ear eventually ended. War had ravaged the countryside, poverty was rife throughout the entirety of Europe, her governments had bankrupted themselves to attain mastery of the continent and civil engineering works ground to a veritable halt, bringing towns and cities back to some kind of dark ages.

Eventually, the war did end, a resounding defeat of France near a small town called Verdun to the east of Napoleons surrogate homeland. The hills, rolling and difficult for a mass attack in dressed ranks, were the unsuitable ground for the final battle, but Napoleon went for it anyway, and the darling of France was defeated by a combination of inferior weaponry – the repeating rifle was pivotal – inferior numbers, and, crucially, the battle hinged on the tiny things, as they often do. A misplaced command here, a squadron that went awry in the chaos there, or just the plain and simple loss of nerve of a single soldier that transmitted itself to his colleagues, and for that to turn in to panic and rout, to leave a hole through which a troop of heavy cavalry could smash a line. It was close, but the rumoured increasing eccentricity of Napoleon overcame his brilliance as a general. The British captured the Emperor and sent him to St Helena, where he eventually died under somewhat suspicious circumstances.

Sir Arthur Wellesley died at Verdun, buried amongst a sea of white crosses. Lord Wellington never did exist.

CHAPTER 10 – THE PRICE OF PIGEON

William awoke to the smell of pine and pork crackling. He vomited to one side before dragging himself to an upright position. Watching him, a green tinge to her eyes, towered Bob. Half a dozen chaffinches were perched on one shoulder.

"Are you alright?" she signed.

"The pig…it reminds me of my own burned flesh, please, take it away."

He took a moment to look around; they were in a shallow depression, surrounded by majestic woodland. It was nearing sunset, and high cirrus clouds reflected a pale golden light onto the woodland floor.

"I have nothing else for you to eat," indicated Bob.

"Where are we?"

"About thirty miles south of Birtles Hall."

"And where are we going?"

"I have no idea, I thought you might have had a plan?" flickered Bobs fingers.

"Plan? I need to think!" groaned William, clutching his head in both hands.

But William couldn't think. He only saw dead bodies and the abomination called Rune.

He had known Chapman fleetingly well – highly strung, a poor boys fervour, and a desperation to fit in with the monied intelligentsia he could never be. He'd never really belonged in any crowd, however:

too haughty for his own people and too self-conscious for William's natural circles. Never humble, never grateful. Indeed, there had been the incident that had seen him black-balled from the Royal Society. Maybe that had turned him into that thing, given him the drive and hunger and the insane lust to be better. William presumed he would never know – he in no way desired another meeting with that.

And Brocklehurst? That demonic laugh and such carelessness regarding life, death and propriety. Brocklehurst was eminent in his field, internationally regarded as a leading light regarding technological innovation and discovery. What was happening? What was he doing? Why kill the very engineers and scientists whom had built him his reputation as a visionary genius? What was to happen to all of his creations? There were hundreds, maybe thousands of the automata shells below the grounds of Birtles Hall, just waiting to be imbued.

William's head spun. He needed food and sleep desperately.

"Bob, I need food and sleep. Are there any villages nearby?"

"I can smell one a few miles south-west of here."

Smell? mused William. And then sighed. Another time.

"Then we had better set off."

Before he could protest, Bob had picked William up amidst a flutter of wings and protesting chirrups, so that he found himself cradled in her arms like a swooned maiden being rescued by her knight in shining armour.

William considered protesting as his ribs ground painfully, but he didn't have the energy. Slowly, Bob began to run, a gentle jog speeding up to an Olympian run. The ground sped by, and in a matter of twenty minutes they had covered the distance and Bob was slowing to a halt. Chimney smoke pervaded and lights twinkled a short distance away.

"I cannot go in to the village," signed Bob.

William pulled a face. "You cannot go in to that village *today*. I promise that soon you will be welcome in every village."

Bob's eyes altered hue subtly but said nothing. William turned and started towards the village. And then he stopped suddenly. "Damn my eyes! Bob, you were his manservant. Practically invisible to a man like Brocklehurst. What on earth is happening?"

"I don't fully know, William. He had no confidantes, and the one time I know of that he met Rune was when he was George Chapman. I was not present at that meeting, although he did take away a serving girl who never returned."

"When was that?"

"In the autumn. I believe Brocklehurst has been anxious for his return."

William's voice rose in volume and pitch until he was nearly screaming, "Why, Bob, WHY? Think damn it, what the hell is going on?!"

"He received correspondence from Paris fairly regularly, but I know not what about."

"Damn, damn and bloody damn, what else? We're missing something."

"He was meant to be going away for a few days, if that's any use?"

"GOING AWAY? GOING AWAY! OF COURSE THAT'S OF PRIMARY BLOODY IMPORTANCE! WHERE THE HELL IS HE GOING?"

A small chattering of tits flew in to the clearing.

"AND WHAT THE BLOODY HELL IS IT WITH THOSE DAMNED BIRDS!"

"You sound a little like him in one of his tantrums, Sir William," signed Bob bluntly.

"LIKE HELL….dammit Bob, I wasn't shouting at you, it's just so bloody frustrating. I'm in Paris having a lovely time with some French chums, when *wham*, I'm a slave on a pirate ship with a captain who's a complete bastard, and then we're shot out of the skies, I'm burned to a porcine crisp, accused of piracy, witness to a number murders on the orders of a man I respected as a brilliant innovator, and then attacked by a monstrosity, before being rescued by an automaton, the likes of which I've only set eyes on in the last few days. I'm frightened, pained, scared, tired. And I'm bloody ravenous, and you're telling me I need to go back to France!"

William's monologue ended with a glare at Bob, whose eyes glared back like lava.

He puffed out his cheeks and sighed a long, deep sigh. "I'm sorry Bob. It's been a long day. And it's going to be a long night. Could you carry me to London?"

"William, I need coal," signed Bob.

"Uh?" said a surprised William. "Lord! I did not even consider your physical needs, How awful of me! My goodness, I am terribly sorry."

Bob's eyes glowed yellow: humoured.

"Errrm, what exactly do you need coal for?"

She opened up one of her thigh plates and William looked in to see, blushing as he did so. There wasn't much to see, but she was a lady nonetheless.

So Bob opened up a small compartment in her foot plate, took out some miniature tools and unscrewed her leg below her knee. She upended it and ash fell out. Raising the stump of her upper leg, William could see a fine grate, her knee glowing gently. Delving inside her thigh, she pressed a knurled bolt and a soft hiss of steam released itself from a small hole that appeared as a result of depressing the bolt. She had been beautifully crafted.

"What the...."

"It's weird," signalled Bob. "At the top of my thigh, and in small capillaries running downwards, is water. The coal doesn't drive the water by making steam, because a far lower heat is required and therefore far less coal. From what I have learned, the engineers and Brocklehurst figured that perpetual motion wasn't possible, so a small amount of energy is required to drive the near-perpetual motion that powers me. Naturally, if I need to react or act more rapidly, then more energy is wasted, so the coals get hotter and I occasionally lose some water, as steam, as a result. But normally I burn slowly, I only really need to stoke myself every few days and I only need water extremely occasionally. Today has been particularly energetic, I'm afraid."

"Brocklehurst told me about the nut-cases he'd found in his locality, but he never really explained how he'd practically used the innovations."

"Here I am!" Bob signed. "The Perpetuality Engine, as it has been named, is apparently remarkable, but it's impossible to defy the small amounts of heat generated – miniscule – due to friction as the water flows around me, so the sunlight capture plate on top of my head supplements the coals. Well, so long as the sun shines, which is only occasional in the north west."

"Golly."

William looked at her for some time with frank admiration.

"You must have been an astounding person when you were alive."

Bob turned away as her eyes turned a melancholic magenta.

William's face turned pale. "Oh Bob, I'm sorry, I didn't mean…."

He shut up.

*

William sat in a plush office overlooking the Thames. In the shadows by the bookcases, Bob loomed accidentally. She didn't really have much choice.

He was very high up, so high that he believed he could feel it sway in the breeze. It was situated in a tall spire that appeared, from the outside, to be based on a Middle Eastern minaret, although the tower was much vaster in its girth and height. It amused William that British architects had taken an object so simple and beautifully elegant in its design, and then bastardised it into a monstrosity, a corruption based on the idea that bigger and more complex must be better. Some of the grander towers were more than a hundred feet around the base and higher than fifty storeys. These spires were interspersed between the traditional government buildings of Westminster. Those buildings were now seen as old-fashioned, but were in truth proper British architecture, and practical to boot, as opposed to this new mania for so defiling a style as to make it hideous in the extreme. The minarets were gaudy and over-elaborate, with the form being so important to the designers that function could not possibly be attained.

The tower that housed the office had an outside that was clad in white marble with gold crenulations at every level. There were at least fifty levels. The roof was of terracotta, stolen from some sort of Mediterranean style and it clashed wonderfully with the Middle Eastern basis of design.

Inside, all of the offices and rooms had curved walls, admittedly quite pleasant, but the further effect was that most of the rooms – unless you were jolly important indeed – were wedge shaped. This meant that meeting spaces were confined, bookcases had to be specially designed to be practical, and carpet layers cursed as they laid each shag pile.

Most importantly, what nobody had considered in their rush to build taller, bolder towers in that trend was the effect of the London particular on marble. The resultant blackened surfaces were ugly and at lower levels, the smog caused the building to crumble, to the extent that scaffolding had been erected around the bases of some of the older towers, which were now some twenty five years old, to prevent them collapsing. London had discovered acid rain.

He glanced at his pocket watch, fingers drumming nervously on the desk. Brandy shone gold before him, even though it was extremely early on. It was a chilly day and the spirit had been gratefully accepted. He had deposited Bob in this office under cover of darkness and then toured the streets, as was his wont, until a civilised hour approached, and his host could receive him. The brandy burned as it ran down his throat, and he grimaced with pleasure. He was running on spirits and adrenaline. He dared not stop now, because if he did he'd sleep for days.

The journey southwards had taken the best part of a day through unpopulated areas where Bob could travel in the open without fear of alarming village folk. Travelling from Marlow, the journey into the early evening had been by stolen boat, via a series of locks, to the foot of the House of Commons. He could barely admit it to himself, but it gave him a thrill of anticipation and excitement to be adventuring once again. Bob played the part of manservant well, even stretching to holding her ex-masters money in a concealed compartment. It had come in handy for purchasing gin the previous evening.

The door burst open and a rotund, red-faced man, heavy with sweat, stormed in to the room.

"Blood and sand, tell me it's not true." Lord William Melville slumped into a massive leather chair. As well as an old family friend, Melville just happened to be rather high up in the more clandestine side of the government.

He glared at the motionless brass figure that continued to loom.

Suddenly, the window smashed. The fresh corpse of an augmented Passenger pigeon wreaked a trail of destruction through Melville's office, where it had been ordered to deliver a sealed package. It had done this as directly as possible, its pistoned, metal wings lending such weight as to enable it to easily break the glass. Unfortunately, it had also broken its neck in the process, and so it was now a dead Passenger pigeon with a sealed package tied to a leg.

Melville untied the letter, calling for a servant to order a repair, whilst cursing quietly under his breath, which became louder and more explicit as he further

William hushed him, before he could continue his rant on a different subject, relating his tale to the new man.

"Shitting death, Hope, it's a bloody disaster! Oh, and pleased to see you safe and sound, we've been worried about you, your sisters and I."

William waved the platitude away. "What's with Brocklehurst, exactly?"

"Brocklehurst, it seems, has made off with a sack load of swag, all of a certain set of technological secrets, killed or stolen all of the people who could have picked up his work, left us with tens of thousands of useless metal shells and defected to bloody Paris, by the sounds of it. Bastard, bastard, bastard. I never should have trusted that lowlife."

"Defected to Paris, sir? But *we* own Paris."

"There's more to this than meets the eye, Hope. I don't know what exactly, but I smell sauerkraut."

"Sauerkraut?"

"Yes, that clever bastard Stieber is in charge in Paris. Sly old dog, always has his fingers in pies, knows everything about everyone who is someone, and hasn't the slightest scruple about applying pressure to their weakest points. Easy with Brocklehurst – massage an ego, supply some cash, promise an exalted standing in a new world order. It's exactly what I offered him, traitorous bastard."

"And what exactly is he going to do in Paris?"

"I've no idea. But Stieber is there, and I've only recently found out that there's been contact between the two. Why the hell I wasn't informed earlier, I've not got a clue. Heads will roll for this debacle, I guarantee it." He sighed. "Probably mine, for fucks sake!"

"I still don't understand I'm afraid," said William.

"Well, there's something going on, but we don't know what. Troubles brewing, and someone is stirring the pot, inflaming all of the usual players. Russia is massing an army on the borders of Pomerania, the Germanies are developing weapons at an alarming rate, France is barely under control, full of malcontents. The Dutch have even increased the price of their blasted tulips. That's not to mention Italy. I presume you've heard?"

William nodded. "And Brocklehurst's involvement?"

"More like that blackguard Stieber. He just can't be on the level. He's up to something, and not for the Germans, although they don't realise it yet. Something is behind all of this and Stieber is the front man – at the moment. But we're damned if we know what exactly. Look at these newspapers."

On the desk in front of Melville sat a stack of newspapers, which the seemingly bluff politician began to leaf through. He tossed a few aside, muttering to himself. "You don't speak Russian William, your German isn't good enough, I believe. No, that's Polish and Austrian isn't spoken by anyone barring myself and the Austrians. Ah. The Telegraph and Le Monde. Here you go." He passed them to William.

"Thank you, my Lord. Do you really speak all of those languages?"

"Yes, I'm fairly fluent in most European languages, although I do struggle with Swedish and Russian. I can muddle through with most of the languages with which we have interests in the Middle East. Punjab, Urdu, Gujarat, Afghan, a few others. Anyway, read!"

William read. The newspaper was dated several weeks previous.

Britain Mobilises 'Eager to Serve' Troops

Bessarabia, Wallachia and Moldavia swallowed by Austrian Empire

Russia consolidates forces in Poland

Kaiser Wilhelm I expels diplomats

In a series of unexpected military manoeuvres, hostilities in Europe continued. Whitehall has summoned foreign diplomats to explain the aggression. It is said that no satisfactory explanations could be gained from the meetings, and as a result, Great Britain has mobilised her navy and those land forces based in Northern France. All leave has been cancelled for soldiers based in various barracks around the country.

This reporter has, however, discovered that several high ranking politicians have disappeared in several countries, including our own. Recent spates of terrorism, including the assassination of a Russian Royal several weeks ago, and the bombing of the Austrian Embassy in Moldavia, have led to this increase in tension across Europe.

The Tsarist regime in Russia is complaining, unofficially, that it fears for its political sanctity and its Royal mandate. The threat posed by Prussia, Austria-Hungary and the Scandinavian and Baltic States has left Russia with no option but to consolidate its borders.

The Austrians cite the Russian warmongering as the reason for the bombing of their Embassy in Moldavia, and that the annexation of Bessarabia, Wallachia and Moldavia is vital for national security.

It has been noted that Belgium has reminded leaders across Europe of the Treaty of Europe, as it fears for its borders if war should break out.

The Germanic states, in a rare show of unanimous unity, have strengthened outward facing borders, leaving borders to each other virtually unmanned. Locally, various commentators have voiced significant concern over the move.

"There's more on pages five, six, seven, twelve, thirteen, fourteen and fifteen. It's the same in most of the newspapers," said Melville. "The coverage in these papers is far stronger." He indicated towards the foreign newspapers stacked on his table.

"The French are petrified. We've effectively hamstrung their armed forces over the last decade or so. Any concerted effort will see them conquered in weeks. We are rather worried ourselves, but unfortunately we've mismanaged the situation so badly, that any buffer the Frogs may have been able to offer has gone."

"Is there any danger of that?"

"There's no forces gathering in the vicinity. Everything seems to be happening to the east. There's some new buck in the Germanies who's organising their confounded union. If they get together, you'll see trouble in a few years' time. More headaches, but at least I'll be long gone by then."

William glanced through other tales from the battles that seemed to have sprung up. A Russian soldier had been tied to a post and had been incinerated to his waist. He had been burned alive.

Civilians had shot at retreating troops, even following a peaceful occupation.

Traders executed for the treasonable act of selling to the enemy

He read an article from La Figaro out aloud.

"Russia has declared war on the independent state of Galicia." He looked at Melville incredulously. "They've declared war on a region of Spain?"

"Don't be a fool, William. It's a small territory on the borders of Austria-Hungary and Poland. Tactically, it's a brilliant move. Politically, it could lead to carnage. Austria-Hungary won't stand for it, and it only leaves the Russians a couple of borders away from Bavaria. That would really test the resolve of Bismarck's attempts to unify the Germanies. He's struggling as it is. Most of the German States are still hopping mad that they're virtually subservient to Prussia. She made a lot of enemies, the day she signed the French agreement with us. And we made enough ourselves."

William looked over at the Thames, sun glowing behind a rising mist.

"But why is Brocklehurst involved?" said William returning to his former point.

"He's our chief technological weapons designer. He's been doing amazing things, designing an undefeatable infantry – but then you know about that. The problem is, is that what he's left us is bloody useless, better for nothing more than a museum. We haven't got any real details of how he was doing what he was doing, and now that he's killed or stolen everyone who knew anything, taken any useful blueprints and equipment, we're left with egg on our faces, a bloody great big hole in our finances, and if Stieber is involved, a bloody great big pain in the arse. No doubt Brocklehurst will be doing the same for whoever is lurking in the background. In the wrong hands, an army of the nature he developed will be big trouble."

"But unless it's being done for a European power, then surely there's no danger; and if Stieber isn't in the employ of the Prussians, surely it's nothing more than playing at power games. The rest of Europe – any of them – won't stand for it."

"Ahh, but you're forgetting the politicking. There's a serious danger of all-out war – everyone is out to get everyone at the moment, and whoever is behind Stieber is making sure that everyone else is being seen as the protagonist; Russia is sure to invade Pomerania, and from there all hell will break loose. And when the smoke clears in a year or two, what happens if a new army suddenly appears? Europe would be on its knees, ripe for the taking."

"There's a lot of posturing, I agree, My Lord, but surely some petty politicking over a few spies is far too petty to escalate to full scale war."

"William, how many times, call me Bill. You're marvellous in your field, if what I know is true, but World Order is a different kettle of fish entirely. The politicians take a similar line to you, not seeing the possibility of threat but in each other. Since Boney was deposed in '43, the spectre of another tyrant has loomed in each country's conscience. And the gears of war have been turning ever since – new and improved weapons, lighter-than-air fleets, subterfuge, spying. By God, Britain alone has a standing army of nearly a million men. In peace time! Imagine how many the Russians have– untrained peasants and inferior arms, admittedly, but by our best estimates, an army in excess of five million. As a standing army!"

Williams eyes widened, and his mouth shaped a shocked 'O'.

"Look out of the window, William, what do you see?"

From up here, he could see across the Thames and on to the Strand. Beyond that further, to the left, was Clerkenwell, whilst beyond the Strand, lay Cheapside, and then the East End, through the smog and fumes. He could see the upright figures on the Strand, gliding ladies in corseted outfits, bustles and frilled bonnets, strutting gentlemen twirling their walking canes, all out taking an early morning turn in the bracing air. But also he could see waif's encroaching the well-to-do streets, cold, thin and frail. Rising his view to Cheapside, he noted at its quietness. It was famed to be the busiest street in the world, with its jewellers, gentleman's outfitters and tobacconists, but there was no throng of suited men: shop fronts were shuttered, the hawkers and pedlars were few in number, their wares frugal, even given the hour. Most telling of all was the number of street preachers, all of them predicting the end of days, famine, or decreeing the rise of the anti-Christ and whatever other tragedy they could call down upon mankind. Fire was his personal favourite, the burning fires of hell. Why would Satan go to all that effort? By William's reckoning, most people would eventually get that from him anyway.

During his early-hours sojourn, he had noticed the dilapidation of even the normally affluent areas, paint flaking on store-fronts, windows broken, and paupers sleeping in doorways. Some of the smartly dressed young gentlemen, those who were not obviously inebriated, seemed to be in a state of disrepair, their clothes not quite pristine, hair not cut with alacrity, moustaches poorly tended.

Further, the much-trumpeted civilian 'steam age' did not progress with anything like the speed that it had been predicted, beyond the staid, mundane inventions like trains and coaches. Truly, the initial inventions were marvellous, but these had stuttered and stopped. William's personal favourite being the steamcycle, invented by a good friend. There had been a lot of initial interest, but his friend had never had the financial backing to further the dozen or so already made at his own expense. Partly out of sympathy, William had spent a small fortune on one. He loved it, although it was entirely lethal. It was heavy, and required automated wheels that descended on the push of a button when coming to a halt. The weight also meant that the brakes didn't work. Added to the immense speed of the thing – greater than fifty miles per hour! – this then required a great deal of planning to even go round a corner. Woe betide any pedestrian should step in the way, the massive wheels left nothing but a bloody, red smear along the cobblestones. William shuddered at the thought of riding over cobblestones. It gave its nickname: the Boneshaker.

William looked out, blinking back his reverie, and said stubbornly, "I don't know. Pigeons crouching on roof tops."

"Smell it William – poverty. That's what you can smell. It stinks. Do you think it's necessary? Why do you think that the British government is so bankrupt, that sanitation is appalling and the people are starving? And not just peasants and paupers, but bakers and nurses – even the successful tradesman and lowly noblemen are having it hard. For what reason? So we can pay for an army and all that it needs, equipping it and feeding it, developing the best guns money can buy, building the biggest cannons, paying the sneakiest spies, bribing the highest placed officials. All for the spectre of war."

"But the inventions, the innovation, it has been extraordinary, surely the benefit of such development must outweigh the financial turmoil."

"Maybe, but when? And at what cost? Think on the augmented animals, they've been an absolute disaster. Messenger hounds whose hearts cannot stand the stress," he referred to the greyhounds that were occasionally used to deliver important messages. Bob and himself had passed one such corpse on their journey south.

"And those Passenger pigeons. Do you know what they cost? We ship them across from America at less than threepence a bird – that's for the capture and then shipping across in decent condition."

"That seems quite reasonable. Far cheaper than a racing pigeon."

"Yes, and we bring back upwards of ten thousand at a time! But then, bearing in mind the cost of that, it then costs another five guineas per bird to fit them out to be of any use."

William spluttered, aghast.

"What were they going to be used for, barring the postal service?"

"Everything from the mundane task of delivering letters, to the less mundane task of exploding on impact. They have extraordinary reflexes and can dodge out of the way of most hazards. They can even dodge a musketball, though they aren't able to see high velocity projectiles." He held up his hand at the beginning of Hope's protestation. "Yes William, I know, only peasants use muskets now. It's why they're being developed as battlefield birds for long range targets. Once we can stop them breaking their own bloody necks!"

Melville stood up, his face purpling, and kicked the dead pigeon before immediately howling in pain. The bird had a great deal of metal work and was both hard and heavy.

"My bloody toe!" Melville moaned, dancing on one foot. He eventually sat down again, eying William suspiciously, as though it was all his fault, before he continued his explanations.

"And that's when they work. The mortality rate for the operation is seventy five percent. Another twenty three percent die early on just because they just don't understand the effects of the additional speed and weight. Ninety eight percent mortality. Life expectancy for those after that is six months. That one," he pointed at the ex-pigeon, "was one of the more experienced birds. There are over three thousand like him. Or her. Whatever, just work out the cost of getting that many to some sort of service."

They both tried and failed at that advanced mathematics.

Bob's fingers twirled. "£162,000 just to get three thousand birds in the air for six months."

"Sweet Jesus. And what about the cost to the populations in America? They must be being devastated."

"They're mostly vermin, William. Vermin."

William was mute and exceedingly pale. Some things were wrong in so many different aspects that it was difficult to know what to be most angry at.

CHAPTER 11 – THE POISONING OF RUNE

Stieber walked in to the room. "So, you're still alive then!"

"Apparently, defiler."

Unexpectedly, Stieber laughed; no maliciousness, just pure joy, a celebration of victory, and, well, sheer happiness. His face lit up and whilst he was still massively unkempt, he became handsome.

"You're in the wrong profession, filth. You should do something that makes you smile a little more often. It may suit you." She was stiff with tension. She liked a happy Stieber far less than the harsh one.

He walked over to her and gave her a big hug, and he meant it, a big happy, bear hug, leaving her shuddering in revulsion. He took hold of Rimbaud's hand, shaking it vigorously.

"My, my, my. I expected to be here for months whilst we experimented merrily. But first time and we're in! I miss Paris and we shall be back there in no time. Oh, how I love her: she is austere and yet merry, ancient and still vibrant. Berlin is a dusty old tome by comparison, full of fusty old men, Rome is frivolous and shallow, regardless of its history. Oh Paris, how I long for thee!"

"Paris?"

"Oh yes. Oh yes, two or three days to confirm our work and we'll be away. A week at most! And my patron, he'll be positively *glowing* with my reports. The time is ever so close."

Amara watched Stieber walk out into stone corridor beyond the room and could feel a palpable sense of his excitement. Not just in the way he seemed to skip, but at the lightness of his step and the sway of his hips. She could almost see the malevolent glitter of his eyes through the back of his skull. That happy look needed wiping from his face. It didn't suit him, she decided. A happy face on this man meant that something was wrong or that someone, somewhere was suffering. At this moment it was her.

She was struck by a dull ache that encased her head. It became a thud and then a searing pain. She shrieked, she couldn't help it and cowered on the floor as she rocked on her heels clasping her head.

Rimbaud bent down beside her, stroking her shoulder.

"Let me give you some more morphine, *ma Cherie*," he said. "The pain will be bad for a few days."

"Leave me alone, you pig," she spat at him, pushing him hard enough to make him sprawl on the floor.

"Herr Stieber expects me to continue my work until we depart. He wants to know why the vacuum jar imploded into fragments in that way and why it that the carbon combusted so spontaneously."

"I can tell you that now, you sadistic *cochon*," she spat. "I prevented a boy, a poor, dead boy from being imprinted in to that chamber. I saved his death."

"You did what? How?" As horrified as he was at her rather bald statement, he was also fascinated. It piqued his scientific bent.

"By telling the poor thing to run away. I made him flee."

"You..." Arthur struggled to put his feelings in to words. "But my work. My life's work. And the danger. What would happen if Herr Stieber found out. Or worse, that beast Rune?"

"Really? What could they do to me that they haven't already done? I may already be dead for all that you know. Should that fill me with optimism or compel me to a sense of duty? What have I to fear?"

"If you should fear anybody, you should fear Rune. He has studied your religion as I have. But his studies saw things that I could never have seen, and he saw something in the flames. My Master brought me his notes and it has taken my work into a different direction. It is astounding."

"Why then is he not performing this work?"

"He was too unstable as the scientist that was, no staying power. He would do this for the cruelty of it and his methods would be unscientific. Herr Stieber needs someone of greater stability."

"Then why is he here?"

"He is Vodun. He has walked in to its midst and he came out that monster. When he visited Herr Stieber in the autumn, he was a man like myself. On his return..." He grimaced. "Something happened between you and him this morning, tell me what it was."

Amara blanched at the thought. "So you were awake? I cannot begin to describe it. We were connected, and that is all."

"He has made it well known that for this service that he renders to Herr Stieber he expects payment." Arthur gazed at her, the first time he had ever met her eyes as an equal. "You are that payment."

"I must have water," she said.

Leaving Rimbaud in the room, she stumbled out in to the corridor. She went quickly to the round chamber from which the steps ascended, and the alcove where the water barrel sat. Lined along the walls were the dozen or so experiments. She could hear Arthur walking down the corridor in her wake. She did not have long.

Fumbling in her skirts as she did so, she dunked her head in to the barrel and drank deeply before emptying the contents of the handkerchief in to the barrel.

Just in time, for she heard also footsteps descending the stair as Arthur rounded in to the chamber. She started to dab at herself with the handkerchief. From the footsteps one of them could only be the devil himself, the other person appeared and was some nameless servant.

So soon she thought to herself, and she lowered her gaze to prevent her eyes giving herself away.

"Ladies, please fill your cups," intoned the servant.

They noiselessly glided over and each took a wooden mug that they filled with water before returning to their places. As they returned, Arthur made to take water himself, but he was shoved out of the way by Rune, who took less notice of him than a jackal notices the earthworm. He did not bother with a cup, and as he started to drink noiselessly through the slit that was his mouth. The servant bade the ladies to drink.

Within seconds Amara heard them. It was in her head, the copper cages that surrounded their heads amplifying the soundless noise somehow.

She sagged, and then a great tenor ran through the middle of it all, blood curdling and feral. Audible, not mental.

Sound stopped from the women almost simultaneously. They all slumped to the floor and Amara was left with a shadow of great pain and loss, a lament for their passing somehow imprinted on her mind. She could feel tears rolling down her face as they passed from being. They had still been alive, even if it had only been a half-life, and she, Amara, a believer in the sanctity of life (excepting that small sliver that wished nothing but death on her captors), had murdered them. Her heart was rent asunder, and she collapsed to her knees for the second time that day.

She could still hear a deep resonating scream, but it was nothing as to the mental anguish that she was feeling. She could not see Rimbaud looking at Rune in abject terror as the beast bellowed in some nameless agony, nor could she see the dumbstruck servant who eyed the dead women who lay on the floor.

She did not see Stieber descend at a hurry with his woman in tow.

Stieber immediately took control of the situation, and, for fear of his life and the life of all of the people in the chamber, he harried them upstairs as Rune fell to the floor convulsing, twitching and flailing around blindly. Pieces of him were falling away and scurrying around the chamber before returning and melding back in to his flesh. One or two pieces scuttled away and then seemed to shrivel, as lifeless as the stone that they lay upon. The nameless servant was too slow in the retreat upstairs. A tendril speared him and it seemed to attract others, until they shrouded the man in a shifting carpet of appendages like great black maggots burrowing their way in to his flesh. He screamed and fell, body wracked with pain. The appendages shifted back to Rune, and as the stairwell started to close, the great shout that still emanated from his lungs dropped in strength, until it was cut off almost entirely as the chamber door sealed shut.

CHAPTER 12 – THE RETURN OF THE BUCENTAUR

"France, William: we need you and your friend to go to France."

"And do what exactly, Lord Melville?"

"Find Brocklehurst, find out what the hell he is up to and bring him back."

"But why me? There must be dozens of people more suitable to the task."

"If we just wanted him back, yes, you're right. But we're not worried about your wellbeing with Bob in tow, and we need someone who can ask the right questions, and, most importantly, in the right circles. We don't just want to bring Brocklehurst in, we want to know his schemes and we need to understand. None of our normal operatives would stand a chance. Frankly, they haven't had so much as a sniff. And one more thing: we need to remove that monstrosity you so graphically described."

"George Chapman," said William, with a rueful shake of his head. "I would never have thought he had it in himself."

"Well whatever, he has and did. There can be no possibility of him replicating his ideas for...whoever he is working for. Understand?"

"Yes, my Lord."

"Start with some boffin friends in Paris, Hope. Your Royal Society credentials should loosen some tongues."

"Yes, my Lord."

"And we're sending you across in secret. We've commissioned a tub called the Bucentaur. That should get you in without anyone noticing."

"The BUCENTAUR?" William asked incredulously.

"Why yes, we captured the wreck of Duval's pirate tub after we shot him down in Cheshire. Somehow the Captain survived along with a few scurvy dogs. We gave him an ultimatum – work for us freelance or hang. He chose the former, so we patched up his boat and we've got him running errands."

"They're the bastards – excuse me, my Lord – who kidnapped me in Paris. They're the bloody reason I'm so...singed."

"Oh well, you'll be able to kiss and make up," said Melville, slapping William on the back and laughing uproariously.

*

A blacked-out horse-drawn hearse drove William along the streets of London. It wouldn't draw attention, unlike the new-fangled automated carriages that only the rich afford. These still drew attention among the poor and working classes, and it was difficult to remove the stigma that natural was best. A decreasing number of required horses meant that stables and blacksmiths were driven out of business, which led to fights and occasionally gangs of men burning the new-fangled carriages in the dead of night. Lynchings were not uncommon. There was also an increase in poverty and an associated increase in crime. Some of this was pretty brutal, with raids from the poorest slums into more wealthy areas. Whilst London still stank, though, the increasing prominence of horseless perambulation had improved the quality of the more popular thoroughfares. Wealthier types frowned upon others emptying personal refuse in to the streets, and because they made the laws, the law upheld it as rigidly as possible. Naturally, this also increased resentment amongst those that still had to live in streets full of horseshit, and pavements littered with turds. Namely, the poor.

The government still refused to see the benefit of a sewerage system that some of the New World cities were seen to be building – Washington and New York being much heralded examples. William now knew better – the money could be found, the benefit eminently recognised, but the New World wasn't on the cusp of being dragged into yet another continental war. It came down to pure strategy – build weapons at all costs, weapons enough to ensure the security of your nation, William mused, and to hell with civil responsibility. New York & Washington also had the benefit of a significant slave population – and therefore the building of a sewerage system, or a world wonder, a dam, or a suburb only cost the government a hefty food bill – naturally all grown for free by more slaves.

The Emancipation act had been uniformly agreed upon throughout the Old World…but in the New World hostilities had ended before they even really began, with the assassination of key political figures by slave cartels. The concessions that the slave masters had promised the slaves were still yet to materialise, however. The slaves had risen up to support of their masters in light of fictitious rumour mongering by the slave masters. Thousands of black slaves had died in countless acts of simultaneous duplicity by their masters. Everyone, but the slaves, knew the truth, regardless of the slave master's righteous indignation at the accusations.

A harsh bump drew William back to the present.

"How can we trust this pirate blighter, errrm, Bill?" William asked of the figure sat to his left.

"Easy. He's actually a distant cousin, classically educated, extremely intelligent, merely bored with a normal life and no clear worthwhile purpose. So, as well as playing on family ties, I've rebuilt his lighter-than-air craft, added a few tweaks at his requests, and given him a sack load of cash. Oh, I've also employed his eldest son around my place, just in case he should get itchy feet."

"Oh, I see."

Silence reigned for a few moments, and then "I do hope Bob is alright."

"Yes, well, a coffin isn't ideal, but there was no carriage at hand big enough or strong enough to take it..."

"...her..."

"... her, yes well," Melville squirmed slightly uncomfortably. "Anyway, the coffin was the best we could do."

"I just hope she doesn't feel too well, errm, at home."

"At home?!" Melville demanded incredulously.

William squirmed uncomfortably. He hadn't gone into the imbuings in any detail, and he hadn't gone into any of the personal feelings that he felt about *les Futiles*. Melville, after all, was a staunch Catholic, for all of his machinations.

"Well, technically she's dead; that is she died once and I think she'd really quite like to die again, only properly this time."

"Dead? Properly?"

"Yes, well, you know that Brocklehurst's work involved automation, right?"

Melville nodded.

"Well, the imbuings are allegedly the souls of the dead, not yet at peace."

"That's IMPOSSIBLE! Positively absurd!" Melville expostulated. Unconsciously, he crossed himself.

"He needed to be up in Cheshire, not for secrecy, but for its proximity to Alderley Edge; it seems that all of those ridiculous nursery stories have some basis in fact, much like lots of other folklore, and he found this out."

"Well, that might narrow things down a bit."

"Sorry?"

"The Catacombs in Paris may be a place you could visit. Every day, all day, if necessary, Sir William." He said with a rather pointed glare.

"Good idea, I do know the place fairly well....ah, it appears we've arrived."

*

The coach and four drew to a halt by a number of low buildings on the edge of a large field that contained a vast number of dirigibles. Hope strained to look, but couldn't see anything that was obviously the Bucentaur. An armed footman opened the door to a dawn breaking on the smoggy horizon of a blustery morning, broken clouds strewn across the sky.

"Check on Bob, would you, please," asked William politely, as he stepped out.

The rugged man gave a most unfootman-like salute, heels clicking together. William stretched his weary limbs. He'd been allowed a day of recovery but he still felt ridiculously tired. William climbed down from the carriage,

There was the sound of footsteps and William turned around to be faced with his favourite pirate.

"Duval, Claude Duval," he said thrusting out his hand. "No hard feelings, I hope?"

"Sir William Hope. And yes, there are several hard feelings, but I will endeavour to put them to one side for the duration of the voyage," he said pompously.

"We'll make sure you arrive safely, and in secret, *my Lord*," responded Duval with a sneer of aggression.

"Gentlemen, gentlemen," boomed Melville. "This is not the time for willy-waving or the settling of debts. The security of the nation is at risk!"

William snapped.

"But he's bloody French, Sir Melville" He's probably one of them."

"His great, great, great, great grandfather was the infamous Claude Duval, gentleman highwayman, who never robbed a lady if she would merely dance with him."

"Pah," spat William, "a chip off the old block, I'd say. He was hanged in these parts, wasn't he, *Claude*?"

Duval's eyes flashed and he started to reach for his cutlass, an old fashioned relic that hung from his belt.

William stepped back, fear in his eyes. He was unarmed.

"STOP THIS RIDICULOUSNESS NOW," bellowed Melville.

William, feeling braver, stepped back forward. Besides, nothing other than slaving would get his back up this way. "He's a goddamn slaver, my Lord, and he will pay, the bastard." He said this quietly, but with the utmost menace.

"Grass before breakfast, when the Queen can spare you, Hope," spat Duval.

William spat in disgust, and no small amount of fear. "Swords it is. You may want to practice, Mr Duval."

The pair glared at each other for a long instant, broken by a terse command from Melville to "just get aboard the bloody boat."

William glared at Duval. "We should be going."

He turned and stalked haughtily to supervise the footman as he extricated Bob from her coffin.

Duval watched the process with amused disinterest, until the lid of the upright coffin was opened. His cheroot fell out of his mouth.

"Lord Melville," she signed politely, William translating, a stiff bow at the waist aimed in his direction. "Mr Duval," she nodded in his direction, "I'm a kind of slave, by the way, but it's only my soul that's been enslaved. My body is dead so they couldn't get that. Nice to meet you." Her eyes momentarily flashed a green-yellow, before returning to blue. She walked somewhat tartly, in William's eyes, towards the dirigible as he translated her message to Duval.

Duval shook his head, amazed, astounded, aghast and unusually silent.

*

In the middle of the common they found Duval's boat. She was no longer a mere rickety pirate tub, but a fully refurbished dog-fighter, a slightly comedic name, for an airship fight was anything but fast and frenetic. William had never seen its like.

The hull was painted patchy greys, from nearly white to nearly black, whilst the sails and decking were painted light greys and blues.

"It's camouflage, or at least that's the word we're using," explained Melville.

"Camouflage?"

"Yes, camouflage; naturally, it's a French word, but it basically means something that's disguised, blending in to its surroundings."

"It doesn't do well against grass, Sir Melville."

"No William," said Melville exasperatedly. "It's an airship. Up there," he looked up exaggeratedly, "it's nearly invisible this far north. Down in the Mediterranean we've painted out spy units blue – blue sky, blue sea. The affect is astounding."

It wasn't the only thing that was astounding. Oar holes, portholes for cannon and jibs for sailing booms were still there, but that was where any similarity to a normal airship ended. There were banks of rotors jutting like porcupine spines, and ropes, not just a few ropes, but many spiders' webs of ropes that were ordered in such a way as to never be a hindrance to the sailors aboard. William's eyes hurt just to look at them.

How many of these damned airships are there?" enquired William as he looked around the airfield. Now that he paid closer attention, he noticed that many contained novel designs.

"Well, this is a one-off, but we have number of squadrons in various parts of the Empire. In fact, we've started specialising the blighters."

"Specialised, my Lord?"

"Yes, quite. The majority are nippy little blighters, like this, but we've also got a fair few vast behemoths designed as air artillery. They tend to need some company though, to keep them in the skies as we've found that a well led pirateer can take them down." He cast a sideways glance at Duval.

"Thankfully, it demonstrates a certain point and Claude here, has helped develop tactics and protocols for various scenarios. Marvellous work, really."

William got to the foot of the gangplank and was met by a smart, middle-aged naval type with spectacular orange mustachios that had three curled strands extending across each reddened cheek.

"You're not a pirate," stated William.

"No, my Lord, I'm the Captain's Number Two. Robert Halpin's the name. I'm a condition of the admiralty." He spoke in a gentle Dublin accent.

"Ahhh, I see," William smiled knowingly. "Very nice to meet you, and this lady is Bob."

"Enchantée, mademoiselle," he said with a twinkle in his eye. Bob merely bowed.

They were led aboard to their quarters only a short distance down a passageway, ironically the same quarters that William had been held captive in. He muttered indistinctly about the matter. Robert offered a tour of the boat, although if William wanted to see it all he would have to leave Bob behind for some parts due to her bulk and weight, and, he added somewhat cheekily, that he was in no way implying anything by that. It would have to wait until they were airborne, however, and would they be so good as to remain in their quarters until they were collected.

William explored his room, which took a matter of seconds. The old rotten beams had been removed and replaced with new timbers to cover the area devastated by a cannonball and no blood stained the decking.

An indeterminable amount of time later, a knock sounded and, without waiting for a reply, the Number Two entered.

"There's been a slight delay getting us airborne. Captain Duval has asked me to start the tour immediately, as we shouldn't be airborne more than an hour or two with such a favourable wind."

William followed Robert and gazed around in awe, noting how the Bucentaur had changed so vastly on the inside. All new planking ran throughout, and all was properly scrubbed using sand in the traditional naval fashion. No longer the mouldering old tub!

William was taken up a flight of steps, past the former slave mess which now appeared to be an open mess. A number of former pirates were playing a raucous game including dice and a sharp knife.

Up another flight of steps, and William found himself on deck. There were no longer any slaves manacled to rough blood stained benches, and the large bosun no longer wielded a harsh whip.

In fact the benches were empty of any people, and it was explained that propulsion was due entirely to the turning of the rotor blades, although the crew would be expected to man the oars given an emergency situation.

Robert Halpin was giving William a running commentary throughout the tour, but he had not been paying much attention, content with letting the words flow over him. Now, however, William started to listen.

"Each rotor blade gives up to five times more thrust than a slave. There are four times as many rotors as there used to be slaves, although obviously we can't run the rotors at a hundred percent, or we'd tear the old girl apart. And anyway, due to the balloon and wind resistance, the thrust doesn't translate directly to speed. We can only manage about two and a half times the old tubs forward speed, although if you note the wheel" – he pointed to the original massive bronze-cast ship's wheel – "it no longer operates in only two directions. It can now be tilted fore and aft to force her up or down, depending on the requirement. Naturally, this induces some stress, with the weakest point, by design, being the rotors. They're of an extraordinarily light metal that allows us to operate such a large number, whilst still allowing us to row in a fashion that, I believe, you are already accustomed with, although the admiralty has ensured that it's only paid tars that are aboard nowadays. The rotors also allow us greater control of direction, with a turning circle somewhat less than five hundred yards at full speed. Anything more extreme would naturally induce too great a stress, causing them to snap. She makes an ideal boat for this kind of mission."

William pulled himself out of his feigned disinterest at being back aboard the Bucentaur, and properly looked around the vessel.

It was stupefying and mind boggling, if not at all pretty. The banks of the rotors were affixed to sturdy poles that slid through the decks supported by a metal sheath tightly packed with grease. Ghastly as a spectacle, they jutted regularly down both sides of the deck, rising like a spectre besides the rower's benches. Tarred cables ran from the poles above head height to a cabin on the quarterdeck, where they gathered like a bastardised mule spinner before running downwards in to the cabin. Great arms of wood struck at an upwards angle from the sides of the ship, mounted on which were folded steering booms. These were painted an ominous red, like blood-stained needles. The massive balloon towered above them all, captured by another web of ropes. William felt like a moth in a trap, and he squirmed somewhat claustrophobically.

"My goodness," he gasped. His mouth opened and closed, nothing coming out, until eventually, "the expense…no wonder the country is bankrupt."

"Quite, but this is a mere bagatelle when compared with some of the heavy artillery ships we've commissioned. And as you're aware, the government believes this level of preparedness is quite necessary, my Lord."

William looked around more closely. Newly forged cannons were fore and aft on great metal plates that were nothing more than large cogs to allow for precision firing. The original brass bow chasers were still present, a small nod to the past. Over the side (William peered somewhat tentatively, although he did not suffer from vertigo, nor had the ship yet become airborne) he noted numerous portholes, currently sealed, which he was informed, were pretty much bog-standard ships cannons that hadn't significantly altered in two hundred years, barring the improved firing mechanisms. There were significantly more than previous, but apparently this had been negated by the use of new metallurgy technologies, which Halpin, thankfully, did not expand upon. William was informed, however, that if they were all to fire at once, it would tear the ship apart.

William noted massive enclosed pipes, all shiny and newly cast, entering the balloon, which vastly improved the lighter-than-air gas delivery system, increasing the ships vertical manoeuvrability. More extraordinarily still, was the fact that a mixture of gases now gave the ship its buoyancy. A new gas, called Helium, had been discovered and it did not encourage ignition, significantly reducing the overall flammability. This added significantly to new capabilities for ordnance, the reason that heated grapeshot had been allowed on the Endeavour.

William's attention returned back to the cabin built on the Quarterdeck. "What's that?"

"Follow me."

He introduced William to a most amazing space. Lining all four walls were what were introduced as control panels. One panel, the responsibility of a mariner sat in front, contained dials around a three feet square pictogram of the Bucentaur. Evidently, the dials controlled the individual rotors, whilst a large master dial on each side could control the entire bank on either side. A larger dial in the centre of the pictogram overrode all dials, controlling all of the rotors at once. Switches beside the dials could switch a bank off, designating their current control status.

It was exceedingly complex; underneath the panel ran a row of pipes emanating a great deal of heat, and attached to each were valves. These fed the main drives for the rotors, allowing the rotors to be controlled in the event of a control panel failure, whilst the spiders web of ropes was controlled by miniature ships wheels, normally commanded by a different mariner sat at that control panel. How these were driven automatically William could not tell, nor was any explanation offered, but the wheels themselves made William suspect that in the event of a failure at that automated station, the rotors could be directed like a good old fashioned rudder.

The young men in the cabin – six in all, at a variety of station – were very stern faced and obviously took their roles extremely seriously. Only highly trained operatives such as these gentlemen could hope to effectively sail the Bucentaur, according to the Number Two.

*

"Take her out!" called a voice from the deck.

The man at the control panel slowly turned the central master dial clockwise, whilst another sailor at a separate control panel pulled a chord and turned a valve. A huge whistle of gas shrieked through copper piping and William's stomach lurched slightly as the ship moved gently up and forward.

William stepped out of the cabin and, in fairly short order, he was able to see over the rooftops of London, bringing forth a most amazing panorama of clean blue sky and the aching clarity of a crisp spring morning; below, counterbalancing this, was the filth and grime of London's streets, streamers of dirty black smog trickling forth from a multitude of residences, many little more than lean-tos and shacks, whilst great ghastly plumes of blackness spewed forth from industrial smokestacks, that threw their filth higher in to the atmosphere, appearing as grey grazes slicing through the blue.

William could feel that the Bucentaur continued to accelerate and rise, the varying hiss of the gas sounding from the cabin behind him.

William turned as the Captain moved to the cabin. "One thousand feet, seventeen knots, please gentlemen. Hope, get your face out of my control centre, this area is now out of bounds to unauthorised civilians."

"Aye captain, I think I've got the hang of it already, anyway," and he moved away with a half-smile, listening to the dressing down that he gave the Robert. He inserted himself for'ard, eyes watering in the cold air, as he watched for the distant shore.

*

The Bucentaur ambled over the lush greenery of Kent, the English Channel twinkling gently in the distance. They had risen slowly through squadrons of hunting swallows and house martins, and now they flew with the swifts, darting and shrieking as they filled stomachs that were empty from their long flight from Africa.

William watched them in gentle amusement, enjoying the aerobatics. Footsteps approached and the Number Two was beside him.

"What do you think, my Lord?" he enquired.

"I'll be impressed when man can fly like those swifts," he said, motioning in their direction.

"Alas, I fear Mother Nature may well never be surpassed in some areas."

"Sail ho!" a voice cried.

"Where away?" the Number Two shouted.

"Two 'o' clock, four 'o' clock!"

William looked quizzical.

We've had to devise a system that can cope with three dimensions, and not just two," he explained to William. "What is she?" he shouted.

"No idea, Sir, never seen her like. She's fast though, and moving in our direction."

"Summon the Captain."

"I'm already here," said Duval, buttoning his jacket and straightening his bicorn hat. "All crew to their stations, if you please Number Two."

"All crew to stations!" he informed a very small, and very young midshipman who had magically appeared at his side.

"All crew to stations, all crew to stations," roared the midshipman with a volume that utterly belied his stature, making William jump out of his skin. Halpin informed William, with a smile, that the boy was only fourteen and nothing more than a streak of piss, so not to worry himself.

"She's a pirate, Captain," said the boy. "No colours, and she's preparing to fire."

"You've got sharp eyes, lad. An extra tot of rum when you're old enough to be issued the stuff."

The boy smiled at the praise, obviously used to Duval's sense of humour.

"There's a lot of them at the moment. We suspect they're being bankrolled to cause trouble."

"Weren't you approached yourself, Monsieur Duval?"

Duval merely laughed at William and Duval watched the approaching ship carefully.

She continued to close and Duval ordered the colours raised and the portholes opened; it was a warning to the approaching ship that they should bloody well consider buggering off, William was informed. The other ship took no notice, however, as a stab of flame and a pencil line of black smoke erupted from her bows. She was still miles away, so William turned to the Number Two with a smile on his face, lips parted as to make comment.

"Rockets!" exclaimed the midshipman, halting William in his tracks. "That's brave!"

The rocket speared towards the Bucentaur before whirling crazily out of control and shooting upwards. A few seconds later, the rocket exploded, the concussion of which could be felt on the Bucentaur which shuddered slightly as if encountering turbulence. Small shards of shrapnel peppered the decks of the ship seconds later.

"Bloody rockets, hopeless unless you get lucky."

The prow of the newcomer was suddenly studded with so many stabs of flame and gouts of smoke that she was entirely hidden from view for a few seconds. William could see a rocket heading straight for him, while another half dozen veered off in different directions, forming grey rainbows across the sky.

William held his breath, he was immobile, staring unblinkingly, as the missile continued to head straight for him. It grew closer and closer. William understood mortality and was too petrified to even loosen his bladder. At the final instant before it struck William between his very eyes, perhaps thirty meters from the boat, the explosive head burst asunder. Somehow, no one was hurt, but a shard pierced the great balloon helping to keep the boat afloat. She merely gave a lurch before righting herself. William continued to stare at the balloon, and back to the dissipating black cloud, and then back to the balloon, waiting for it to collapse upon itself or explode as the gases ignited, and for them all to plunge to their collective dooms. He still wasn't breathing.

A voice in his ear, rather smugly amused told him to breathe. "We've compartmentalised the balloon," Duval said rather gleefully, "it stops most punctures being fatal, and there's sufficient helium that we should be safe from fire."

William looked around to see Duval and Robert Halpin rather pale in spite of the fact.

Duval suddenly sprang to life, barking orders to the crew and the rotors shifted slightly with one side speeding up, which William recognised from the change in pitch.

She swung round to show the enemy her broadside, roller-coastering first up and then slightly down to gain the advantage of altitude. As each canon came to bear, an almighty crash reverberated through the ship and each section in turn disappeared in a cloud of black smoke.

The round shot were more accurate by far, and rather than aim at the hull, the gunners were firing at the balloon from a height advantage.

It was all fairly simple – the first two balls screamed past the enemy airship, traces of smoke showing their courses. The third smashed in to the deck and the fifth ball smeared itself down and through the heavy material of the balloon.

Whether there was a scrap of burning wad attached to the ball, or whether there was a spark as the ball contacted cabling, William never knew. The balloon burst in to flame, a gentle whisper of sound, a caress of warmth, and suddenly a hundred screams could be heard, as she suddenly fell downwards, plunging noiselessly in to the twinkling sea far below.

*

Some semblance of normality returned to the Bucentaur in a remarkably short amount of time. There had been no time to clear the decks, so a flurry of activity resulted in the closing of portholes, lashing down of canons and inspection of any damage by Duval and his senior officers. They didn't even consider it necessary to repair the balloon. She was hale and hearty.

William was quietly impressed at Duval's decisiveness and tactics. It could be risky to bare her broadside against high explosives, but the risk had been calculated, activity rapid and there had been no undue fuss. The crew did not cheer such a decisive victory, they all understood the horror of that few seconds as the enemy plummeted to the blue below, and they went about their remaining tasks with a grim efficiency.

He was vaguely aware of the bustle on board, but he only had eyes for Duval and the grim memories of destroying a Pirate Captain many miles away surfaced.

CHAPTER 13 – THE PIRATE CAPTAIN

They were in a ramshackle bar, more of a house that served some form of alcoholic spirits. The Pirate Captain did not recognise William, now broad shouldered, well-tanned, fully a man. The captain was trying to recruit William, whom he quickly realised, could be a remarkably good pirate; sharp and innovative turns of mind were obvious, so straight enslavement was his last option.

William was dressed in well-worn clothing that was both practical and piratical. The look on his face during the year long hunt had people turn away or avert their gaze. Five crusty looking tars flanked the captain and they wore ragged clothing and were hard eyed. He had been forced to hand over his longsword. The Pirate Captain had looked on it with interest, assessing its nicked edges and well-oiled gleam.

William felt anger clench in his belly and he struggled to keep his exterior calm and nonplussed.

"What happened Mr Gloom?"

"She's going soft," William sneered. "People had seen us and she was about to let them go. I'd rather we left no witnesses." At this last he hit his fist into his palm. That means no price on the ship, or my head."

The large black man In front of him chuckled a deep, rumbling chuckle. "You surprise me. She hardly has the reputation for humanity in these matters." His thick creole voice surprised William. The voice he had remembered for all of these years had been that of a pirate, full of curses, gruff and ill-educated. Now though, whilst still rough and coarse, there was a definite edge of intelligence, his vocabulary seemingly extensive. There was no culture though. He supposed that a man who effectively owned a small ocean and controlled a ravenous crew of sea-dogs must have some nascent intelligence. He shouldn't really have been surprised, but then his childhood memories were strange at best.

"They were children," William said. "She was going to set them free leaving us no spare boats."

The Pirate Captain laughed out loud at this. "That bitch isn't going soft, Mr Gloom. That was a form of the most terrible of tortures you are describing. Alone in a small boat." He shook his head. "They may have lived for days, slowly burning in the sun, freezing under the stars and all of the while becoming wilder and more insane. That was no release. Even I would kill them straight and not resort to such barbarism. Not for poor children."

To William's surprise, he felt some empathy with the man, who looked genuinely perturbed at William's tale.

William ad lib'd. "Land was in sight and some of the children were older, at least ten years old. I think they would have made it to shore."

"So what happened next?" The man studied William shrewdly through all of his responses, looking for any slip, any excuse to run him through. You did not get to be a King of the Seas without some guile. He liked the boy but didn't entirely trust him. Not yet. He'd seen this sort of ruse before. A small candle was alight at the back of his mind, gently illuminating an unnameable suspicion.

"We disagreed. Badly."

The Pirate Captain smiled a pensive smile at William.

"Bill, it was worse than that. She's got all sorts of people looking for you. She even sent one of her agents to me. Unfortunately I didn't really like him very much."

William could attest to that. A terribly brutalised figure had been nailed to a tree outside town, although William couldn't tell if had died beforehand. Whichever, it hadn't been an easy passage to the next life.

"Indulge me. I'd like to hear the details. I am, after all, your only source of salvation."

William grimaced, not even an attempt at theatre as he truly meant it. Just not in the way that the Pirate Captain thought.

If you were my only source of salvation, William thought, *I'd still kill you.*

"I insisted that they be put to death. She insisted that they have their freedom. She's the Captain, so what she says goes and even stinking of her sex, still she didn't appreciate me yelling blue murder at her, for undermining her authority on the quarterdeck of her own ship in front of the entire crew."

"I'd have killed you, myself."

"It may be shows her weakness that I'm here."

The Pirate Captain grunted and motioned for William to continue.

"I rarely get angry. She seems to have a knack of pushing the right buttons."

"That she does," the large man laughed. ""That she does."

He had a sympathetic look on his face. The candle in his mind was guttering. He relaxed a bit. The bitch was, well, she was a bitch.

"Anyway, she slapped me and punched me, even ordered my arrest and an immediate lynching from the yard arm. She hadn't needed the last order, her men were already champing at the bit." William smiled quite ruefully, slightly abashed at his own behaviour, although it was all part of the plan, a plan hatched in her head for her mastery of the seas and for his revenge for his sisters. The crew hadn't known about it, not even the bosun who was her closest confidante.

She had tried to take the Pirate Captain several times before, but he was careful and she didn't have the strength to meet him ship to ship. So whilst they lay there, sweat glistening on naked bodies, the scent of her in his nostrils, they'd plotted.

And they'd had to make it real.

"I punched her. Hard. There was a crunch as her nose splintered. It left me no choice but to leap overboard. It's just a shame that I didn't get the chance to kill her."

"And then you rowed all of those children back to shore, bringing me all of those beautiful gifts?"

"Just so. I'd never get an audience without them. Some of them must be worth good money. Others good sport."

"The pale little blonde girl. I've reserved her for myself. It's just a shame they don't retain their innocence for long."

William's face grimaced.

"What? Squeamish?"

"Slavery is not something I'm comfortable with. Gold and fighting, yes. Children, no. But I could think of no other way to guarantee an audience."

The Pirate Captain was surprised at his honesty and it showed.

"It's why I'm the richest of all the Caribbean pirates, Bill. I have the contacts and the sources that none of the others have. It's why my crews are the best. I pay the best and expect the most."

They regarded each other for many moments and it was the Pirate Captain who first averted his gaze.

"I think we can do business, Mr Gloom."

"What's on offer, Captain?"

"You'll be on the quarterdeck. We can see where it goes from there."

"A generous offer. Why? I've betrayed one Captain and I'll never support you in slavery."

The candle in his mind gutted and finally extinguished. His men could sense it and they relaxed. "I like your honesty and there's more to me and my operation than mere slavery. Don't forget, I hate that bitch too, and it amuses me mightily to have you on board. I would so like to see that mangled face of hers when she hears of your employment."

He handed William his sword belt. "Welcome aboard."

William raised his eyebrows in surprise, looking up as he fastened the belt around his waist.

"What were you expecting? A deal sealed with blood? I'm not a damned barbarian." He laughed at William good naturedly.

But William still hadn't accepted his offer.

"So then, son."

It was unfortunate that this had been his closing gambit, for his ending would be worse. He was no-one's son, and the cause sat before him.

"I am no-one's son," William spoke low and cold, gravel in his tone, echoing his thoughts.

He drew his longsword. It was a butcher's weapon, crude and lacking all finesse, and even though William's fencing abilities were renowned within his own circles, he enjoyed the bludgeoning effect of this particular brutal weapon.

It grated like a body being dragged over a stone floor as the long blade was slowly exposed, the effect mesmerising the Pirate Captain's men.

The Pirate Captain broke the mesmer with a scream.

The man on the far left raised a brass blunderbuss, its speaking trumpet aimed at William's head. The frizzen sparked and an explosion filled the room leaving them all blind from the flash and the smoke. All apart from William, who'd moved like a ghost, facing away from the blunderbuss as he went, ignoring the man as spent for a few instants, disembowelling another man who still levelled a pistol at his former position with a great upward hew of his sword. The man was still levelling his pistol when the blow struck, his screams filling the room.

The down stroke caved the skull of the man next to him with a dull thump, like that of a clapper on a broken bell.

The remaining three tars were stunned and blinded by the blunderbuss, but William still moved, elegantly drawing his sword against the throat of the fourth man and pulling with some effort as the tip ground against the man's spine. The fifth man had a cutlass out, swinging it wildly around himself in a parody of insanity and William merely thrust at the man, the point beating the edge, skewering the man neatly through the chest, trapping his sword in the bone. William merely looked at the man wielding the blunderbuss, little more than a boy, and even with William's sword jammed, the boy blanched, dropped his weapon and ran. He jerked his sword from the pirate's chest, hearing bone splinter as he did so. Blood welled and a great sucking sound emanated as the man tried to draw breath. He exhaled and expired at the same time.

It only left the Pirate Captain.

William was breathing heavily, but not from the effort, only from the pent-up frustration that had built up over the preceding three years.

The Pirate Captain stood, a wry smile on his face and it was only at this that William realised he'd not sensed one flinch of movement from the man.

He stood and it seemed to take an eternity. He was at least a foot taller than William, massively broad in the shoulder with an impressively large stomach that barely moved as he stood, belying its cumbersome impression.

"You bastard," spat William. "I am nobody's son. Murderer, rapist, defiler I name thee."

The smile became a broad grin. "You're the second man to recently attempt to fillet me. The first hangs from a tree. How would you like to die, little man?"

William dragged his sword discordantly across the floor before hefting it upwards: it dripped blood. He realised that he shouldn't tarry because the cowardly sailor would no doubt fetch help. And the Pirate Captain knew it too. He'd placed the table between them, drawing his weapons, a long knife in his left hand and a machete in his right. Neither was a match for Williams's sword unless he was so inordinately fast that he could get round William's guard. He didn't have the look of someone gifted with speed. He was just too big. But then, both the pugilist and the swordmaster who had taught William had been old and fat, vastly beyond their prime, but both moved… eerily. It was the only word William had ever been able to ascribe to them. One moment they were reeling or too far away, the next William was sat on his bottom, stars around his vision or a sword was nicking his throat like a razor.

And with astonishment, he found it thus with the Pirate Captain. One moment there was a table between them and William had his longsword, his prey at his mercy. The next, William found himself reeling away, a deep gash in his left shoulder.

"Who was it, little man? Did I fuck your mother?"

He taunted William and his youth rose to the bait, a young man's impetuousness fired by fury. Presented with the central figure of his ire, he did not reply. He lunged with the point directly at the Pirate Captain's chest. The large black man, bald head glistening with sweat, merely stepped back. It was his mistake, his sole mistake. He stumbled over the corpse of one of his crew as he did so. William was already turning his thrust, following it through, swinging the edge hard and true, hacking through a flailing left arm and smashing the ribs of the man. The Pirate Captain's arm flopped to the floor, sliced clean through at the bicep. The stump pumped great spurts of claret high in to the air.

"Yes, you son of a bitch. You murdered my father and brothers, whored my mother and I personally saw you dash my baby sister against a wall. You sold my sisters." He took the long knife out of the Pirate Captains dismembered hand.

The man still lived, although his life blood pumped from the rent in his chest. It was starting to fountain less and less.

"Mine will be the last face you see on this earth." And with that he flicked out both of the Pirate Captain's eyes. He started to scream hoarsely, the adrenaline that had masked the pain starting to fade with the blood that pooled around his body.

"And with your own knife, you'll know what it is like to be violated, you filth." He rammed the Pirate Captain's long knife through the seat of his pants into his anus, as deep as the hilt would allow. He left it there, rising as he spat on the man, leaving him to his agony, not even bothering to entertain his wildest vengeances, both those during his nightmares and those whilst he plotted during his waking hours.

He left him alone for one reason:

There was no such thing as a revenge that gives salvation to the soul.

None.

None whatsoever.

Tears streaming, he left by a window.

A clatter came from the front, the sound of a furore of men, whilst further along in the direction that he headed, was the boy who had earlier run away. He was guarding the back door, alone. He was guarding it so well that he had no mind for his surroundings.

Not twenty feet away was a black stagecoach, ancient beyond the beginnings of this century. Out of this stepped a lady. The Pirate Queen. She was beautiful. The most shapely leg stepped forth, lightly muscled and ever so long, the colour of lightly milked coffee. She had a narrow waist and her hips swayed gently as she walked, and even though she was clothed, William could see her naked. So could the cowardly boy, who suddenly forgot about the back door. His nervous aspect vanished and his strain became a swagger.

She was looking at William through her periphery and William shook his head. He needed the boy alive. She strutted over to the youth. William had a partial erection just watching her. God knows how the boy felt. He'd probably already ejaculated into his adolescent pants.

Her lips parted as she reached the young man. He was looking into her eyes, unable to tear himself away from the bottomless clarity of her brown eyes, which is why he didn't see her fist crack into the side of his jaw. His legs collapsed beneath him and William ran over, hoisting the streak of piss over his shoulders. They were halfway to the coach before William saw the first pirate exit the sordid building, and they were in the coach and away before a pirate could come close.

William had defeated his nemesis. Only he still felt hollow.

INTERMISSION

Please, go ahead, stretch your legs. Empty your bursting bladders. Buy an ice cream from the lady with the lamp-lit tray and the short skirt. Don't worry about us. We're just going to have us a little *history lesson*.

*

Nobody was quite sure how it came about. It kind of just happened, like osmosis or the slow creep of an invasive species of weed that worked itself southwards. By 1819, the Russians *had* crept slowly southwards, and rather than just inhabiting the steppes and the East, they had also inhabited parts of the West.

In their outrage at the depredations inflicted by the French during the early years of the Long War, they'd licked their wounds and then allied themselves with the Prussians and the British, closing off an alley for Napoleon to escape down when it had been his turn to run.

But that had meant them oozing south to do so and they'd just never left. Hardly anybody seemed to mind, there was virtually no fuss from even the Prussians themselves that some of their coastal region was now an annex of the great Tsarist empire and that their magnificent, historic lands were split in two.

The cause of their wroth was this:

During 1812, Napoleon had personally driven his army north, a vast army of more than six hundred thousand souls, an army that had no concept of the vastness that lay before him. It was perhaps his greatest failure of logistics and planning during the whole of the Long War. His army went hungry on the way north, regardless of the number of farms pillaged and the other unnameable depredations caused upon the populations as they scoured. On the orders of the Tsar, roaming bands of Cossacks burned crops and fouled wells. Napoleon's supply train could not cope, and the raids upon the French were frequent, crude and grizzly.

But remarkably effective.

And then there had been the winter, not the soft southern winter of a Corsica, or the mild Gulf stream winter of a Britain. It wasn't even a chilly central European winter of a Germany. This was a *Russian* winter, where the river through St Petersburg froze itself solid. The Russians were used to this, they wore great bear skins and great piles of wood were stacked in strategic places. Holes were dug in the ground long before the freeze occurred, within which they sheltered from the killing winds that froze blood. Even with all of the preparations, the Russians suffered terribly, frost bitten extremities, dehydration because all of the water was frozen, hunger because a soldiers rations were never enough, and they were peasants – slaves – of the Tsar. They would do as they were ordered, and atrocities against its own troops were Mother Russia's greatest killer in that terrible place.

The French had nothing but crude shelters and tents that offered no protection. Where the Russians might suffer the loss of toes and fingers, the French suffered a whole body freezing, not just to individual soldiers but to whole company's. One evening there would be several hundred men. The next morning? Nothing but an encampment of rictused sentinels. Stone cold corpses.

Of the vast army that had set out to persuade the Tsar to cease trading with the British, that army defeated by cold and hunger as much as skirmishes and raids, fewer than five percent returned. That's right, you're reading goggles are focussed just fine. Of the six hundred thousand that set out, less than thirty thousand returned.

The French had headed ever north invading the Southernmost reaches of the Russian people. In fact, that's inaccurate. They didn't conquer because there was nothing *too* conquer, only a long hard chase, a chase where Napoleon attempted to catch one enemy army after another, to corner them between the three prongs of his own *Grande Armee*, but ever onwards the Russians ran before the advancing French forces. And as they went they razed their own fields, fouled their own wells and burned their winter caches.

It rained, terrible rains that flooded the ground, whilst lightening lit the sky like Armageddon-come.

And when the rain was a morass, a marsh that rotted the hooves of the horses pulling supply wagons, the sun came. It was June and so the sun was hot. Not a British heat where the wind whips in from the seas, cooling the land, but a Continental heat. It baked the land and where a glutinous mud once churned, the land sucked in the moisture, drying the trails to clay. It baked the wooden wheels of wagons hard in to the ground and snapped horse's legs as they became trapped within that drying mud.

The way was never clear, there were no roads, merely trails through heavy woodland and barely readable tracks through dense grassland steppes. Driven hard, more animals became lame, stalling the convoys of supplies until the stalling became legion.

Normal French tactics in a normal land would have meant a hungry army, but Russia was no normal land, not like the Continental Europe that Napoleon was used to. It was vast, and so the people were sparse and widely spaced, even given their enormous population. There was, therefore, no foraging, especially as the Cossacks raped their own lands as they fled northwards.

The French army starved and baked and rotted. Dysentery was rife. So was desertion, leading to gangs of outlaws who fought the Russian cavalry and the Russian peasants until, eventually, in the years that passed, some even settled to become those self-same Russian peasants.

The French army bled. It bled from the outside and the inside. The latter from the contrary weather, disease and the speed of march leading to chronic supply problems. The former was from peasants and cavalry raids, because as their plight became worse, so the number of desperate groups of French soldiers grew, and these *Monsewers* foraged further and further afield, cutting themselves off from the safety of the main force, then being trapped, cornered, massacred. In small numbers, perhaps, but over the weeks this was not insignificant.

Again, that's an inaccuracy. Relatively speaking, these numbers *were* insignificant to a force of six hundred thousand men. **600,000** men. Six cent mille hommes. Шестьсот тысяч человек. Shest'sot tysyach chelovek. Men, human beings, conscripts. People. Everything was insignificant compared to the supply train, a summary lesson in the very basis, that infamous adage that describes the running of an army. It runs on its stomach. Old, corny, unoriginal.

But true.

TRUE!

There were battles at Smolensk and at Borodino. The latter was the most murderous of all Napoleon's battles throughout Europe, yet still the losses were as nothing compared with the logistics; the fighting a mere bagatelle. A mere forty-five thousand French died.

The supply train, the logistics they'd been sufficient. What was insufficient was the planning. Imagine looking at a map – poorly drawn, and with little accuracy in scale – and considering that Russian could be taken in a month, give or take a gnat's minim. That was what the greatest general in Europe had planned. A month. He expected the Russians to stand and fight. Neither happened.

The French even took Moscow. That's right, you can still read. They inhabited Moscow, the spiritual heart of the Motherland, even if not its recognised capital city. Moscow was the heart that leapt at the Motherlands tender touch. And rather than see it in enemy hands, the Russians burned her, rent her heart asunder.

For a month it was French. One month, and then Napoleon decided to chase the Russians back south, fearful of the onset of winter. September had waned, October was on the rise.

This far north he was again too slow, too late, partially due to his own ill health.

Winter came, mild for the Russians in their bearskins, but terrible to the French, who, two months overdue, found themselves horrendously unprepared. The horses had summer shoes, the men summer clothing. The weather closed in and unlike a British winter, where the wind howls in from the sea to warm the land, this far inland the temperatures plummeted. It was only October, not especially extreme, but to the French it was murder beyond the fighting.

And still the army bled, it continued to desert and starve and now it froze. To sleep was to die, men begged to be left to their slumbers, to sink in to their cold induced stupor that left them as glacial corpses.

So what did Napoleon do? Did he rescue his men by a divine master plan on which his very reputation was built? Did he inspire his men to warmth, holding them close and delivering them the heat of his very own body?

No. He did not.

He fled.

He fled for his own throne, he saved his own bacon. He was home within a fortnight.

And his men?

They were left to the command of Murat, the King of Naples. Did he save his men? No! He ran for warmer climes, all the way back to Italy to rescue *his* own throne, to lounge in his own lap of luxury, to that lap which was the mild, moist thighs of the Mediterranean.

And the men froze and were massacred. They died.

A fighting force of thirty thousand men, give or take that gnats minim, returned as a cohesive force. More found their way back, but many of these were not French and they fled to their European homes of Prussia, Austria and Poland whilst the French coalition crumbled. No longer did France hold sway over continental Europe. Never let it be said that some British Duke won the day. He didn't, Napoleon defeated himself in a Russian winter.

The Prussians and the other Germanic states coalesced, defying the Emperor, the Austrians thumbed their noses, not for the first time, the Dutch grew their tulips, but none of them fought for the bloody tyrant.

It was the end of Napoleon. Not the very end, because after his defeat by a combined allied force of Prussia, Austria, the Netherlands and Great Britain, a fight in which he'd managed to amass three hundred thousand men, made up mostly of boys lucky to find their collective backsides with their collective hands and a torch, he was defeated. And yet still he returned from his exile on Elba.

And from there, there was Waterloo. And Wellington fled.

Napoleon chased him when propitious. And then fled himself when it wasn't.

Russia never forgave the tyrant.

Millions had died because of the invasion, partly due to the atrocities performed upon them, partly because their own cavalry had burned all of the food and fouled all of the wells. They did what the

French did, drinking from polluted puddles and dying nameless deaths, freezing as they starved and starving as they froze.

So they pervaded slowly south, implicit permission of the land owners through parts of Prussia and Poland, supplied by the seas as they hugged the coast and then the population as they moved inland. Within a few years, the Russians had inveigled upon swathes of the Germanic states and most of Poland, almost to the borders of Austria. All in the name of neighbourly love and mutual aid. And few people seemed to be bothered.

Some folk minded, though. For years, there was a steady rise of forts along the border with Pomerania. Well, hardly a rise, more of a fall. Great bastioned castles sunken into the ground and a killing ground a hundred or more meters long.

The Russians had no intention of ever leaving the lands they borrowed. They excused their actions by claiming that they were a part of the alliance, a part of the force that enveloped Napoleon's army: even as the Tyrant broke through again and again, they claimed they were denying space to the French army as it split to flee, combined in retreat, divided to pincer and joined to crush.

This was a loose alliance against the French following the débâcle at Waterloo, what should have been a stunning victory. The allies were all damaged and dented, licking wounds, unable – or unwilling – to commit to the defeat of France and so Europe became a battlefield, from Brittany to Bordeaux, to Barcelona to Brussels, to Belgrade to Brescia. Sometimes there was a pause for breath where a winter started early or finished late, all of the opponents tucked up by July, perhaps oversleeping until April or May, but every year more deviltry was planned, new weapons invented, always by more destructive and inhumane methods – impersonal, even – the longer that the war enveloped a continent.

But all things end. And sometimes these are the beginning or the midpoint of another tale.

A   tale   such   as   this.

CHAPTER 14 – MA CHERIE

William and Bob disembarked the Bucentaur in a large park at the dead of night, unseen by anyone of importance. Determination crossed his face. He needed to exact vengeance for the murder of the innocent folk of Birtles Hall. And once he had killed Rune, he would hunt down Brocklehurst, make him explain his actions and then commit summary justice on him.

William was still confused – why France, why desert? Who was behind it all? Stieber? It seemed unlikely, the more he considered it. He too had to be serving someone – he was good at sowing seeds, distributing half-truths, gathering information, disseminating that information, but from all William had been told, Stieber wasn't a leader, a person that people would follow and love and die for.

William led the way, he knew this area of Paris, and he led Bob to an empty stable behind an inn. He'd taken the back ways, never via popular thoroughfares, passing only beggars and drunks. Bob's presence would soon be known, but he hoped that by the time it became an imperative, that they would have completed their mission, made a successful rendezvous with Duval and be back in Britain, and possibly in time for a late brunch.

William entered the inn. He'd stayed there previously, but not for some months. The owner had a soft spot for him and he'd never really disillusioned her of his lack of anything but carnal interest.

Still, he hadn't expected the reception he got – a full blooded slap to the face, followed by a fierce hug with head buried in a shoulder becoming slowly damper, followed by a rather painful kiss that crushed his lips. And then another heavy-handed slap.

"You bastard! I heard you were dead!"

William rubbed his rather frizzy beard and stroked the stubble slowly growing from his top lip.

"Almost, ma cherie"

Perhaps he should try a little harder with the girl – she was beautiful (if rather short) with a full head of bright red hair, bright hazel eyes and, as normal, a corseted bodice illuminating magnificent breasts. He sighed inwardly. It would never work, she was so common, even if they did get on so well.

She shook her head and disappeared behind the bar, reaching underneath the counter for the best ale that only went to the most cherished customers. Hoppy, bitter, strong. He sighed with pleasure – it had been a while since he'd had beer so good. She brewed it at the inn…maybe it could work, after all.

"Cherie, I need to introduce you to a friend of mine" he said, after taking her to one side. "She is staying in the stables tonight, please can you make sure it stays free of visitors? Equine or otherwise?"

Both William's cheeks smarted rather painfully, but then he also realised that his trousers were feeling a tad tight at the moment. She really did have an effect on him.

She raised a quizzical eyebrow, just the one, but she followed him and then gasped in surprise when she saw Bob.

"She says hello," smiled William as Bob twirled he fingers. He was becoming quite re-accustomed to their speaking thus, and they'd even started creating shortcuts for regularly used complex words. A glow of green-yellow and a quick flick showed that she understood his fascination with her particular female form. He had also learned her eye colours as they reflected various moods – magenta for sadness, blue was normal, green-yellow tended to be rather difficult as it could be sultry, humorous, darkly so at times. William wasn't sure if she'd been designed to show emotions – he didn't expect it prevalent in Brocklehurst's mind – or if she did it naturally, so to speak. He'd stayed away from her emotions to a certain extent, as he realised she was really rather sad with her lot, but William still found himself fascinated by her, and quite attracted in an odd sort of way because she had a true depth of character within that metal shell. He was fairly sure that she was now in for the fight and William had promised her he would find a way to release her from this body – as soon as he knew what was going on and she could have some form of revenge. Anger and hatred tended to show red, but they too could dip into magenta, violet and purple, depending on the association.

Actually, Bob had signed "Bonjour," and it slowly sank in to the multilingual William. He glanced at her; she would be remarkably useful and he signed to her to keep her signing to English and her ears open to French.

Yellow…humoured…and there was even a humanoid twinkle to the colour. She must have been a most remarkable woman when alive, not just in spirit but also in body.

William explained very briefly about 'his friend' and swore his cherie to secrecy. He doubted she would keep it. He certainly would have struggled.

*

Next morning, she arranged hot water for a bath. For both of them. They both stank of sex and William was slightly hungover and extremely tired, in a most contented fashion. He could still see in his minds-eye her breasts swaying heavily over him as she came repeatedly, a most remarkable woman, who's orgasms were more liquid than his own. Actually, he could still see her udders now, shamelessly naked, orange bush proudly prominent as the young serving boy tried his best to fill the copper tub without overtly gawping at her nakedness and his steadily rising erection. He was a bit sore as he lowered himself the tub, but she did not care as she none-too-gently lowered herself on to him and moaned deeply. She came almost immediately, the stinging hot water and his manhood taking effect, but still she rode him, the steam of her scent acting as an aphrodisiac as it drove him into a rutting frenzy. Her large nipples dragged up and down his chest and he watched her bosom bounce and heave in a most gratifying manner. They both came more or less at the same time, and even through the hot water, William could feel her hot juices on his penis as she could feel his seed burrowing itself deep inside. He was impressed with himself at his own quantity of juice, but then it had been a while.

They dried each other down whilst the poor serving boy emptied and then refilled the bath with fresh water which, this time, was used to only clean themselves properly.

William could feel the pregnant pause in the atmosphere as they eventually dressed some time around mid-morning. She had already expressed her interest in marrying William, mostly because they got on so well, partly because of the excellent sex and partly because of his obscene wealth. He blushed with some shame as he ignored the barely disguised request for a proposal.

"Cherie, something has happened and I don't know what. Can I reside here in secrecy until I get to the bottom of things?"

She opened her mouth to speak but William hurried on.

"It's of national importance. No, that's not true, it's of international importance, but I've no idea why. Whatever it is, it will affect the whole of Europe and cannot possibly make France happier."

William was a lover of the French way of life, and she knew this and trusted him. Her lips pursed themselves in a rather sour fashion, but she wasn't entirely serious about being angry. Her heart, however, did sink. He still hadn't asked her to marry him. She relented internally and allowed that his presence would remain secret. He'd explained over post coital cigars in the dead of night what had happened to him since he'd last left Paris, although he did leave out some of the more sensitive political aspects. She knew what he needed to do, more or less, and it shouldn't present any danger to her. She still hoped that she may still become Madam – nay, Lady – Hope once this escapade was over.

CHAPTER 15 – LEARNING TO PLAY NICELY

Amara attempted to escape.

She had been treated perfectly well following the experiment. Like a Queen, to be fair to Stieber. There were the tailored clothes of western styles unlike anything she'd previously worn, tight fitting garb that hugged her slender figure, exaggerating her waist and accentuating the sway of her hips as she walked. There was no bump starting to show, and Amara was unsure if anyone but Stieber and Rimbaud knew of her situation. And the quality of the clothing! My goodness, they were sometimes delicate and sometimes sturdy, but for all that, the seamstress must have been a perfect goddess. She'd had good, nutritious food, containing vegetables of all shapes and sizes, all alien to her eye and taste buds. Beetroot was her personal favourite, an earthy sweetness that tasted like nothing else in her experience. The drinks she imbibed were new: fresh and cloying, rich and dry, harsh and smooth, cold and warm. She stayed in luxurious hotels or grand houses that contained bedrooms larger and more luxurious than her entire house in the hills. The beds were soft yet firm, and she delighted in the chaise longues upon which she could laze and read the multitudes of literature in various languages that filled entire walls in great libraries. She spent weeks utterly flabbergasted during their slow progress through Italy. Everywhere they went Stieber appeared to know – and command – all of the town notables, and so they had the best of everything.

And of course, Stieber could not help but parade his prize through these safe places, and she was fêted through the fashionable parts of towns at hurriedly thrown parties, at theatres and restaurants, and they made her wear the finest clothes at these gatherings. A gift from Rimbaud placed proudly upon her head, that of a tiara that sparkled like sunlight through spring rain, helped disguise her copper crown, but many people commented on her head that was clad in chiffon and topped by the tiara. It could not hide the fact that something ungodly seemed to reside below that mantle. Her beauty and exoticism were legion with the throngs, but throughout all of these engagements she remained silent. Yet this only added to the mystique that followed her ever northwards. Rumour of her coming spread before them and the well-to-do folk flocked to see her and marvel at her beauty.

She was sold to those throngs as a Queen from abroad, not as some ungodly experiment. They loved her and placed her on a pedestal, yet they did not pity her, as they most surely would, had they but known the truth.

She had a servant girl and Rimbaud acted as her charlatan medic and he was always at hand to tend to her condition, which still refused to show through even her slenderness.

She had everything that a lady could want. Even Rune was absent as he recovered in Rome from his poisoning. It had taken days for them to dare re-open the underground chambers, and when they had, Amara had been out of the house as a safety measure. She did not know what occurred, and no-one would speak of it. She hoped − vainly, she knew − that he would never return. Stieber had warned her in friendly terms that he would brook no repeat, and as if to try win her by bribery, he set her upon this road of splendour and luxury.

She had everything that a lady could want. Except freedom.

And then they had left her alone. Just this once.

So she attempted to escape.

Her only option was to climb out of her bedroom window four floors up. She managed somehow to balance on a window ledge made wet from an afternoon shower, and scramble fearfully on to sturdy looking vines that clad the great house. There was a slight tear as part of a vine parted itself from the wall, but it was too ancient and well-established to allow itself to be displaced entirely by this mere slip of a girl. She descending, sliding and slithering on the wet foliage to the floor below, grasping gables and vines, using ledges on the lower storeys alternately as foot and hand holds. It was all too easy, she was free. Once down, her wits gathered, she started loping, a long legged, stamina saving lope towards the mansion walls that were almost at the horizon, through row upon row of grape vines shining in the late spring sun.

Suddenly she screamed, a searing pain flashing through her skull, blinding her vision, sending a charred metallic smell through her nostrils and then she fell, lying still, unable to move, gazing up at clouded skies. Unable to blink even. Tears came unbidden to her eyes as the dryness stung.

Then, standing over her, was Stieber. He smiled a darkly benevolent smile.

"I don't know how my man thinks of these things, even more how he actually does them."

He turned around and strapped to his back was a container the size of a cushion. It was made of some dark wood.

"You see, my dear, when you remove yourself from the vicinity of this machine, or I press this switch here" – he motioned towards a small number of controls dials and switches that adorned the box – "all those probes in your head simply stop working."

"Frankly, my dear, I still don't even know if you're technically alive or not. My Master certainly isn't – alive that is – and my man really doesn't know what will happen to you when – or should I say IF" – Stieber smiled slyly – "we ever remove them. Interesting isn't it?"

He pressed a button on the side of the container and suddenly everything was normal again. She could even feel the warm sensation where she'd uncontrollably soiled herself when all of her muscles had ceased to function.

"Now, shall we play nicely, my dear?"

She rose unsteadily, staggering slightly as her legs regained control of themselves.

She launched herself forward, attacking Stieber, gripping his neck at the sides and biting deeply in to his cheek, tearing, tearing. Rough hands gripped her from behind and a sob escaped from Stieber to the front as he vainly attempted to fold back a flap of cheek through the blood that teemed down his face and poured through his fingers. Panic was in his eyes: he clearly wasn't used to being on the receiving end of such treatment.

Shaking, he levered a switch on the rucksack and once again Amara was rendered paralysed. More importantly to the Prussian, he was rendered safe.

*

Some days later Amara smelled of her own stale self, no longer perfumed and bathed each night, and no longer clad in elegant clothing. She was tied up each and every night to the foot of her gaoler's bed. The only thing Stieber allowed her in any good measure was wholesome food after a well-reasoned argument that Amara had to be well fed to ensure that there were no complications with the baby. She had no idea if the thing growing inside her came from the seed of her husband or the rapist. A sick dread grew stronger each day that it must be the rapists because, after so long, she and her husband had never managed to conceive. She did not know what she would do with the thing if it came out white or milky. It would not be the fault of the baby, but after such a start in life, its omens must be poor, and those of the mother even poorer.

A baby of such origin would never be accepted in black society or white, and in that there would be even less chance of a happy life, never mind that it was a rapists get.

Could she love such a creature? Or every time she looked in to its eyes would she see the spectre of its father, every time it clamped on to a breast to suckle, would she be terrorised by the things that its rapist father had done to her breasts? And how would such a child survive if it ever became aware of such a father? How could it ever feel it belonged? How could it ever truly believe that it was purely loved, like any normal child felt of its mother? How could a rapists get survive the guilt?

IT. She couldn't give the thing a gender in her mind's eye, nor bring herself to even acknowledge *it* as her child.

As they moved further northwards, Italy grew steadily wilder. Two-score troops guarded their journey and these deterred the numerous outlaw bands that seemed to line their way, although they rarely caught anything more than a glimpse of a man peeking over a hillock, or a hint of colourful clothing in a dense copse of trees. It was slow, tedious going and it was now extremely uncomfortable for Amara as she lay cramped at Stieber's feet. Sometimes they only covered as little as twenty kilometres along lumpy, uncomfortable tracks and lanes that slowed their progress as they journeyed along those wilder, less travelled paths.

Whether Amara had been pampered or as she was now, trussed, through every village that they passed, children were thin and malnourished, women were haggard and weary. The menfolk cast sly and greedy eyes towards the caravan, watching for any perceived weakness they could exploit. But whilst the caravan guard was reasonably low in numbers, they were hard faced men, armed to the teeth with revolving pistols, long-arm rifles, wickedly serrated bayonets, gleaming swords, razor-sharp knives and exploding grenades. They stared all of the menfolk straight in the eye, and none could return their gaze.

People were poor, extremely poor and their respective governments ignored them, because they were gearing for a war they could feel but not see, so ran the commentary from Stieber, who dearly loved the sound of his own voice, full of pride for his own smug cleverness. To Amara, his voice sounded like a nail down a chalkboard, and she cringed at the grating sound, loathing it more every day.

"We ride before the flames of revolution. We are the vanguard! All Italy will soon be enveloped and we will go forth as its standard bearer. And from out of the flames, will come my Master's army. She will envelope the whole of Europe, a new European order. Why stop there I asked my master, and do you know what he replied?" He chuckled. "He laughed at me and said that he had no intention of stopping at Europe. A new world order! We will run it for the good of the people. We shall give them exactly what they want and they will love us!"

He paused and smiled at Amara with that smug smile that Amara detested so much.

"The rest of Europe will join Italy in their revolt. This will not be such a small thing as happened in France all those years ago. This will be *all* of Europe. As we travel to Paris, the French will start to mutter and murmur, and those rebellious heartlands of Marseilles and Lyon will throw down the towers of the establishment. The Austrians will find Russia knocking on its door, and she will rise in fear, and as she does so, her armies will cause great fear in her neighbours, and so the remains of Poland and all of the Germanies will rise up. They will demand too much of their peoples and all will refuse. They will see the phoenix that rises from Italy and they will see a better way. They will demand that it should be theirs also. They will dethrone their masters and even the papacy will tremble in fear, because my master will appear before the world as a God. All will fear him. All will love him. All will flock to his banner."

He smiled triumphantly, his eyes burning with insane zeal.

He was happy, she could tell. He became happier as they entered France. They are angry, he would tell her, simmering and stewing. Dangerous. Imagine a forest in a drought. A spark – that is all it would take. A spark, and the whole place would be aflame. France alight, anger and spite released, Europe beware.

Stieber laughed and glowered as he spoke. He was the spark, he would say, he was only in need of the flint to desire it and he would be the spark, and France would light up and subsume Europe. His Master victorious at last.

Outwardly dispassionate, Amara continued to watch Stieber, never offering a glimmer of emotion, not a widening of an eye, nor the flaring of a nostril. But she was scared, because she knew from his self-absorbed ramblings that she must be the key to the whole, possibly the flint as *he* spoke. Stieber may be insane, clearly he was, but his eyes burned with a bright intelligence when he spoke and his goal was crystal clear, unlike Rimbaud, who barely seemed to comprehend exactly what Stieber was up to. War. Conquest. Power. Or for Stieber, the power behind the power. Those were the things that Stieber wanted, things that were incomprehensible to Rimbaud who was in love with learning for the sake of learning, and damn the consequences.

She was becoming to know Arthur better, indeed he was the only person with whom she spoke. She almost felt sorry for him. She had tried to explain in quiet conciliatory tones of what Stieber was, how this would all end, but Rimbaud didn't seem to be able to grasp the meaning of the facts, he just stared in to her eyes like a small child.

He was smitten, she understood, and she tried to use her sex, that desire to have her, but he was too scared of Stieber and too in love with his learning, and she was too scared of her own sex to try and even do a half-decent job of mesmerising him with her beauty. It was barely an effort at all, and for that she was inwardly relieved.

She railed at him and harried him, but he only shook his head patiently, as if she was a child and tried to explain that she was mistaken.

She hated Rimbaud for what he had done to her, for his stupidity, his blindness, his fear. But, a small part of her *did* pity him. Whilst he was the cause of her rape (well, Stieber was, or his master, if you wanted to go to the top of the tree), whilst his hirelings had murdered her husband, he was nothing more than a pawn in Stieber's game, and the more she talked with him – in spite of her pain and her hatred – the more she pitied him. And once, when she saw Stieber looking at Rimbaud, she also realised that once his usefulness was done, then he would be discarded in the same unfeeling, thoughtless manner as her rapist had been murdered. Almost as an afterthought.

Stieber loved neither man nor nature. His megalomania grew more feverish as every day passed, and with every day that those plans came closer to realisation, his tyranny and cruelty were elevated so that it hurt Amara to look at him.

Rimbaud was a pawn, as was she. If only she could make him see that before she murdered him for her pain.

*

Stieber led Amara in to the Catacombs via a private entrance that was away from prying eyes. She stared around at the alien-ness of such a place. Never mind Paris itself, which had been a teeming mass of poverty, with the stench of human filth rampant. She had gaped at tall ramshackle hovels that twisted upwards in precarious spirals, bending and twisting in creaking agony, and she had watched the people, so many people, as to make Rome a fishing village by comparison.

No, the Catacombs were alien in such another way; never before had she seen so many sarcophagi, inscriptions, tombs, statues... and bones.... so many skulls, femurs, ribcages, finger bones and spinal vertebrae. And like most of Paris, it was in a state of crumbling disrepair, the musty smell of ancient decay throughout. Some areas were so poorly kept, that rotting corpses lay strewn across pathways where the walls had collapsed. In these places the stench of putrefaction was such that Rimbaud was left retching and even Stieber seemed to go a ghoulish shade of green.

They moved deeper and deeper and Amara shivered as the air got colder and damper. Water dripped from the stone ceiling to form great puddles that soaked their feet until they were so cold that their feet went numb. After perhaps thirty minutes, they were suddenly at a locked door that Rimbaud opened into a well-lit tunnel, the lighting provided by, in Amara's eyes, magic lamps. Water dripped steadily from the ceiling. The smell of decay faded and after a mile or more of the long straight tunnel, they came to an iron door with three different keyholes. It wasn't locked, and on the other side was a large anteroom filled by nothing more than an alien, a monster.

Amara screamed at it. Shining black eyes stared without emotion straight back at that scream.

Rune smiled and took her hand.

CHAPTER 16 – AMARA & WILLIAM

Brocklehurst sat in a luxurious office of his own design, a motorised seat massaging his lower back. One eye was no longer white, but was a crimson red, filled with blood. A large furrow ran down the length of his scalp.

"Where the hell are they, Hope?" screeched Brocklehurst.

A servant entered his room to lay the fire; it was still chilly as the afternoons wore to evening, and Brocklehurst watched with a dissociated pleasure as the newly designed firelighters were lit underneath the kindling and coals. A green phosphorescence glowed for a few minutes, sufficient to set a merry blaze and the creep of warmth could be felt through the room.

"Where are what?" William enquired with a pert politeness that was belied by his face, which contained a vast smile. He had no idea what the man was blathering about nor was he particularly bothered. It humoured him to see Brocklehurst anguished, more so to see his physical condition.

Brocklehurst threw a heavy paperweight at Hope in rage, missed, and scrunched up a piece of paper that it was securing, and succeeded in hitting Hope with that.

"The bloody automatons at Birtles Hall! You know damn well what I mean, or you bloody-well wouldn't have been sniffing me out."

It had taken William several weeks of searching – and enjoying his lodgings, including all of the hors d'oeuvres that went with that particular inn – before he had gotten a proper whisper on where he might locate Brocklehurst, and then, whilst snooping around, he'd stumbled, quite literally, into Rune. It had been a dark, wet night and he had slipped in an indescribable pile of filth on the street, pitching him right into the beast, who'd literally just picked him up and thrown him in to a cell in the factory.

"I'm sorry Brocklehurst, you'll have to explain."

"The bastards were waiting for us – fourteen dirigibles left from Le Mans a fortnight ago, myself as commanding officer. You should have seen them Hope, magnificent. Two of them were vast behemoths, their size beyond belief. And now they're destroyed and Stieber will have his revenge."

"On who, exactly?" smirked William, finding Brocklehurst's alternating smugness and hysteria setting him on edge. Bloody commander indeed! Still, at least watching him squirm was fun.

"I'll make sure you go first."

"You were going to tell me what happened, and, I presume, what caused your injuries."

"We arrived at Birtles Hall – I need those blasted automata, damn it! – and everything was quiet. The hall itself was bereft of everything. Not a painting, nor statue, nor any of my other belongings. And then in to the basement. Nothing….nothing…" Brocklehurst shook his head ruefully.

"Then we heard explosions from up top and we ran like the wind to see what on earth was happening. Both of the giant dirigibles were aflame, and of the others, only my Bucentaur was not engaged in combat…"

"Duval! The double crossing swine."

"...I was ushered aboard, but there were hundreds, perhaps thousands, of foot shoulders trying to board her also. Duval's men fought like devils as we took off, hurling dozens overboard to their doom." With a melodramatic wistfulness, he raised his eyes skyward. "The poor souls."

"And your injuries?"

"One of Duval's men was knocked whilst shooting and managed to crease my skull. An inch lower and it would be me being imbued. A splinter from where the bullet struck did this," he said, indicating the blood-red eye.

"Shame." William managed to keep a straight face for a second before bursting out in laughter. "But it is good to see that even your own side want to kill you. I've been right about you the entire time."

He wasn't good with dormancy or boredom. The last three weeks had been an agony to the point that he was itching to cause some form of mischief, even it was only taunting the man in front of him. Deeper still, he was seething, his blood slowly boiling more furiously at the prolonged inactivity and he yearned for any chance to smash Brocklehurst's face to jelly and burn the factory, and all within it, to the ground. And so he laughed, pointed, laughed some more.

William's throat was seized from behind, the tears of uncontrolled laughter turning to tears of pain, and he was lifted and shaken like a rag doll.

"Rune, put him down," ordered Brocklehurst. "I need the information out of him.

"Tell me then, dear William. Where are my automata?"

"Whatever makes you think that the British Government would leave such assets either undefended or, worse still, in a place where they could be taken? It seems like you're losing your touch."

"Stieber ordered it. He said that they'd be there. He had assurances."

William laughed. "So Stieber's been compromised?"

"I'll allow you to tell him that to his face. So. Where the hell are they?"

"I have no idea." He looked straight at Brocklehurst.

"Rune, help the man remember."

A fleeting look of panic crossed William's face as Rune flicked his hand and an appendage snapped off. It ran over to the chair, ran up its leg, across his lap and on to his arm.

"I tell you, I don't know anything!" His voice had risen an octave.

"Not so superior now, eh, Hope?" sneered Brocklehurst.

The appendage turned in to a pincer as a steely hand gripped William's arm to the chair. The pincer moved to his hand, down his little finger, gripped the nail and tugged.

William screamed as the nail tore free.

"I don't bloody know!"

He screamed again as a second nail was forcibly removed. He watched as the appendage moved to his middle finger, blood running freely to the new carpet below.

He managed not to scream this time, he just grunted because he was already in a sea of pain. As the fourth nail was parted from its finger, he again pleaded his ignorance.

"Please Brocklehurst, believe me, I do not know." He partly feigned the pleading tone: his repose with the Pirate Captain had been far less pleasurable, and he'd been interrogated far more expertly. This wasn't all that bad in comparison, but it was in no way pleasant.

"Pathetic," spat Brocklehurst. "Take him back to his cell."

The pallor of Brocklehurst's face told its own story.

*

Stieber, through the tone of his correspondence, was less than happy and Brocklehurst had been forced to increase the numbers of workers, taking on a mixture of French and German engineers, as *recommended* by Stieber. The few engineers he had brought from Cheshire, those whose loyalties were assured via some kind of personal debt, were having to train these foreign engineers in the new rules of engineering, physics, chemistry and mathematics that the Cheshire crews had laboriously developed over a number of years.

It had put back Stieber's plans by a number of months and Stieber's master was even less happy.

The pressure was on Brocklehurst, and it noticeably reduced his swagger.

A stringent timetable had been given to him and, in his opinion, he had six months to complete twelve months work – namely to entirely rebuild his terracotta army. Production was also occurring in Italy, Spain and Austria. The armies of automata would be massive.

Foundries around Paris were given orders on strict deadlines to produce exoskeleton items. Brocklehurst had been forced to supply some of the raw materials because the poverty around France had led to metals of such poor quality that many of the original orders were rejected and thrown in a large scrapheap. Added to this, the skills of the Parisian foundry workers were atrocious when compared against those of their Lancastrian and Cheshirian counterparts. made had been rejected due to weak casting, specifications not being met and he'd even had to apply pressure to some as they'd tried to substitute sub-standard metals from those that he'd supplied, which they had then sold to line their pockets. The pressure had necessarily been quite direct and forceful, and that sort of behaviour had quickly stopped once the rumours had circulated of the outcome of such activities.

The French and German engineers, thankfully, were quick learners, although their basic knowledge was lacking in some areas. The first shells of the automata lay on shelves in the warehouse and now all he needed was Rimbaud and the girl.

The warehouse was in a large abandoned factory built in the middle of the previous century, well used until recently, but drafty and run-down. It was made of orange brick over several storeys with perilously worn stone staircases throughout. It smelled of something so rank that it even managed to partially mask the odour from the Seine running close by. Brocklehurst's office sat on the top storey. He had endeavoured, in classic self-importance, to ensure that it was the most expensively renovated part of the building.

White plaster gleamed throughout the rest of the factory and precision tooling lined the walls. The top floor contained several workshops, and he had designed it use for the most intricate and ingenious parts of the automata. There was a bustle of activity throughout, whether it be the micro-riveting of body parts, manufacture of minute springs and hydraulics by bespectacled engineers, or the sweeping up of swarf and debris by grubby urchins.

Pressure test equipment hissed gently, drills whined piercingly, large hammers thudded resonantly and the smell of hot oil and burning metal masked the background smell of Paris and the pervading odour of the factory.

The floor below contained the assembly area where the first few automatons were already assembled. It also contained a living area and a small brewery as all of the staff were required to live on the premises. William had been informed that this had been non-negotiable – as had the refusal to accept the contract. However, the smell of hops and malt on that level was a wonderful reprieve from the rest of the factory.

The ground floor held the warehousing area, where raw materials were received before being sent to foundries and then received back. The floors in between saw less use, usually for a bespoke experiment or a trial of some update to a design where space was required.

There was also a basement area. It only connected to two places: the first floor, where almost nobody was allowed to enter, and the Catacombs, from where only few ever arrived. Heavy metal doors protected the two entrances to the basement. The room looked surgical. It gleamed white and silver and it was spotlessly clean. There were large and complex banks of machinery and power transformers that hummed violently. Gas valves taller than a man and miles and miles of cabling ran around the room into the Catacombs themselves. And at the hub of the machinery was a great control panel containing gauges to measure electricity, automated paper feeders that drew lines corresponding to brain activity, lights that flashed a multitude of warning colours, klaxons that detected the shades of the dead, under all of which lay an ominous metallic tang that clung to the taste buds for hours afterwards. Tall electric lights loomed from the corners of the room. In the very centre of the room was a metal chair without any form of salute to comfort. Ankle and wrist manacles had been welded in place and a torc-like circlet was attached to a telescopic pole at the rear of the chair. It looked positively medieval, with needles pointing inwards and thin wires spiralling outwards. A passive observer would shudder at the likely use of this creation, hairs would rise at the nape of the neck.

It was where Amara spent most of her days.

*

William looked at the black girl with a mixture of pity and dislike. She was black, which in his mind took him back to his Pirate Queen, her love, treachery and betrayal. Never again. He thought of the Pirate Captain, who had sold his sisters to slavery, murdered his mother, slaughtered his father and brothers – all for a few gold pieces. His year-long imprisonment as a child had been a torment of filth, starvation, disease and humiliation. Very few of the blacks he met had any decency – most were wilfully ignorant of what was happening, the important minority were thieves, murderers and rapists... only the wizened old lady who cleared his cell every few days had demonstrated any kind of moral fibre, probably the only black person he had ever met with such as that. Old and grey, stooped almost double and wizened beyond belief by the hardship of her life, she had sneaked in extra morsels of food on occasion and murmured words of consolation, not that there was any consolation, in truth.

And he thought of le Clerc, that hugely fat man, with the gleaming bald pate, his oil-on-water manners and his affectations. He grimly recalled the place at which that black man had kept his sisters.

And now, before him, was a spectacularly beautiful and alien-looking black woman. She was similar to his Pirate Queen, who had been flawlessly beautiful: this woman, though, was more beautiful still, and yet her beauty was deeply marred, both physically and psychologically. But her beauty was untamed, her spirit luminescing through her dark skin and her blood-shot eyes. She exuded beauty that was so much more than skin deep.

Her alieness, the electrodes piercing her skull, the jagged rents of scarring about her scalp, eccentric tufts of hair growing back to show that she would never have a full head of hair again, they all added to an exoticism that William found wildly attractive, and yet... his prejudice was stronger.

And she just sat there, eyes closed, ignoring William's presence. William promised himself to ignore her in return.

He lasted less than five minutes. His natural curiosity won out, he was fascinated and just had to know what on earth she was doing here, what she was doing here like *that*.

"Errrm, hello, my name is William Hope."

There was silence from the girl, in fact no reaction of any kind.

"Parlez-vous Français?" he enquired. His travels had taught him that there were many languages and dialects spoken in Africa, both European and local.

Still nothing.

Bugger it, he thought to himself. *I need to talk to someone, just for my own sanity.*

So William embarked upon his story, and although he made it brief, it lasted longer than hour, starting with his imprisonment at the hands of pirates, his Pirate Queen, the Pirate Captain, the rescue of his sisters, enslavement at the hands of Duval, Brocklehurst, treason, Rune, Bob the catacombs and finally recapture. He needed a glass of port, he thought, as he finished.

There was a long silence.

"It's well that I speak English, or that story would have been in vain, Mr Hope," she said in a beautifully lilted accent. "It was a shame that you could not keep the distaste of my skin colour out of your tone."

"Do you blame me?" he asked bitterly, once he'd come overcome his own surprise at the hostility in her tone.

"You are obviously educated, Mr Hope, and I would have thought that a man of your intelligence would be able to see beyond skin colour, or at least analyse those of your own skin colour."

"Meaning what exactly?" he enquired harshly.

"From your very own story, there's Rune," she shuddered as she spoke his name. "And Brocklehurst and Duval. All have performed exactly the same crimes as those committed against you. And yet, you do not extend the same level of discourtesy to those people based on their skin colour. Let us not forget, Brocklehurst was employed by your own government who seem to have had no desire to know of his techniques for gaining results."

"Your command of English is really very good, Miss...?"

Do not patronise me, you bastard," she snapped, eyes blazing. "You white folk have murdered my husband, defiled ME and then experimented upon me without even knowing if I am alive or dead."

The thin copper wires that connected to the electrodes glowed faintly as her ire grew.

"For over a hundred years, you white folk have plundered our lands, killed our people, enslaved the rest, empowered brigands, and given us your blinkered version of governance and civilisation. All across the known world – the Indies, Africa, India, the New World. Everywhere you tread there is murder, rape, theft. And to what end? So a High

Lord like yourself can be fed sweetmeats by concubines, smoke cigars and drink brandy. Pah! You disgust me with your narrow-minded ideals and your studied indifference of your own people."

She was crying now, nearly hysterical, and William was aware that it was likely that he wasn't the real target of her tirade, only that he was there.

She ended her tirade with a long, long sentence containing many expletives, some in English, some in a language that he did not understand, but were clearly expletives all the same.

They sat in silence again as her body heaved with the effort, as she attempted to gain control of her emotions.

Awkwardly, William shuffled his bottom closer to hers and put a tentative arm around her shoulder. She stiffened briefly before glancing up in to his eyes and then falling into a sobbing, hysterical wreck on his chest that rapidly became wet with snot and tears. He held her close, stroking her shoulder tenderly, until her sobbing stopped and then, quite remarkably, he felt her breathing regulate into slow deep breaths: she had fallen fast asleep and he didn't dare move for fear of waking her, even when his left arm went numb.

He mused over her outburst. His father – and now he, himself – had interests in the Indies and William himself had reviewed the figures regarding employment of workers – virtually slaves if you like – but he'd never considered it as slavery before. The costs of that employment were laughably low for such a large workforce and he commanded large profits from these interests. Well, it *was* too good to be true. William had travelled far and wide in his role as knight-in-shining-armour, but the connection between that person and Sir William Hope, gentleman and scholar, was never made. He had visited the plantations and ignored the state of the workers, as had ignored the hovels they lived in. He had pirated across faraway lands, but never as Sir William Hope, never as a privileged individual, just as, well, a pirate. He had sailed the seas as Sir William Hope, plant collector and scholar. The two disparate selves never seemed to meet, and it was over this that he mused constantly in the days that followed.

Slavery as a practice may have been illegal in Britain, even if owning slaves abroad was not, and at home worker rights were negligible, pay was poor, scandalously so, and work was rare enough that people took what they could find and cut their cloth accordingly. Judging from the streets of London, life as a commoner must be atrocious, but even in his own country, he turned a blind eye, concentrating solely on his studies and interests, most recently his photography, which he'd not mentioned to the girl.

Still, he was fairly sure that the magnitude was of a different order in those other places. Whilst Western behaviours were not ideal, their desire to bring civilised governance was out of an altruistic desire only and if a firm hand was occasionally needed, it was only because that was what the indigenous populations understood. No, there really was no comparison, although he did concede that she may have a point; maybe he could revisit some of his attitudes. It was, at least, the scientific thing to do.

Eventually, he just had to shift his position. She'd lain there for over an hour and at his movement she awoke somewhat groggily. She looked around herself searching for her bearings and when they were found, she rapidly removed herself from William's arms, jerking away self-consciously.

She peered suspiciously at him and seeing nothing to find fault with, her gaze softened – slightly.

"You never did tell me your name," said William.

"My name is Amara. And I am here to commune with the dead."

She stared at William defiantly before amending her statement.

"Actually, no, that's not true, I am here to capture the dead. They need me to make tens of thousands of your friend Bob."

"Oh my," said William. "We do have a lot to talk about. Shall I start with photography?"

CHAPTER 17 – WILLIAM GETS SPANKED

Over the next few weeks, Amara and William talked a lot, whenever they were together. They were slowly becoming friends, a common cause breaking through their natural suspicions towards each another.

One such conversation blew his horizons wide open.

"How are you here, how were you chosen? Why *you*?" William asked her one evening. He knew the practicalities of the matter and he was painfully aware of the why. But the choosing of her over the multitudes and how they had found *her*, William did not know, nor could he begin to comprehend.

"I am Vodun," she said simply.

He looked at her, mystified.

She shrugged before continuing. "My mother was the Vodunsii for our village, for many of the villages around. You would call her a witch doctor," she scoffed at the words. "Her followers numbered in the thousands. I was to follow in her footsteps. I had been chosen."

William raised an eyebrow quizzically.

"You either are or you aren't a Vodunsii, a priestess you may call it in your parlance, not to be confused with the Queen Mother. You know when you are and I was. I knew, as did my mother, from a very young age, maybe before I could even form proper thoughts, perhaps even at conception." She shook her head slowly, a movement somewhat wistful in its manner.

She continued after a long pause. "I was to take over from my mother, I had been learning my entire life to take over from her and I was better than her, more aware. We both knew it. But I saw too much, I learned fear, but most importantly, I found love. Taking lovers is expected as a Vodunsii, for how else is the talent supposed to be passed on from generation to generation? But *love* is not expected, no not at all." She smiled wistfully. "I loved them both so much, my husband and my mother, but in the end my mother drove me away with her bitterness and her hatred towards him. She railed so hard that I ended up taking his side in everything until I was left no choice but to choose between them. The only decision I could take was to be with him."

A tear rolled down her face as she momentarily lost focus, delving somewhere inwards, somewhere painful. There was more, though, William could see it hidden deep in her hooded eyes.

"We left before the strain became too much, and she…never…spoke to me again. She never even uttered my name I'm told, not once, before the end."

William placed an arm around her. There was nothing unusual in this because she was often quite emotional after dealing with the souls of the dead each day. That sort of thing tends to take its toll.

She recovered rapidly. "I've wept all of my tears for this. It's an old tale." She shrugged, knowing the pointlessness of dwelling on matters long since decided, even if she did so anyway. "I gave up being a priestess and moved high in to the hills, and now the villages have to live with some sham priestess."

"Then it's even more puzzling. How were you found?"

"Our village was studied by white men some years ago. There were several of them – Arthur was amongst them. He had been there several times, but I was only young at the time and his presence did not seem to matter to me then. I didn't recognise him as I recovered after the murder of my husband, but he reminded me of it on the voyage over here whilst he was sneaking me the tiny amounts of water he could get away with."

William felt the blood drain from his face.

"It makes some sense now. I vaguely remember reading something about this within the Royal Society, although I didn't take much notice. I generally prefer studying plants than mankind, at least they make sense." He offered a weak smile. He received a weak smile in return.

"Of course!" He slapped his thigh hard, making Amara jump at the sound. "It was the reason that Chapman was blackballed from the Royal Society! He'd run pretty close to the wind a few times , but this was the final straw – especially as old Sabile had only just taken the reins. The gossip was rampant for weeks afterwards."

"Chapman?" Amara enquired, rolling the word around her mouth. "I think there was a Chapman with the party. George Chapman?" William nodded in ascent and she paused to think further. "Yes, he most surely was. There was some foul play with one of the women in the village and my mother couldn't abide the man, always looking at her sideways, never openly. He asked some most curious questions, far too insightful for a mere man."

"What does that mean? And how did he become that beast Rune, then?"

"THAT is Chapman?" Horror was upon her face. "How long have you known?"

"Since the altercation at Birtles Hall. The monster was about to kill me!" He pointed at the minute red mark on his forehead, the remnant of a spinning appendage.

"It explains so much. Why didn't you tell me!"

"It wasn't a secret, I just mustn't have mentioned his name. What does it mean?"

"I don't know yet, I must think on it, if I'm ever allowed to have any thoughts of my own again – *undisturbed.*" She looked at him pointedly.

He ignored the look. "What is there to think on?"

"Rune is an incarnation from the flames. A dark incarnation, one that is avoided at all costs by the Vodunsii. I must think on that. In silence."

She turned away from him, and, on this occasion, he took the hint.

*

The conversation was returned to some nights later.

"What you must understand about Vodun is the implicit recognition of grey, that is that each person is manufactured of both black and white. It makes grey, and it seems to me that this is something, from the little I know, not allowed for in your bible. People are either good or bad, no?"

William nodded his ascent, although the dubious look on his face showed that *he* wasn't sure either.

"Vodun recognises that grey and embraces it. But, as I said, there is black, though never pure and there is white, also never pure. Unless you are a God. Or touched by one that lies within the Vodunsii."

"Hold on, you're telling me that Chapman is basically a God?"

"No, merely touched by one. One is not made in to a God. A God just becomes." She shrugged, obviously not fully comprehending it herself."

A look of confusion passed over William's brow. He was in way deeper than his knowledge allowed. His Christian piety was almost non-existent. How was he supposed to know about an alien religion?

"My religion worships deities and Gods. There may be minor deities that govern the elements or the rocks; there are deities to whom we perform rituals for good health or a peaceful passing. And as the Priestess you are the conduit."

"Right." William paused, looking slightly embarrassed.

There was a pregnant pause.

"Conduit?" he eventually continued, unable to bear the silence any longer, nor the look of amusement on Amara's face as she watched his mind try and catch up with the conversation.

"Exactly. The conduit. The one who communes with the dead. The dead are the messengers of the conduit."

"I'm sorry, I'm hearing words but they sound all wrong put together like this."

"I'll put you out of your misery then. The conduit tends to talk with an ancestor, usually someone of significance. Mine was my Grandmother, a devious and manipulative woman, spiteful in the extreme, but also powerful in the talent. She may have been mean, but she was a blessing for the community, and wealth and fortune visited us for some time."

Amara smiled at the recollections of her grandmother. "She was a horrid in the extreme, but charismatic and perversely loved for her meanness, almost like it was that quirk of her character that was endearing to the villagers. It wasn't harmed by that certain aura she had, a force of personality that made people need to love her."

She laughed suddenly. "Her and mother certainly didn't get on. They were too alike. I suppose all three of us are, or were. Are, I think. They're both still there." She tapped her head.

William listened rapt in fascination. He didn't think he'd ever heard anyone open up so freely, so easily. He'd barely spoken of his adventures abroad, not even to his sisters who had been there for at least a part of it.

She seemed more relaxed for it, as if it were a catharsis, like marigold on a burn.

She looked in to his eyes and held his gaze. He couldn't break the stare because she wouldn't let him, and he wondered what she saw. Did she see his shallowness, his selfishness? Or was there something deeper, something that he himself didn't know about? He felt penetrated, as if she was judging his worth. Was he a man who could be depended upon? He didn't really know himself.

She smiled at him kindly, like a mother to a child, and he suddenly felt small and lonely, orphaned all over again, in need of his mother's arms gently cradling him. Inexplicably he began to cry, silent tears trailing slowly down his cheeks. He'd never had the opportunity to mourn his parents, he'd spent the subsequent years imprisoned, planning revenge or enacting vengeance. After that there had not seemed to be the need. And now this lady, this o-so sorrow-laden lady had brought his grief forward from a recess of his mind, a recess that he didn't know even existed. And so he wept his grief, his grief for his mother and father, for his baby sister, dead these many years, and for the harm upon his little sisters and for his older sister, so long absent from his world, gone to heaven knows where in that shell of a body that still breathed.

She took him in her arms and cradled him until his tears stopped, and then she continued her story, sensitive to the fact that he wasn't yet ready to tell that particular tale. Although he would. They both knew it.

"In the ritual we commune with the dead, directly and coherently. But in the background all manner of things…swirl. There is no word to truly describe what happens. It is not even truly in the background. You need a point of reference to understand."

She held him closer, her lips caressing his brow, a contact that gave electricity. His eyesight tunnelled, darkness central, brightness all around, and he was falling, falling into a depth of blackness that knew no light.

He felt himself touched, and he was speaking to her, yet not speaking, and all around the darkness boiled and broiled and rolled and roiled. He was touched again and again, although nothing came through. *She* protected him, and he understood, although a description of those touches eluded him, certainly in any way that allowed elucidation in any satisfactory manner.

There were caresses and thuds of contact, not necessarily pleasant or disturbing in either case. There was a singing that attempted to inveigle its way in to his mind through his subconscious, but Amara – he presumed it was her, it felt like her – merely wafted it away in a breeze of psyche. She was so comfortable here, and like her arms around him, he felt safe, once again that child protected by a parent. Nothing could hurt him.

So he reached out and pain stabbed in him. He wasn't here, but his body seemed to hurt, all of his appendages seemed to quicken at the sensation, almost like a shot of adrenaline thrust around the body at the moment of fight or flight. But no limbs were here. Only a mind, and he realised that the pain had been caused by her, by Amara.

Apparently, he'd had his bottom spanked, and he could feel her amusement as he thought this.

He was shocked – *she could read his thoughts*. Logically he should know this, but where the hell had logic gone? Certainly not into this Vodun dreamscape.

Maybe she could read all of his mind, his deepest thoughts, his greatest sins, see even deeper than those eyes that had so held him.

There was humour in the darkness, and perhaps a lightning of the gloom. *She* caressed him this time, a touch that said *Fear not, naughty child*

He laughed in spite of the fear and with it he relaxed. As he did so, the space became lighter. It seemed grey with swirls of white and black with the occasional stab of red or yellow or blue or green, small pinpricks that hurt his eyes. Nothing touched him however, he floated in a bubble that was almost tangible, something manufactured by Amara. She was giving him a glimpse of the ritual, nothing more, a nursery rhyme of the authentic rather than the gritty reality, and for that he felt grateful.

He could discern shadows that were vast and dark. These tugged at his innards, they enveloped him in a sense of misery and despair, sometimes of such malevolence that, unshielded, it would have torn him apart, whipping him across this nothingness like grains of sand on a sea breeze.

Only it wasn't nothingness, it was somethingness.

And as well as the shadows, there was the white, or so close as to it as makes no difference. This pierced him, trying to fold him inwards into his own unworthiness to exist, a haughty superiority equally as lethal as the darkness. It would doubling him up again and again, leaving him…nothing. As if he had never been. As if he deserved never to have been, so lowly was his existence, less useful than a worm in the ground.

But always the white and the black were overtaken by the grey.

This is what exists in everyone. A greyness. And in that, he felt better about himself, because it let him recognise the darkness within himself, let him accept it and then be thankful that he rarely acted upon it.

Maybe that was humanity.

The darkness reappeared in the centre of his vision and for one moment Hope panicked wondering what on earth it could be, but then he saw that he was being sucked out of that tunnel, whatever it may be, light blooming around his vision until the black appeared nothing more than a pinprick.. He was drenched in sweat, Amara's lips still just touching his forehead... and then it went altogether, and with it the last vestiges of all sensation completely removed.

"There, you have a point of reference." Her voice sounded husky, full of emotion. For what, William did not know.

"I do. But what does any of it mean?"

"It's a reflection of life. It gives you some equanimity when things...." She searched for the right and finding none she could only manage "...happen."

She smiled. "You can see very well what we are made of, what you saw is effectively that. It's what makes us all, and sometimes the white is as bad as the black, sometimes more terrible, so very judgmental. I've yet to see any goodness In the black, though. I think that it is what Rune is made of, or at the very least, he is an aspect of it."

"What of the colours?"

"They are the living. All of the grey is death. The pinpricks are those that are passing through, those like us."

"So we would have also appeared as colour?"

"Yes."

A long pause ensued whilst both gathered their thoughts and brought their emotions back into check.

"I presume then, that your talent is the reason for Rune's interest," said William at last

"I can see no other reason, William. I have shown you what I was, once upon a time. I gave that power up, that sovereignty over the dead, and with it that influence over the living. It is more than just being respected, the living would probably end their lives if I had demanded it of them. The responsibility was just too great. I left from fear, not the love of my husband, as great as that became. I ran away, scared of myself."

She looked exceedingly pale as she spoke. William guessed that this had been the first ever admission of her reason for fleeing her Vodunsii.

"What does he need you for?"

"I don't know for sure, but given what happened in Rome, when he touched my mind," she paused and shuddered at the recollection, "I guess that he means to milk my talent. His is an immature and unnatural talent."

She stumbled, unsure of herself. William pressed on.

"What happens if he takes you?"

"It could be the birth of something never before seen by a white man."

There was a long silence before a sly smile crossed Amara's face. "The Frenchwoman. Is she very beautiful?"

William blushed. Amara laughed.

CHAPTER 18 – LUCAS FULL CIRCLE

Lucas had decided to walk. It seemed right, somehow. Running was taking him home too quickly.

Since his contact with …well…whatever it, or rather, she was, the land around him had become real, three dimensional even. He no longer felt like a character in an oil painting, he now felt that he belonged to a part of a living world, one that he recognised, one that he almost felt he belonged in.

Almost.

He plodded on and on and on, occasionally attempting to speak to people who appeared like ghosts and always ignored him utterly. Sometimes he saw figures that weren't ghosts, but they couldn't, or wouldn't, see him either. Very occasionally, he would see a being that was brighter than the sun itself, infinitely more painful to look upon and if they saw him, they in no way acknowledged him.

At no point did Lucas become upset or dispirited. He had Mudasir, and the beacon beyond the horizon was everything. If the truth be told, any attempt at interaction with any of the others was pure mischievousness on his behalf. He had always been a cheeky monkey, at least that's what his had mother told him. He wondered if she still lived, perhaps occasionally remembering that she'd had a son. He ought to feel sad himself, remembering his mother, his father, his brothers and his sisters, but he could not summon the enthusiasm. He felt happily grey.

Lucas passed through villages where the buildings were bright and vibrant, whilst the numerous inhabitants were grey and dull. He passed through cities with thousands of drab and insignificant beings, whilst the market places they haggled in were ruddy and vibrant and azure. Graveyards contained spirits that had more colour than the grey priests that tended them, and the graveside flowers positively burned the backs of his eyes with life.

He stopped often, usually at a place where the colour effervesced and overflowed in its excitement. He could sit for days basking in the glow. Mudasir would come alive, and even following the setting of the sun, the colours pulsed and sparkled, and he and the dog would play or lie down together, feeling at peace as they soaked in the blazing glory.

Sometimes the mists would come, and these he avoided. Even from the outside, he could see that they were wrong. He shuddered at the memory of the fog on the lake, the corrosive burn, and yet he bore no recollection of what he had seen.

He continued to travel north with a small amount of west. He never conversed with a person, and he never heard a word spoken in return, he never heard a word of any sort spoken, but he knew that he passed through Italy and eventually in to France. Wellesley had fought, run and chased throughout these lands, from the English Channel to the Mediterranean to the Atlantic Ocean. And it was whilst fighting a retreating defence that he, Lucas, had been killed, somewhere on the outskirts of Rome, his physical body now lying in its catacombs. Now, however, he approached a northern star, its light was bright, its light was beautiful.

As he moved closer, it burned ever brighter in its intensity, a blazing star, an equatorial dawn, and he was drawn ever towards it.

When he arrived its brightness increased, achingly so, both with beauty and with pain if he concentrated for too long. And then suddenly it became more bearable, as if he stood within its sphere of luminance. It was Paris and he'd always dreamed of arriving here at the head of a column of troops, even if only in the centre of the column, unable to see anything, merely as a rank and file soldier, just to be in the midst of a conquering force, the defeat of the Tyrant celebrated even by the French themselves.

He stared about himself in wonder. The city lived, it shone and glowed, it was incandescent, but Lucas barely saw and certainly did not register the grey people, any of them, the rags and the emaciation, the languor and privation, the sullenness and anger.

All Lucas had eyes for was the splendour and the burning hub that fired the gossamer web of light that had once so blinded him. The hub was warm and comforting.

It appeared as his journeys end.

And when he arrived, he greeted friends, for it was.

*

Amara was led to the chamber in the basement. The cold chair sat expectantly, its chill beckoning. The chambers hissed and the stench of adulterated steam pervaded throughout. The buzz of electricity was still a most alien sound to her, a million bees buzzing in torment struggling to escape, and more, it had a physical presence, it throbbed and thrummed at her flesh, which crawled at its touch.

Rimbaud sat her down, his puppy-dog eyes pleading for forgiveness whilst gleaming with the immense pleasure at his successful research which now had meaning. He implored her that this was only transitional, and that once their work (yes, he'd said "*their* work"!) was done, he would make it all better.

It made her angry and sad. How could he think he could make it better? She'd spent months with him and he was basically *nice*. He wasn't angry or brutal. He didn't do this to force the conclusion, merely to find what the conclusion could be. He wasn't evil, he was naïve and slightly insane.

She almost liked him, certainly pitied him, barring the fact that if he hadn't been so brilliant – and insane – she wouldn't be sat here in this chair.

He pampered her, he'd bought her a plush cushion to remove her discomfiture, Earl Grey, scones and jam awaited her arrival. A further multitude of apologies, doe-eyes and more apologies still, followed that arrival. He loved her and she, in her pride and humanity, pitied him. But in her pride she also hated him and recognised him for the tool that he was. If she could only use him as that tool. There could be no other way out of this dungeon, nothing that she had been able to plan and William, when they had both been there, had not managed anything realistic either, although she had seen him watching and listening intently whenever they were outside of their cell.

She sat her posterior upon the cushion, and Rimbaud connected her iron crown to the bees that hummed around the room. Steam hissed and washed around their feet, a cloud upon which they seemed to float.

Sometimes her sessions lasted hours, taking only a single soul through the wires before being imprinted upon the carbon black. Sometimes, she would take many in a matter of minutes. It was all about her, and she was never fully in control.

That was then, when they had the luxury of time, but now she knew of Brocklehurst's desperation. More technologies were introduced daily to increase the number of souls she could collect. Everyday she pulled in dozens. She had stopped being able to remember the individuals, their sins and hates, their kindnesses and loves.

This time, however, it was different. She knew him.

She resisted.

Lucas, run you fool, run

Lady, I love you, your light shines eternal

Damn you, boy, run! Not all is at it seems, it's a trap. RUN!

He walked towards her, ignoring her words. His trusted her implicitly because Amara had no malice towards him, but he could not see that the trap was not of her making. There was nothing to *see*. He smiled as he approached her. He came willingly and she pushed him back, but the tug was inexorable, he pulled her back in turn, arms spread trying to embrace her, and he kept coming forward. She pushed back again, screaming incoherently at the boy. He ignored it all. He came on, and next... and next he had become one of *les Futile*.

CHAPTER 19 – WITHDRAWAL SYMPTOMS

William and Amara were often separated for days at a time, occasionally left to their own devices in separate cells, and once they had spent three entire days with nothing to do but talk.

Sometimes they were led down to the cellar together, where Amara would be shackled to her chair and William would photograph these sessions using his specially prepared photographic media. His prints were vastly superior to those taken by Brocklehurst's scientists. All throughout, they were both aware of each other's roles, although William's was minor in comparison.

Whilst he was unable to capture any captured spirits in the chamber although there were numerous occasions of a faint glow around Amara's head when the complex equipment that surrounded her would clunk and whirr, valves would glow with a mechanical hiss and pop. Other things appeared on his exposures, although what they were, William could not tell. They appeared as faint smudges or blurs of motion and contained an intangible, tip of the tongue, *something* about them.

To say that the process was painful to Amara would have been an understatement. The electrodes caused a great deal of pain, but this was nothing to the emotional pain.

"I know them all," she wept one evening in the cell. "Their hopes, their fears, their wives, husbands and children. Their petty crimes. Their heinous crimes. But worse than that, they are all so forlorn, so helpless, so lost. Frightened. Futile."

"Then stop," William said simply.

"I can't," she responded. "Once attached to that machine I cannot stop. And I cannot escape, I tried that once."

She described the incident where she'd escaped from the hotel.

"Let's try something different then," said William. "It may be painful though."

He explained what he wanted to try.

"It may kill me," she said.

"You've got nothing to lose, you may already be dead, and there's no other way to get out if you are alive."

She stared into his eyes for long moments before closing her own and setting her face firmly. "Do it," she said.

William moved across to her and tested an electrode. It was only attached via the iron crown, and he began the intricate process of removing the fixing that held it in place. After a few moments he removed it and ever so slowly started to withdraw the copper electrode that pierced her skull.

The second it was moved, Amara shuddered and then fell away from Hope, fully dragging the electrode free. She immediately went in to convulsions, screaming an unholy scream. At the same time a klaxon sounded in the corridor outside, followed by the sound of heavy feet. A rustle at the door, the click of a key and it was suddenly thrown wide open. Three scientists entered the room immediately followed by Rune.

The scientists snatched the electrode from a pallid, motionless William and started to carry the black girl out of the room even as she continued to shudder and convulse. Rune moved forward, however and William didn't see the fist that impacted his midriff and threw him across the cell with a cracking of ribs. He only had eyes, until that moment, for the girl, who was now seized in a rictus of spasm, the piercing shrieks ceaseless.

That night William barely slept, the pain of his beating from the unnaturally strong Rune keeping him awake. He was in despair, also. He didn't know if Amara lived, and their cause seemed helpless.

*

Early one morning, several weeks later, William was struggling awake, still suffering from lack of sleep due to his broken ribs, when one of Brocklehurst's scientists entered the cell bearing a white envelope.

"May I discuss these, Sir William?" He simply bounced up and down with excitement, and curiosity piqued, William assented. Besides, he had nothing better to do, he was bored having spent very little time out of his cell since the electrode incident and only recently had he been allowed to see Amara again.

"Oh," said William, his eyebrows raised high, mouth in an astounded 'O'.

The envelope contained William's photographs, those that he had presumed lost when press-ganged by Duval's crew. They were dog eared and water stained, but the results were still fairly clear.

As the scientist engaged William in discussion, he showed a suspicious amount of knowledge, and more, discussed them with a measure of glee that bordered on the insane. They discussed unlikely and downright absurd theories on why the particular chemical blends should so apparently capture the spirits of the dead. Hope became more reticent and introverted as the conversation moved on.

They strayed in to Brocklehurst territory.

"What I don't understand, is why Brocklehurst needed to move premises and in the manner that he did. Why such butchery?"

"Well," said the scientist, who, in his only lack of etiquette, had so far failed to introduce himself. "Most of the engineers up there were staunchly patriotic and those heathen druids were starting to get very sniffy about the so-called desecration of the dead. Anyway, I don't believe that there were enough souls for our requirements."

"But why the cold blooded murder?"

"And leave traces, evidence of what exactly we were up to?"

A sudden thought came to William. "I don't recall seeing you during my convalescence, I must say."

"No Sir William, you didn't. You see, my name is Wilhelm Stieber, and I'm the second-in-command of this project. My master directs all of course, but only in the broadest sense. I have an eye for detail, you see, those you see here, and those that you most certainly don't."

William paled, but it was coupled with high red spots on his cheeks. He struggled to maintain his emotions and so he digressed to cover his temper and fear. "Your knowledge of my techniques is thorough, Herr Stieber, for your being one of the most feared men in Europe. I thought you would have minions to perform such tasks."

"I like to have a hands-on approach, I always have. I had to admonish Brocklehurst for his actions against you in Cheshire. I would rather make sure that all use was made of a person before disposing of them."

"Rumour has it that you're a butcher, Herr Stieber," said William with a studied lack of expression, the high red spots on his cheeks continuing to bloom.

"Only when necessary," replied Stieber, with a faint smile. "I much prefer fear, it's a far more potent weapon. But then, I suppose a few deaths are necessary to earn that fear. It allows me to make use of people while they are alive, you see."

The final point was directed most pointedly at William.

He had nothing to say in return. What could be said to Wilhelm Stieber, the most feared and notorious man in all of Europe?

Stieber continued. "Take Chapman, for example. I requested that he visit me, and knowing what I know of him – for example, that he's the East End murderer called Jack – he positively threw himself in to the task set before him." He smiled to himself in self-pleasure.

"Actually, as Rune he is rather useful and entirely faithful, although I do not know why. If he'd remained as Mr Chapman, I would have tired of him long ago because Brocklehurst has mastered the craft I required of him. I may even let Rune have the girl eventually. He is so desirous of that."

Finally, William *did* have a response for Stieber, the worst insult he knew to a German.

"Your mother was a sow," and with that he turned away, disgust overriding both fear and anger.

Chuckling, Stieber left the room.

*

William was alone in the chemistry laboratory. He'd been there regularly over the past few weeks of his captivity, manufacturing and developing his photographic plates. He'd never shown any ideas of escape, but his mind was a foment of ideas, each one as rapidly dismissed as it arrived. *If only Rune would bugger off*, William thought, *I may stand a chance, but the bastard is always lurking*. The factory was like a gaol, no way in, no way out, unless permitted. *I need time to get out and away, which just isn't an available option with Rune on the loose. Why doesn't he just bugger off? Why didn't I bring Bob on the scouting mission? If I'd had her, I'd have been out in a jiffy. Hell, I'd never have been here in the first place*. These latter thoughts were an oft-repeated one. Bob was still based in the stables back at the inn, smouldering gently behind her kneecaps. Subconsciously, he was quite enjoying the challenge of hatching an escape plan, it was like being set free with nothing in the way of responsibilities – but the lack of any viable plan frustrated William in the extreme and his mind whirled at the potential for innovation with the use of the tools at hand.

There was a murmur outside of the laboratory, and William, ducking underneath the small window, opened the door a tiny touch.

There was an air of relief about the place, and from the way they were whispering, Rune and Brocklehurst would actually be away for several days. A number of additional armed guards had been brought in, but compared with the monstrosity that was Rune, this could well be his best chance of escape. He had to try and get the girl out too. She was key to their plans. Anything to thwart the bastards.

He re-closed the door properly and ducked back to his chemical bench. He looked around. He needed an impromptu decoy. He smiled. He had a plan. He was innovating.

*

Rapidly, he completed a number of photographic plates, and left another few unfinished, so that he should have something approaching a reasonable excuse for being there should someone enquire as to the inordinate amount of time he was spending in the laboratory. He took some blank photographic paper and spilt some chemicals on these to add weight to it.

He looked around more closely. There were some thin sheets of magnesium, five inches wide and ten inches long. He shaped these into small hollow balls with a large hole at one end, and caked the inside with white phosphorus. It was stored in water to prevent spontaneous combustion, and William prayed that it would remain moist enough for his requirements. He hid the balls in a box in the laboratory.

He took a large jar of red phosphorus powder, and inserted several metres of string, placing the jar back on the shelf.

William then took hold of a bottle, uncorked it, winced in anticipation and then poured a small amount of the sulphuric acid on his hand. It burned, going from a prickly nettle-sting sensation to a nasty bee sting. He hurried from the laboratory, out to the busy engineers in the workshop.

"I'm awfully sorry, but I've spilt some of the sulphuric acid on myself, would you mind if I treat it in the medical room? I'll give it a wipe and then treat it with some of that marvellous petroleum spirit – it's meant to be wonderful for treating burns."

The engineer didn't appear to care a jot, he just peered interestedly at the reddening blisters forming on Hope's hand, and grunted, which William took as assent.

He went across to a smallish office in the corner of the topmost floor and went inside, closing the door behind him. There was a large cabinet, a narrow bed, and a tiny desk and chair. It was the large cabinet that he needed. He raided it for some cloths that he used for wiping off the sulphuric acid. He then smeared the burn with petroleum spirit and receiving instant relief, he smiled with pleasure. There were several small jars of the jelly-like material, and he hid these about his person before returning back to the chemical laboratory, with a nod of thanks to the surly engineer.

This time, he barricaded the door with the simple expedient of a tilted chair leaned underneath the door handle. As crude and amateurish as his chemistry.

He took the magnesium balls from their hiding spot, praying that this experiment would work. He inserted as much petroleum jelly as he could into each ball, leaving a hole to the top of the ball. In to this hole, he sprinkled red phosphorus powder to the top, before inserting a length of string into each and crudely closing the soft metal around the string to hold it in place. He didn't want the ball to be fully enclosed; it wasn't designed as an explosive. Strategically placed – for example, attached to the lubricant containers used by the maintenance urchins – they should give him the diversion he needed, and the means of escape for himself and Amara from the prison. He had a dozen of the small balls. He secreted them about his person, taking care not to displace the phosphorus-infused fuses.

A guard watched him exit the laboratory and eyed him suspiciously, for all that he was one of the better mannered guards about the place. He was one of only two English guards. William smiled at him, shaking imperceptibly in his boots.

The guard marched over, preceded by his Neanderthal brow. "You done? I got me orders to get you back in that cell of yours, when you're done. That bastard will 'ave me guts for garters if you've been allowed to try owt."

William smiled weakly, "My head hurts, I'm taking a turn before I go back and finish. I'm afraid I may be late tonight, as I spilled chemicals on some of the plates. They are rather ruined."

The guard eyed him even more suspiciously and poked his head in to the laboratory. He could see the spoiled plates and nothing more, as William had taken great care to hide any other mess that he had made during his incendiary device manufacture.

"Well, I'm on all night, so s'ppose it makes no difference ter me."

William lingered for the remainder of the afternoon, taking regular breaks, whilst complaining of his hand and citing Rune as his excuse for having to complete his work. The guards were clearly terrified of the beast, and so held their collective peace. Hope burned inside and he had to force himself to breathe deeply to stop his excitement bringing and eager gleam to his eyes.

On a whim, William returned to the medical room and stole the bottle of chloroform that he'd seen there, along with some swabbing cloth. An alteration to his plan was forming. Whilst the lad was clearly misguided, there was no malice in him and he'd always treated both William and Amara with respect. Sometimes he even betrayed a sense of pity, unlike some of the other guards that were around the factory. It stood to reason that the lad had a key to his cell, and well, needs must. He needed to get Amara out.

By early evening, the upper floor was deserted. It was Saturday, so the majority of the staff would be in the leisure room playing chess, gambling at cards, or merely drinking and gazing in to nothing. One of the incendiary devices would be needed for each of the entrances to the common rooms.

William was starting to get feverishly excited: his plan could bloody well work! With an effort, he calmed himself. He didn't want to give himself away, he could already feel his face flush with excitement, but he needed to leave it longer. "Patience!" he said to himself. As many of the staff as possible would need to be in the common room, and the more intoxicated the better.

Then, a horror hit him. There was a thick sinking in his stomach, and he felt nauseous. He'd not considered it at all. Amara couldn't leave the old mill, or she'd be struck down with convulsions and prone-ness once she was out of range of that blasted device of Brocklehurst's which had so affected her on her previous escape attempt. Damn and blast!

He took another stroll out of the laboratory. The entire floor was now completely deserted, with even the guard having disappeared for the time being. He hurried over to Brocklehurst's office and almost laughed out loud. It was so easy! Brocklehurst really was a careless, arrogant, arse of the highest order. There it was! Sat on one of his shelves, a small red light blinking on its face. He tried the door handle, and found that the office wasn't even locked. The cretinous imbecile!

He ran in to the room, took the wooden box and ran out again. A bag – he needed a bag to put it in, but he didn't have one, and he'd not seen one. He constructed a hasty web sack out of some of the bandages that he'd stolen, placing the box in that.

It was time. It was now or never.

*

"Hey, Wilson, I've finished," he shouted from the laboratory. There was no reply. "Wilson!" he shouted louder.

There was the tread of feet, and Wilson came in to the laboratory, still adjusting his waistband and cast his eyes about for any signs of mischief. "Call of nature. Time to get back to the clink?"

"Yes, I think so."

Wilson turned his back to exit the room, but as soon as he did, Hope jumped on his back, forearm around the guards throat and the other hand, gripping the chloroform-soaked cloth, over his face.

It didn't take long to subdue the young man. He was a bit fleshy and had absolutely no unarmed combat training. Against Hope's wiry strength, he didn't stand a chance, especially with the element of surprise. Wilson slumped to the floor unconscious, but William continued to hold the cloth over his face for another minute before removing it. He needed to make sure he had plenty of time to perform the rest of his dirty deeds. There was a single room without windows, a storeroom, which was also lockable, so he dragged the weighty body across the floor to the storeroom, tied Wilson up and then gagged him and took his revolver and keys before locking him in.

He sneaked out of the top floor on to the staircase. There were a number of other guards, more than usual in Rune's absence, so he needed to be quiet and, more importantly, lucky until he was ready for the hullaballoo to start. He got down to the ground floor, where, as well as the warehouse area, there was also the large gaol area where he and Amara were stored. William wondered how many people Brocklehurst thought to capture, and for what reason. He unlocked the large iron door that led into the cells. It was well lit and whitewashed, almost clinical in appearance.

The cell that he and Amara usually shared lay at the very end of a passage that ran a length of almost a hundred paces. All of the cells, both left and right, were empty. Some were barely bigger than the bed that they contained. Some did not contain a bed at all. Theirs was spacious and large by comparison, but with no home comforts. Not for the first time, William wondered on the propriety of his sharing a cell with a woman, and Brocklehurst's reasoning for it. He hadn't mentioned it to the girl, but he didn't trust the innovator, nor especially his puppet master.

Reaching his cell, he unlocked it quietly. Amara was inside, eyeing the door with wilful spite in her eyes. The expression changed to one of amazement, but before she could speak, he hushed her and rapidly explained his plan to her.

"Oh William, I can't go anywhere with these in my head," she shrieked, obviously distraught at having the possibility of freedom so harshly taken away.

"Worry not! And keep your bloody voice down!"

She looked ready to react again, but he gestured at the makeshift sling he had over his shoulders and around his back. Strapped there was Brocklehurst's controlling contraption. He concealed it by putting on his jacket.

"Brocklehurst! He's such an arrogant bastard that he's actually gone off for a couple of days, and he's just left this in his office, with his office unlocked!"

"I don't trust that man. He could be up to something," said Amara.

"What have we got to lose?"

"Do you remember what happened last time?" she enquired. "I almost died."

"As did I! Amara, do you want to stay here?"

"Idiot!" she laughed. It was the first time he'd heard her laugh. It was like the cheery babble of water flowing down a small brook, beautiful, full of life and energy as it tinkled throughout the cell. The hairs on the back of his neck stood on end and he gazed at the girl in front of him. She appeared not to notice and, still laughing at him, pulled his arm towards the cell door.

At that moment it opened and a pair of guards appeared, investigating the reason for the open door at the other end. They were not expecting trouble.

William and Amara reacted instantly: a quick glance at each other and they leapt forward to attack the surprised guards. Neither William nor the guards had time to draw their weapons. It was a fist fight.

Or, in Amara's case, a talon fight. With absolute viciousness, she jumped on the man, wrapping her legs around his waist and with her left hand grabbed a handful of hair to help haul herself aboard, knocking his hat off in the process. With her other hand, she gouged his face, long red welts opening up. Having found full purchase on the man, her right arm then went behind his head also, grabbing another handful of hair.

He screamed in pain.

She yanked his head backwards, and using his own resistance, heaved it forwards again, her forehead smashing the bridge of his nose. He went down, and she sprang lithely to one side before hammering a right foot in to the side of his jaw. She watched his lights go out as his head bounced on to the white floor.

William had made even quicker work with his pugilist training. He jabbed a couple of rapid left handers in to the guard's gormless face, stinging him awake somewhat, without doing any real damage. Then the fool tried to rush forward and William met him with a massive uppercut that floored the man immediately.

Amara turned to find William watching her after delivering her final blow.

"You fight well!" he laughed. "A proper little harpie."

Amara merely spat on the unconscious man.

They dusted themselves down, tied and gagged the unconscious pair and then left the cell, taking care to lock the door behind them. William also snapped the key off in their cell door, before locking the main door to the cell corridor. They hurried to the warehouse doors.

There were very large double doors that allowed carts in to unload. It was even large enough to allow some of the some of the new motorised wagons that were starting to appear in Paris. However, only the small portal within one of these large doors, which allowed people in and out, interested William. It was made of iron, with the frame and hinges made of the same.

"How on earth are we going to break that down?" Amara asked incredulously, a deep flush entering her flawless cheeks.

"Wait and see," said William, who mentally crossed his fingers in hope.

He struggled for a good few minutes with four of the round incendiary devices. He prayed that the phosphorus was too damp to go up in flames right away, taking him with it, but not so damp that it wouldn't light at all. The malleability of the magnesium eventually allowed him to distort the devices sufficiently, with some pinching and creasing, into the sizeable gaps between door and door frame. He placed the devices on either side of the two rustic hinges that held the doors in place. He then passed the fuse wire over to Amara, with strict instructions not to pull on them, as that would tear the fuse free. They agreed on a safe position behind some large crates that they could both hide behind once the fun began.

William then bounced up the small set of stairs that led to the rear exit of the second floor. This door was metal also and had no lock on it, so William jammed a device in between the door frame and the handle. Amara had joined him, and again, she trailed this longer piece of fuse down the stairs, whilst William ran ahead to the main second floor entrance. He approached cautiously, aware that there may be a larger number of people within hearing. He could hear a good natured card game being played, and a small piano being thumped very badly indeed. It sounded as if they were all enjoying themselves, aided by some good liquor. They were not due back in to work until midday the following day, so most would partake of a good quantity, and this William hoped, could be the difference between success and failure.

The door was wooden, again with no lock. He cursed, and swept past to the top floor, from where he swiped some of the engineer's tools, and sneaking back downstairs again, he jimmied the door shut. He hoped it would be sufficient. He attached another couple of devices, and trailed the fuse down after him. Its length only took it to the landing below.

Running full tilt downstairs, he nodded to Amara, who was beginning to look concerned at his prolonged absence. She grabbed the fuses for the warehouse door, and lighting a home-made lucifer without any fanfare, simply set them alight. Lurid red flames danced extremely rapidly along the phosphorus-impregnated string far more swiftly than William had anticipated. With a yelp, he ran to the fuse that led up the main stairwell, and quickly lit it, before sprinting as fast as he could, weighted down with Amara's contraption and two pistols, to the back stairwell.

When he returned to Amara, she was mutely watching…nothing. He could see nothing more than a wisp of smoke rising from the device to indicate some sort of activity. Absolutely nothing more. She glanced at William rather forlornly. Suddenly, from the stairwell, there came a monstrous hiss, followed by a 'whoooosh' and a blinding light. This was followed almost immediately by four seemingly spontaneous eruptions from those at the warehouse portal. They both had to turn away from the unbearable blue-whiteness of the burning magnesium.

It was now too loud to hear if anything was happening, and the shadows cast by such a bright light were stark and eerie. They were so deep, nothing could be seen in their darkness.

"I hope to God this works, Amara. That mixture should burn hot enough to melt the hinges and just allow us to walk right out."

Shielding his eyes, he ran to the portal. The heat was fierce, but thankfully discreetly placed, so that he could approach closely. He choked and retched on the fumes, which were foul and irritating in the extreme, and he had to move away a small distance. Amara stood at his side, one arm lay on his, the other shielding her eyes. William looked behind, back in to the building, but could see nothing untoward.

He heard an audible splutter, and, again, almost simultaneously, the four devices went out. Their departure left them in pitch darkness, light blinded by the ferocity of the magnesium light.

"Damn it," William swore, whilst he heard Amara mutter something in a foreign language. He covered his nose and mouth with his sleeve, shook off Amara's arm, and ran at the portal, kicking at it with all of his might. He couldn't allow it a further second to cool down. To his surprise the hinges broke, brittle with the heat. The door pivoted on the locked side, before the portal swung outward and fell to the ground with a large, heavy thump on to the walkway outside.

Amara gave a very female shriek like those he was used to hearing from his sisters and he turned around to see her outline sprinting towards him, an immense smile on her face. She leapt on him. For a moment he felt fear as her legs wrapped around his waist, but this was in pure excitement, as she also wrapped her arms around his neck, and buried her head in to his neck, before sobbing loudly and hysterically.

Cursing good-naturedly, and with an extraordinarily beautiful and somewhat grotesque black girl clinging to him, he turned for the streets of Paris.

The slap of a gun bullet hitting the door frame by his head brought him back from the moment.

Another struck the ground at his feet. There was the ratcheting of gun bolts sliding as the next rounds were slotted into breeches. William could see two of the French guards, older men, standing tall. They were side on to William and Amara in classic infantry poses. They were clearly more experienced than Wilson, even if their gunmanship was woeful. They were probably more used to muskets where aiming was almost pointless.

Without even dropping the girl, William raised the pistol he had taken from Wilson. It was rifled, and he was used to firing rifled weapons. He took aim as another round crashed from a rifle. It whined in to the darkness beyond the doorway, causing William to flinch.

He took stock, re-aimed at the guard who still struggled to engage the next round in to the breech, and fired. Blood bloomed from the man's neck and he collapsed, twitching.

William shifted his aim by a few degrees. The revolving pistol meant that he had no need to reload. A look of fear crossed the man's brow, he knew he was too late, much too slow, but he still managed to fire before William. The shot went badly astray, he'd squeezed his trigger far too soon and William saw the round spark from the cobbles twelve feet from the gun that fired it. William squeezed and watched the centre of his face dissolve.

Without waiting to see him collapse, William turned and began to jog gently.

William was not in any real shape to do this. If he hadn't been poorly fed for the last weeks, poorly exercised for longer, and wasn't still recovering from the severe burns he'd received, he may have had the stamina to get further. One thing that hadn't been removed from him was his personal strength of will and an iron determination.

He managed about fifteen minutes of the steady run, the entire time Amara sobbing helplessly in to his collar.

Amara stopped her hysterics as William drew to a ragged halt, panting gently, his thighs and calves burning, and his lungs on fire. She looked at him with those impossibly large eyes of hers, and he felt himself falling in to them, falling, falling, the legs and lungs entirely forgotten. *My God*, he thought, *but this girl is beautiful*.

She brought the moment to a stop by unwrapping herself from him. She turned to stare in the direction of the old mill, but there was no sign of a larger conflagration, much to her disappointment, only a strange white smoke that was clearly not dense enough to be anything serious.

"I wanted the whole place to go up!" she exclaimed.

"I had to think about us first, Amara, and some of the people in there are innocent of crime."

"Not to me they're not," she said viciously, swinging round to face him. "Where are we going?" Her eyes had gone cold and glassy.

William looked around. They were in a more populated area of town now, still close to the Seine, and not far away from some of the more popular riverbank café's. They were still open at this late hour, nearly eleven, because Paris never really slept. And their surroundings were well lit.

William turned back to Amara, looked her over and said "Shit."

"What?" she said rather defensively.

"You've got a rather interesting head, girl."

"Well, what are you going to do about it? And don't call me girl." She was evidently quite a feisty one.

He looked around some more, and up a narrow lane, he noticed clothing hanging from the lines that stretched between the two sides of the street. The clothing wasn't pretty or fashionable, but it would have to do. Unfortunately, it was also a storey up.

"Stand under that tree, in the shadows," he ordered Amara, pointing at a large, and rather lonesome, oak tree.

William, also keeping to the shadows, climbed on to a window ledge and then hoisted himself up on to the lintel above the window. It was somewhat precarious, but a shawl hung almost within reach. Almost, but not quite.

"Sod it," he said to himself, and jumped. He grasped the shawl and landed a second later, sprawling on to the cobbles below. He ended up on his back, and a low crunching noise came from the wooden box. He had completely forgotten about it!

He spun around, peering in to the shadows of the tree, and he could see her outline in the gloom underneath. She hadn't reacted, it must still be working.

Hurrying over to Amara, he draped the shawl over her head, so that it also acted as a veil. She complained of the smell. If he could get away with no-one noticing her skin colour either, that would be ideal. Negroes weren't especially rare on the streets of Paris, but there were still few enough to occasionally turn heads.

They strolled casually away, trying to make it seem as if they were out for a romantic evening stroll. William's destination was the little inn.

An itch at the back of his mind – Amara related, no doubt, if he'd had the courage to admit it to himself – made him sneak in to the stables, retrieve Bob and then leave without saying a word to his red-headed lover inside.

Coward, he said to himself. And then: *This is becoming a habit*. Was talking to oneself to this degree entirely normal?

CHAPTER 20 – ACHILLE RICHARD

William had friends in Paris. One of them was an eminent natural philosopher named Achille, a former plant collecting mentor of William's who lived on the northern outskirts of the city. He left Amara and Bob in a nearby graveyard whilst he visited his aging friend. He had no wish to give the man a heart attack by turning up with both Amara and Bob.

Achille had taken William on his first plant hunting voyage some eighteen months after rescuing his sisters. It became the prelude to William's acceptance into the Royal Society. During that eighteen months of recuperation he had taken on the schooling and, frankly, healing of his sisters. He'd also studied hard about the things that he'd seen on his travels, and he read with growing awe and wonder about the flora and fauna that he had seen but never had the opportunity to study. Much of the fauna was well documented, but flora fascinated William more than anything else, and he realised that there were a vast number of species still to be discovered. The break had done more. It had allowed him to rediscover an itch for travel, and learn things that couldn't be gained merely from the study of a good book.

He'd cultivated many contacts whilst becoming embroiled in the subject, and following a journey to the Himalayas, he had been accepted, along with a number of his papers, in to the Royal Society. William himself had discovered a number of significant species, and he'd made a study of the plants and their interactions with the species around them. Much of this had been guided by his friend, but the study and papers had been his own

– not forgetting Achille's peer reviews to help him along the way.

And, well, all told, this man was probably the reason that William was still alive. In William's eyes, Achille was a great man – no, make that a Great Man. Without his patronage, William would still have found himself abroad, but instead undertaking far less noble activities. Most likely this would have been the frequenting of brothels and inns, fighting his way across barbarian lands, until one day being skewered by a spear, or knifed over a game of cards. He'd given William a purpose at a time when he was most vulnerable, instilled a respect for indigenous peoples and furthered his awe at his surroundings. Even those surroundings at home now contained a multitude of fascinations and not just something to be ignored. Take his sisters, for example. Now in their twenties, they lived together, already confirmed spinsters (not that they could be blamed for that, of course) and they were rather wild and benevolent, by turn. They were more the former than the latter, if anything. Victorian England wasn't a particularly kind place, especially to its women, and with William's tutelage, they learned the things that he himself had learned; unarmed combat, armed combat, martial arts and more. By far his most difficult task, however, had been tending their compassion. When they had returned, they were all about revenge and damn anyone's eyes who said otherwise, they really didn't care about other peoples' opinions. But throughout all, William had developed a subconscious sympathy for some of the protagonists, and, more latterly, Amara had brought this out in to prominence during their long conversations. If it hadn't been for the abstract poverty of those conquered lands, the rape and pillage of the people and resources, there would have been no need for the rampant slavery, the murder, there wouldn't be a market that fed the repulsive desires of the paedophiles. And William passed this on, piece by piece, to his little sisters. They now only ever really exhorted to violence when there really was no alternative. Which in his eyes, was still a bit too frequent for his liking.

William knocked on his friend's front door. He didn't have a card to present and he felt rather naked without either that or his topper as the butler answered the door. It was past dawn, but not by much, and so it was still ridiculously early for his friend to be expected to accept visitors, especially as unkempt as William undoubtedly was.

The butler raised an eyebrow, a typically Gallic motion. "Oui, monsieur?"

William was well past speaking French, he really couldn't face pussyfooting around with required levels of social etiquette. He spoke in a harsh-toned voice.

"Tell Achille that Sir William Hope awaits his pleasure."

The butler had evidently heard of William, for he immediately ushered Hope in to the hallway, and thence in to the breakfast room, which was set and ready to receive the master.

The butler started to order the maid to set an additional place, but William stopped the man. "Coffee and toast." He paused and added," And a big bag of extra toast and another coffee also."

The butler took a second look at William, barked at the maid in her native tongue, and then hurried from the room.

Ten minutes later, William's friend arrived. He'd dressed in a hurry, but was still far more presentable than the scruffy man before him. To his eye, Achille had aged a lot in the intervening period since they had last met, a mere year ago. He *was* old, Hope realised, very old. He face contained an unnatural pallor and he had gone entirely bald. His stoop had become more accentuated and his prominent nose sprouted thick white hairs. His beard appeared thin and straggly. His flesh hung from his bones. His eyes were still a fresh, spring blue, though, and he was still a handsome man...just old. William didn't know how old exactly, but he did know that he had fought for Napoleon during the Peninsular Wars, having risen from a drummer boy to a *Garde Impériale.*

Achille had a look of distinct irritation; it seemed as though the butler hadn't entirely believed that he was who he said he was. It took the old man a few seconds to recognise William, but recognise him he did, once he'd seen through the paltry excuse for a moustache, the lack of coiffured hair and the remnants of scarring and burns. He looked and blinked at William and muttered indistinct expletives under his breath before he exploded.

"My bloody, dear, God, William. What in the bloody blue blazes are you doing here?!"

William's face registered surprise. This was not the welcome he had expected, nor was the use of language learned in the ranks of Napoleon's Imperial France.

"Get the hell out of my house, you imbecile." His English was perfect. "Where is the first place that you will be looked for?"

"What the...?"

"You've obviously escaped, are you entirely backwards? And you have come to the first, no sorry, second, place that they'd expect you to go!"

William had the decency to blush. He obviously wasn't thinking straight.

"I can't hide you here. There's a horse being readied. Get on it and bloody well bugger off. Write me a letter when you get home. A bloody good one." His blue eyes sparkled with a vigour that belied his physical appearance.

"It's not that simple, Achille," said William, shaking his head morosely. He really could be dense, he realised. Their great friendship was public knowledge.

"Yes it is! Get on the horse. Avaunt, skedaddle before anyone gets here, you moron." His English really was very good.

"I need a wagon."

Achille slapped his forehead hard. "How the hell are you going to get away in a bloody cart?" Colour flushed his cheeks in his growing irritation.

"I don't know, I was hoping for some constructive help, not justified abuse."

Achille relaxed a bit, and let out a bit of a chuckle. He smothered William in a hug that squeezed him short of breath with love, even though he could feel the old man's bones grate as he did so.

"Take care, old friend, I'm feeling slightly frail."

"By God, William, you look like death warmed up and you're as thin as a stick. You haven't got time to tell your story, so make that letter good, bloody good." He had always been one to repeat himself. He stalked up and down the breakfast room.

"You don't know the extent of my plight. You need to know before you can suggest something." Or rather, William thought to himself, *before you get me out of this bloody business*.

Achille raised a quizzical eyebrow.

"A quick stroll. Believe me it will be quicker and much more effective than mere words."

The Frenchman continued to appraise William, shrugged, and ordered his boots and largest overcoat. He required the overcoat to hide his morning clothes, as his attire was entirely inappropriate to be seen in public.

They walked side-by-side the half-mile to the old church. It was hundreds of years old and had clearly been repaired repeatedly over the years, although with a great deal of care to try and retain its spirit and character. This far outside of the centre of Paris, lichen clung to many of the older headstones. As William walked towards an ancient Yew tree in the centre of the graveyard, he realised that a shiny new cross may be required for his friend when he saw Bob.

He felt, rather than heard, Achille stop dead. William had been eying Bob for a few seconds, but his friend had only just spotted her.

"Jesus Christ," he said in flawless English, before hastily tracing the sign of the cross on himself. "What is that?"

"Who is she, I think you'll find," said William. "Her name is Bob, and she's dead, but I'd appreciate it if you didn't mention it."

Too late. William saw the colour of Bob's eyes change to a melancholic magenta. Her mechanical hearing must be far superior to that of a human. He cursed himself inwardly.

"Bob?" enquired Achille.

"Yes, I realise it's a male name. Her former master used her as a manservant and had to pretend she was a man, you see."

"Ahh! The misogynist Brocklehurst?" he added somewhat mischievously.

William looked at Achille, his mouth agape.

"As I said, I'm the second person they'll come to visit, after that ginger strumpet in town. He visited me here some weeks ago, but I don't think I entirely convinced him of our purely professional relationship."

"Unfortunately, that's not all."

The ground shook a little as Bob marched forth, and the Frenchman had only eyes for her at first. And then, like a wraith floating on mist, Amara glimmered forth from the shadows of the great tree. William was struck by her elegance, her straight back and perfect posture, with the veil shrouding her decorated skull to look like a crown-in-mourning. She looked like a Queen. He was mesmerised by her womanliness, even though he couldn't see her face.

Achille, on the other hand, presumed he looked upon Lady Death herself. This was death incarnate. She (for she was obviously female), would look in to his soul, find him wanting, and then reach in to his chest with a vaporous hand, to stop his heart with a squeeze.

He could feel his chest thumping unnaturally, a pounding through his ribcage and dark spots were forming in his vision.

She will be beautiful beneath the veil, he thought to himself. She radiated magnificence, but William broke the spell, relieving Achille from his trance. He felt his heartbeat slow and regulate itself

"Achille Richard, I have the honour of presenting Miss Amara...?" He realised he didn't know her surname.

"I am married, and you may call me Amara. That will suffice." She spoke aloofly.

Much to his own surprise William bowed rather formally. His friend was doing the same.

"Enchanteé, Madame," he said gravely.

"Now do you understand, Achille?"

"Yes, I do. Follow me." He had a determined look on his face, and he evidently knew exactly what to do.

He led them through to the opposite side of the graveyard, through a rusting, ill-used gate and then down a cobbled lane, straight to the blacksmiths. They left Bob and Amara in a shadowy corner, the now-bright sun casting stark shadows.

There was a large Shire horse and a derelict-looking gypsy caravan mouldering in the sidings of the yard.

Achille arranged it all.

CHAPTER 21 – A SPY IN THE CAMP

They greeted each other like old friends, which they were fast becoming since William's return from France. Both looked older and more careworn than they had a mere few weeks ago.

"I'm sorry I'm late, Hope," said Sir William Melville. "The London traffic this morning is horrendous. Some poor sod on a Boneshaker managed to smash himself into a gas lamp. The explosion was catastrophic, buildings have been toppled, and the heat is so great I think we'll be lucky to find even a brass button from the poor sap."

They were seated alone in the bar area of a large theatre, its high ceilings ornate and gilt in blue. There were roaring fires at either end, even though it was July unpleasantly warm outside. Somehow, the old building managed to stay cool whatever the weather outside – unless it was freezing outside, and then the theatre itself became an icehouse.

"You look slightly careworn, Lord Melville," said Hope.

"Bill, just call me Bill, man. And yes, there's trouble a-brewing, all the way from Cheshire to Corsica."

William raised an eyebrow. Melville really did look careworn, lacking so much as an expletive, or his usual ebullience and energy. He had large bags below his eyes and he even appeared to have lost some weight.

"Trouble?" he enquired.

"Yes, trouble. Big trouble. And the hell of it all is that we don't even know what the trouble is. Our network of spies seems to have contracted somewhat. Some have simply disappeared, others seem strangely mute."

A well-tailored man brought Melville a telegram. He put it to one side without reading it.

"Where's your usual servant, errrm, Bill?"

Every time they met, it started the same way. Melville insisted on a familiarity that astounded William from someone so far above his own social station. It wasn't something he was at all comfortable with.

"Gone. Vanished. Puff," he gesticulated with a wide raising of his arms. "Like a tree in a mist." This was one of his more obscure sayings, which left William mystified He declined a request for clarification.

"I may have some more information regarding that. I think he was in the pay of Stieber."

"RIDICULOUS!" yelled Bill Melville. His normal self returned with a vengeance and he thumped the table so hard that both pots of tea spilled all over.

Once the mess had been cleared up, and the tea replaced, he continued in a much quieter tone.

"Please explain – carefully – Hope. Jennings has been with me for many years, his loyalty is doubtless."

"Well, you've read my reports into the goings on with Brocklehurst and Stieber?"

"Yes, damn your eyes. The German consulate refuse to believe any of it and it seems they also refuse point-blank to have Stieber removed from office. We've even complained to the Kaiser himself, but all for naught."

"Well, in the report you will recall that Brocklehurst boasted about inside information regarding the whereabouts of the automata?"

"Yes, yes, go on!"

"Well, I took the liberty of using the *carte blanche* you have seen fit to give me since my return and I've done some investigating behind the scenes, so to speak," he gestured about him, indicating his theatrical surroundings, just in case Melville should not get his subtle drift. Sir William was not, to all appearances, an especially subtle man.

"Yes, yes, man! Bloody well get on with it!"

"Well, naturally, Sir, I started at the top. That is you, my Lord, and I'm pleased to report that you don't appear to be in any way implicated."

Melville choked back his tea. "You bloody-well investigated me, you odious little toad?!" There was a return of corpulence to his cheeks. And then: "Forgive me, Hope, my temper occasionally gets the better of me."

Hope knew this and succeeded quite admirably at keeping a cheeky grin from his face. How Sir William Melville kept his job, he wasn't quite sure. He'd, allegedly, and somewhat infamously, sworn at the Royal Princes when they were little, and in the presence of the Queen.

"No offence taken, my Lord. Anyway, after reviewing – very discreetly – nothing more than correspondence entering and exiting your department, as well as those sent personally by your staff, I followed a paper trail that led from Jennings to an address in Southend. Having read his files, I know he's an Irishman, so I was naturally suspicious that he would be sending mail to the south coast. It seems that the resident of that particular address is that of a postman. An interesting come-down from a former German embassy worker, I believe."

"By God, Hope."

"He was apparently sacked by Stieber himself, but I think that we would eventually find that if we could follow the trail of the correspondence further, that in all likelihood, it would lead all the way back to the man himself."

"Do it, man, do it!"

"I have taken the liberty already, my Lord."

"Good, good. Anything else?"

"I've got my eye on another couple of your people."

"Hell and damnation." He spoke quietly for a change. His ruby red cheeks were now so white as to be virtually transparent.

"Why am I only finding out today?"

"Because the information has only just been collated, and I wanted to talk first. I believe the subtle approach may be the *correct* approach to take in this case. We don't want Stieber aware that we know. We can only feed him false information when it's either vital for our cause, or, if it comes to the worst, when we are absolutely desperate."

Melville nodded thoughtfully. "Quite Hope, quite."

There was a lull in the conversation as Lord Melville reviewed the information.

To give him longer to mull it over, he enquired "and Jennings?"

"Probably dead. Stieber likely thinks him a double agent after the ambush at Birtles Hall."

Quite suddenly, Melville laughed a great, hearty laugh, the colour returning to his cheeks. They really were quite expressive, William thought in a fit of good humour. A man with expressive cheeks. There was a first.

"By God, Hope. They ARE still there – how the hell could we move so many of those damned things without alerting half of the North of England? We've had a few subtle men do a small amount of extending and re-decorating. If Brocklehurst was half as clever as he thinks, he might have surveyed his surroundings more carefully and noted that several of the larger rooms below ground were slightly smaller. I took a calculated risk on his bluster at seeing the removal of all of his personal belongings from the Hall itself to hide the matter. It worked."

"By God, so Jennings was right?"

"Yes, quite right. Do you know why he did it?"

"Not yet, but I suspect Irish nationalism or debt, quite possibly a combination of the two. I expect the results of his family and financial situation quite soon, along with those others in you department."

Melville shook his head and noticing the telegram, he picked it up and read it.

"Bloody, bloody hell," he exploded, using his favourite expletive.

"My Lord?"

"Our naval intelligence – if that ain't a contradiction – at Anglesey reports a large force of dirigibles heading eastwards. Further intelligence from the docks in Liverpool has confirmed the sighting. The forces in Cheshire have been warned, but this," he shook the telegram violently, "states a force of more than fifty ships. There must be some mistake." He shook the telegram violently, his jowls wobbling in time with the movement.

"What if it's a two-pronged attack? The automata AND the nomads?" William asked in a sudden flash of inspiration.

"By Christ," Melville said. And after a second "but why the Frogs?"

"Well, with all of the unrest in France at the moment – there's been some pretty serious riots reported in The Times – half of the population craves the return of their Royalty, even they did chop most of their heads off." William shrugged. "At least under their heel they weren't this desperately stricken. The other half is outraged at the thought. Why not introduce a lucifer in to the gunpowder mix, and then stand back and profit from the outcome?"

"Yes, but Stieber must have other reasons. He's already the most powerful man in France."

"Maybe out of the conflagration, he thinks he can unite the two factions?"

"Hmm, it could be far bigger. Russia is flexing its muscles, more bloody troops on the Pomeranian borders, Prussia and Austria at each other's throats again, God knows why, they're practically one nation anyway. And that leaves Britain an island in a sea of foment that it can't do anything about. But why? Why all this trouble for those brass things?"

"They're practically indestructible – well, until they run out of coal. Maybe that's his way of pacifying France once they've had enough of revolution. Or even to use as a force that can't revolt. Let's not forget that Stieber himself has a master. Who, and what's his plan?"

"Damn, damn, damn. I don't know." Melville thought quickly. "William, get yourself to the barracks at Knightsbridge, and take yourself off with the additional forces I'm about to rouse. It'll have to be by train, as the weather conditions won't allow us to get an airborne fleet there any time soon. Hopefully, it will delay those bastards too."

There was yet another pause as Melville scribbled a note which he handed to Hope. "It's another *carte blanche* that gives you more authority than the Queen, William, use it wisely. Your experience in the matter may be invaluable."

He gestured to his new servant. "Take Sir William Hope to the Knightsbridge barracks immediately, and don't delay for fire or brimstone."

"Or luggage, Bill?" William asked tartly.

"Quickly Hope, quickly! Every second counts!"

Rather rudely, Melville swept William out of the empty theatre house and in to his hansom cab.

CHAPTER 22 – THE RESCUE OF ELISABETH & VICTORIA

Amara was hungover again. For the last three nights she'd drunk stupid amounts of gin with William's sisters Elizabeth and Victoria. Rather like William, their formal names seemed to indicate a reserved, British nature, of which she had seen quite a lot of in the last few weeks.

But not from the sisters themselves. They were quite an odd pair, in a most endearing manner. They'd met her and William in France, following an augmented passenger pigeon from Achille, and it was they who had single-handedly smuggled them out of the country. They had managed it by ferrying them across the English Channel and up the east coast in little more than an old bath tub. Thankfully, the prevailing winds had made the journey a short one, despite which, William had been furious at his sisters' recklessness at sailing such a small boat over such a notorious piece of water as the English Channel.

They'd merely laughed and cussed at William like hardened brigands.

And they'd immediately taken Amara under their collective wing. Which was odd, because most women were insanely jealous of Amara's beauty; admittedly it was now marred, but her face was still flawless, her figure extraordinary, her natural grace without peer.

Once home, they'd introduced her to their drinking culture – and four or five nights each week, they got outrageously drunk together.

Whatever happened tonight, Amara was never drinking again, she promised herself. It was early afternoon, and whilst no longer nauseous, her legs felt oddly independent from each other and her brain. She giggled slightly. It was good to smile again, but even thinking such a thing brought her back to earth again with a good, solid, thud.

*

The four of them (William included) shared a town house which an agent, a very discreet agent at that, of the sisters was renting for them. They considered it too risky to stay at either William's estate or town house, or the sisters' cottage in a leafy suburb on the outskirts of London. The town house they were in was more of a mansion, with glorious grounds containing massive flowerbeds and – importantly – a high wall with discreet patrols on Melville's orders. She liked the man – fat, ugly and quite funny with a number of scandalous tales about those that inhabited his upper social circles. He used words like "shag" and "roger", both of which had a particularly funny ring to Amara's ears.

It was also hot and sunny, early July brightening the skies until late in the evening. A wet May had given the grounds a verdancy and the warm June had brought the flowers in the gardens into peak bloom. Amara loved it, happy to feel the warmth of the sun once more.

Bob was also free to roam the grounds and, once again, she demonstrated an extraordinary affinity with nature that confounded all logic – but there she was every day, with a few crumbs and a little jam, mobbed by blackbirds, thrushes, blue tits, robins, bees, hoverflies, wasps and more. Her head became a perch and, for some reason, they never left any droppings on the bronze woman. She seemed happy, her eyes a constant turquoise blue, often veering to yellow with humour during their evenings with Elizabeth and Victoria – or Liz and Vic, as they insisted upon being called, which still felt a little too informal to Amara, regardless that they'd each seen the other vomit at some point.

In between the hard drinking, Amara had spent time with William. They often walked the grounds. William impressed her with his knowledge of the plants within the garden and she was amazed at the global diversity of their origins: balsam collected from the Himalayas with its seed pods that exploded in the autumn, Japanese knotweed that grew twice as high as a man, with its red stems and fluffy cotton-like flowers, Burmese rhododendron that lit up the spring landscape. William expressed some concerns, in that they needed to be ferociously controlled to keep them ornamental and not have them turn in to pests. The prettiest by far, to Amara's eyes, were the native species, the nodding heads of anemones with their furry leaves, sweet smelling roses, Love-in-a-Mist with its pretty seed pods, the starbright blue petals of the cornflower; there were so many. And the whole time they spoke of their respective history, each becoming more comfortable with the other until they realised that they had a sibling-like relationship, laughing at each other's jokes before they'd even been completed and thinking the same thoughts at the same time. The colour of her skin faded to immaterial in William's eyes, and to Amara's she began to respect his previous difficulties with her skin colour.

One afternoon he completed his tale to her as he knew would, that of his Pirate Queen and the monster, Francois le Clerc. He did something that he had never done before, with anybody. He told it all, every last word, including the part where he actually rescued his sisters, and he had such a skill at telling his tale that she could feel herself in it...

*

...He had the Pirate Captain's ledger, and they'd had the opportunity to study it between the three of them. The boy was the third. He seemed reticent at first but he became increasingly amiable over the next few days, partly due to the fear of pain, but mostly, William suspected, due to the young man's ebullience and enthusiasm. It came naturally to him. William liked him, if you could forgive his coarseness, which was hardly to be unexpected.

The ledger itself was thick and bound in a cracked, brown hide. It smelled. Not badly, it just had an odour of history. Opening it, William was surprised to see an elegant copperplate script, so at odds with the very coarseness that had left such edges to the boy. The boy had taken every character and number and crafted them into a beautiful work of art. He had made everything entirely legible. Unfortunately it was also entirely unintelligible because some form of code had been used to cover his business interests.

Underneath William's calm study, his anger burned, an ire that blazed brightly in his eyes. Both the boy and the Pirate Queen could see it.

Somewhere, those pages contained the location of his sisters. But more, flicking through the coarse pages of paper, there were hundreds of entries. It meant hundreds of children, probably women too, all sold in to some form of servitude, whether it be a simple worker, a common whore or a toy. It didn't really make much difference, once you removed the innocence of the children from the emotional equation. They were all toys, mere baubles, each life a bagatelle to be cast aside or buried in a shallow grave.

The Pirate Queen quietly sat opposite him studying him carefully. He was painfully aware that she saw it as a business opportunity, or at the very least, as an opportunity to imprint herself in a most indelible fashion onto the seas as *The* Pirate Queen. She knew of his desire to smash all of those slavers into oblivion but he hadn't told her the reason why; she wasn't an idiot, however, so she must have at least guessed some of his motivation. Did she think it was his wife? His lover? His mother? He didn't really care, for now they could only wrestle as much from the boy as possible and then wreak mayhem. After that, William feared there would be a reckoning. He would need to be mightily lucky to escape with his own and his sister's lives intact, should he cross the woman.

They finished questioning the boy and then the Pirate Queen simply slit his throat before tossing him overboard. William hadn't even had time to protest before the barbaric act had been completed.

He'd liked the boy.

Only, immediately afterwards she'd thrown William overboard, and for real this time. She laughed as she did so. She had what she needed and then she was heading off towards an island where she could rest, regroup and then plot and conspire her way to the top of the pirate mast.

It hadn't worked out that way, and although William had cried – she was, after all, his first proper lover – his focus had never shifted from his sisters.

Only it was now more than that. There were so many people in the hide bound book, and William cursed his mortal memory that he could only remember so little of the information contained within it. William felt honour-bound to bring deliverance to as many of these debauchers as he could whilst he also rescued his sisters: at the same time, he would try to save as many of the enslaved as possible.

He watched her hang, tears on his cheeks regardless of the fact that she'd cast him overboard.

What William did have, snapping his thoughts back to the present, was a starting point. He steeled himself as he sat in a Caribbean inn, drinking a dark ale spiced with ginger and chilli, and he formulated his plan. The second phase of the plan started in Madrid and worked its way up to London via the major cities of Europe – Barcelona, Perpignan, Marseille, Lyon, Paris, Dover and then finally on to London. There were even names he recognised.

The first phase started locally, a man that probably held his sisters.

*

It was a short sea journey from this island to a small island that held a very small number of natives and absolutely no white overlords. It had nothing of value, and, whilst it had been explored, mapped and indexed in some weighty tome in some government archive as *mostly harmless*, it was of no further interest to the white djinn.

Mostly harmless. Mostly. But William new better.

The island contained a handful of tiny villages, each of a dozen or so huts or mud shacks. It also had one large mansion partially sunk into a hillside to protect it from the hurricanes and tornadoes that frequented this part of the world. Today, however, the skies were blue, nary a cloud in the sky with a hot breeze rustling through the trees and vegetation. He could hear the occasional alien squark of an exotic bird, but apart from that the island appeared to be blissfully peaceful, an idyll that was impossible to imagine in even the remotest regions of England.

The mansion was low, only a pair of unconnected outhouses reaching to a second storey, but it sprawled neatly over a large area, starkly gothic in its structure, regardless of its inability to ominously loom. It looked out of place given the jungle-like backdrop. Smoke rose from several chimneys and from one outhouse – there were about a dozen in all – a black spire of smog dirtied the sky and from it, the sharp-dull clunk of a hammer on iron could be heard. A number of black women, poorly clothed but well fed, scurried around the grounds on some errand or other. But mostly it looked sleepy in the early afternoon heat.

William approached a pair of gates. Of everything, this aspect sent a cold shiver down his spine. They were tall, made of very stout iron bars and a heavy padlock secured a thick chain keeping the gates securely closed. And the ironwork then stretched out around the circumference of the grounds. It felt more like a prison, and William suspected that this was exactly what it was. It had been designed to keep its inmates in and not to keep folk out. It puzzled William because the island was small with nowhere for anyone to run, should they have the urge to escape from the estate. He presumed that even those free folk living in the villages paid some form of fealty to the man who lived in his own gaol.

A pull chord dangled from a heavy bell that was attached to a pole adjacent to the gate. Hope straightened his clothing. He had worn his best, specially cleaned for this errand. A rich purple waistcoat adorned with gold buttons – real gold, too – and a pure silver length of chain disappeared into a pocket, at the end of which hung a gorgeous English verge Moser pocket watch that had been the prized possession of his great grandfather. It was a family heirloom worth a great deal of money. Beneath the waistcoat he wore a white silk shirt frilled up the front. The baggy sleeves tightened at the cuff and he finished the ensemble with tight black trousers, tall boots with silver buckles and a well-worn tricorn hat.

He looked every inch the pirate, with a cutlass that hung by his side, but he also appeared to be a gent, or, at the very least, very wealthy. Purple dye was very expensive and that, along with the cut of his clothing, gave his proud bearing a more regal air, giving his image true dignitas.

He pulled the chord and the bell clanged low and dull. He didn't have to wait long. Indeed his arrival may have been expected, word being passed up from the village of an unscheduled ship heaving-to, weighing anchor and sending out its boat to the paltry harbour, where half a score of raggedy fishing boats were moored, because he was greeted by three men. Two guards flanked an enormously fat black man, his bald pate glistening in the sun. He too wore purple, a long smock reaching down to sandaled feet. Each of his fingers was adorned with a golden ring, most of them thick and heavy, some of them set with precious stones of such size that he must have worn a small fortune on each hand. Other than that, he wore no adornments, if you can forgive the affectations – eye liner and a beauty spot just above his top lip.

William fought to keepa neutral look on his face, the glint in his eye impassive, for upon seeing the man he was filled with revulsion. He had jowls that swung gently as he moved forward and huge pendulous breasts swayed beneath his purple dress. His great stomach appeared to sag almost to his knees. William noted his gait, which appeared purposeful and he didn't seem to be particularly disabled by his obesity. More, a sense of power emanated from the man, a dark power that seemed to gleam from his eyes as he drew closer to William.

He stopped as he neared the gate and they studied each other, neither of them showing any expression as they stared in to each other's eyes, one set hazel, the other mahogany brown. There wasn't a furrowed brow, or a hardness to either study, but William felt a malevolent humour shining out from the man before him, a malevolence that made his skin crawl. William fought to keep the sensation of revulsion and utter disgust from his features.

"Bonjour monsieur," spoke the man. "Je m'appelle Duc Francois Etienne Louis Charles le Clerc, mais dit moi Francois. Puis je vous aidez?" His voice was oily and almost whispered, an affected inaudibility forcing William to strain his ears. It was as if he spoke to a small child.

William understood perfectly, but feigned ignorance. He had used the tactic before when he didn't trust a person. It made them careless as they spoke to others, seemingly totally in confidence from his English ears.

"I am very sorry, sir, but I only speak English and a smattering of Creole. I am William Gloom. I have come looking for employment from one with such a reputation for honour as your good self."

It was utter horse manure and William felt dirty speaking words, but he needed to get in to the compound. Hopefully, once inside, he could go on a killing spree, followed by a rescue. Whilst it didn't show, his blood was up. He had been itching to get here following the death of the Pirate Queen.

"Mr Gloom, your reputation precedes you. How well did my niece die?" He spoke perfect English. He could have been schooled at Eton.

"So *you* were her patron? I suspected as much."

"I helped her out once, years ago. She is family after all. And you did not answer my question. Did she die well?"

"Better than she deserved."

"It is as well that she died how she did. She murdered my son."

"I'm sorry," said William, feeling anything but. "She tried to murder me also. However, that is all in the past. I really do need employment."

"We shall talk over chai. I will then decide."

He clapped a hand and one of the guards withdrew a large iron key which turned easily in the padlock.

William entered, surprised that he hadn't been asked for his sword. He strove for an easy gait, trying his hardest to show no tension. Sweat dripped down his back, and he cursed inwardly as he wiped his palms on his pants, a small betrayal of his anxiety.

There was another nod followed by a dull thud on William's head. All of the lights went out.

*

The lights reignited gently and allowed a brief discourse only.

"Mr Gloom, I apologise for the crudeness of our first encounter. I promise that all of my other dealings will be far more sophisticated. I'll introduce you first to my pharmacy." le Clerc held up a large glass syringe with a barbarically large needle at the end. He shoved it forcefully into William's shoulder and depressed the plunger. The amber liquid emptied from the chamber and flowed coldly into his arm.

The lights dimmed slowly and then were extinguished entirely.

*

He came round again. It was a warm day, although which day, William could not be sure. He smelled of himself rather strongly, so he suspected that it had most probably been several days. He could not move arms or legs, although his head was free to move, and a glance showed that he was tied to a large four poster bed by leather restraints. The curtains in the bedroom were open, and a single door too, which faced out on to the sea by way of a small terrace, upon which sat a chair. Sat upon the chair was a grossly fat black man smiling beatifically at the panorama before him. He drank from a china blue tea cup, one small finger perpendicular to the others as he drank.

William looked around for a chance of escape or some sort of clue that could give an advantage. He could see none. He was in a bedroom that appeared entirely normal – it contained a non-descript painting of the sea, a bedside table with a couple of small ornaments, a wardrobe and a dressing table that held some accoutrements for self-grooming. A chair and a chaise longue were next to each other below the painting at the end of the bed.

He turned his gaze back to the figure on the terrace. It now regarded him. The same beatific smile still adorned his face, although now that his eyes were upon William's he could note a sense of smug superiority in his eyes. He regarded le Clerc as impassively as possible. The man eased himself out of the chair and moved over to regard William more closely.

"Monsieur, you have very beautiful hazel eyes and a lovely face, if not classically handsome. You need fuller lips and more prominent cheekbones. You could possibly pass as a pretty lady, although before your youth passes much further, if you would like my advice. Most male faces become more masculine with age. More weathered, I think may be more accurate. Now, why are you really here?"

"Work, monsieur. I am rather at a loose end and find myself fairly unemployable on most of the islands. There appears to be a price on my head. Is this method of questioning really necessary?"

"I believe so, Mr Gloom. How long have you been in the Caribbean?"

"A while." William couldn't help a whiff of suspicion from crossing his brow. le Clerc smiled at him.

"About a year, Mr Gloom, if I can do my mathematics correctly. I remember the first report of you with my niece fairly clearly. You are, after all, a white man."

"And that matters how, exactly?"

"You appear to have an ulterior motive, my young friend. All of the people you have taken up with seem to have expired, and that makes me suspicious. Is that what you require of me? Why are you even in the Caribbean? You appear to be a young man of means. If nothing else, your accent is far too gentile for a pirate."

"I have an education, is that a crime?"

"You have far more than an education, you have breeding," scoffed le Clerc. It was a gentle rebuke, but the first. William could feel, with a sense of dread, the way that this conversation may go.

"A bastard son. Nothing more. Scorned, pitied, patronised. I am bloody angry about it, and I felt that anger may be a prerequisite of this trade. I cannot stand those bloody bastards. At least here I know when I expect to be knifed, and it will be front-ways rather than in my back. Do you not agree?"

"Oh Mr Gloom, I agree more than you could possibly know. My niece was my favourite. She, umm, grew to hate me."

"Why?" William knew of this detestation, and he knew that the Pirate Queen's hatred of her uncle was legion. She would not say why, but he could guess. Her quest wasn't solely for mastery of the high seas.

"It is a family matter."

William smiled. "That's what she told me, although I can hazard a guess. Maybe I am not the man for you."

It was a bluff, and they both knew it. William would not be allowed to leave, no matter how hard he insinuated.

"It was I that told the Royal Navy of her whereabouts. She was a wanted criminal. I decided to exercise my civic duty."

William was astounded, and the shock showed on his face.

"Do you think she was driven by nothing more than mastery of the high seas?" He laughed out loud. "I can see by the look on your face that this wasn't all she wanted, although your naivety shows that you know not what it was she actually wanted. I doubt she did either."

"She was family!" was all that Hope could manage.

"Mr Gloom, you humour me. You should have spent more time in school before visiting me. Now, I must find out exactly who you are. Will you tell me to save us all your pain and unnecessary effort?"

William's voice came strong and deep. "Who am I? I am your worst nightmare."

At this, le Clerc laughed in deep amusement. "My worst nightmare? Mr Gloom, you are not even close."

*

Oddly, the torture did not start with physical pain. It began with a wakefulness that had to be endured and an emotional pain that needed burying deep beneath the surface of his countenance.

For seventy-two hours he had been kept awake, not allowed any moment of sleep, and throughout that period, he'd had a number of visitors paraded before him, all of them painfully young, both female and male alike.

His sisters were among several such parades, both together and singly at different times. Either due to their incarceration, or due to their intelligence, neither appeared to recognise William. He himself struggled to hide any expression on seeing them both. Inwardly he was surprised, a surprise borne entirely of relief. They were alive, in good health, and bore no visible signs of abuse. One thing he did note on all of the children paraded before him was the lack of eye contact. They cast their eyes downwards, with nothing more than an occasional upwards flicker of inescapable temptation to look at this new thing before them.

The seventy-two hours became ninety six hours and more, until a new dawn hit the horizon, the sun casting its shadow from behind seeming to cast his small room in to greater gloom than when it had been at night.

His head drooped of its own accord, and a sharp nudge by a scrawny woman brought him back. She refused to meet his eye or be drawn in to conversation.

le Clerc entered the small room, fully dressed, affectations and all, even at this early hour.

"Mr Gloom. I think it's time for you to sleep, now."

A pair of guards unstrapped him from the hard, metal chair and led him down a flight of wooden stairs. He reached the bottom of the house and they led him down further, by way of a roughly hewn mud staircase. Through his tiredness, Hope stumbled, only prevented from falling into the gloom by the hand of the guard who had stunned him at the gate. It all seemed so long ago. His clumsy attempts at conversation were ignored entirely.

It grew cold as they descended. They seemed to travel for an age, but they couldn't have done, because there was no way that the fat black man could ever ascend back up. At least, that's what William's mind told him strangely, as his head spun with clouds and queer thoughts, trivialities like whether his butler had shaken off the cold that he'd had when William had left for the Caribbean, or whether his journals would be waiting for him when he returned home, or if... it was all too much. He could feel the walls closing in metaphorically, not just physically, through the descent.

The stairs eventually led to a chamber. In its middle was a small wooden bed. It had a mattress that bowed at the pretence of being such. A dirty cover scruffily covered the thin mattress. There was nothing else. A bed, a rough floor, sloping mud walls and a stairwell.

The guard shoved him over to the bed. A heavy wooden door, unnoticed through his sleep-deprived haze. The gaolers pulled closed behind as they left the room. The sound of a heavy bar being put in place was the last sound.

It was dimly lit, and William noticed candles on the walls, big, thick candles that would last for many hours.

He lay down. He closed his eyes. He opened them again, shifted on his bed, and closed his eyes again, keeping them shut even through the wakefulness beneath.

He stayed like that for perhaps five minutes, and then flung the cover off himself. He prowled around the small room and noticed the food and water placed on the floor on the blind-side of the bed. It could only be described as functional. It offered no thoughts of taste or flavour.

He ate some of the food and drank some of the water.

Hi exhaustion was such that he could not rest his mind to an extent that would allow sleep. He paced the room, sat down, lay down, paced again.

Such a time came when his head hit the pillow and he did sleep. When he woke, the candles were still burning, although lower. He had no idea just how long he may have been asleep, but the candles still had many hours of burning left. On a whim, be blew out half of the candles. It left enough light to pace by.

It turned out that his whim was prophetic. He slept again and when he awoke, one of the candles had extinguished. Two were left burning, both very low. He left them to burn, and he watched in fascination as one guttered and then went out. The room was now almost dark. It was mesmeric to watch, and he had no choice but to watch. Until the third candle started to gutter, when he moved and lit one of the remaining three. It flickered and took hold. Carefully he put it back in its place

Four became three, and somewhere he slept and ate a little. He could hear no noise, in fact no sensory input of any kind other than the sound of his own boots on the floor and that of his own mastication.

Three became two, became one. He slept, he woke. Time moved slowly. Or quickly. He could not be sure. There was no point of reference.

His nerves were becoming more threadbare the further the last candle burned. He paced the small cell incessantly. He swore violently at the spent candles, at the cell, at le Clerc and at anything else that sprang to mind.

The last candle went out and turned William's hysteria on. He fumbled across the floor finding the wooden door, and he hammered on it, hitting it repeatedly with first his fists and then the flat of his hand once he could feel blood oozing from the knuckles. He continued hitting at the door until enough of his frantic energy had been expended to bring him partially to his senses. This brought him, by parts, further to a rational mind.

He was a young man of only twenty one, still malleable and mentally flexible enough for the situation to be redefined in his own mind, for a sense of rationalism to enter, and he was mature enough for any immaturity at simple night terrors to be easily quelled.

He had also travelled enough, even at this age, to understand, now that his mind was quieter, to scry what le Clerc did to him. First, he had been subject to sleep deprivation and now he had been put through the impending doom of watching his lights extinguish one by one, his fractured consciousness fraying still further. And now there was this. Utter nothing, no sense of anything other than a sound or smell of his own making.

le Clerc probably had more games waiting for William, but now that his mind was quieted, the logic of the situation comprehended, he needed to devise a strategy.

Should he feign terror or some form of apoplexy of the mind?

He could present himself as the living dead, nothing more than being in an awake coma at the mental pressure received.

He wasn't sure that his acting abilities were up to it, le Clerc seemed clever and resourceful. He was sure to see through a sham such as this, so William felt that his best device was to be himself – just a self who was full of fear, sullen and eager to cooperate. Presenting hysteria would not be believed, but a failing attempt to hide fear would be realistic, and an openness to answer le Clerc's questions would make his lies more plausible. That was, those lies that he would slip through in a multitude of truths.

These understandings and decisions were made in a matter of moments and he felt his way to his bed and liberated his dwindling supplies of food and drink in a majestic, bland feast. It made him feel better to have a full stomach. He located a corner and made his first ablutions since arriving in the chamber. It didn't improve the atmosphere, but it amused him that this was part of the degradation planned by le Clerc. May be the fat man did not quite understand his slightly immature pleasure in the obvious grossness, nor did he know of William's previous incarceration at the hands of the Pirate Captain, which had been more disgusting by far.

More time passed in the utter darkness. He could hear his breathing and the breaking of his own wind. His defecations no longer assailed his senses. He slept more than once and now the sound of rumbling could be heard: he was hungry and thirsty.

Eventually though, he detected something different through the sensory deprivation. He had kept himself sane through further of planning his strategy for how he would face le Clerc once the door was opened. There was no doubt that that time would arrive. It was the manner of the man. He knew it, and that too stilled his mind. It fed his determination to best the man.

And this is what he detected. A shift in air pressure or a vibration through the floor. Something. The door opened. The light was dim, but to William it was incredibly bright. He squinted, lowering his eyes and ensured that his shoulders were slumped in a dejected fashion. His eyes were red-rimmed. He looked and smelled awful. Most of the sham was genuine.

le Clerc remained silhouetted for many seconds before entering the room. A small child bore two lanterns, and these were hung on the candle holders. The light shone bright and warm, and William could feel his own wanness in the orange glow.

Hope looked up. The fat man before him – no armed guard evident – smiled pleasantly at William. He felt his anger rise at the smug bastard. He was here, head immaculately shaved and oiled, his purple smock beautifully fitted and tailored, his affectations and eye make-up present.

William dropped his head in submission staring at his feet. Into his periphery appeared painted toe-nails from below the hem of the purple dress. They too were purple, but were swirled with fine gold leaf in some form of emblem.

It made William angry. Very angry.

He swallowed and then swallowed again, forcing the anger down. The bastard might not have his bodyguard, but he had foresight. There was no way that he would come here alone unless he had a reason. He swallowed again, hoping it appeared to be fear. He could feel the smile emanating from the man above him. He resisted smashing the man in the face, but only by the very skin of his teeth. He could feel his body trembling. Again, he hoped it appeared as fear.

"So then, young man, are you ready to tell me the truth?"

Hope shook his head resignedly. "What do you mean?"

"*Why* are you here! It is a very simple question. I have a strong desire to know why you and my niece were together and why she is now dead, along with every other person of significance that you have had dealings with since your arrival in the Caribbean. You are not a desperate criminal and you are not a bastard son."

"I know," said William. "I am an enigma. Try living inside this." He tapped the side of his head and snorted ruefully. "If it's any consolation, I don't know either."

le Clerc sighed. "I don't know, Mr Gloom. What am I to do with you. I *could* turn you in to my servant – I have my ways to make you compliant, never fear – but I do not believe that I quite believe you."

William remained silent.

le Clerc sighed, more deeply this time. "Come with me, boy."

William looked up sharply – perhaps too sharply – at the command. He was being watched and immediately lowered his gaze whilst he roused himself painfully from his cot. His feet dragged across the floor and the young boy followed them both.

A guard was at the door and in the shadows behind, another two lurked. William had not seen any of them before. It made him wonder at the forces he may need to overcome.

In quite a sprightly fashion for a man so big, they ascended the stairs and went out on to a veranda. The day was still young, perhaps mid-morning or sooner and it shone its beauty without a cloud in the sky. The sun twinkled off the sea in the distance as a fitful breeze excited it.

There was no breeze where they sat because of the windbreaks erected, silk sheets of a gorgeous crimson.

They sat at a stone table and on it was a spread of food and drink. William inspected the feast which was a multitude of sweetmeats, canapes, cakes, breads, jam, honey, sliced meats and a wealth of morsels that William could not identify. There was enough for a dozen people, and yet le Clerc seemed to be alone, barring himself and one of the guards. It was doubtful as to whether the guard would be indulged.

The one thing that did exist at the table were a wealth of forks, spoons and knives of types that

Hope had only ever seen at the most proper of formal dinners, cutlery for every eventuality. Which meant that some of them would be sharp and pointy. It was an opportunity to let him at least disable the guard, should the opportunity arise. There seemed little harm in fortifying himself first though. He hoped that he would need the energy.

He looked quizzically at le Clerc.

"Please, dear William, tuck in. You must be hungry."

"Why the kindness?"

He received no reply, just a rueful smile and a small shake of the head, as if he was a small child being indulged by benevolent uncle. He motioned at William to eat. le Clerc himself donned a tailored and initialled napkin, took a small plate and placed a single item on the plate, which he then cut in to smaller pieces and ate one by one. He sighed in pleasure. Again, the beatific look crossed his face. He really did seem to be enjoying himself.

William stood. As he did he heard the guard shift, but William merely copied le Clerc and placed a single item on his plate. It was a pâté of some sort, so he placed some bread on the plate with it, and using a blunt knife of some sort, he spread a small amount on the piece of bread. It was perhaps the best pate that William had ever tasted. It was bold with subtle undertones of fruit, garlic and black pepper. He helped himself to more food, attempting to try one of everything as time wore on. The only thing that disappointed William was the drink: there were many cordials and fruit juices, along with selections of chai and coffee. He could find no wine, never mind a more fortifying spirit. Monsieur le Clerc did not hold with alcohol.

Footsteps on the veranda disturbed the look of pleasure on the black man's face, and as William turned in that direction, he saw that there must be some business that required the Masters attention, something that did not meet with this part of the plan for breaking William.

"Mr Gloom, please avail yourself of more food. I shall return shortly." He passed a significant look to the guard, who straightened himself and became outwardly more alert.

It was clear, however, that after five more minutes he stood day-dreaming again, staring out to sea, perhaps thinking of some girl or other.

Which is probably the reason that he was brought round to full awareness with a knife in his throat, a short, sharp paring knife that had only just been slicing an apple in to quarters. The knife in the throat had the effect of silencing any possible noise other than a guttural groan, which was soon cut off when William rammed the knife into the man's face, audibly smashing skull as he did so. William helped the man to the floor, making sure that he lowered him behind the windbreak so as to take him out of sight of the house. He took the important things. The unsheathed sword he resheathed and belted around his waist. He took the two musket pistols and checked and reprimed them. They were primitive, but serviceable. And he now held them threateningly. He didn't bother searching for further ammunition, he wouldn't have time to reload any weapons for what he intended: carnage of the most unsubtle form – no plan, no silence, just death.

He strode for the door through which le Clerc had removed himself, his bare feet slapping gently on the warm stones, the scent of the warm sea in his nostrils.

The door slammed open when he was ten yards away, and another guard raised a pistol towards William. He died before he could pull the trigger, a musket ball slamming through his chest.

It had begun. The sound of gunfire would have raised the whole island. He dropped the pistol that he'd fired and picked up that one left by the dead guard.

William entered the house. A musket ball flattened itself against the wall three feet from his head. A house servant stood with his mouth open a mere six feet away. William emptied a pistol into her head. He drew his sword, last pistol in his left hand.

There was a sound to his left, and turning, William shot without registering at what or who. A fleeing servant dropped noiselessly, a musket ball in the back. William felt nothing. Regret would come later.

Two guards skidded round a corner further up the corridor to his right, and he strode at them, flinging the last pistol at one as he closed. It was enough to allow him to dispatch the other with a neatly feinted slash that became a lunge, piercing the belly of the man. William twisted the blade as the innards sucked at the blade, threatening to trap it within. It came out noisily as a rush of blood and visceral fluid emptied on to the stone floor. The second guard aimed a thrust at William, but he was poorly trained. William could tell just by the way he held a sword. William forcefully knocked the lunge away leaving the entire body open to any form of killing stroke that he could desire. He merely turned the parry in to a hew as it came back and the blade hammered in to the head of the man, jamming deep in the skull. William let go and picked up a different sword. He strode back the way the men had come.

A manservant approached William. "Mr Gloom, please." Cold fury silenced the man permanently.

There was a scream as a house maid saw the action. She made the mistake of freezing in her fear. She died also.

William didn't know which way to go, so he stood still. They would come to him. He chose a place where the corridor was wide enough for sword play, but narrow enough to restrict the number of opponents he could face at any one time.

There was no need. The next person he saw was four feet tall, pale and evidently scared. But it was also his sister.

"Elizabeth!"

"William, you must leave. Now! More men will be here soon."

"Where's your sister? Where are the rest of the children? Where is le Clerc?"

"William..." she began.

"Shut up and answer my question." He spoke harshly to her because he didn't have the time for a discussion. She burst in to tears.

William dragged her in to a room. It turned out to be useful, because there were no other exits and the lock had a key.

"Elizabeth. Tell me where I need to go. Now. We will all leave this island together, this very day."

She sniffled and told him. "But be careful. There are at least a dozen soldiers raising themselves. I saw some of them coming this way."

"Don't worry about them. Now stay here. Lock yourself in and don't open the door for anyone but me."

She nodded.

William left the room and almost came to an end there and then. As he strode out of the room he collided with a man wielding a sword in one hand and a curved dirk in the other. It sliced through his jerkin opening a shallow cut in his chest. The fellow looked as shocked as William, which had spoiled the killing blow intended for William's throat. William smashed the hilt of his sword in to his opponent's face. He felt the cheekbone break and the man screamed shrilly. He grabbed the hand wielding the dirk and with a sudden jerk, forced the arm back in to the owner's face. His scream ceased instantly. William took the dagger.

He followed his sister's directions. The guards appeared to be acting independently of one another, because they came on him individually, and before he'd reached his destination there were another three corpses.

He found himself before a large antechamber that led to a large wooden door. The door was closed, but more importantly three guards stood between him and it.

They didn't have the look of green, wet-behind-the-ears boys that were now littering the corridors of the mansion. They all wore similar black leather jerkins and carried good quality swords and they all bore a number of scars and walked easily. None of them showed the slightest bit of fear.

William remained in the entrance to the antechamber. It was his most defensible position. The men spread out, one each coming from his left and right, the third directly towards him. Each carried a sword only. For some reason they bore no guns. It was good news for William, because he would already be dead if they had.

The one on the left moved first. It was nothing more than a probing thrust and William parried it with ease, before whipping round to parry a far more determined attack from the man on the right. The man over-extended himself due to his eagerness to take advantage, and it would normally have meant his end, but William was unable to riposte, as he desperately turned back to the man on the left, who was thrusting again and then back at the man in the centre, who was far less subtle, aiming a massive overhead sweep at William. He barely parried them all. They worked well as a team, and William could feel panic rising in stomach. They would be too much for him if they carried on like this.

The man on the right had regained his balance and attacked again, but this time, the other two had not recovered sufficiently to press home an attack, and William parried again, and, fed by his desperation, he flung the dirk at the man in the centre. It did not hit him squarely. William was right handed and had never before thrown a knife with his left hand. It did, however, hit him on the head hard enough to force him back a step, and as it hit him, it skewed from his forehead, opening up a shallow cut. Like all scalp wounds, it began to bleed profusely.

Once thrown, William followed up by attacking the man on the left, who was just about to strike out.

William left his back undefended because he could see no alternative. It took the man by surprise, and before he could fully extend his arm in to a stroke, William was on him, clubbing down on the top of his skull with the pommel of his sword. A crack reverberated up William's arm and he watched as the eyes of his opponent dimmed. He collapsed, and blood began to leak slowly from his ears. Desperately, he spun round, just in time to partially stop the blade of the guard from his other side, the point of his weapon only skewering a fleshy part of his waist rather than taking him in the abdomen. Hope slid down the blade and head-butted the man savagely in the face before kneeing him in the groin with a force that sent black spots running through the guard's vision. With a great deal of pain he withdrew from the sword speared in his side and contemptuously swatted aside a slash from the man in the centre, who was having some difficulty due to the blood running in to his eye. It made his death a formality. A feint, a thrust and finally a backhanded slash saw his throat opened, and a sheet of blood covered William.

Breathing heavily, William turned back round to the only guard who remained conscious. He was on his hands and knees with no thoughts of William, only the pain in his groin. The pain stopped presently when William stabbed him through the top of his skull with a force that wedged his sword deep in the bone. He merely took another.

William moved over to the door. It was not locked. In the room, looking petrified, was le Clerc. There was the bodies of eight children in the room, each with his or her throat cut.

"No, you shan't have my children," he sobbed, tears glistening in his eyes. "They are mine, and no other man may have them, my poor, dear things."

William scanned the room rapidly. Victoria, his other sister was cowering in a corner. None of the children dared to shriek in le Clerc's presence, even with William covered in blood and other nameless bits of gore.

William strode over to le Clerc.

"Stop, or this child dies." He had another child in his arms, cuddling her gently whilst holding a knife to her throat.

"Let her go and I'll let you live," William said.

The fat man panted in terror. The thing before him was an apparition from the abyss.

"You will spare me?"

"I will."

"Do you promise on your life?"

"I promise." William's face was as hard as granite through the blood. le Clerc took it for a man telling the truth.

He let the girl go.

"Up, fat man."

le Clerc did as he was told with an enormous effort move his bulk, where previously he had seemed so lithe.

"Move this way, away from them."

Again, le Clerc complied in meek submission. He moved to within about six feet when a voice screamed.

"Look out William!"

A knife appeared in le Clerc's hand from somewhere in the folds of his robes, but William was wise enough to understand that the entirety of the performance had been nothing more than an act, and he simply raised his sword to the horizontal and shoved gently as le Clerc flew at him. His massive weight did the rest. He slid gently up the length of the sword. He tried limply to stab at William, but Hope merely slapped it away.

He thrust le Clerc backwards and sliced his blade deep into the man's groin. With such bulk, there came a lot of blood. An awful lot, because William was covered in the stuff as the artery pulsed great, crimson gouts in to the air. Children shrieked at the blood and at what was being done to their uncle. For some, he was the only family that they could remember, and regardless of his behaviour, there was a sort of dependence on the man. Cognisant of the noises, William heaved the sword from the glutinous flesh and hewed the blade of his sword in to the top of his skull. The bone splintered momentarily, and then blood was sheeting down le Clerc's face and he shuddered and heaved. It lasted a few seconds.

le Clerc died.

*

William tailed off.

"There is more, so much more to tell."

He looked weary, and Amara felt pity pouring out of her every pore and a great welling in her heart at what the man had been through.

"Stop. Tell me more another time, if you feel up to it."

He nodded wearily and they sat there in silence until the sun went down.

*

Amara was still sat down trying her best to both ignore and quell her churning insides. She was really, truly, never letting Elisabeth and Victoria feed her drink again. She had pride and bearing. She did not have hangovers, they weren't for women like her. She should be better than this.

Her skull throbbed. It had nothing to do with her trepanned skull or the electrodes that pierced her brain.

The front door slammed open and then slammed closed. She flinched at both sounds. She vowed never to drink again. She swore to keep the promise this time.

Footsteps thudded up the stairs and she felt a tingle of irrational fear. Her door burst open without so much of a knock, and she tried to stand at the intrusion. Pain and nausea ran through her as the door thumped into the wall.

William strode in. "Pack your bags, Amara, we're going to war. Where are they?"

"Asleep upstairs. And what war?"

He didn't reply, he stalked up the next set of stairs, a determined spring in his step.

"Liz, Vic, get up you lazy cows! Pack, we're going to bloody war!"

There was a groan, and Vic stuck her head out of a room, blurry eyed, whilst a shout of "go to hell," emanated from the next room along.

"I'll bloody well wash out your mouth with soap, you little harlot! Get up and pack!" He offered Amara a wink, as she stumbled to the top of the stairs.

"My God, you bunch of lushes. Hurry up! It's urgent! We're off to wipe Brocklehurst's eye! Hurry up! Hurry up! Vite! Vite! Vite!"

There were shriek-groans, and then excited movement in the occupied bedrooms. The hangovers of the three ladies rapidly diminished at the prospect of action.

"Let me at him!" Liz strode out of her room in a most unladylike pair of nubuck jodhpurs, with a gunbelt fastened around her waist. A tightly fitted blouse and scarlet waistcoat accentuated her ample breasts. Over this, she wore a large, black, fitted overcoat that partially hid her guns, but only exaggerated the shape of her breasts.

William stuck his head out of his room, which was also on this floor. "It's no wonder you don't get invited to society balls. If father were here, he'd be apoplectic at that ridiculous garb." William couldn't bring himself to enforce society rules on the pair, they'd been through too much, and so they drank like men, rode horses like men, and belched and farted like men.

She stuck out her tongue.

"Pack the metalwork, we've got a train journey before that lot will be of any use."

Vic came to her door, only half dressed, looking slightly disappointed. William turned away at seeing his sister in her under-garments. She started to disassemble her crossbow, and Amara laughed at William's discomfort.

"Where are we going?" she asked, also with a gun in her hand.

"Cheshire. It's grim up there – pack something warm."

He grabbed his suitcase and strode down the hall, before turning and disappearing downstairs. "And bloody well hurry up!" he shouted behind himself.

A chorus of expletives followed him down the stairs. They all burst out laughing: Amara had joined in.

*

A coach and four was waiting outside. He'd ordered Melville's new man to upgrade the hansom – it simply wasn't big enough.

He groaned as he saw the suitcases that his sisters had brought. They were simply huge. He'd argued with them so many times about what to pack, what was reasonable, and what was simply excessive. He'd never gotten past the simply excessive, and so he'd simply refused to help them with their luggage anymore. Let them suffer.

They smiled tartly at him. "We've only packed bandages for you, William, you always end up bleeding everywhere," said Liz, smiling sweetly.

Stoney faced, William was trying his best not to laugh at the quip. It was old but not tired and, in all honesty, probably right.

Amara also carried a suitcase obviously loaned from a sister. With some sympathy, he did help her, but one of his sisters caught his eye. Her look said everything, and he had the good grace to blush. Another look passed between the sisters and Amara didn't miss it, either and also had the manners to blush. There was an awkward silence between them as Liz and Vic disappeared round the other side of the coach in a fit of giggles, which had entirely disappeared when William helped Amara aboard.

Bob merely stood immobile throughout all, and clambered clumsily in to the coach. Her eyes radiated sadness as she could not easily join in. But then she had not really attempted to. She had an air of mystery about her that seemed to grow the more they spoke and he wanted to know those secrets. She had obviously been someone of importance and the more he analysed her foibles of speech, he realised that she probably wasn't English, and that it wasn't just a facet of signing. It certainly explained her excellent French. And she was intimate with the subtleties of politics and diplomacy – certainly not a common trait for women, and positively not of the middle or lower classes. Evidently a Lady – but who? She wouldn't tell and the suspense was killing them all, not just William.

The coach eventually set off, piloted by a taciturn soldier at a break-neck pace. Thankfully, it wasn't one of the new-fangled steambulators. That would probably have exploded at this pace, or at the very least smashed into something leaving them all dead or maimed. William preferred to be at the reins himself, so even if he felt the need to go this fast, at least he would be in control.

He briefed them on the way.

"Why are you inviting us?" asked Amara.

"I can't let you out of my sight," – a stifled giggle from the sisters – "and these two hellcats are rather good in a scrap. In fact, because they are women, most men are loathe to even engage them. Seems like a terrific advantage!"

"Well, apart from that hidalgo in Spain, William," said Vic.

"Yes, he *was* a bastard!" said Liz. "Bloody Spaniards."

"You can tell Amara about it on the train. We'll be there shortly, no time for one of your stories right this second." He turned to Amara, "Honestly, they can turn taking their toilette into a saga, these two can."

They all laughed uproariously: William had made a joke.

CHAPTER 23 – A CHANGE OF MIND

Lucas felt himself disassemble, all of his conscience seemed to spring apart, spouting forth like champagne from a bottle. Something – himself, somehow – expanded. Gravity departed. He *spaced* out.

He screamed through pure terror. There could be no pain, because there was nothing to hurt, but still Lucas screamed.

He could see parts of himself from afar, not a hand or a lock of hair, but a memory. He watched a feeling from a disconnected recollection float before his eyes, before springing away to co-exist with a disparate part of his mind.

He realised that what he saw was his life as he had lived it. His central intelligence still seemed to be in one place.

He saw a woman's face as it swam past amongst a host of his life. He felt the deep vacuum of a cannonball as it swatted past to spray him with the bloody remains of his best friend in the rank next to him. He could see a winter sunrise outlining the spires of Constantinople as it sparkled beside the Black Sea. Bright stars illuminated snow-capped mountains. A woman sucked at his engorged manhood, black hair glimmering in candlelight. Lucas could feel the pleasure. Goose-bumps raised as he recalled the chill. He could smell the spices in the marketplaces as the sun rose. He remembered vomiting as the stench of shit hit his nostrils. The lady was black, and he had never seen her in the flesh.

Panic flew across his vision, pure and unadulterated. He yelled at the fear. He moaned at a pleasure that coursed through him. He felt hot and then cold, dry and then wet. Fearful. Angry. Sad. Happy. The emotions, smells, touches, all of it, whirled through him and around him, away from him and towards. It sped faster and faster, until Lucas could feel his mind beginning to split like the cracking of ice before an avalanche. He could feel the wisps of snow start to rumble down the hill. They started to take boulders of sanity with them, tumbling into a ravine far below.

His fear and panic started to ebb away as his grip on a reality started to diminish, as his mind started to flow away from him. The memories, the smells and touches, the emotions, all overcame him. His mind could take no more. It cracked and slid downwards.

Until everything just stopped. Everything but his central intelligence, which sat there numb and mute, ravished and dark.

Light bloomed in a sharp electric shock. Memories reordered themselves into something that reflected chronology. Strong bars dropped down separating him from them.

He had memories, he could see them caged and tamed.

He could not reach them. He needed to reach them. He did not know why. He had to regain them.

Heavy vertical bars closed around his central core. Electricity coursed through it, and he screamed in anguish as it flayed him, ripped in to him, bursting his being asunder.

He could see who he was. The grey, the white and the black. It did not seem to have any relevance nor significance. The memories. Through the bars he could still see them and he yearned for them.

More electricity scourged him. But it did not matter.

He watched as shades became attracted to bars that seemed to be a prison. There was no pattern, but still, it had no relevance.

He approached a bar. It hummed. He touched it and flew backwards as a shock ripped through him.

More white and black clung to the bars, as well as all of the shades in between. He felt propriety leave him. He felt all sense of wrong and right depart. Despair and fear drained from him and he began to feel invincible.

He could take on the world and nothing could defeat him.

He did not notice his ability to discern leave, nor his shades of right and wrong. They stuck themselves to the bars of his prison and Lucas did not notice.

A physical thunk reverberated through *everything*. He suddenly had vision. He could see a metal statue directly in front of him and more in his periphery. They were giants and yet he seemed to be of equal height. He tried to move his head but could not.

A whistle sounded, surely beyond the range of human hearing, but Lucas could hear it anyway.

He about-turned right, much to his own amazement. A crash sounded in unison to his own footsteps. The whistle blew a different tune, and this time he marched. Facing him, now outside, was a brick wall, and lined up in front of it stood a row of people, a mixture of women and men, adult and child, soldier and commoner. The whistle sounded and they stopped. A voice roared a series of numbers and Lucas had a gun at his shoulder, aimed at the people in front of him.

He felt nothing, although he knew he should. A surge of power ran through him, awful and exhilarating.

A last whistle sounded.

Lucas fired and the people died.

CHAPTER 24 – RIDING THE RAGING BEAST

They arrived at a compound in a part of west London. It had evidently swelled to huge proportions, encompassing the entirety of what used to be a large public parkland. A high wall of orange bricks, reaching to a height of perhaps thirty feet, encircled the compound making it impossible to see inside. Guard towers were spaced around the perimeter with armed guards in each.

A lieutenant inspected the driver's paperwork, raised an eyebrow and allowed them to pass without further ado. Inside, the complex was not what William had expected, although he supposed he should no longer expect the mundane – he no longer lived in a world where the mundane truly existed. He had considered that perhaps they would be taken to a normal railway station, perhaps even one inside a regimental barracks. It *was* both of those things, but also so much more. He had expected a train. One of those green, blue or black affairs that hissed steam and was driven by a red and black faced old timer in coal stained overalls. One of those things that you saw everyday with small children beaming brightly, suited men reading serious papers and old ladies gossiping quietly. These things were pleasing to the eye, a place where a man could relax in comfort knowing that, as long as he had his copy of Bradshaw's with him, he could be anywhere in the country at the stated time, fresh and ready for anything. They smelled beautiful, they were big and comforting, they were *home*.

The monstrosity in front of the company certainly hissed and its one saving grace was that it *smelled* like a real train. Other than that, it gave no cause for comfort.

It was a raging beast, a fortress on wheels. The engine stretched longer by half than a normal engine, and it was black, cold and hard. Thick armour plating clothed all of its surfaces and a stumpy funnel peered a mere six feet in to the air, a jagged crown set on its top. The cabin seemed completely enclosed, made of the same armour cladding as the engine itself with a tiny porthole on either side. A cunning sight-glass extended upwards from the cabin, an array of mirrors allowing the rotating scope to give a two-hundred and seventy degree view, only the ninety degrees behind being blind. Appended to the top of the rear cabin hunched a gun turret housing a pair of stubby cannons large enough to down a charging rhinoceros. There was a vast cow-catcher at the front, matt black and spiked. Even its wheels were ominous, larger than normal, and black and foreboding, the steam licking around them creating an aura both terrible and beautiful.

A dozen carriages were attached. Like the engine, they didn't give any of the innate cheeriness of a normal steam train. All of them were menacing, the same gunmetal grey and armour cladding, windows were mere slits to allow weapons to be fired, with the exception of the officers coach, where daylight was expected, and servants would put up removable armour in the event of a battle. Raised bunkers appeared on top of each carriage, in which sat a pair of soldiers armed with a small cannon and powerful rifles that were new and queerly designed.

It was a fortress on wheels: it had artillery, fortifications and infantry. It was colossal. Her name was Black Bess.

William, Amara, Victoria and Elizabeth gazed on mouthing a silent 'O'. Bob would probably be doing the same if she could. They remained motionless and astounded until a young lieutenant cleared his throat. They were shown to the middle carriage, which was deemed the safest carriage. On the way they peered through the tiny slits in to the other carriages, and it became obvious that this was a large force, perhaps a hundred or more to each carriage, crammed in in a most uncomfortable sardine-like fashion. They were all clad in red jackets and white trousers, well pressed and clean-shaven. All of the soldiers carried a smaller version of the same queer rifles that the men above them carried, of which William had heard whisper of, but never seen in action. Sam Browne belts contained grenades and spare ammunition. A low muttering was evident, but these were obviously serious soldiers on a serious mission.

Their carriage was partitioned. The rearmost contained more tinned soldiers. The forward half, however, was quite luxurious, and it contained the commissioned officers drinking Earl Grey tea or expensive brandy.

They were introduced to the commanding officer. Or rather, William was. Lieutenant Colonel James Estcourt obviously wasn't a compromising man. He stood tall and lean, with black hair and large grey-streaked mutton chops that made his fierce gaze and heavily lined face all the more uncompromising. He had a nose reminiscent of Wellington. Medals adorned his left breast and his eyes showed permanent suspicion.

"Pleased to meet you, Sir William," he said, entirely dismissing the others. His tone was clipped and martial. "We're glad to have you along, but we will not be able to babysit the ladies, I'm afraid."

Estcourt looked Amara up and down, not bothering to try to conceal his disdain. Her pregnancy was now quite visible and he continued brusquely. "They should disembark immediately. As for that," he motioned at Bob. "Is it any use in a scrap?"

William hid a smirk, the ladies bristled and Bob's eyes turned a malignant red. It was a depth of colour William had rarely seen before. He'd hate to see her truly angry!

"Lieutenant Colonel Estcourt, may I introduce my sisters, Vic and Liz. They are extremely capable. In fact, they are a distinct advantage, as men seem to hesitate before engaging. The Lady Amara is my ward and there is simply no discussion over her embarkation. Bob is her chaperone. She, too, is a lady. For propriety, I believe that will suffice for our needs."

He didn't often get hot under the collar but, irrationally, he was quite angered by the man in front of him.

Estcourt opened and closed his mouth. Dealing with civilians was not his forte and the way that Hope had emphasized the word *Lady* regarding the black woman was very far out of his sphere of understanding. She clearly was not a high-born lady and even though she wore a head shawl, there was something distinctly unusual about her cranium, even if he wasn't quite sure what. He shrugged. "Very well, but I am not responsible for anyone but you, Sir William." He turned to an aide. "I want that recorded, Smith."

The aide reddened slightly and cleared his throat. He was obviously nervous in his superior's presence. "Sir, I believe that it may be prudent to place a small guard on the Lady Amara. I believe she is in Lord Melville's plans." It was prettily put and the man had one of those unfortunate faces that flushed a beetroot red, belying his confidence of tone.

"If she's in Lord Melville's plans and not in my orders, she can bloody well get off my train then," he barked at his aide, and swinging round to William. "Immediately."

William smiled and rooted in his jacket pocket, producing Melville's *carte blanche*. It was literally a small white card with minutely written orders. He felt rather smug as he presented the card. Estcourt snatched it out of his fingers and he reviewed it through a rather heavy-looking brass monocle. He handed it back.

"Harrumph," barked Estcourt. He turned to his aide. "Half a dozen men, but note my chagrin, if you please, Mr Smith."

He about-turned and strode to his table. Smith made a few notes, looked up at William with a wink and a smile. "This way, if you please, Sir William, Ladies." He showed them to an empty table next to that of the Lieutenant Colonel, who studiously ignored them as he studied a map of the terrain from Alderley village, where the closest station was situated, to Birtles Hall.

It was undulating terrain with no significant hills via the direct route, but it seemed to offer plenty of cover to allow his men to approach without detection. Equally, he was concerned about those same copses of woodland that were generously interspersed along the way. These could quite easily contain an effective ambush by only a couple of men and some light artillery pieces, such as a Gatling gun, or some other similar ordnance, and that could lead to disaster should a trap be effectively sprung.

The plan was obvious: the garrison from Capesthorne Hall, less than a mile from Birtles Hall, would contain the invasion and then, in a classic pincer movement, their force would smash in to the rear of the enemy should they arrive on schedule.

The most obvious and easiest route for Estcourt's men to take was the direct country lane, and he clearly considered this his favourite option, regardless of the opportunity for ambush. William cleared his throat.

"I recently walked those hills quite extensively, Colonel, and if I may offer some advice, don't take the easy way. It will only walk you to the front door, as there's no easy way to traverse from here," he indicated an area on the map, "to the back door under any form of concealment. If I may be so bold as to suggest this route, it will take a short while longer, but it will drop us down from this cover here," he indicated some rolling hills and some more light woodland, "right into their blindside. It's not obvious, but the paths down are suitable for a force of this size, as once we reach here," again he indicated a raised area on the map. "We can group as you require, and attack forthwith. We have no idea of their disposition or if they expect us to arrive in such a fashion. If they do expect us and we take the easy way, a force this size will be decimated *en route*."

Estcourt merely grunted without saying a word.

The train when it pulled away did so with sonorous screams of agony, its immense weight making it feel like she would never be able to move. The stresses and strains of the machine vibrated through each and every carriage. But move she did, and Black Bess rumbled heavily through the suburbs of London, eventually passing into a more rural setting. Even after several miles of travelling, the vast behemoth still seemed to be accelerating, until eventually the train rattled along at a fearsome pace. William hoped that the strength of the lines was sufficient for such a load.

The journey was mostly dull because there wasn't a lot for them to do, the main interest being shown towards Bob, a novelty to all of the officers in the compartment. Frankly, they were slack-jawed with amazement, and whenever she moved, there was a slight pause amongst them. Having witnessed what had passed between Estcourt and Hope, and by dent of their martial training, no questions were levied of the company.

They ate a hearty meal, the food being served to the officers vastly superior to the rustic nature of the fare eaten by the soldiers on the other side of the partition. Wine, brandy and port were offered, but the ladies were still a little too fuzzy to consider it and William wanted a clear head.

Estcourt, having considered the maps more fully, as well as his own boorish behaviour, requested William to describe his proposed trail to the target. He kept his aloof and military bent, but some of his arrogance melted a touch as William described the way with precision, pointing out bottlenecks and likely places for sentries, should any be posted. Estcourt became steadily more impressed at the orderly nature of Hope's mind and the keen intelligence that pinpointed the relevant details.

The Lieutenant Colonel mused for a few moments. "She's a beast is this train, faster than anything else in the world I'm led to believe. And secret, very secret. We'll arrive at Alderley hours before they could possibly expect, but if they have sentries, the careful route makes more sense."

"They also have Brocklehurst, Sir. A traitor, but he was very highly placed for anything technological. He's probably aware of this train and its capabilities, which means that any force may well be forewarned. I'd suggest that your caution is signally sensible."

Smith informed them that the journey would be completed in record time, but it was still gone midnight by the time they arrived at their destination. It was chilly and quiet, the terrain slightly foreboding as a bright moon cast stark, spectral shadows around the place. The village centre contained nothing more than a small row of houses down either side of the main street and the necessary shops – a grocer, a butcher, and a blacksmith, the latter of which was looking quite run-down as the requirement for horses became far more reduced from old. Moving up the hill in loose formation, they passed secluded abodes, large houses with even larger grounds, which were contained behind railings and thick hedges, wealth evident in vulgar splendour as the self-made middle classes tastelessly raised themselves above their station.

They moved up the hill in the direction of Alderley Edge itself, before bearing right down a farm track that wound first upwards and then downwards towards a still-invisible Birtles Hall. It was a tricky passage with over a thousand men in tow, especially for those who had to shoulder the burden of light artillery pieces that all hoped wouldn't be required. A stroll that would normally have taken an hour took three times as long. Estcourt displayed his displeasure because the direct route would have only take forty-five minutes. William remained silent, praying that it was a moot point.

Half a mile from their destination, after descending several dales and climbing several hills, the main body of men, hidden on the blindside of one such rise, halted. Estcourt, Hope and the other officers surveyed the Hall from the edge of a copse of trees as it gleamed dully in the moonlight. If it hadn't been for the moon, nothing would have been visible and even with it, as large as it was in the sky, nothing could be seen but the vague, wavering outlines of buildings.

William described it all for the benefit of the officers, pointing out the snake of the road on the far side of the hall that led from the lane to the main entrance. There were informal living quarters − large and impressive buildings that had housed the engineers and scientists − to the low scruffier buildings that would have been the residences of the farming folk in the previous Lord Hibbert's day. The Hall itself was rear-on to them, but William described the various approaches and the lay-out of the building itself from entering the large portico entranceway. Privately, William was wondering if this was all a wild goose chase, as the estate was quite obviously deserted.

CHAPTER 25 – HUMBUGGED

And that's when it began. Just not at Birtles Hall. Another half-mile or so beyond, invisible in the moonlight, was the larger estate of Capesthorne, where most of the French royal family lived. Only a few of them were pure-blood French – the oldest – whilst the younger ones were bastard half-breeds of French and English. In some eyes, this was a disgraceful turn of affairs. The hero of many years of war, Arthur Wellesley, had married a Frog. It enhanced the taint on his reputation amongst the upper echelons of society, adding to the blot for the time it had taken to defeat Napoleon, and the vast numbers of casualties that now crippled Britain. The results of their union were present at Capesthorne. Whilst not exactly a prison, the constant danger of assassination meant they rarely left the estates, seemingly happy with their lot. If he'd survived a few years longer, he would have been bouncing a cherub-faced toddler of three on his knee, his grandson, the newest addition to the French royal family.

It was sudden: one moment the night lay silent and eerily moonlit, a soft mist rolling along the pastures. And then there came a distracting flash of orange flame that turned in to many flashes of orange flame. The unsynchronised compressions of sound that were the stuttering reports of small arms fire echoed and rolled over the hills. William could make out the gruff of ancient muskets and the crack of modern rifles, interspersed with rapid machine gun fire. In between were vast gouts of flame and the subsequent dull, thunderous booms of artillery pieces.

Rapidly, Estcourt called for a squad of one hundred scout troops. Dumping their haversacks, they were ordered to quick-time their way to Capesthorne Hall, assess the situation and engage only if urgently required to assist the sizeable garrison stationed at the Hall. One of his senior officers led the squadron.

The remaining troops set forth in a rapid, but more measured pursuit. He left no-one at Birtles Hall as it was so patently deserted. At one point during their journey there was an explosion of massive proportions, and William could feel the heat from a quarter-of-a-mile distance as a dirigible went up in flames, a vast rolling fireball sweeping upwards before rapidly disappearing, leaving everyone partially blind by the extreme brightness.

They stumbled on, hurrying as fast as they could, to the tune of automated rifle fire rising and descending. There were many more flashes coming from the invading force. Fire from the Hall returned in a desultory fashion, erratic and without order.

Then, there was the sound of rifle fire rolling left to right in a continuous half-company fire: the light troops that had gone ahead were engaging the invaders in a well-drilled, well-disciplined, hail of bullets. The darkness receded as they advanced, a number of fires taking hold within some of the buildings illuminating the way. They were close enough now to hear the screams of pain whenever there was a lull in the crack of weapon fire. It was, William knew, the real sound of battle. He hated it. He had given Bob surreptitious orders to keep Amara safe; in fact it was Bob's sole mission, and she had been made quite aware of this. Estcourt had made it perfectly clear that none of them were supposed to engage the enemy, he didn't want the discipline of his well-oiled units disturbed by the actions of mere civilians. William and his sisters were all well-armed, however, and they all had weapons drawn, even though they were at the rear of the unit.

A substantial force of invaders returned fire at the small squadron that they now approached. Estcourt's men were well positioned behind the brow of a low rise, lying down to prevent them becoming easy targets. There were, however, a few unfortunates. The sights of war. William shuddered.

Estcourt deployed his men. He had a substantial force but was significantly disadvantaged by not knowing the terrain. Thankfully, the dirigibles were negated by the lack of daylight and weren't firing their cannon, where a small error in judgment could lead to catastrophe for their own raiders. What's more, he could not fight a normal battle, where two lines of men shot at each – with automation came a substantial change in the tactics of warfare and Estcourt, for all of his seniority, didn't have a great deal of practical experience in this type of battle. An aide standing next to Estcourt died abruptly, a small bullet hole in his forehead. A morass of brain tissue and bone exploding from a hole the size of an orange from the rear. He had soiled himself as he fell and it mingled with the smell of gunpowder. The odour of war.

Estcourt's men split into groups of two hundred. Two of these groups supplemented the scouts on the low rise, whilst the other two groups went left and right, scurrying from cover to cover, firing blindly in to the night. It was here that William could see the benefit of the uniform – it seemed to shine in the moonlight and it meant that there was little chance of being confused for an enemy trooper.

Hope felt a metal hand on his shoulder and turned to see Bob gazing back the way they had come. A small number of dirigibles, two of them massive beyond belief, were silhouetted by the moon. They were landing at Birtles Hall.

"Christ," said Estcourt, following William's gaze. "They're trying to bloody-well humbug us!"

William thought rapidly. "Colonel, give me fifty men, we'll reconnoitre."

Estcourt snapped at an aide, and within a minute, William had a force of fifty under the command of a young Lieutenant, a boy called Jones. Hope smiled, he could barely be shaving yet and he appreciated the subtlety of Estcourt, effectively having handed command of the unit to William himself whilst satisfying the hierarchy of the military.

They dumped all of their extraneous baggage where they stood. Bob shadowed Amara, who was armed with a pair of modern revolvers. Vic had her loaded crossbow, with a large quiver of bolts fastened to her back. A pair of pistols were in holsters at her hips. Liz had her pistols and had managed to liberate an automated rifle, along with a magazine belt. Their features were pale in the moonlight, although William presumed that they would be pale in any light, the skin of their faces drawn tight against their skulls. They were scared but determined and they received many an admiring glance – both for their beauty and for their obvious fortitude – from the troops that they were now travelling with.

Stumbling in the half light, they travelled as quickly as possible, hugging treelines and not exposing themselves along the ridges of the rolling countryside. This was where the British uniform was a liability: William thought that they shone as loud as flaming beacons, a burning red that crept on ghastly white limbs.

Unencumbered they made surprisingly quick time back to Birtles Hall. Even in this light, it was obvious that the force they faced was small – two large dirigibles for carrying the men of bronze, and two more as an escort. Obviously, they had hoped to sneak in and out again undetected. They almost had, just a small matter of the moon and a wandering eye from Bob having rumbled the deception.

The force may have been small, but it still outnumbered the fifty men that approached. And then there was the small matter of the added advantage. They also had Rune present. He was immediately visible to all, although only Bob and William recognised him for what he was. His blackness transcended the darkness, occupying a place under the unlit portico that exuded darkness, or perhaps sucked in light. It hurt William's eyes to gaze upon the beast, a strange sense of dissociation in his mind.

Bob snapped him out of it with a nudge and a twirl of her fingers. "Stay with Amara," she signed rapidly, "and direct the forces. Only I can match Rune."

She didn't give William any time to respond, but thrust a surprised Amara into his arms (which was quite a thrill, as well as deeply embarrassing) and started down the hillock they were positioned behind.

William barked orders for the ten best marksmen to stay put and pick off the invaders as best they could. The rest were to follow him. He glared at his sisters, but said nothing. He knew that anything he said to try and keep them safe would fall on deaf ears. If anything, they would try something stupider or more dangerous to spite his patronising them so. He passed Amara to them in a flash of inspiration, and ordered them to keep her safe.

"Especially from that beast," Amara added, shuddering. Evidently, Rune still had an effect on her. The sisters closed in on her, serious in their duty. William was relieved. By rights, all three of them should remain safe.

There was a crackle of gunfire now, and beneath his feet William could feel a rumble as walls collapsed. Brocklehurst's men were wreaking destruction in the cellars below. A redcoat in front of William collapsed in a mist of blood, and a hundred yards ahead, an enemy pirate fell shortly after the hum of a bullet hissed overhead from the hillock behind.

The darkness at the portico moved. It slid, it floated in their direction and Bob moved towards the shadow, a clumsy, thumping beast in comparison. There was a crash and a thud as they met, although in this light and shadow it was impossible to see who held the advantage. Rune staggered back one moment, and then Bob would be sent flailing to the floor the next, rising beneath a flurry of blows that appeared to have no effect.

Meanwhile, William's force had taken cover behind a wall and was peppering the enemy force. Ten of their number ran forward, crouching low, whilst being covered by the main force. and disappeared behind some laurel hedging before splitting into two teams of five, each one heading for a large dirigible. The harsh staccato of gunfire blinded and deafened them. Where five men had moments before run from cover, there now lay only corpses, wiped out by a salvo from a machine gun mounted on one of the airships. The other force fared better, making it to the cover of a small building adjacent to the closest large airship. There was a pause, a brief, eerie silence. Even the grunts and clangs of battle between Bob and Rune seemed to dim.

The silence disappeared again, and, as one, the remaining five moved, two firing their weapons randomly in the direction of the dirigibles, the other three running and hurling heavy sacks over the decks of the ship. They turned and sprinted back. A bullet tore through one man as he retreated. A huge explosion rocked the ship, vaporising the other two in an instant. William watched in horror as the building that offered cover to the last two riflemen collapsed, burying them underneath heavy rubble. Ten men had dead in a matter of moments, and still the battle raged.

The airship detonated a second time as the balloon caught, and William and his men instinctively ducked as a searing wave of heat blew past their position.

It cast Bob and Rune apart. Without a glance, Rune was ran, careless of the flames, towards the remaining dirigibles. As he ran alongside the second large behemoth, it exploded, the balloon superheating to spontaneously combust from the combination of heat from the ordnance and the heat from the exploding balloon of its sister ship. The temperature soared tremendously, scorching William's still-sensitive skin from where he stood, but Rune staggered on, seemingly unaffected.

There hadn't been time for a scream from the first airship. It had been destroyed utterly. From the second, now a pile of burning deck and canvas, nothing but terrible screams could be heard.

The smaller dirigibles were further away, ladders descending to the ground, mooring ropes holding them down.

Twenty or so burly men appeared on the portico from the inside of Birtles Hall. Half a dozen brass man were being carried between them. The pirates reached for guns when they saw the devastation. The bronze men clanged audibly as they fell, even over the crackle of weapons fire and the horror of the exploding behemoths.

The dozen men retreated back in to the building but a single solitary figure ran from the building and William immediately recognised it as that of Brocklehurst. He could not afford to be taken by British forces.

"Kill that man!" Hope bellowed, and, turning towards the hillock, he gestured towards the mound where his sharpshooters still lay.

He aimed his weapon and fired, all of the men around him did the same.

With the flames, the greyness of dawn, and a spectacularly disjointed running style, Brocklehurst led a charmed life, because not a round hit home, nor did he stumble or fall. Until a bloodcurdling scream pierced the darkness and a dark figure ran from their cover, rushing straight for Brocklehurst, who, unable to help himself, turned at the inhuman noise.

A crossbow bolt thudded in to his thigh, and he went down silently grasping at the limb.

Amara reached him, screaming audibly still, a dagger gleaming in her hand, but before she could plunge the weapon in to him, an extended limb wrapped itself around her waist, and a dark shadow loomed in the firelight. The tentacle lifted her high into the air, and Amara froze in shock and terror. Her knife fell from nerveless fingers to the ground. Bob, who had retreated back towards the hillock, started her rumbling run back in their direction, but it was obvious that she could not catch Amara, Rune and Brocklehurst before they reached the dirigible.

Another crossbow bolt flew through the night, a twang coming from William's right, but Rune merely swatted the missile from the air, and even though he was struck many times in the back by bullets as he retreated, none seemed to have any effect.

Amara's screams, which had ceased temporarily, returned anew, but now with desperation and fear in those tones. William led a sortie of his men towards Rune. They were too far away and Rune was too quick. Another tentacle had grasped a moaning Brocklehurst into his embrace and he simply sped to a rope ladder. A young boy waited by the mooring rope, a harness around his waist. As soon as Rune was on the ladder, the rope was released and the dirigible, mooring rope boy swinging beneath, swept up in to the grey sky. William could only watch in frustration as it rose majestically, prettily silhouetted once again against a falling moon. It was, William saw with no surprise, the Bucentaur.

They had saved the automata, but they had lost Amara. A hole appeared in William's chest as the thought filled his mind. *He'd lost Amara*. He fell to his knees in despair and anger at his failure.

CHAPTER 26 – THE CHASE

Suddenly there came the sound of nearby gunfire and several of the men around William fell. He swung round towards the mansion house and saw that his force stood between it and the remaining small dirigible. William had completely forgotten about it.

William's hope and despair blossomed at the same time. If only they could secure the dirigible, but they first had to stop the crew hiding in the house and then somehow board her. Like the professional, well-trained soldiers that they were, his men were already returning fire as they scrambled for cover.

His sisters appeared at his side. Victoria now held a pair of revolvers for the simple fact that she only had a few bolts left. Elisabeth retained her rifle, aiming and firing in a calm manner. William joined in, although he was much less careful, aiming in the general direction of the enemy and letting off a small blaze of lead in that general direction. Liz's approach to the firefight, and that of the soldiers, gave better results. Within a few minutes, fortified by those men who joined them from the hillock (William had entirely forgotten about them, and thanked the evolution of the army for now allowing their men some freedom of action, within certain boundaries), they had pinned the ship's crew inside Birtles Hall. Bob then proceeded to haul down the columns that held the portico aloft, the wanton destruction sealing the entranceway. She was seemingly oblivious of the occasional bullet that came her way. The collapse of the entrance was rapidly followed by another satchel of explosives – the men were clearly in a grim mood after the brutal little fracas and not in any sort of mood to take prisoners. The room through which the bomb was thrown seemed to jump in a blur of vision, and then abruptly caved in rapidly, gracefully followed by the whole front of the house, which slowly disintegrated in whorls of dust and a hail of mortar.

Satisfied that they had nullified the threat from the Hall, and in extra quick time, William ordered Liz to shoot the trembling boy who waited by the mooring rope of the remaining dirigible. She did not hesitate, even though it was clear that he was barely out of short pants. The boy crumpled to a heap, some fifty feet away, never stirring again.

Dawn gleamed far more closely now, the cloudless sky lightening to a pale blue on the eastern fringes. William beckoned the young lieutenant across, thankful that he still lived.

"Do any of your men know how to pilot one of these?"

"No, Sir William, not directly, although a number have served on naval frigates."

There was a snort from behind. "William, we need a few men to do exactly as we say and that damn thing can be airborne in five minutes."

William turned round, registering some surprise because it was his sister, Elisabeth, who had spoken. Victoria swept the battlefield for used crossbow bolts, unerringly flitting from corpse to corpse, knowing exactly where each had been shot.

"Since when could you fly?"

"We've been helping out at the local airfield. It's boring doing nothing but learning how to behave like a lady. Even fencing and boxing get a bit dull after a while. So we decided to go down a year or two ago whilst you were away plant hunting." The last bit was said quite scornfully.

"It looks like a bog standard scow, from here, it's not even fitted with heavy armaments or any of the more up-to-date motorised contraptions," Vic continued from her sister having collected as many bolts as were serviceable. "They're simple to fly, especially as we've got the prevailing winds. That is, presuming you want to follow that ship?"

William could only nod.

"Excellent, a few men to alter the sheeting once we're away, should be quite easy. You just need to capture it first." She smiled sweetly at William.

He blinked. He shrugged. He turned towards the airship, and reaching it shouted "Ahoy the ship!"

"Bugger off, you bastard," came a northern voice.

"You can't escape, you fool. Your crewmen are all in that house. I presume that only leaves you?" Before the man could reply, he continued. "I'm coming aboard, and if you're reasonable about it, I swear no harm will come of you."

"I said bugger off, you bastard!"

Liz and Vic watched as William started to ascend the rope ladder, regardless. He whistled, rather tunelessly. What appeared to be a tune from the deep south of America. A former rebel tune. A face appeared at the top and Liz took careful aim, but Bob stayed her. Somehow, she had sneaked up on them.

He reached the top. The northerner took a single look at him, his grim visage, the blood and powder on his clothes, and most importantly, the look in his eye. He gestured William aboard, standing to some semblance of mock attention as he did so. His rheumy eyes watched Hope warily.

With a shriek, the two girls ran over and clambered up the rope ladders like seasoned riggers. William had gallantly allowed the man the liberty of his ship (he was the Captain after all), especially on learning that he could fly the damn thing blindfold. *Sod my sisters*, he thought.

They were less forgiving, however, and they were certainly a lot less trusting than William. They cared even less about honour, they hadn't promised anything, and they were most obviously not under William's command.

Their first order, given at gunpoint to the protesting man, was to land the airship gently because it was the only way they could get Bob aboard. Grumbling loudly about "bloody toffs", he did so. Bob came aboard and calmed the sisters to William's train of thought immediately, although he didn't see any communication. They did, however, let the man be, whatever she had done.

The remaining soldiers alighted also. William could see that the young lieutenant was shaking, pale and extremely quiet, but given his brave conduct, in what was probably his first combat situation, there were no nudges or anonymous teases from his command. They studiously ignored his moment of weakness, remembering their own first time and William became even more impressed at the body of men before him. The boy was pleasant and obviously had a good rapport with his men in peacetime, those self-same soldiers who could be tricky when they were bored, spending every last ha'penny in bars and brothels. He had repaid the trust that they had put in him, fighting hard and commanding intelligently, although William could not remember any of it.

A few moments of silence passed awkwardly between them. Everyone looked towards one another for what to do. None of them were truly in command – William was a civilian, and the boy should await for word from Estcourt.

Jones shouldered his way forward. "We're coming with you, Sir William," he said. "I was ordered to stick with you, so that's what we're doing."

His men looked at him with pride. They would look after him with their own lives. It was odd how it could work like that, a single moment such as this and a legend could be borne, for in years to come old codgers would tell tall tales of their times with the legendary Colonel Jones (for that was surely his destiny), and watched him grow from boy to man, how they'd helped his star flourish.

"Send a message to Estcourt, we're heading south, I'm considering Le Mans as the most likely destination."

William also ordered a check on ammunition, which turned out to be paltry, leading to a further delay, as some of the men were sent to search the corpses and the wounded. In the end they had a decent amount, although the ammunition wasn't ubiquitous, which meant a number of enemy weapons were also collected, most of which were quite inferior to the modern weaponry carried by the soldiers.

The airship itself had plenty of victuals, so soon after the order was given to set sail.

As they rose, they were greeted by a growing panorama of destruction, highlighting the short, but brutal, affair that had just taken place at Birtles Hall. The sun had still not quite risen, although it was quite light and a vast swathe of debris initially caught their gazes. There wasn't a murmur from any of the crew as they stared down at the pall of smoke, inhaled the stench of sulphur and a lingering acridity of burnt hydrogen. Dust still settled from the collapsed frontage of the hall and it was obvious that somewhere inside, a fire had taken hold. The hulks of the two ruined behemoths, like vast skeletons, were strewn across the grounds of the estate. Corpses and the groaning wounded receded as they rose.

But then, the spectacle unfolded further.

Vast gouts of flame rose spectacularly from Capesthorne Hall, where dozens of enemy dirigibles burned, small but bright figures in the near distance. They saw more explosions as errant flames ignited pockets of lighter-than-air gases. Great swathes of wreckage could be seen where vast detonations had erupted, plumes of black smoke darkening the skies. William wondered how he could have missed such things, until he realised that he was half deaf with their own pyrotechnics, and that subconsciously they were all shouting loudly whenever they spoke. The devastation at the further estate dwarfed anything at Birtles Hall. Not a building stood unscathed. The beautiful bridge that spanned the lake had burst asunder, and dozens of bodies could be seen, even at this distance. There were still bursts of gunfire apparent. Estcourt appeared to have won, but there were still pockets of fierce fighting taking place and they witnessed a number of the Colonel's men crumple as a grenade landed at their feet.

William suddenly felt sick to the stomach and he sat heavily from where he stood, a wave of faintness sweeping over him, dark spots blurring his vision. Only a brass hand stopped him collapsing completely.

"William, stay with us," she signed. "We have to get Amara back. You have no idea of the cruelty that will be done to her if we don't get her out of that beasts hands."

"I can guess," he signed back.

"No, really, you cannot." Her signing abrupt, eyes red.

"Explain."

"No."

William cursed and shrugged. The spell of weakness passed and, realising that he was famished, he ordered for food to be prepared for all of the men, including the captive.

He could feel the smoulder of anger starting to ignite deep in his stomach.

"Just where the hell do you think we are going?" he shouted furiously at Bob. He turned and stormed off to the deserted quarter-deck, where he everyone left him undisturbed to pace out his frustration, until thirty minutes later, Jones brought him a large plate heaped with food, accompanied by a large flagon of ale.

With a full stomach and the ale in his veins, the fire burning deep inside the pit of his stomach was temporarily extinguished. His sisters recognised the subtle signs, and they now approached him.

"We probably won't catch the other dirigible before Le Mans, William," said one.

"They won't go there. We're not going there," he replied tersely. "We're going straight to Paris, and so are they."

"Why?"

"I don't know, but there's no point going to Le Mans."

"We need a plan for when we get there," said the other.

William looked at them both mutely and nodded. He signalled an apology to Bob, who stood watching at the other end of the ship, a non-committal pale colour in her eyes. He then summoned the sisters, Bob and the young lieutenant to the captain's quarters, along with more ale. He bade them sit whilst they discussed a plan of action.

*

William stalked up and down the ship. It was quite small, so it didn't take long, and given a longer journey, it is quite likely that he would have worn a deep furrow in to the oak decking. The more he walked, the angrier he became.

They weren't flying especially high, but low cloud scudded in and with it came cold rain that soaked William to the skin. It did not dampen his ire or cool his passions.

He had to get the girl back and Brocklehurst would pay. So would Rune, Rimbaud and everyone else in that damned prison. His fists were clenched tightly. From the shelter of the captain's cabin, his sisters watched him, all thoughts of their normal levity banished. They had only seen him this way once before, and they'd then been children. On that occasion, he'd been unrecognisable from their brother. After he'd finished with *that* man, they'd looked upon a stranger, an alien almost, covered in gore and blood from a head split remorselessly apart, and from where an artery had gushed and pumped.

They recognised the same fire; and they were a little afraid.

Bob watched also, and her eyes emanated a fiery red: she seemed to be in a blaze of emotion, and any signings shared between the three had been tense and abrupt, ending any thought of continued communication with her.

Bob looked a little worse for wear after her tangle with Rune. Her breast plates were badly dented, and from somewhere inside, wisps of steam leaked. The solar plate on her head was shattered, pieces of it missing. Some of her fingers were slack, the minute springs over-stretched or merely damaged beyond repair. A thigh plate was missing from her left leg and she favoured her right, as if limping from invisible damage. Considering the force of the blows they had witnessed, she had survived remarkably well, the heavy plates protecting the majority of her inner workings, even if she did limp and grate and hiss as she moved.

The plan was simple – get there as soon as possible, land on the roof, smash their way in through a skylight, rappel down, rescue the girl and kill everyone else. The sisters had a few embellishments of their own, but William had, by this time, wound himself up in to a proper lather, and found himself beyond any subtleties or refinements. Hard and simple, it had always worked previously.

Eventually, William realised just how cold and wet he had become, so he came back to the captain's cabin. Without any self-consciousness, he stripped naked, hanging his garments on steam pipes that ran around the room, making it quite warm – all for the price of a few extra lumps of coal. The room was designed such, that even in battle, when the cabins were dismantled, the pipes themselves could be shut off at a valve, and the pipework removed and stowed.

They crossed the English Channel, mountainous waves rolling across and, even up here, they could smell the tang of the sea and taste the salt in the air.

Naked, he serviced his guns, nimble fingers taking the weapons apart, carefully cleaning the mechanisms, coating with oil, re-assembling and checking their operability before reloading. The sisters had already done this, Vic's crossbow gleaming gently with a fresh coat of linseed oil and Liz had serviced her new rifle under supervision from the young lieutenant, who could barely keep his eyes from her corseted figure. It was a little unfair to expect him to behave otherwise, but she'd still made him blush deeply after catching his eye and glaring at him in such a way that made the other sister laugh and give Liz a playful slap. After that she'd only pouted in a most unladylike manner, pink turning to puce on the young man's face.

And then they were back over land, and even this high, they could see a ravaged land, a ravaged people, both beaten and down-trodden.

There was no sign of the Bucentaur, but then they never expected to as she had only recently been fitted out with the newest technologies, and she'd probably extended her lead over them. They were probably warm and safe in their factory in Paris.

It felt slightly warmer this far south, and as they approached smudge on the horizon that could only be Paris, William dressed. As the sprawl came closer, so the stench began – after only a short time out of the city, in the fresh airs of rural Britain, they had forgotten the rank odour that such a mass of people generated.

And then it was there, they could see the top of the factory but could not see the Bucentaur. There were four pylons constructed on top of the building that William had not known about during his captivity. They were designed for airships to be moored to them and their captive expertly flew the dirigible whilst relaying commands to those soldiers who were at his beck and call for the procedure of docking in such a way.

It was afternoon following the night of the battle when they arrived and William's only thought was to get in rapidly. So, once docked, they disembarked immediately down rope ladders that extended from the hull of the ship. Not long afterwards, once all was set, ropes secured and with the hope of surprise still with them, three skylights were shattered by gunfire. Fifty men, the sisters and William descended in to the engineers' workshops. It looked deserted, but William's hackles rose. There was to be no surprise attack, they were expected.

Four soldiers ran over to the main doorway, and it was here that all hell broke loose.

An explosion and the four soldiers were no more, a tripwire trailing across the doorway triggering a series of grenades. A few seconds of shock ensued, followed by the doors bursting inwards and the rapid crackling of gunfire. They threw themselves to the ground, diving for cover behind cast iron engineering equipment, benches or whatever they could find. More soldiers were hit in the process. Groans sounded from the injured and sightless eyes, gazing whichever way they fell, from the dead.

More explosions as a number of grenades were thrown to follow the hail of lead and then more gunfire. Those lucky enough to have found good cover returned fire and suddenly it was a more cautious affair between men hiding behind doorways against those hidden behind benches and engineering equipment.

William, perceiving that the enemy were few in number, gestured to a dozen men that they were to follow him and that they should be rapid when they attacked. He counted down on his fingers...three...two...one...go. They leapt up, covered by their comrades and overcame the six enemy men holding the doorway. It was more of an execution, the sharp crack of weapons, the groan of wounded enemies and they were done. Beckoning for the rest to follow, he bounded down the stairs to the floor that contained the mess and sleeping quarters. A padlock secured the door. William made a snap decision to ignore the floor, although he thought it likely that they would have to come back...never mind the possibility of leaving an enemy force behind them.

There was a sudden, loud, crash behind them, back from where they had come, and certain of the source, he ordered Elizabeth and Victoria to investigate. Only one thing made that much noise and he was happy to send them away, allowing him to complete this stage of the mission without worrying about their safety.

He hurried the soldiers downstairs to the warehouse area. It was here that William feared the most, as it was here that it was easiest to convert to a good defensible position. They reached the foot of the stairs and his fears were realised. Racking had been tipped over with loopholes punched through to allow the enemy to fire from cover. To get in to the large space proper, they would have to squeeze through an opening. Someone had funnelled the entrance using a metal barricade. William peered through and noted the raised gantries where enemy guards lay. A bullet whined past closely by his ear as he showed his face slightly, causing him to jerk back. The funnel could not be moved by human hands. It was simply too heavy. Reluctantly, he ordered a man to get Bob down here at double speed. Her strength may be able to remove the barrier.

She arrived with his sisters, and simply wrenched the metal away, ripping it like a tin opener, peeling it backwards to widen the aperture. Vic and Liz were handing out a few grenades that they had managed to liberate from the enemy dead on the top floor, and those, along with the very few that remained from the battle in Cheshire, were readied.

Several were thrown in on William's command, and the soldiers ducked back in as bullets whined back at them, thankfully hitting no-one.

The grenades went off and a dozen soldiers rushed in undercover of the blast, aiming to use the barriers for their own cover. Bullets poured through the opening, and three men went down in the headlong rush, one with a wound that that entered through the forehead and exited through his groin. The remaining men made it unscathed, and started to let off shots, concentrating on those men separated only by the thickness of the barriers, as well as anyone that was stupid enough to poke out a head on the gantries higher up.

Visibility was terrible and constant flashes of light kept them blind. The percussion in the confined space deafened them and it also held on to the smoke from the grenades, making men gag and retch. Bit-by-bit, all of the soldiers were able to get through, and with minimal casualties. They secured the first section of barricades. William made it out and saw that the corpses of the enemy were young guards, not seasoned troops. There were far fewer of them than William could have possibly hoped and, following a few brief flurries, he saw one drop his weapon. More rapidly followed his lead. Fresh faced, scared youngsters came forth, hands high above their heads. The first part of the liberation of the factory was complete, but there was still no sign of Rune and Brocklehurst. Or Amara.

CHAPTER 27 – QUATRE NEUF TROIS NEUF

Amara was dragged, literally kicking and screaming, thrashing uncontrollably, utterly mindless of her fragile electrode crown. It made no difference because she was in the inhuman grip of Rune. They were followed, and she was fussed over by Arthur Rimbaud, who blathered about having to perform an emergency procedure. As usual, he apologised repeatedly and he even attempted explanations that did nothing to Amara to reduce the fact that she was still being violated once more.

Rimbaud sweated heavily as they made their way to the basement and he cast fearful glances at Rune, who's aspect oozed more taciturnity than usual, if that was possible from someone who's only emotion exuded from his eyes. He'd never even heard the beast speak! It made no difference, truth be told, because Rune scared the living hell out of him, and the day that Rune smiled would be the day of his death, for on that day, Satan himself would be present.

Behind them, he could hear gasps of pain, the rattle of keys and a lumbering thumping footfall down the stone stairs. It was Brocklehurst, and he remained in a bad way. They'd had to snap off the part of the crossbow bolt that protruded from his leg, but they did not have the medical equipment to draw it out and then not watch him bleed out. He still had a tourniquet around his leg, on which they occasionally released the pressure, so that his leg wouldn't just go blue and eventually fall off. He thought is possible that the femur was cracked or chipped. Rimbaud quite purposefully used the word excellent, as he was almost at the end of his journey to detesting the cad. He had, after all, been tricked and then left in a position of such insecurity that he had been unable to find an escape, nor any exit that would allow him credibility, potentially even his sanity.

Brocklehurst had wooed him, first with his scientific papers – well, Chapman's at any rate – and then, of course, there had been all of the financial aid. And then. And then. That was the crux of it – small steps further in to this madness, to the point where he found himself drilling holes in to the heads of innocent women... by God, just how many small steps had Brocklehurst encouraged him to take? How much perspective had he, Arthur Rimbaud, had removed, or more likely ignored in his pursuit of this thing? During moments of clarity, he could barely look at himself in the mirror, he felt like Lady Macbeth, driven insane by the blood that he had spilled and the torture that he had visited. He had even found himself washing and scrubbing, the image of the Lady removing imaginary blood from her hands foremost in his mind.

And now they required a last procedure for the near future, one last mass imbuing, because they were found out and had to flee this place.

Arthur wasn't sure he could go through with it, but he also felt that he might not even be needed for this anymore, so if he kicked up a fuss, then he would simply be killed out of hand. Brocklehurst had been most precise in his instructions that all work must be meticulously detailed and recorded, which included any input that Rimbaud had on the machinery that forced the spirits in to the carbon black.

As a compromise to himself, therefore, he'd decided that he had no choice but to comply with their desires, even if it was only to reduce the pain and suffering that Amara would endure. And if he found a safe opening to sabotage the work, then he must take it. For his own soul, he had to do something righteous, even if that did mean his very end. For now though, he must bide his time.

*

Arthur winced as Rune sat Amara forcefully into the metal chair. There was no cushion now, as he had failed in his first two attempts to seat her. The cushion was now over the other side of the room, where the chair had also been. It had bounced off some machinery, which was now being fussed over by Rimbaud and a couple of engineers. There were half a dozen other engineers in the room, all of them specialists at one or other aspect of this new form of science. They bore with them no luggage, but the unbolted door to the catacombs spoke to Arthur of their escape route, and most likely where any accoutrements would have gone.

Forcefully Rimbaud took over the checking, snarling at the engineer to get out of his damn way, and to his surprise, the engineer moved away from the diminutive scientist. When he moved away, Arthur slowed the checks to a snail's pace, unfastening and refastening various connections, muttering overtly that the only way to perform the job effectively and with minimal delay was for this preparation to be done properly.

Brocklehurst had surmised that any pursuit would give them a day to get out of the damned place. Hope would surely go to Le Mans. A lookout on the rooftops had scuppered that, though, and all manner of rushing ensued. They didn't even have time to get the additional men to engage any armed force and drive them back to their dirigible. One engineer had gone as far as to ask why they didn't just blow the pursuers out of the sky, but Brocklehurst had slapped him down. Any chance of a quiet getaway from Paris would be impossible, even with Stieber's patronage, should an airship simply blow up. Brocklehurst wanted a few days head start before any bodies were found, and by then, they would be nearing their new destination.

Rimbaud spent many minutes performing the checks, with the occasional cloud of dust dropping down from the ceiling as some impact or other rocked the foundations, heightening the extent of Brocklehurst's own misjudgement.

He could finally delay no longer, and somewhat tenderly, he started connecting the wires from the machine to Amara's crown. Somehow, she had been allowed to retain the controlling device that could kill her if she strayed outside of its sphere of influence. As hard as she tried, Rimbaud utterly refused to catch her eye, and very deliberately completed the task.

There was no gentleness as the engineer placed a rack of carbon black discs into a vacuum chamber. This was one of Rimbaud's own refinements – why do one at a time? And Brocklehurst, his brilliance in that field of technical logistics and extrapolation, had expounded this by setting up a dozen such bell jars, from which a vacuum could be pulled. They had, however, never used more than one bell jar, because soon after the set-up had been completed, Amara and William had escaped. Rimbaud had seen the strain that a dozen imbuings had placed on the girl. The souls of one hundred and forty four – one gross – being dragged in at one time from the catacombs, to the shining beacon that was the black witch may kill her. Or worse.

*

It also meant that Amara, for a short instant of no more than ten seconds, had dozens of souls running through her. Only the brevity of each encounter stopped her going insane. No-one truly understood the procedure, but the use of a human conduit was a pre-requisite, and those poor souls in Rome had been driven utterly insane by the capture of a single soul. Yet here, in Paris, Amara had enveloped thousands from the ready source of those that populated the catacombs.

Thirty minutes passed, and now the explosions and gun fire had ceased, but no-one had yet attempted to enter into the crypt below. If they had, a further explosion would have rocked the room. The door at the top was rigged to blow. In fact, all that could be heard were the angry bees infesting the brutal machine that was slowly sending Amara insane, even if the weeks of freedom had been a temporary catharsis. The walls crumbled in her mind, and they were crumbling more quickly now that she had the pain of recapture and that glimpse of freedom with William and his sisters. In some ways, the re-incarceration made it worse.

And that vast number of souls squeezing through the tiny place in her mind: she could hear them, feel them, as they were brutally transferred. Some gawped about, innocent and unknowing, whilst others fought. It made no difference. Amara imbued them all.

Les Futiles.

She could smell those same queer smells that had enveloped her when the electrodes had been introduced, and she could feel a side of her face slacken. These were the physical manifestations of the process when so many were coming through at one. She was suddenly free as the carbon black slides were filled and the machinery temporarily halted the transfer. A minute passed as engineers emptied and refilled the jars. She slumped slightly to one side because she no longer had the strength to sit straight. She felt numbness spread through her left side. The machine began to pull again and a blood vessel burst in her eye, filling it with blood. The next set of vacuum jars were full.

A crash soundedfrom above, but no explosion ensued. It didn't stop the engineers exchanging nervous glances between themselves.

"Let's go," snapped Brocklehurst, and he himself, grimacing in agony, started to remove Amara's electrodes. Several of the engineers helped, but Rimbaud merely watched, occasionally glancing at Rune, whose glittering eyes were affixed on him.

Arthur's hands were clammy, no, worse, they were dripping with sweat and he could feel a line trace down his back, following the crease of his spine. His vision became tunnelled and his ornamental sword suddenly weighed him down. His legs became leaden as he gently shifted his weight from one to the other. And then the expected command came, and to Rimbaud's ears they came as if time had slowed down.

"Kiiillll…tthhhhe…ffrrooog." Brocklehurst gave the order, speaking as if through treacle.

Suddenly, time whipped back to normal speed as the doorway imploded. One engineer was buried in the rubble, and no-one, not even Rune, moved with the shock. The debris scattered across the chamber, and dust danced powdery motes through the harsh lamplight. Funny, it had never seemed harsh before. His attention slammed back to the doorway.

There stood Bob, her eyes shimmering painfully to his gaze, although they appeared colourless. Still, even though she was a robot and utterly motionless, Rimbaud could sense her anger. It was more than that: she was apoplectic with rage. Behind her, a small force of armed men were gathered, ready for action as soon as Bob cleared the entrance.

A mere second or two had elapsed in the time since the doorway had burst asunder, and the first to react was Brocklehurst. He screamed, not in in fright, but in anger.

"What do you think you are doing, bitch? You twice traitorous whore." He hurled a piece of stone at her, but it only glanced off a breastplate.

"Obey me and serve me, like I programmed you."

Bob's fingers twirled and she strode forward towards Brocklehurst, although only Amara could understand exactly what she said. She blushed that Bob should know such language.

"Command: four-nine-three-one."

Bob stopped. Dead.

"Rune, kill the rest. You lot," he gestured towards the engineers, "bring the girl."

An engineer grasped Amara by the throat, and started to drag her along.

Rimbaud amazed himself, seemingly forgotten in the mayhem. His sword was in his hand, gleaming madly in the lamplight, and he proceeded to skewer the engineer through the back, a runnel of blood trailing down the centre groove of the blade. Amara fell gasping and Brocklehurst whipped around at the shriek from the engineer, whose legs suddenly lost all control, and he collapsed, paralysed. It didn't matter too much, as he only had a few minutes left to live.

Brocklehurst roared at what he saw, drew his gun and simply shot Rimbaud at close range. It hit him in the chest, and he was knocked to the ground at the impact, still grasping the sword as his body tensed utterly at the shock.

It was obvious that he considered Rimbaud done for, because he crouched next to Amara, grimacing in pain as he did so, totally ignoring the whimpering Frenchman.

It was his downfall.

Brocklehurst had the girl by the scruff of the neck dragging her up, the pair of them fought. Rimbaud struggled. Something major had been nicked by the bullet – not his lungs or his heart but an artery somewhere. His clothing was starting to get heavy with the blood. But he persevered at his attempts to rise. He very nearly passed out with the pain.

The frantic struggle put up by Amara drove him on. The injured Brocklehurst, who, in spite of the damaged leg, was still stronger and bigger than the girl. Desperation drove him on also. In no way could he allow himself to be captured, although he suspected that Rune had a similar command for the Englishman: watch Brocklehurst, kill if necessary. In his desperation, Brocklehurst slapped the girl cruelly across her face, taking her breath away. It caused her to cry out in pain and in shock. With that distraction and pain, he managed to haul her upright, noticing with surprise that she seemed to have given up the fight. Her eyes, though, were only on Rimbaud. The Englishman followed her gaze.

Rimbaud had managed to crawl the necessary yard to be within reach before using his sword to lever himself to a kneeling position. He watched Brocklehurst's gaze reach his own and then he switched his gaze to that most beautiful black woman, her with those violet eyes that contained wells that overflowed with feeling, with sadness and melancholia. And forgiveness. Those eyes, that forgiveness. It gave him strength because it was for him, he roared with the knowledge, although it cost him dearly as the pain lanced through his body. The steady flow of blood turned to a sudden gush. He groaned in triumph, a yell that pierced the entire chamber bringing everyone's heads swinging around. He thrust the sword once more – and for the final time – up through Brocklehurst's right side, up, up , up, out of his splintering left collarbone and together he and Brocklehurst collapsed to the floor facing each other like dead lovers, although only Brocklehurst was currently dead. Shakespeare came unbidden to Rimbaud's mind, that of Romeo and his Juliet as he faced Lord Brocklehurst and he coughed blood at his own black humour.

In an instant Amara was at his side.

"Oh Arthur." She was crying, tears streaming down her dusty face, ebony skin gleaming where the rivulets flooded.

"Quatre neuf trois neuf." He smiled at her and died.

*

William and his troops poured in to the room. They were just in time to watch Brocklehurst die and just as that happened there was an inhuman shriek at which everyone turned. Everyone spun round, everyone but Rune. He had already spun a circle and a half to bring himself facing the passageway that led underneath the Seine. It was he that had shrieked. In that pirouette, arms thudded and tentacles became razors. Men fell dead, friend and foe, without realizing that they'd been struck.

He, it, bound forward hauling a prone Amara in a vice like grip, her flailing hand still caressing Arthur Rimbaud, and then she was tucked under his arm.

The pregnant pause lasted several seconds, except for Amara who struggled futilely, like a dervish within his grip: mentally though, she was deciphering Arthurs parting words. It was the difference in French that threw her for a few moment, the difference in accent puzzling her understanding of the words spoken, something so painfully simple. And then she built the bridge across the French, just a few microseconds really, and then a second for her to realise the significance.

A command.

Rune was at the doorway now. She started to shout. Her first attempt came unintelligibly hoarse. She coughed, rasping, a needle-like pain enveloping her throat. Her second attempt was a little more coherent but nothing happened. And just as she was being bundled down the passageway, she realised that Arthur was French and Bob was made in England. She screamed the words.

"Four Nine Three Nine."

Bob became instantly operational. She didn't waken as if from a slumber, it was just as if she continued her actions from when she was previously conscious. Operational.

Alas, she was too late. Rune had disappeared. Nonetheless she ran through the open doorway after him.

William and his remaining men surged further in to the room with an ire driven more by the room itself, its clinical nature and obvious use. They dispatched with alacrity, casually almost, the remaining engineers that were loyal to Rune.

Hope considered following Bob and the monster, but realised the pointlessness given the pace that both could move at. With a flash of inspiration he realised that in no way could Paris remain home to Stieber and his clandestine operation. Which could only mean that thet would be looking for the quickest way out of the city. He ordered the remains of his small troop back up the stairs and thence to the roof. The small trek strained already weary bodies, but the rappel up the lines to the domed roof itself was tortuous. It took an age, William squirmed with desperation to get underway and refused to countenance the suggestion that someone should tend to the wounded, until Jones damned his eyes and ordered four of his men to do it anyway.

CHAPTER 28 – AND THEN THERE WAS ONE

Eventually they were away, although it seemed to take an age to the impatient William. Almost immediately, the captured captain pointed south-east at another vessel that rose from a Parisian suburb. It was only a mile or so away, but it could mean a long chase if the airship was airworthy.

There was, however, something obviously wrong with the dirigible for she fairly limped away, and the boat that William was on had virtually no-one in to slow her down. Twenty five men and women, nothing more.

Even given the fact that the renegade dirigible was injured, it took hours for them to oh-so-slowly close the distance and in that time adrenaline flowed away. An almighty realisation struck. They would be outmanned and outgunned. William didn't have a clue how to storm a ship in the air, and despair struck him a hammer blow again and again in the knowledge that he had virtually no chance of rescuing Amara. His heart felt heavy in his chest. He felt nauseous to the pit of his stomach when he thought of her.

The distance decreased so that after several hours they had closed to within almost half a mile. Their prey became identifiable although William had had the sneaking suspicion for some time that she would be the Bucentaur all along. Which, naturally, she was.

William was numb: the armaments on her were frankly brilliant. Against which William had a dozen twelve pounders, an old brass bow chaser and his sister with a crossbow as the only ranging weapons.

An idea struck William.

"Quick, a fire. I want a fire. Now."

The captured shipmaster looked at him slack jawed. Only a fool ordered a fire on a hydrogen-filled dirigible.

"A fire damn it. A wet one at that, one that makes lots of smoke, one that looks a lot worse than it is. And then slow her down."

It was a trap, obviously, but Duval had a monstrous ego, an ego the size of a planet, a superiority complex greater even than the former Lord Brocklehurst.

It worked. Duval's Bucentaur swung about and approached cautiously, but William had the crew running around frantically, those that he hadn't hidden below decks. Victoria and Elisabeth were screaming histrionically, although through fits of giggles it became difficult to distinguish the two. They were looking feral and dangerous within that laughter.

The brass bow chasers had been primed long before, and William could see that the bow chasers on the Bucentaur had been carefully aimed: they were generally more accurate on an airship than a proper sea going vessel, especially on a day of light weather like this one. There were no waves up here and the main variable, the wind, was almost non-existent.

In a vagary of the moment, William found himself peering directly at Duval through a telescope as Duval peered directly at him. The traitor sketched a sardonic bow at him. Surprisingly, William could see few sailors aboard the Bucentaur, although that monster Rune loomed ominously on the quarterdeck.

He'd briefed the crew. No heroics: jump on board, rescue Amara, straight back and away. Simple, no fuss. Anyone who fell was to be left at the mercy of the enemy, to murmurs of unease from the soldiers. No one said anything though, too many of their comrades had been killed and maimed, and Amara was beautiful and exotic. Loved. His sisters were to remain on board and as if by some psychic link, they peered at the ship master. Their job was obvious.

The bow chasers on the Bucentaur suddenly disappeared behind a bright flash and a pall of smoke. William heard the whine as an iron ball passed over his head, and as the enemy had the altitude, he spun round to see where the ball had struck. Splintering wood cacophonied and he reeled as the tub lurched.

He gazed in horror.

Only one of his sisters now stood where moments before there had been two. Half a torso – the lower half –toppled. Bloody splatters painted the deck beyond to a great rent in the deck. Blood wept from the torso instead of coursing through veins and arteries. There was no heart left to push the blood high in to the air in great bloody gouts.

Victoria stared. She was sheeted with her sister's blood. She did not scream. She could not scream.

CHAPTER 29 – THE FINAL RESCUE

William felt a rush of anger, both at his sisters and at Duval. The girls had been ordered on more occasions than he could recall to places of safety, chided to become ladies and always they had disobeyed. And THIS was the reason why he had tried to protect them, smother them from danger and the brutality that hung over society like a blight. Not only did the paupers steal each other's wine and wrestle over the dregs, but the commoners brawled, the middle classes schemed and connived, and the upper classes caused nations to embattle their lands, murdering all indiscriminately. Everywhere he looked, William saw violence. He had wanted to protect his sisters. And he had failed.

The greater anger was at Duval. The chivalrous, brutal, traitorous, turncoat bastard was the worst of them all, no nation, no pride, no morals. No honour. And at this instant, rather than freeze, William plunged in to action.

"Fire," he screamed and their own bow chaser fired along with the three portside cannons that could be brought to bear. The prow was wreathed in a stinking fug of black powder smoke, the cheapest that could be found because the Captain was unwilling to pay for anything better. The balls struck and with an audible clang as one struck the Bucentaur's bow chaser. It was thrown from it ropes and sailed over the side plunging to the countryside below.

Rockets screamed across the space from the Bucentaur, the space closing as Jones yelled in his high-pitched barely adult voice "full speed ahead." He snatched the rudder from the shipmaster and turned the ship gently on to a collision course with the enemy boat.

The rockets strafed wildly, one veering crazily upwards, another equally so downwards and a third just fell like a stone. All three exploded simultaneously and peppercorns of shrapnel fell on to their heads from the detonation above.

A moment of silence, William mused distractedly, *not that there was ever silence up here*: the wind whistled and the wood groaned, gases hissed from pipes and men grunted with exertion as cannonballs rolled down long barrels, water splashing and hissing as they were swabbed.

They were close now, very close, Victoria was stood by William, still wreathed in her sister's blood. She gripped a loaded crossbow, face taut with pain. William glanced at her. She had to have revenge, so he said nothing of the fact that she was armed for war, part of the boarding company.

He could see Duval clearly now. And Rune, holding Amara. She looked calm. What Jones had put in to place could not be undone and it would most likely lead to all of them dying.

The shipmaster had not been idle, in fact he had been the only one with any sort of initiative. He had realised the need for altitude and gassed the airbags, the boat rising gently.

Jones turned on the man, unaware of what the captain was doing, even whilst massing the crew close to the gunwale for slaughter. He pointed his gun at the man, who placated Jones with a wicked grin before hitting a valve that caused a piercing whistle as it vented gas and she plunged rapidly, smashing into the deck of the Bucentaur fully amidships.

A great crash sounded and wood groaned and collapsed. Men staggered whilst some were hurled overboard at the force of the impact.

There was a moment of strange silence as the two ships paused, a collective holding of breath before one finally began to settle on the other with a great groan of twisting timbers, and Jones led his men screaming for each man to do his duty. He was the only one capable of leading the charge, William still ran cold and Victoria looked vacant except for a grim tightness around her mouth and lips, her crossbow clenched tightly in her hand, a gun at her waist.

If the ships had been sea-faring ships, the Bucentaur would be terminally holed. The Captain would be surrendering, suing for peace. They were in the air however and there was virtually no damage to the Bucentaur's balloon.

The impact *had* sent her crew reeling, but she outnumbered Jones' small crew of marines beyond the point of superiority of weapons and training. Nevertheless the fighting began fiercely, and Jones had a mission which wasn't the destruction of all on board: Rescue Amara, get the hell out of there. The determination of the marines momentarily unbalanced the pirate crew. William and Victoria moved utterly silently, running slantwise to the battle, leaping from the highest point onto the deck below, as close to the quarterdeck as could be managed.

Rune was on one knee and his grip had momentarily loosened on Amara enough for her to start hitting his head, wild, fierce blows with the base of her fist. Somehow there was enough impact for her to escape his hold, although how she could possibly hurt the beast, William did not know.

There was a click from beside William and a bolt buried itself into the forehead of the beast. Rune looked stunned for an instant and then toppled over, his eyes growing dim and he spasmed and spasmed, over and over.

William reached the quarterdeck grasping Amara about the waist, lifting her in his arms. Close by there was a crack as Vic fired her gun. A pirate spun a graceful pirouette, blood pluming into the air from a hole in his neck.

"Jones, Jones, back to the ship," William roared over the furore, but Jones could not hear for the battle was too fierce. And then suddenly there was a vacuum at his side as Vic leapt towards Duval, who carried an injury, although whether from the impact or from battle, William did not know. He held an arm close to his chest and his sword dangled loosely from a sash around his waist.

From somewhere Vic had a sword of her own and William saw a sudden glitter overtake the look of pain in the pirate's eyes, a dark cruel glitter. Without warning he had his sword in his left hand and he thrust forward, screaming in triumph, because Vic was raising her sword to deliver a vicious swing that would surely decapitate the pirate.

She had read the look in his eyes and twisted away as best she could from the full force of the thrust, but she had over-committed and couldn't dodge away entirely. Duval's triumphant scream was cut short as the pommel of Vic's sword smashed in to his head knocking him unconscious.

William watched in horror as the sword appeared from his sister's ribs, low in the side. Unceremoniously he dropped Amara to her feet, towards his sister and picking her up, cradling her in his arms. The battle was between them and their own ship, but the pirates were fighting defensively having seen first Rune and then Claude Duval toppled. William could not care less for the pair, nor the fate of the Bucentaur. His only goal was to return to his ship and find some medical attention for his one remaining sister. Fortunately, the battle was set in close lines, neither force willing or able to try something innovative, the battle sword to sword. Not a single crack of firearms sounded now, because to reload at these quarters was to die. So William merely skirted the fight with Amara leading the way. They leapt aboard at the lowest point.

Jones had been made aware of the fact and, with a sudden rush, forced his men to hit the pirates hard. It gave them a moment of respite, enough to turn tail and flee towards the waiting ship, supported by some grenades. They were cheap and lacked power, but they were sufficiently effective for the pirates to choose not to press at the exposed backs of the retreating soldiers. Ludicrously, a cannon went off from the Bucentaur, and a massive crunch of splintering wood uttered from their ship. There was an almighty lurch as the Bucentaur seemed to be pulled off the ship that was lying on its larboard decks.

The soldiers leapt as the boats parted, and suddenly everyone was aboard, at least those that were still alive, and they streamed to the oars hauling away to open up a gap. And suddenly they were entirely free of the Bucentaur, a final scream of tortured wood and the Bucentaur lurched upwards due to a differential in lift.

Rune.

There he was stood on the rail of the Bucentaur as the gap widened ever so slowly, achingly slowly. His Vodun control was much improved from the days in Cheshire, even with a crossbow bolt still jutting forth from his forehead. A mere twenty yards separated the boats as a single tentacle stretched, splinters of nail flew at William's crew and ravenously the tentacle speared towards the black woman who could do nothing but stare, mesmerised in fear.

Again, Jones was the only man – boy, really – who reacted, slashing down with his sword with a veracity and viciousness that belied his years. He cut deeply but the flesh was strong and it whipped him aside, a great gash appearing in his cheek, hurling him against a bulkhead. The action sparked William into life. With his greater strength he hewed at the tentacle, he barely saw Amara as she concentrated her entirety on the appendage that suddenly couldn't close that final gap towards her.

He slashed down again and severed the tentacle. There was a shriek as if he had wounded of a multitude of unearthly beasts, the sound both high pitched and deep. It went further, as if it also reached beyond the range of hearing, and it resonated through them physically.

There were marines firing guns at the balloon of the Bucentaur and she started to drop, but like a great whip curling around his waist, Rune's tentacle encircled William, lifting him bodily, dragging him along the deck, smashing his head in to the side of the deck with a sickening crunch. He was overboard, somehow still conscious,

"Save Victoria. Save my sister. Flee! Protect Amara!"

They were the last words they heard him speak, anything else whipped away by the noise of the wind and the dull shock.

Jones ran to the side, his cheek leaking blood still, and he watched as the Bucentaur plummet. But it did not crash. It righted itself, its plunge becoming gentle like a leaf caught on the wind. It was away, beyond any pursuit.

Jones stood watching forlornly. His first command was a complete failure. William captive aboard the Bucentaur. Duval escaped and Rune alive. A sob burst from Vic as she had her sword wound tended. It wasn't for the injury, even if a bruised rib hurt like hell. The raw emotion of the sound meant it could only be for her brother and her sister. Amara stared into space, it was all she could do.

EPILOGUE

1. Wellesley, France, 1817

They were on the trail of a princess – or rather, an ex-princess. Rumour had it that she had been abandoned as a mewling baby at a convent in the middle of nowhere.

The convent itself, had had its fair share of trouble and strife during those troubled times. Back then, few of the nuns had remained virgins.

It was more peaceful now and, as normal, Wellesley was adamant on the discipline of his troops. He kept a strict rein on them, having witnessed first-hand the way that the Spaniards had treated French soldiers: the French had taken *anything* that they wanted, and the guerillos had exacted as much revenge as possible on the French. Wellesley, therefore, had insisted on the British paying for anything they took from any nationality. Whilst not ubiquitously adhered to, it worked for the most part. For the rest, the provosts were kept watchful and busy.

The arrogance of the French monarchy and nobility – the absolute cause of revolution in France – had, of course, meant that they had left the girl with tokens of who she was – a heavy gold ring, identity papers and a long sojourn from a maudlin mother on how she loved her daughter, goodbye sweet princess, we love you, only a matter of days before Madame Guillotine had taken the head from her shoulders, a baying crowd of French citizenry cheering as the royalty was murdered. The Mother Superior had been made to swear to secrecy until the girl came of age, and then introduce the poor, indoctrinated thing to a life she could have never even imagined. Without the reality, the girl would probably have led a peaceful life of spiritual contemplation, maybe losing her virginity to a sister-nun and nothing more. The letter was written though, and at the allotted time, the head nun broke the news to the girl.

The princess wanted to know none of it, and she remained, secretly mulling on her heritage in the convent for several more years, before secretly writing to an agent detailed in the maudlin letter. As it turned out, the agent received the letter, and sent it onwards to Wellesley, before being taken as a traitor by one of Napoleon's spy's. The sudden break in contact with the man sent Wellesley into raptures of a most unbecoming type, and this was why he was now whipping the horses into a furore through dangerous territory to a secluded convent in the north-east of France. The game was afoot, and he was determined to get there before the French, and so prevent the murder of yet another innocent.

And then suddenly, the two-hundred strong force found themselves in a pitched battle – galloper guns deployed by both sides – and a massed cavalry charge ensued.

The next thing that Wellesley knew, he lay on the ground unseated and dazed with only a young cavalry sergeant nearby. But let's not forget the five chasseurs, also unseated on the first pass, advancing on the prized possession that was the enemy General's head.

The sergeant swayed gently on the brow of the hill, no wounds immediately evident. He clumsily parried a sword thrust sent in by one of the Frenchmen, swayed some more, and was then skewered through the neck from his blindside by another chasseur. The first Frenchman opened up his belly, and as his guts spilled out of the gaping fissure, Wellesley understood that, yet again, his soldiers were drunk, as the odour of rum pervaded the air.

With a snarl of rage – mostly at the dead sergeant, but partly at his own impotence – he leapt at a French chasseur. He swung his blade in a most unconventional manner; so unconventional that the guard put up by the enemy was inconsequential, too weak to stop the blow, and the man could only gape in surprise as his head toppled from his shoulders, before his body collapsed in a gout of blood.

Wellesley swayed past his attackers, but he swung round, and in a more formal display of swordsmanship, he feinted and then lunged. He skewered another Frenchman, before deflecting a thrust from an officer, a young lieutenant who would not grow a day older, because, with a dazzling display of speed and ferocity, Wellesley riposted with the point of his sword. The tip hammered against the spine of the boy. The sword stuck firm, and left with no choice, he dived and rolled, picking up a heavy and poorly balanced cavalry blade from the first soldier that he had killed.

A pain lanced in his side, as an already bloodied sword speared through a section of flesh. He twisted, jamming the blade in to his flesh, and hewed down with the heavy blade, taking off the attackers arm at the elbow.

He now faced only two Frenchmen, both heavily bearded Crapaud, scarred and fierce looking. But no, there was only one, as the ground shook and a British cavalryman galloped past, opening up a face with a classic reverse stroke. It threw the man backwards and he did not rise again.

It left just the one, and they advanced warily towards each other, swung and riposted, thrust and dodged. It ended quickly, Wellesley was too fast, too well trained. He turned his man deftly, side-stepping a clumsy thrust, and gently slid his clumsy blade in to the man's back, piercing his heart.

A further thunder of hooves, and Wellesley noted that his cavalry had utterly defeated the French. As usual, the enemy steads were poorly fed, and the odour of rank saddle sores emanated throughout the battlefield. They were no match for the grain-fed mounts of the British, and it was this, rather than pure skill, that had defeated the enemy, regardless of sobriety.

None of Wellesley's aides had survived, which was why he had been virtually alone.

"You look like hell, sir," said a cavalry major.

Wellesley didn't look himself over, he merely glared at the man, who had the decency to blush.

"We've lost seventy eight men, sir, twenty two dead, forty one with minor wounds, the rest may, or may not, survive."

"Get those who can ride ready. We leave immediately."

"Sir."

Later that afternoon, a warm afternoon, where Wellesley became aware that every flying insect in the vicinity was interested in the blood and gore that coated him and his men, they arrived at the convent. It sat in a steep valley that was heavily wooded, and with a rather lovely turquoise-blue river running by its north wall.

Without any further ado, Wellesley hammered on the door, not even considering to make himself presentable.

A porthole opened in the door and, aghast, the nun listened to his perfectly fluent request for the princess. After some protests he became angry and demanded, unequivocally, the lady in question.

They didn't really have any choice but to present a hefty, plain girl, who happened to be a princess, dressed in a most unbecoming black habit that did nothing to hide her thick-settedness, or her heavy breasts. Only her green eyes betrayed anything approaching prettiness. At that moment Wellesley was smitten, as was she, even through the gore and supercilious manner.

Within a year, Wellesley was divorced and remarried, sending shockwaves through the nobility, but only increasing his popularity with the common people.

2. William

William heaved and the bank of oars moved. Sweat rolled down his back. His skull still creaked from the battle. The crack of a whip sounded and he felt a sting on his back as the lash bit. He continued to heave.

The Bucentaur moved inexorably south.

IF YOU'RE INTERESTED....

Waterloo

On the 26th February, 1815 Napoleon escaped exile from the island of Elba. By June of 1815, he had managed to gather a relatively small force of around 70,000 men. He was quite outnumbered by the Allied forces. However, he 'stole a march' on the Allies, and it is theorised that had the initial offensive at the Quatre Blas crossroads been heavily pressed, he may well have gained the field at Waterloo before the Allied forces came together (note that this was the most likely route for the German forces to arrive in support of Wellington, so tactically quite important). As it was, Marshall Ney, who commanded the vanguard of Napoleon's forces, didn't press the attack, allowing for a hasty defence of the crossroads, from which Waterloo did occur...and Napoleon was defeated.

Napoleon

Perhaps the first great conspiracy story....how did he die? Most logically, he died of natural causes – some state stomach cancer. Others state an English 'plot' to slowly poison the Emperor, with arsenic a commonly held conspiracy theory. The reason? Fear that he may rise again, such was his popularity.

The Passenger Pigeon

An American bird wiped out by hunting. At one point they were considered to be the most populous bird on earth. Flocks would consist of millions of birds (quite literally), and were said to be up to 3 miles wide. After the American Civil War, the improvements in railroads led to hunters and trappers having greater access to populations of them, and huge nesting sites were utterly destroyed by a number of rather inhumane methods. It's written that 50,000 birds were killed every day for five months in 1878. In the space of 30 years (1870 to 1900), 30 billion birds came zero.

William Hope

A William Hope did exist, and he was a photographer by trade – he's the one that took photo's of fairies, ghosts and the like. They were doubtlessly faked. He had quite an eminent following, however, including Sir Arthur Conan Doyle.

Photographic Media

There was, at the birth of photography, numerous different types of light sensitive paper existed. I've bastardised one of these to allow William to photograph ghosts!

Wilhelm Stieber

Wilhelm Stieber was Otto von Bismark's Spymaster General. He is credited – along with Fouche – of 'inventing' modern methods of information gathering. An unremarkable looking man, he did disguise himself and passed himself off as both a valet to a senior French statesman and a pedlar of cheap goods behind enemy lines – all in the name of 'intelligence'.

Arthur Rimbaud

The one thing that Arthur Rimbaud was not was a scientist; he is a fairly famous poet, and he had the fortune of being in Africa (and therefore meeting Amara), although some thirty years after the story is set. The joys of re-writing history means I can do this. Honest.

James Estcourt

James Estcourt was a parliamentarian who joined up for the Crimean War. He was promoted to Major General, despite having no experience. He was blamed – probably unfairly – for the privations of the English soldier in the Crimea.

Achille Richard

Was a renowned botanist whose books are still in use today. He has a number of orchids named after him.

Francis Brocklehurst

Francis Brocklehurst was a modest landowner in the Macclefield area of Cheshire. Nothing bad is written about him, so I fear I have done his memory a disservice. If it's any consolation, his character didn't start out as a 'baddie'. Indeed, all of the information I have read reflects on his altruism with the local poor (alms) and other 'charitable' work.

Birtles Hall

Is a rather pretty hall in Cheshire. It did burn down in the 19th Century, but a little later than happened in the book. There are indeed a number of rather beautiful walks around the area, including up to Alderley Edge, where there is a strong druidic mythology. There are also a large number of grotesque houses that have absolutely no consideration for the far more austere roots of the village, nor the surrounding countryside. I think these are a later addition to the village than the 19th Century!

Hare Hill

A beautiful National Trust garden, especially during Rhododendron season. Again, there are some beautiful walks down to Alderley Edge, where there is indeed a narrow gauge rail that goes in to a cliff face.

Printed in Poland
by Amazon Fulfillment
Poland Sp. z o.o., Wrocław